WHAT THE EYE DOESN'T SEE

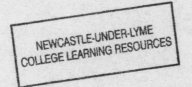

Born in 1966 and brought up in Gloucestershire, Alice Jolly now lives in Brussels with her husband and son. *What the Eye Doesn't See* is her first novel.

WHAT THE EYE
DOESN'T SEE

ALICE JOLLY

POCKET
BOOKS

LONDON • SYDNEY • NEW YORK • TOKYO • SINGAPORE • TORONTO

First published in Great Britain by Simon & Schuster, 2003
This edition first published by Pocket Books, 2003
An imprint of Simon & Schuster UK Ltd
A Viacom Company

1 3 5 7 9 10 8 6 4 2

Simon & Schuster UK Ltd
Africa House
64–78 Kingsway
London WC2B 6AH

www.simonsays.co.uk

Simon & Schuster Australia
Sydney

A CIP catalogue record for this book is available from the British Library

ISBN 0-7434-5071-X

Typeset in Bembo by M Rules
Printed and bound in Great Britain by
Bookmarque Ltd, Croydon, Surrey

In memory of Verity Sylvia Pease
of Hook Park Farm
1927–1997

ACKNOWLEDGEMENTS

My thanks to: Stephen Kinsella, Amanda Holmes, Kathryne Andrews, Lucy Hodgson, Clare Andrews, Simon Pettifar, John Lash, Ian and Fran Twinn, Max Hill, Tom Walker, Xandra Bingley, Sibyl Ruth of The Open College of the Arts, Susannah Rickards of Real Writers, Victoria Hobbs of A. M. Heath, Kate Lyall Grant of Simon & Schuster, The Arvon Foundation and The Brussels Writers' Group.

FEBRUARY

Maggie

I don't know why I lied for him.

At the time so much else had gone wrong that I just thought – oh yes, this as well, and I didn't take it seriously. Now I should be tortured by what I know, but six months have passed, and the world spins onwards, just as it ever did, and I get out of bed in the morning, and carry on the Normal Life Game. I'm shocked by my mind's capacity for evasion. After all, Tiffany is dead. No matter how often I tell myself that, I never quite believe it. Perhaps I learnt that from Dad – the art of unseeing, of unknowing.

The newspapers have been full of it, but don't believe all you read, words hide as much as they reveal. Even I don't know everything, although I was at the wedding with Dad when Geoffrey married Tiffany, and I was there four years later when she died. If only knowing was a process you could put into reverse. The irony is that I've always believed myself to be honest. Now I ask Nanda why honesty is so hard and she says it's because all stories are lies. Once there's an audience, then there's a reason for the telling, and the facts are altered to fit the case.

Things don't happen in words, but words are the only way to explain them. And that's what I'm left with now. Words.

My treadmill mind goes round them again and again. Questions and answers, the case for and against, justifications and explanations. A court of law inside my head, the judge's gavel pounding the back of my throat. Sometimes I just want to take my head and shut it up in a cupboard, lock the door, and enjoy the silence. It was such a small lie – in fact, it wasn't really a lie at all. I just looked back at the wrong moment, then I failed to disagree with what had already been said. And the punishment is that I'm left with a power I don't want. The power to protect or destroy all of our lives.

To see him, to see him not. So many decisions, and no way of judging what's right and wrong. For four months I've left his letters unanswered, his phone calls unreturned. But yesterday he called and said he wanted to meet, and I didn't even try to resist, because he's spent all his life in the persuasion professions – barrister, stock-market fiddler, politician – so he always gets his way. And anyway, what do I care, now that I'm going away?

Which is how I come to be waiting for him at Embankment tube at four o'clock, on a February day which appears to be happening inside a parked cloud. There's half-melted snow on the ground, and the light is already failing. For once he's on time, my chameleon father. I see his car, torpedo-shaped, sliding along the road, with cigar-shaped headlights, and an oval grin. Not a car you'd be likely to forget. An E-type Jag, Series 1, made in 1964 – he likes to tell you all the details. He parks it askew in a disabled parking space. In the mist, the pinstripe height of him is blurred, and he walks crooked because of his foot, his overcoat toppling, one shoulder lower than the other.

My stomach has switched onto spin cycle. I shouldn't

have come. I imagine him as a devil – his overcoat flicking around him like the cape of a pantomime villain, hiding perhaps a forked tail. His silver hair, parted in the middle, rising from his head like wings – or horns? Somehow those images don't work. At the station entrance he looks around, but he can't see me, because he's short-sighted and too vain to wear his glasses.

'Maggie,' he says, 'sorry, I didn't see you there.' His face is half in the light, half in the dark, and as he smiles his mouth reaches from ear to ear, revealing teeth which slope backwards. I offer my ear for him to kiss. He smells of laundered shirts and shoe polish. Nanda always says that he's been corrupted by the ease with which he charms.

Feet echo past us in the mist. My hands are pushed into my pockets, and water has seeped through the soles of my boots. I wear a beret but it doesn't keep my ears warm, and the wind pulls at my hair, twisting it in spirals around me.

He wants us to go for a drink but I won't, so we walk along the Embankment. Usually he talks all the time – anecdotes, in-jokes, having a dig at anyone and everyone, the cabaret rolling on – but now he's awkward. Our words tumble out in the wrong order, as we both talk at the same time, and then stop. He tells me that I look good, although he doesn't think that. There's a greyness to his skin, and a brightness in his eyes. Drink, I would think.

As always he's an extravagant display of good taste. A sleek Savile Row suit, a shirt in the same indigo as his eyes, a striped silk tie, long narrow shoes which squeak. His nose is large, and he looks sideways over it, and it's hard to tell whether that look is humorous or forbidding. He's watching me now with a glinting eye, which hasn't got a monocle in it but should have.

'Anyway, listen, Mags,' he says. 'I want to ask you a favour.'

I say nothing. Our eyes meet obliquely.

'You know there's this book being written?'

'No.'

'Oh, I thought I might have mentioned it. Well, anyway, there's this book being written. It's not really about me, not as such. But it's a biography, of a type, a biography of a group of us. You know – Geoffrey, Hugh, Buffy, Angus. All the boys. The Citadel Club. I mean, it's just a political book, nothing more . . .'

'And who's writing this book?'

'A journalist. Adam . . . Adam . . . Damn, can't remember his name.'

In the distance a barge hoots, and traffic rumbles past. We walk under a bridge and our feet make an underwater echo. A pigeon nods across our path, squawks and flies away across the river. My glasses have steamed up, so I have to clean them, and I don't even need to wear them, except they're useful to hide behind.

'Dad, is it a good idea to encourage anyone to ask more questions?'

'Well, the problem is, Mags, this was agreed two years ago, before . . .'

A lorry speeds past, drowning the pavement and his sentence.

'Anyway, as I say, two years ago it didn't look like such a bad idea. In fact, I thought it was rather a good idea for someone to write a book about me . . . well, about us. Now, of course, I'd rather not be involved, but I don't want to make a fuss, and I can't let the others down.'

'No, of course not.' I hope he detects a tinge of sarcasm in my voice.

I've stopped walking and we stand by the side of the road. There's a dead rat in the gutter. 'So what's this got to do with me?'

'Well, actually, what I really need is for you to talk to him.'

'Talk to this journalist?'

'Well, it wouldn't be much. Only a few questions. Actually, I've given him your number.'

'You've what?'

'Your number, yes . . .'

'And what shall I tell him, Dad? The truth?'

For a moment his eyes turn to mine, and they're hollow, and open into his head like long tunnels. He flicks at the cigarette he's smoking, hot ash falls onto his hand, he winces, and brushes it away. Then he turns, shrugs, half-laughs. I should speak, accuse him, tell him what I know. Speak, speak – but I remain silent.

So we walk on, listening to the rhythm of our feet crunching slowly along the pavement, on and on, until the streetlights come on and we stop at a stand where a man is cooking chestnuts over an open fire. Dad's shadow on the pavement is as long and spiky as the branches above. He wants to buy me some chestnuts, and I say no, but he insists and I'm hungry. The chestnuts come in a paper bag and I hold them in my gloved hands, feeling their heat unfreezing my hands. They're too hot to eat.

'Maggie, it's not just me who thinks it would be a good idea,' he says. 'Geoffrey was saying that you ought to talk to this journalist.'

'Geoffrey?' My teeth shiver and I look down at the chestnuts in my hands. 'So how is he?' I ask.

'Oh, he's not too bad. Much the same as ever. In fact, things are working out rather well for him. You know he's been recalled and promoted to Energy Minister?'

I wasn't asking about his career, but of course Dad thinks of that because that's all that interests him – yea, though we walk through the valley of the shadow of death, it's onwards and upwards just the same.

'So you and Geoffrey . . .?'

'Yes, yes, of course. Why ever not? We get on like a house on fire . . .'

Dad looks at me, half-laughs, stops, knows that he shouldn't have said that. My face smarts, outrage gathers in a lump in my throat, refusing to turn into words. I want to make some gesture of protest, but instead I stare at the chestnuts, their brown and shiny skins split open. There's something pitiful about them. I feel they've been dragged into this unfairly. Dad never knows when a joke's gone too far. Humour can be far more deadly than malice – that's what Nanda would tell him, if he ever listened to her.

I feel his hand on my arm and I start trying to peel one of the chestnuts, just for something to do, and because I don't want him to touch me, but it's hard to do that and hold on to the bag at the same time, so Dad takes hold of the bag, while I unpeel a chestnut. The chestnut has split open on the fire, but still I have to slide my fingernails under its hot, fibrous skin, and inside it's pale and looks like a brain. I imagine it turning round and round. 'Maggie,' he says. 'For God's sake. It's finished, you know that, don't you?'

Finished? Perhaps for him, but not for me. If only it had stopped, just as it was in those first newspaper articles. It sounded so simple then. I read those articles when I got back to England – that night confined in a box of black and white print, distant and stingless.

The Junior Arts Minister, Max Priestley, described last

night how he was driven back by a ferocious blaze at a Gloucestershire holiday cottage that killed the wife of the MP for Ealing, Geoffrey Drummond. Priestley, a neighbour and friend of the couple, said he fought to get into the cottage in Brickley after his daughter, Maggie, had called the fire services. Tiffany Drummond, 36, was the daughter of the American oil millionaire John Farrenden. The couple married at a lavish ceremony in Houston, Texas, four years ago. Geoffrey Drummond, who was told of the tragedy this morning, was at his London home during the blaze, which is under investigation.

Dad and I pass a pub, and he wants a drink. The pub is halfway underground with cramped windows, low beams and a smell of damp wool and melted snow, like skiing holidays. It's stacked full of suits, dark grey and pinstripe. Chapped hands grip beer glasses and folded umbrellas drip onto the floor. We push through to the bar and Dad orders whisky. I feel eyes watching him. Roll up, roll up. Accused murderer on view. You'd think it was a day out at the zoo. I want to hide him from them, but perhaps it's all just in my head. Dad doesn't seem to notice.

I look at his hands, resting on the bar. Oddly thin and white, they have no grip. Like something stored in formalin in a biology lab, they make me curl up inside. It's not that I'm expecting to see blood. No, nothing as obvious as that, but I feel that somewhere Tiffany's mark is there. Perhaps a speck of her pale and perfect face powder remains, caught in the grain of his skin, making a part of his fingerprint, black lines on white paper. It would help a lot if I had liked her but I never did.

He's got to go to a meeting at six, he tells me. It's some

committee, something to do with pedestrianisation. Can you believe it? Pedestrianisation, he says. Time was when pedestrians were simply people who parked the car too far away. I laugh because already I'm beginning to feel the whisky in my cheeks and fingertips. He burbles on, trying to tell me news about the family. Fiona my stepmother, James my half-brother, exiled to prep school, poor little devil. But Dad's no good at family news, because he's always been pretty detached from all that, and usually I deal with family stuff. Like all roads lead to Rome, and all trains go via Preston, all communication in our ramshackle family used to go through me. Before, before. 2 October. The night of the fire. Yes, everything divides there.

After a while Dad's more serious. 'You know,' he says. 'Fiona has bought *The Which? Book of Divorce*.' He turns his head to one side slightly and wrinkles up his nose. 'Of course, I can hardly claim to be surprised. But buying a guide to divorce – I mean, really.'

'Well, if you're going to get a divorce, you've got to get the right one, haven't you? You don't want any old divorce.' Our laughter is shallow and bounces back at us from the low ceiling. 'Don't worry, Dad, I don't think Fiona would return you to the wild right now.'

'Well, let's hope not. I'm not sure I'd know how to feed myself.'

He orders another whisky and one for me as well. The whisky tastes of ginger and cloves, and we find a table to sit down at, side by side. Suddenly Dad is gloomy. 'Of course in the past I'd have been expected to do the honourable thing. Out into the barn, an accident with a gun, that was always the excuse, wasn't it?'

He shrugs and then tells me that he's giving up his flat in London. The lease is up and he's got to be out, that's what he says. Probably the truth is that he's got no money. He signed everything over to Fiona when things were looking bad. She, I think, has sweetly declined to give it back. She never did like him having a flat in London. Fiona, who has always been one of life's defence players, suddenly on the attack.

When I say I've got to go, he says, 'Well, I'll drink up and come as well.' He won't let me leave first. We step out into muffled air and cold which grips to the bone.

'People used to run away and join the Foreign Legion, didn't they?' Dad says. 'Do you think there's a modern equivalent?' He slips on black ice and steadies himself against a railing. I have to stop myself feeling sorry for him.

'Couldn't you go and live with Rosa?' I ask.

'Perhaps,' Dad says. We don't normally talk about Rosa because I'm not meant to know about her. Although I could hardly fail to know since I walked in on them having sex, when I was ten years old. Sitting upright, her naked back was shaped like a cello, Dad's hand resting on the strings of her spine. The twisted sheets, his white knee, held in the light from the half-curtained window. Always I have known what must never be mentioned.

He drives me home although I don't want him to. Sunk low in the slippery leather seat of his car, the whisky makes me feel like I'm wearing a balaclava inside my head. The car growls over Westminster Bridge. Dad drives too fast, with the window open, blowing in sharp air, as he smokes, and then tries to flick ash out of the window, except it blows back in, and the wind makes his hair stand on end. As he spins around a corner his hand touches my leg and I hold on to the handle of the door.

'And your job,' he asks. 'How's that going?'

I'd been hoping to avoid that subject.

'Actually I've given it up. Just recently. A week ago.'

'What?'

He swerves and grinds the gears. 'You must be mad,' he says. 'Two years of law school, then you get a good job, and now you're chucking it in?'

'Dad, I just didn't want to do it any more. I don't like the law. I don't want to be involved in judging other people.'

He gives me a laser-beam stare and wags his head. He'd have liked a beautiful daughter, but since he can't have that, then I'm expected, at least, to be successful at something.

'So what are you going to do now?'

'I'm going abroad.'

He assumes his grumpy bigot act, which he uses so frequently that it's almost become who he is. 'I don't hold with abroad,' he says, pulling down his mouth and shaking his head. 'All those babbling voices and sticky heat. Dreadful. I prefer places to be Northern, grey and guilt-ridden.'

'Dad, I'm not going to Spain. I'm going to Brussels.'

'I don't see why you can't stay here.'

For him I don't really exist unless I'm playing a role in one of the scenarios he creates. He likes to be able to go to his club and boast about me to his cronies, and use me in their endless games of one-upmanship, so it's fine when I'm a success, and doing what a daughter should do, but when I don't fit in, then I slide from his field of vision.

'So when are you going?' he says.

'Three weeks time. I leave on the thirteenth of March.'

I don't know why he's surprised about me going away, he knows I never wanted to be a family law barrister, I wanted to work on crime or human rights. But at the time when I finished law school jobs were hard to come by, particularly for a wild-haired woman, with the wrong clothes, a recognisable surname, and awkward opinions. I was always so determined not to be just a fucked-up little rich kid with a well-known father but now it seems that's what I've come to, all the same.

Welcome to Malden Mansions, or Moulding Mansions, a sixties planning disaster, like piles of egg boxes with muddy grass in between, and mostly deserted, because it's sinking into the earth. Dark windows glitter all around us but all of them look out on concrete, not like where Nanda lives, where I used to live as a child, and where Dad lived as well. You can see for miles from there.

Dad follows me under the arch, where the light is broken. On the strip of grass outside our front door, translucent snow slides from abandoned yellow beer crates, and drips from a deck chair, which stands naked and shivering beside the path. Next door music pulses from a church which has been turned into a night club. Inside, an inflatable champagne bottle blocks the door to the sitting room. I move it and shuffle two tomato-sauce-smeared plates into the kitchen.

'What a desirable residence,' Dad says.

'Dad, Dad, be careful.' I scoop up Biggles – a honey-coloured rabbit with floppy ears which are dirty where they trail along the ground and a pair of teeth which have finished off the Internet connection and most of the hall carpet. Biggles' nose twitches as he sniffs at the collar of my coat. Under his fur, I can feel the knobbles of his spine and I put him against my shoulder, like a burping baby.

Dad stands under the shadeless hall bulb and asks me if I live here on my own. No, I tell him, I live here with Tyger and Sam and Druggy Dougie. Dad knows them from when I was at law school and they used to come and stay at

Brickley Grange for the weekend. Dad was still an MP then, and Geoffrey used to live nearby, at Hyde Cottage, just across the fields, and he used to come over to play tennis and swim, and Tiffany used to come with him.

You should wear things that emphasise your waist more, honey. That's the kind of thing she said to me – and I used to be amused at the leisurewear ghastliness of her. Lei-sure. Pronounced like seizure. Tan-coloured tights which made her stick legs look orange. Pink would be such a good colour on you, honey, and it goes with so many things. Yes, but not as many as you seem to think. No problem was so big it couldn't be tidied up with a cheerful little homily from a self-help book. She used to draw smiley faces on letters and produce packets of tissues from her handbag. Perhaps I judge her harshly, although you can tell a lot from these things. But how can I say that when she's dead?

As Dad walks into my room he stops. 'Oh, the bed.' He jumps back with a laugh, as though he's only just spotted it, which isn't likely because the bed takes up most of the room, and the headboard is five foot tall and made of dark wood as thick as a tree trunk. The foot of it is scallop-shaped like a seashell, and the sides are twisted spirals of wood with knobs like urns on the top. All over it's carved in a chaotic mass of leaves and vines and if you look carefully the heads of small animals – monkeys, or mice, or mythical beasts – peer out from between the vines. When I was little I dreamt about the animals.

'I suppose you're taking that to Brussels,' Dad says.

'I want to.'

The bed belonged to my mother and it's the only thing she left me. I've never gone anywhere without my bed, although it's a devil to dismantle, and took five of us to get it into this house, after we'd taken a door off its hinges.

When I took the job in Brussels I was worried about the bed. Now Dad stands beside it, and for once he's still, except for one hand which rests on the bed, his finger moving over the head of one of the tiny animals. There's dust and wax now around those twisted vines. When he sees me watching him, he puts his hand in his pocket.

'Look, Mags, I'll have the bed sent out to Brussels if you want.'

'Well, you don't have to.'

'I know, but I will. It's not much fun driving that bed across Europe in a van.'

That's how the bed first came here – Dad drove it all the way from Spain, with my mother. I only know that because Nanda told me. It was in Seville that Dad and my mother met. In this London winter it almost hurts to think about Seville – gold fish in green ponds, cool patterned tiles, bougainvillea and smoky wine. That's where my mother grew up, and she refused to come to England without this bed, so Dad had to buy a van and it took days to drive, and at night they slept on the mattress in the back, and I suppose I slept there too.

Now Dad hitches up his trousers at the knee and sits down in a pink leather armchair. The elegance of his ankles always surprises me. One of his socks is grey and the other black. My bedroom has a Bedouin-tent look, with yards of Indian cotton, a light shade shaped like a star, and kelim cushions all over the floor. I switch on the electric heater which belches out burnt-dust air. Outside, snowflakes glitter white in the light from the window. Taped to the wall by the bed there are postcards – one's from a friend on holiday in Zambia and shows a bird sitting inside a crocodile's mouth, eating bits from between the crocodile's teeth.

There's a pile of letters on my dressing table. The

handwriting on them is as prickly as a thorn bush and spreads all over the envelope. They're all from Nanda – news from her cheerful Grannies' Commune in Gloucestershire. The latest talks about Brussels – too many small dogs and lace handkerchiefs, she says, and the Common Market is a misguided project, markets are only valid as a means of social development, and on and on like that. A sniff is audible in the spiky letters.

As usual my bedroom is a mess, so I'm piling hat boxes into a corner, trying to make a bit more room. Dad gets up to help me push a box under the bed. His eyes are near to mine, indigo, deep-set and too close together.

'So what do you think?' he says.

The journalist, of course, we were certain to come back to that.

'I don't mind,' I say. 'I'll talk to him if you want. But there's something I want you to do for me in return.'

He leans close to me. 'But Maggie, of course, you know I'll do anything for you.'

'OK, right. Then go and see Nanda.'

'Nanda? Yes, of course. Of course, I will. I've been meaning to go. I'll go as soon as the weather clears,' he says. 'I'd be going to see her soon anyway.'

Except he wouldn't have been. He went to Thwaite Cottages once, just after the fire, and he hasn't been in touch with her since.

'It would help a lot if she would answer the telephone,' he says.

Then suddenly he looks at his watch and groans. 'Oh God, I must go. I'm hopelessly late. What a bore.' He stumbles out into the hall, hopping over Biggles, who's eating what remains of the hall carpet. This is how it's always been and nothing has changed, even though he doesn't have a job any more. Daughters have their slot, after a committee meeting, between two important votes, speak to my secretary and get it in the diary, and afterwards please send a letter confirming the details and put the papers away in a file.

'Before you go away, Maggie, you should really go round and see Geoffrey.'

'I don't think so.'

'He needs you, Maggie.'

The floor quivers as a Northern Line train worms through the ground below us. Dad's eyes wrap themselves around me. For the first time today he's really looking at me. He raises his hand, touches me, the tip of one finger massaging the point of my shoulder. 'Sorry, sweetheart. Sorry.'

He hasn't called me that since I was a child. We say goodbye and I watch him dancing away through the shadows, towards his car. He stops under a streetlight, and turns round in a complete circle as he waves a hand at me.

As I turn to go back inside, memory falls open at the night of the fire. I'm running into the flagstoned hall at Brickley Grange, breath snagging in my throat. Dad is in the sitting room, his socked foot propped on a stool. From the television there's a sudden gale of sitcom laughter. A new cigarette burns in an ashtray, an amber glass of whisky gathers the light. A twist of pain as though I've pulled a muscle inside my head. The scene is as shallow and fragile as celluloid. Our eyes join, but they are too naked, and we both look away.

I slam those memories shut and go back to my room. Sitting on my bed, I look in the mirror, arranging myself as though for a portrait, taking stock of the situation I'm in. Girl, twenty-eight, dressed in old-fashioned clothes, grey and black, convent clothes of another era, a statement of not belonging. A girl at once substantial and ethereal – nothing

more than a mark on a mirror. All the things I've tried to
make my own – my friends, my job, this flat – they're only
cardboard props. Like a moonstone, I have no colour, I only
reflect the colour of those around me.

I always used to think of myself as a good person, but then
I'd never had much opportunity for evil. Most people don't,
they aren't called upon to make the choice. In my generation
the Gestapo is not at the door asking if you've got any Jews
hidden in your attic. Evil is surprisingly hard to come by and
hard to imagine as well. Which is how a person can put ten
bodies in their drains, or seduce dozens of children – just
because nobody can think that they would.

And that's how I am with Dad. Is he a victim or a villain,
a man of principle or a murderer, a fallen angel or a fraud?
Whatever anyone says, I'm not able to think that he might
have done wrong. He's a fraud, a fraud. I must believe it –
but I don't. I can never quite give up on him. I've made a
bad investment and now the only hope of getting any return
is to invest still more. Good love after bad. For twenty-eight
years I've tried to believe in him as a good man. But if I'm
wrong about him, then I'm wrong about me as well. The
mark on the mirror will disappear.

Max

Bugger. No cabs. Pissing with rain, and cold enough to freeze the blood. Foot giving me gyp and bowels in an uncertain state. Ghastly meeting, of course. Pedestrianisation. I mean, really. What do you expect? I was only asked to go because Angus couldn't, and I know the form. That's all I do these days. Make myself useful, be seen around the place, keep my nose clean. Bide my time.

And now no cabs. A bad end to a bad day. I light a cigarette, raise my hand to shield the flame. Nothing to look forward to this evening either. Just Gus coming around, clearing the last of our stuff out of the flat. I abandon the search for a cab and walk back along the river, where Maggie and I walked earlier today. Tiresome little madam. Her eyes boring through to the marrow of my bone. Awful place she lives in. But what can I do? She'll never take a penny from me.

What did I do to deserve a daughter like that? I blame it on Nanda. I should never have left Maggie with her and her cranky friends. But there wasn't much choice. Eighty-five, Nanda is now, yet still she never ploughs a straight furrow, never does anything the easy way. And then Maggie, poor girl, was cut up by all that stuff about the fire. Didn't do me much good either, come to that, but there's no point in dwelling on it. For me, the problem is that I don't convince her, never have. Difficult when even your own family doubt you.

Back at the flat, I climb the stairs, turn the key, open the door, then flick the hall light. Dead. I flick the switch again. I don't believe it. Those buggers have cut me off. Small-minded, penny-pinching bureaucrats. You'd have thought privatisation would have put a stop to that. In the sitting room the glow of a streetlamp slants in through the window. There's the usual smell of gravy wafting up from below. Pictures have been taken down, and the bookcases are empty. The atmosphere is gloomy and expectant, like prep school end of term.

Until recently I lived in a world of too much light. The constant click of cameras. My face staring from a page of print. My voice catching me unawares from the radio or TV. Journalists trying to trap me in a net of words. Looking at everyone, suspecting everyone. Measuring every syllable. You'd think I might be glad to have a break from that. And perhaps for a week or two I was. But now I want the show to go on. Because what's the point of life if no one is watching?

On the wall there's still a pin board stuck with press cuttings and photographs. I can't see it clearly but I know anyway. A photograph of me with the Duke of Edinburgh. A newspaper article about some Disability Award I received. A picture of me chatting with some drooling pensioner during an election campaign. A letter addressed to me, signed by Bill Clinton, with a spelling mistake in it.

The phone rings, shrill and insistent. I look into the darkness. That sound makes me twitchy. Who would it be? Tiffany. I always think of Tiffany. Still if I pick up the phone

I think it'll be her. Then every time I feel the shock of her death again. She came to this flat – once, or was it twice? During that fateful Christmas two years ago when snow brought everything to a halt. Often she tried to come here again but I never let her. This is my lair and I guard it jealously. I stand by the phone, let it ring on and on, hear her voice. You lied. You lied. You lied. An evil corner of my mind is glad that she's gone.

Oddly, it's her kneecaps I remember. They were perfect, shaped like tear drops or petals. I saw them as she sat down beside me at dinner, the shape of them emphasised by her thin black stockings. And she had earrings like gold leaves, which hung down below the line of her jaw, resting at the point where her neck and jaw bones joined, where there were soft blonde hairs, and a small scar of puckered skin.

From below I hear the front door open, the shuffle of heavy feet. I peer over the stair rail. A slick of hair bobs up the stairs towards me, asthmatic breath coming in puffs. Gus. 'No bloody electricity,' I tell him. 'And they've never even sent us a bill.'

'Oh, no. Shit. Sorry.' He's wearing a mackintosh, the belt stretched round his spherical shape. Drops of rain glisten on his glasses. That skin condition of his is worse than ever. Scaly and scabby, blotches all over him.

'How can they possibly cut off our electricity when they haven't even sent us a bill?' I ask.

Gus fumbles towards the kitchen. A match is struck and his moon face appears above the flame of a candle. 'I think there was a bill, actually. Several.'

'Then why in God's name didn't you tell me?'

Gus flaps his arms, steps backwards, stumbles on a box. Taking the candle, I go into the kitchen, reach for the Talisker. I pour myself a glass, and drink it, then pour myself another. In the hall the candlelight touches on flock wall-paper and beige plastic wood. I take the bottle back to the sitting room, pour a glass for Gus. 'Sorry,' I say. 'Sorry, to be so bloody.'

Gus takes the matches from me, lights the gas fire.

'Perhaps we should get the last of this stuff into boxes, and then go for a drink, what do you reckon?' he says.

'Good idea.'

'So did you see Maggie?' he asks.

'Yes.'

'So how is she?' Gus asks.

'Oh, fine, fine. Moving to Brussels.'

'Brussels? Why?'

'I don't know. Some pointless do-gooding, I suspect.'

'I thought she liked being a barrister.'

'So did I. But there's no explaining her. She needs a man, that's what I think.'

Gus disconnects the computer on the desk where he's always worked, snuffling and puffing in the dark. Then he drops piles of paper into the wastepaper bin. I drink and feel defeated. I should be packing but I don't know where to start. If only I could ask Fiona to come and do it for me.

Gus passes me a pile of post. I throw it in the bin. 'If it's important they'll write again, and if it isn't they shouldn't have written in the first place.'

I sit down on the lid of a metal trunk. The end of an era. It'll be strange to go. Farewell to brown lino, brown skirting boards, and a carpet with a pattern that looks as though someone has vomited on it. I rented this flat when I was first elected, because it was cheap and within the Division Bell area. Then Gus came to work for me, and we moved our office over here. All the important work anyway. So much better than the Commons, full of snoops and gossips. Only

my secretary – the dreaded Mrs Mimbers – was left in the
Commons as a decoy.

I think of this journalist who comes to see me. Adam . . .
Adam . . . Anyway, the book journalist. Of course, I don't
find it difficult to tell him what he needs to know. The
Official Version. Anyone can read it in *Who's Who*. Father a
senior army officer, killed in the war. Mother still very much
alive. Winchester, Cambridge, the Citadel Club. Called to
the bar in 1964, elected to Parliament in 1979. Junior
Minister for Health. A short spell at Transport. Minister for
the Arts. Maverick, controversial. Those were the words
they always used. Resignation on a point of principle, coin-
ciding neatly with the leadership crisis. A switch of loyalties
just in time. And so I go on. But of course, that isn't the
information he wants. Truth is, there's a lot of my past I just
can't remember. Drink, I suppose.

I cross the room and stare down into the empty blackness
of a filing cabinet drawer. 'So you've taken your files?'

Gus squeezes his hands together and the dry skin of them
rasps. 'Yes, but you needn't worry. They've been stored for
future use.' Gus is all very cloak-and-dagger. Keeps files on
everything and everyone, and I'm at least as bad. Mainly it's
just a game, and most of the information Gus has collected
is pretty harmless. Only a few small snippets of really saucy
scandal, kept in reserve, in case of dire need.

Gus has a great talent for information, presentation, finding the right angle. Appearance is reality, that's his creed. It's
important in politics, as in life. For ten long years he and I
worked together. His talent for information was the making
of me, I admit that. He's clever, much cleverer than I am.
There's very few people I'd say that about. He has an incredible head for detail. But he's wasted on that. Public relations
are his real talent. For me, having him around is like having

a brain outside my head, not always a comfortable sensation. The Magician and the Magician's Assistant. Together we could make anything possible. Coins out of the air, doves from the sleeve of a coat, a woman sawn in half and put back together.

It was just after he left Cambridge that he came to work for me, just for a couple of months, to get some experience. He was meant to be helping Deadly Dull Browning, my then assistant. First morning he arrived, I remember the shock of his appearance. Oh dear, oh dear, I thought, there's been some genetic mishap there and left Browning to deal with him.

After that I never gave him a second thought, until one morning Browning and I were talking about an inquiry which was causing a real stink – something to do with food poisoning. We were in my office at the Commons and it was stiflingly hot. There hadn't been a breeze for days. Everywhere the air had been in and out of several pairs of lungs, and several exhaust pipes. Gus was sweating away at another desk, head down, with too many clothes on. Suddenly he cleared his throat loudly. 'I've got a copy of the draft report if you want. It's a week out of date, but it might be useful.' Then he reached into his desk drawer and, with both his raw, shaking hands, he held out a sheaf of papers to me.

I was stunned. Any of my colleagues would've given their right arm to see that document and there was this misshapen lump passing it to me across the desk. 'I had lunch with someone,' Gus said. 'There was a draft lying around . . .' I hesitated, looked over at Browning. Then I put my hands in my pockets and chuckled, uncertain what to say. Gus watched me, his left eye clicking open and shut. Open and shut. Time passed, footsteps came and went along the corridor. A photocopier whirred. I cleared my throat. The ends of my fingers itched. Browning pursed his lips and I shrugged. Even the wallpaper was sweating. Gus's opaque eyes did not move from my face. As I took the document, his fingers touched mine. A Faustian pact, if ever there was one.

After that I intended to give Gus his marching orders. But somehow it was Browning I got rid of instead. Then within six months Gus got me into every newspaper, and into the right meetings, and onto the right committees. Operation Brown Nose, that's what Gus and I called it. Those were good times. I was a rising star and Gus was my stage manager. Photo calls, radio interviews, high-profile scraps. This place seemed like the heart of a secret operation. I always thought we should have a huge map spread out on the table, and little red flags to move across it. Often we worked all day and all night. Gus stayed here sometimes, because he lives in some Godforsaken place out in the sticks – Peckham Rye, or Balham, or somewhere. Ghastly.

Two years after Operation Brown Nose started, I got the call from on high, and became a Junior Minister. Not that it is so very difficult, mind you. When the competition is all men with Sellotape around their glasses and clumps of wax in their ears. In politics you can go a long way just by being personable. Then the leadership crisis. Gus had already made sure that I was not on the sinking ship. After that, plain sailing. Minister for the Arts. I was en route for the Cabinet, poised on the brink. Then there was the fire. Tiffany was dead. And my constituency organisation deselected me, just a couple of months before the election. And there I was, suddenly no seat in the House, nothing. Only a few months ago, but it seems like another century.

Whenever I'm in this flat, I think of the morning after the

fire. After Tiffany's death. The whole world was upside down and back to front. I sat on a chair in the kitchen with my head between my knees. I was in such a state I couldn't move. Everything was black. My mind was elsewhere. Far back in the past. They say that lightning doesn't strike twice in the same place. Believe me, it can.

Eventually I realised Gus was still with me. I could hear the sound of his voice, but I couldn't understand the sense of his words. He was cleaning his glasses again and again, hands shaking. He was asking me questions but the words were all jumbled up. Then slowly I began to understand. Gus was plotting and calculating, finding an angle. My jacket? The packet of photographs? Maggie? He knew what had happened because I'd called him from Brickley. And he knew because he had telephoned me the night before. The rest he didn't ask. Of course, I'd been in some scrapes before but this was different. Small boys really shouldn't play with matches. Jokes, jokes. None of them worked.

Gus made me take off all my clothes and lie down in the back bedroom, the one he always uses when he stays here. The bed smelt of him. I lay there, shaking. In my head the future was like a smashed-up car, broken and bent. Gus went out to the laundrette. He was gone a long time. I lay and listened to the silence. Was it unusually silent that morning? Or was it just that I noticed the silence? It was an autumn day but the sky was bright. I lay and watched clouds moving across the skylight above the bed. After a while I stretched myself out and tried to think. I knew I'd have to go back and explain.

But when Gus came back he had another plan. He sat on the side of the bed, rubbing his hands together. He had it all pieced together in his head, told me what I'd have to say. I was shaky and ready for surrender, but he didn't want me to throw it all away, all that we had worked for together.

It won't work, I said. It would be better for me to come clean now. He turned away from me, walked back and forth up and down the small bedroom. The tic in his left eye made the flesh of his face flutter. His eyelid clicked open and shut over his small, pale eye. It's already too late for that, he said. Your decision was made last night. If you didn't explain it immediately then you can't begin now. No one will believe you.

Gus is more than twenty years younger than me but that morning he was older. He made it into a neat package. He talked about it as though what had happened was Tiffany's fault. And, in truth, it was. He put his hand on the sheet. I could feel his fingers through it. It'll hold, he said, it'll hold. So I put on the clothes from the laundrette, bristling with static, warm and smelling of soap powder. He stood at the door, watched me go. To Geoffrey.

Problem now is that Gus doesn't accept that my career is over, at least for the moment. Strange, really. You'd think he'd be glad to move on, work for someone else. What good is it to him, watching me piss my life away, when men with half my brain are climbing the greasy pole?

'Listen, Gus,' I say. 'Have you accepted that job yet?'

'No, I thought I'd wait.'

He's been offered a job with the Party. Some research on pension and social security. They're always short of people who can do sums.

'Well, what are you waiting for?'

He shrugs. 'I'd rather keep working for you, that's all.'

'Gus, I've no money to pay you and no work for you to do.'

'Yes, but Geoffrey is going to get you that Inquiry job, isn't he? So I might hang on and see what comes of that.'

'That job's a very long shot. And even if I get it I doubt I'll have any budget to employ anyone else. Anyway, it's not the kind of work you want to do.'

I watch him trying to close up a cardboard box. It's too full, he can't get the lid down. His parsnip fingers are struggling, his lips flapping in frustration. He gives up, looks up at me, the light from the candle glinting on his thick glasses

'It's a good chance, that job,' I tell him.

'Maybe.'

He runs his tongue over his lips, the only bit of him which look really human. Red and round, in the pasty skin of his face, they're like lips painted on a rag doll. He's always biting bits of dry skin from them, or licking at them nervously. The room is getting warm now. There's a smell of gas and candle wax. The fire clicks. A police siren wails in the street below. Gus picks up the whisky I poured for him, cups it in his hands. 'So you're going back to Brickley Grange, are you?' he asks.

'What else can I do?' I push a box out of the way, sit down in an armchair by the fire. The springs squeak. Gus is still watching me, scratching at one of the scabs on his hands. 'I mean, if I need somewhere to stay in London, I can always go to Geoffrey's, but I can't put up with that for long. So it's back to Gloucestershire, Fiona and the Doghouse. Life in the country, doing the gardening. The sunset years. I may even take to writing whingeing letters to my MP.'

For the first time Gus looks as though he might smile. He finds the proposition ridiculous, as I do.

'Look, what I'm telling you, Gus, is that you shouldn't wait around on me. You've got to think of yourself.'

I stand up and start shuffling boxes around aimlessly to avoid Gus's glum and stubborn look. I wish to God he wouldn't make this so difficult. The problem is that he's sharp, and he knows me well. This isn't really about jobs.

'Remember Mrs Mimbers and the wardrobe?' he says, with a smile of reminiscence which annoys me.

'Yes,' I say, and turn away to pour myself another drink. I hope he's not going to get sentimental. I can't put up with that. The last thing I need is a Trip Down Memory Lane. But I do remember, of course. One afternoon Mrs Mimbers turned up when Rosa and I were having a bit of a fiddle. Usually we made clear Mrs Mimbers should never come here. Anyway, Rosa hid in a wardrobe. I went to deal with Mrs Mimbers, doing up my trousers as best I could. Unfortunately the wardrobe was one of those home-assembly jobs and it decided to disassemble itself noisily, while I was trying to have a reasonable conversation with Mrs Mimbers in the sitting room.

Gus picks up something from the desk and holds it close to the light of the candle. It's a stamp and an ink pad. The stamp says Blah! Blah! Blah! Gus bought it for me as a birthday present ages ago. Stamping Blah! Blah! Blah! in red ink across turgid documents was always a good way of cheering up a rainy afternoon. We used it so much that the knob broke, and the ink pad dried up. Anyway, no point in thinking about that now. We pack. The silence between us fidgets.

The phone rings. I give Gus a look and he answers it, says I'm not available. Then he changes tack and hands the receiver to me. 'It's Rosa.'

I snatch the receiver. Rosa. Rosa. At last. 'Hello.' Silence, then a brief rustle. 'Hello,' I say again.

'Are the swallows flying south?' Her voice is soft, uncertain. I imagine her lips close to the phone.

'Yes, certainly. How about the Flag? Eight o'clock.'

'See you there.' She's gone. I stand holding the telephone. Draw in a deep breath, as though I might be able to catch a scent of her, twisting along the phone wire.

'So are the swallows flying south?' Gus asks.

'Yes.'

It annoys me that Gus should use our code. Probably I should ask him if he wants to come for a drink as well, but there's no point in drawing this out. He picks up the Blah! Blah! Blah! stamp and it moves back and forwards between his fat fingers. In the half-light I can see him chewing at his thick bottom lip.

'Look, don't worry. If you want to go I'll pack the rest up and you can just come and get it later,' he says.

'Well, if you wouldn't mind?'

'No. I don't mind.'

'Thanks, that would certainly help.'

I shouldn't let him, but all the same. I look at my watch and pick up my coat. His hands are pushed down beside him, fists clenched. But he smiles, picks up the stamp from the desk, throws it towards me. I reach for it in the dark, but miss, then bend down to pick it up from the floor. 'You better put that in,' he says. 'You might be needing it.'

God, I wish he wouldn't do this. I toss the stamp into the bin. 'I don't think so. It's broken.' I pick up the ink pad from the desk, throw that in as well. I turn to go, Gus follows me onto the landing. Under the bright hall light, he's standing with his hands clasped, looking at the floor.

'Well, give us a call then,' I say.

It's like that day when he gave me the document. Except now he has nothing to give me and I've nothing for him.

Nanda

One can only bear so much of the truth and this, now, is enough.

I look around me at this new doctor's surgery which has red-brick walls, both inside and out, and white light, reflected from snow, shines through a high window, bright enough to blind me, and Dr Dervitt sits opposite me, his lips snapping open and shut, like a cine film being played too fast. He talks of options, and treatments, and his hands expand and contract as he explains the operation of the stomach. He is a young man. The sound of his voice goes on, although the morning has stopped.

I knew, of course, deep within, I knew. Three weeks ago – perhaps four – I went to the hospital in Gloucester for some tests, but even before that I knew. I watch Dr Dervitt's arm, below his short-sleeved shirt, and it is white and smooth, exactly the same as the plastic top of his desk, yet there is life in that arm and not in the desk. He watches me from under heavy lids. 'Miss Priestley? Are you all right?'

On the wall behind him there's a painted children's jungle and a chattering monkey is stationary on a swinging vine, his mouth jabbering, as he raises a paw to wave, and an elephant's trunk is frozen, curled upwards, squirting a grey splatter of water through the palm trees. Dr Dervitt clicks the top of his pen.

'Yes, of course I'm quite all right.'

I must not snap at him because really he's managing admirably. Even the professionals are shaky in the face of oblivion. Death is the one fact of which we can be quite certain and the one fact we can never accept. I don't want to continue this conversation and neither does he. Somewhere in the distance a door slams and children shout and I can't seem to remember the words one says to doctors, it is so very long since I have encountered one. The winter of 1972, it would have been, six months before Lucía's death, and they took me to the cottage hospital – now, of course, defunct – and they said it was pleurisy, but I only stayed one night before Freddy and Theodora came to take me home.

'I think perhaps I'll leave it for the moment, if you don't mind.' My vision becomes cloudy at the edges and when I start to stand the blood has gone from my feet, and the floor is no longer beneath me, and a rush of cold floods me, and a throbbing starts in the side of my neck . . . I see a vision of myself stumbling, grasping at the desk, and the walls, then my body lifted onto a trolley, with me trapped inside, shouting silent words. My bloodless fingers fumble with the clasp of my bag. So finally it has come to this.

'Yes, why don't you think it over and make another appointment?' Dr Dervitt's hands smooth over papers on the desk, his head nods back and forwards, and his eyes are turned away.

I find a handkerchief in my bag. 'Thank you so much for your help.' I must make this easy for him, even though his defeat is so much less absolute than my own. My blood has started to flow again, and the floor is solid beneath my feet, and with my hand on the side of his desk, I can stand. He opens the door and I walk out into the caustic corridor.

'Now book another appointment as soon as you've had some time to think.' My feet pick a careful path over the carpet, and Dr Dervitt raises a hand in farewell, knowing I will not return.

I find my way out of the low red corridors, and into the winter sun, and the warmth of it gives me strength, and I blink as the weight of it lies heavy on my eyelids. I let sensations wash over me, while my mind rests, preparing to search for a strategy to outwit despair. My breath rises in frozen clouds in front of my face and my eyes are full, but the tears are only the sting of shock, and I keep walking, feeling my way through their fractured light . . .

It is early still, but despite the snow, the market is opening up in the square and wheels crunch through the ice, horns beep, children cry and dropped tomatoes are crushed in the gutter. I pass the school, where I taught for twenty years, time gone in the twitch of a cat's tail, the years carrying out their deadly work, and I see Max, seven – perhaps eight – years old, standing beneath this very tree, looking down at a baby bird, fallen from a nest. On the pavement, in the rain, the baby bird was little more than a smear of blue mucus, one half-formed leg spread out from its first fluff of feathers, but, oh, how he wept over that dead bird, his face twisted with anger, his arms flapping up and down as though he might fly away, in place of the bird that never would.

There are cobwebs stretched across the black branches of the trees, they glitter with frozen dew and one branch hangs low, and I stop to look at a cobweb which links one frozen twig to another. I stretch up a stiff arm to touch it, tenderly at first, feeling its trembling resistance, then pressing my hand against it, so that it yields under my hand and dis-integrates into nothing. The past, so close, so very close, yet I cannot cross the divide.

Colonel Bampton passes me carrying bags of meat from the butcher's. 'Good morning to you, and how are the Miss Priestleys?' That's the way people in Burrington refer to Freddy, Theodora and me, having tactfully decided years ago that we must be sisters. He touches his hat and walks on, then Young Mrs Briston calls a greeting from one of the stalls, and their smiles shock me. Time should freeze and there should be silence, people should stand aside and let me pass, but instead they turn away, smoking cigarettes, chatting, swinging plastic bags from their hands. I stand on the kerb and Shirley Biggs stretches out a black leather arm to me. 'Shall I help you, Miss Priestley?'

I shake my head, and pull back my arm. 'No, no. Thank you. I don't want to cross the road.' I turn back across the square. I must get away, there is too much life, too many people, they can do nothing for me. As one nears the end, the road narrows, until it is single file only, and one goes on alone . . .

It is a long, long walk home, two miles and all uphill, and when I reach Frampton Edge I stop to rest, and below me is the Medlocks' farm and the stream. And how the land rises and falls, thick with snow, white against white, dissolving into the distant morning sun, and further down still, the crooked roofs of the town of Burrington are hidden in the bottom of the valley. Doubtless somewhere there Dr Dervitt still clicks the top of his pen, while behind him the frozen monkeys chatter.

I walk on and around me the air is so still that I can hear the distant sound of a hammer on metal, ricocheting across the valley, travelling upwards, before it is released into the still air. My flesh hangs heavy but inside I'm floating and floating, as though my soul is already detached from my body, and the thought comes to me that today has been strangely similar to the day when I found out I was pregnant with Max. There is that same knowledge of something growing inside me, that same sense of being driven back inside myself.

At home Freddy is out in the garden scraping snow from the path and she puts down her shovel. 'So what did the doctor have to say?' There's disdain in her voice because, in her view, anyone who goes to the doctor is rather letting the side down.

'Oh some bug or other. Not much they can do.' My legs feel suddenly weak and I move towards the front door, frightened that I might fall, and I turn my face away from her, wiping my handkerchief across it.

'Well, it is a bore,' Freddy says. 'Too bad of you to be ill when I really need some help getting this snow cleared.' She walks away down the path, her shovel swinging in her hand. She never was any good at other people's illnesses but as long as she can clear the snow then all will be well.

Inside the kitchen is bitterly cold, and melting snow drips and drips through a crack in the ceiling and onto the kitchen table. For five days now we've been frozen in, and the pipes are solid, but the electricity mercifully continues, despite the winds that batter us. Bullseye is snoring on a pile of washing, his tail curled around him, and I put a bowl under the drip and start to make tea, my hand shaking as I load more wood into the stove. The water in the kettle is melted snow and makes tea which has a bitter taste of wood, but now my hands are too cold to manage the mugs and the tea bags, and the room is breaking up into shafts of light . . .

I stumble back into the sitting room and look around at

the debris of our various projects, at the books which are spread everywhere and topple on every surface, and the floor which is stacked with boxes, journals, Arms Campaign leaflets, pamphlets about Prison Reform. On the desk there's a review I'm proofreading for Theodora, several unfinished articles, piles of letters and photographs, the new book on Thomas More, a broken cup I'm trying to mend for Freddy and my German dictionary open and ready. But whatever is the point of all this? I pull myself up, decide to take a positive approach, and then realise that there isn't one, that the fact of this will not yield to all my mind's guile.

For so many people life is just a slow process of giving up; they bed down for death as early as forty or fifty, and they stop fighting for any improvement in themselves, or in other people. Theodora, Freddy and I have watched our friends picked off, one by one, and in truth we have almost felt some contempt for them for surely they simply didn't try hard enough? We have kept ourselves alive by working, struggling, and searching, and at every junction we have chosen the scenic route. To begin with, in that far, far distant world of our youth, the search was all about people and every problem would be solved by the liberation of women and the triumph of the communist cause. A just society could be created if only the full potential of every human being could be released – that we decided while at Oxford, cycling to and from tutorials, through foggy streets beside the canal, where armies of women were trapped in mean terraced houses, their shoulders permanently tipped to one side by the weight of shopping, or washing, or babies. We would never live like that, we decided, and neither should they.

But then war came and after that there could be no grand

plans, no more poetry, and so we came here to Thwaite Cottages, fifty years ago – longer even than that – and although work, friendships, lovers have often taken us away, we always return, caught on the hook of this place, and reeled back in. The space, the gaps, the expanse of nothing reflecting always the emptiness above us, that is what calls us back again and again – the unconscious realisation that what is important is not the grand plan, but the gaps in between, the space where an outstretched hand is not met, the meaning which lies in between the black typed words on the page, the weed that sidles up unnoticed in the carefully sprayed and clipped garden, and suddenly bursts into flower . . .

Gaps – yes, the gaps – that is where I search now, looking for that nameless something, whatever is beyond – Jung's collective unconscious perhaps, or the Buddhist nirvana, or Plato's ideal world to which the soul yearns to return, or perhaps even plain old-fashioned God, who as a young woman I strived so hard to discredit. I don't know, and I have never expected to know, doubt has been the foundation of my faith, but now suddenly questions of belief can be deferred no longer and I feel that I must come down on one side or another. I need a magnet to bring together the scattered filings of my mind, I need a geometry for the random elements of my beliefs. Always we are running and running from that fearful thought that we might be intelligent beings doomed to live in a meaningless world . . .

Of what use have they been, so many years of striving and questioning and searching? I thought that death would bring some final enlightenment, but now I fear that it will not be so, and I stumble towards it with no more understanding than those ignorant millions who have never given it a single thought. There is, perhaps, nothing beyond, and now the thought comes to me again of those Oxford women we so despised, and I realise that they, at least, ensured that some man had a properly laundered shirt and a hot dinner. Perhaps, after all, such achievements are not to be so lightly dismissed. This is the beginning of despair.

I go upstairs, feeling a click in my hips, placing each foot carefully, then I cross the landing and go through the door which leads to Theodora's cottage. As always, she sits at her desk, amid piles of books, starting work early, writing with a fountain pen, despite all that new technology which is now available. Her books are biographies of famous women, or women who should be famous, and at the moment she is researching, sorting through the life of her latest subject, Lou Andreas-Salomé, one of the first women psychologists, beloved of Nietzsche, Rilke and Freud. Theodora is organising that life into a pattern, identifying the themes, working out the main route from the side roads, showing what in the early life proved significant in the later . . . if only one had been able to see the shape of one's own life from the beginning.

Light shines on her cheek from a lamp with a jewel-encrusted stem. When we were at school she was considered quite a beauty, and she still looks as though she expects to be admired, and her hair has strands of red in it even now, and every morning I put it up for her, tying it up into two separate buns on either side of her head, leaving a dip in between, just as she likes it. Her ears lie flat against the side of her head, and their length is emphasised by drop pearl earrings, and her pale skin is smudged blue by the veins beneath it, and her eyes poke forward above her long nose. I watch her mauve hands, with perfectly manicured nails, moving her tortoiseshell pen across the paper. Those knots of hair bob up and down as she works. Her regal bearing, and the high white ruffled collars she always wears, ensure that she resembles nothing so much as a portrait of Elizabeth I, and this room, her study, is also decorated with a touch of luxury which might befit a queen. I watch, and watch . . . I thought that I would be able to watch her forever. How I long to go in and rest my head on her shoulder and talk to her, but what is there to say? There's nothing to discuss, the finality of this is brutal, the knowledge of it drips down my spine – the minutes, the hours, the days are already tipping away. As I'm turning to go Theodora looks up over the top of her spectacles and her grey eyes pierce me, then she opens her mouth to speak but says nothing. Her eyes close and then open again, she lays down her pen, and her hand flutters as she moves to touch the collar of her blouse, and her face seems to be falling, all of it moving, like a landslide, and I turn away, unable to bear that sight.

'No, no,' she says. 'Come in and sit down.'

'Oh no, really.'

'Yes. Yes, please do.'

I move down the one step into her study and sit on the sofa by the low window and outside the snow is silver where the sunlight falls on it, and there's a dip in the land which marks the route I have just walked, the track across the fields, and the turning where the road drops over the side of the hill and down towards Burrington. There are no clouds and the sky is pale, pale blue with only the vapour trail of a plane stretched across it, disappearing beyond the hills, and on the windowsill a green glass vase is filled with holly and mistletoe. Inside the vase the sun magnifies the shadows and separates the stalks into myriad shades of green. The beauty of it grips at my throat.

In all the many, many years we have spent together I have

never seen Theodora like this. Her head hangs down and her eyes watch a patch of sunlight which falls on the carpet, framing the dainty shoes that she always wears although her ankle bones bulge to the side of them now. I feel our eyes meet on the floor, and the world is turning and turning, and time holds us in its grip. Theodora picks up her walking stick, rises and takes hold of a cardigan which is on the back of her chair, then she puts the cardigan over my shoulders and I pull the sleeves of it straight, and she moves to sit beside me on the sofa.

There is a joy, a strange warped joy, in seeing her so broken, for in all these years I have sought her love and yet I have never been certain of it. Now the strength of it is revealed, finally, in the pain that she feels. From outside we hear Freddy dragging a shovel along the path, and a shiver of wind in the trees and, in the far distance, the sound of a tractor. We stare down at the frozen fields, and the trees, black where the snow has melted, silhouetted against the snow-flecked land – and, oh, how life is distilled now, and stripped right down to the white of the bone.

Maggie

Today I'm having lunch with this journalist Adam Ferrall – Adam Ferret.

On the telephone, he was shifty, red-haired and long-nosed, sniffing around in other people's lives. So now it's a surprise that he isn't much older than me, and that his face is pale, clear-skinned, with dark eyes. Certainly not sharp-and-seedy journalist. Perhaps more earnest-Englishman-with-plastic-bag? He's got those wide-open kind of eyes, slightly red at the rims, which don't blink for five minutes, then blink twice, then stare again. His hair is cropped very short, which normally I don't like, but above his mournful face, it looks all right.

'Maggie?' He squeezes my hand so that the bones of my fingers cross over and stares down at me as though concerned about the state I'm in. Or perhaps it's just that I'm not what he had in mind? He runs his hand over his bristly hair and smiles. His teeth are even and white, except for one at the side, which is crooked, and triangular in shape. He carries a soft leather briefcase – and yes, a plastic bag. He's dressed in jeans, a woollen jacket over a ribbed rollneck jumper and a striped scarf. His eyes draw like magnets. I turn away, shrugging, staring around me.

This café – just off Fleet Street – is his choice and it's all stainless steel, like a school canteen, with pale wood and spotlights on wires stretched across the ceiling. I told him on the telephone that I wouldn't have long. Now I say it again, but he's brimming with charm, indicates a spindly table near the window, and folds his legs underneath it. Does the fact that he is not sharp-and-seedy journalist make this better or worse? Just get it over with, that's the important thing. He starts to talk about his work, mentions various newspapers. Probably I should have heard of him but I don't read the newspapers.

He's trying to put me at my ease. Where do I live? Where does he live? Fulham. The weather's been awful, we agree. More snow is still possible. His voice is flat, with a paper-bag rustle, and no emphasis anywhere. I watch his mobile phone on the stainless-steel table. In the space between us a white tulip wilts in a milk bottle. I grip my hands together in my lap so I'll remember not to eat the sides of my nails and my eyes buzz around his head, not settling on his face.

Of course, I'll have lunch? No. No, thanks. I'm in a hurry. His hands are large and capable. Plug-wiring and bottle-opening hands. His nails are neatly cut with a shine to them, as though they've been polished. Perhaps I'll have a cup of coffee? Yes. A hot chocolate would be better actually. A waitress squeaks over to us in platform trainers. He orders a toasted Mediterranean ciabatta sandwich, with some salad, not on the side, but on a different plate, and a cappuccino, made with double coffee, and mineral water, flat not sparkling.

He talks about Dad and it's clear he's swallowed the lot – hook, line, sinker, fisherman and river bank. The person he talks about is a man in the newspapers, not my dad – or perhaps it is my dad, and I just don't know that. His hands rearrange the cutlery as he talks, lining up the knife and fork so that they're the same distance from the edge of the table. My eyes move to the steamed-up window beside us and across to the few other customers, media types, sipping coffee, huddled together in hushed conversation. I'm worried that they'll hear.

I cycled here, so my skirt is wet and my russet-coloured scarf – the carefree gypsy look – keeps slipping off my shoulders. My hair is damp and hangs down like a witch and my boots are dirty. It's deliberate, that. I want him to know that I am not to be charmed. Odd clothes are always useful for that, they put other people at a disadvantage. I peer at the salt and pepper pots, shaped like chrome pyramids. My nose is running, I haven't got a handkerchief and the napkins here are linen so it seems a bit much to wipe my nose on them. I'm loaded down with two plastic bags of overdue library books. Under my skin, I'm shivering. I look at my watch.

Adam Ferrall asks about my early memories of Dad and I tell him that I don't really have any, because I lived with Nanda, and then I went away to school. He asks more questions. No, I don't think so, I say. Yes, perhaps. I'm sure you're right. Yes. No. Probably. It's surprising how many questions can be answered in one word. The waitress returns and I stir hot chocolate with a swirl of cream and cinnamon sprinkled on top.

What actually can I remember about Dad? Mainly weekends when he used to come to Thwaite Cottages and I used to describe colours to him, because he's colour-blind, and I felt sorry for him, because I didn't understand and thought that all the world looked black and white to him. Blue tastes fresh like peppermint, or a sharp winter morning, and it sounds like a running brook, and feels like a feather brushed against your face. Red screams and burns your fingertips and smells like pepper. I used to go on and on like that.

And one day he taught me to smoke, sitting on the front wall at Thwaite Cottages, looking down over the valleys, in the summer, with his cigarette making a curl of smoke, as he showed me how to inhale it, and everything went fuzzy and blew up like a balloon inside me, and we laughed and laughed until I nearly fell off the wall. Probably I won't tell Adam Ferrall that.

Silence now, except for the squeak of the waitress's trainers, and the mumble of hushed conversations from behind over-coat collars. I watch his eyes and wait for them to blink but they don't. Like a good barrister, he's knows that silence makes people indiscreet but he's got the wrong person because I've seen all that before. I imagine myself like a cartoon character, hanging on to the edge of a cliff, sliding down on elongated fingers. It would be better, I decide, for me to come to the point, because I won't have him thinking I'm scared.

'Presumably, what you're really interested in is the . . . fire and Tiffany and all that?' My voice catches on that word and stumbles.

He blinks twice and swallows. 'No. Not really. The book I'm writing is a political commentary, or the biography of a group of people. I'm not looking for scandal, but I do need to look at the people I write about from all different sides, so I can show the truth about them.'

'Oh really, is that what journalists do? They reveal the truth?'

He sits back in his chair, smiles, shakes his head.

'Maggie, perhaps you don't think much of the media, but

all journalists are different and some do important jobs. Some journalists even die for what they do.'

'Only in the same sense that some shop assistants get run over by buses.'

'Isn't it really a bit easy to criticise the media?' he says. 'I could do the same. Most of my colleagues do. But strange though it may seem, I happen to believe in the value of what I do.' The waitress arrives with his sandwich, which smells of hot bread, and basil and olive oil, and he starts to eat it with his knife and fork, cutting neat squares in the crusty bread.

'But how you can be so sure that people want to know the truth?' I say. 'There are plenty of facts which happen to be true but are better kept private.'

'Do you think so? I'm not sure I agree. I think people aren't damaged by what they know, only by what they don't know. It seems to me that people are attracted by the truth. They may try not to recognise it, and they may take time to accept it, but finally it's all that they want.'

My mind moves around that idea and stores it for future thought. I hadn't expected him to say anything interesting, because I always assume that good-looking people aren't intelligent. For me people divide into those who might say something which interests me and those who definitely won't. He just might fit into the former category – a rare find.

'And behind all the opinions,' he says, 'there are facts, don't you think?'

'No, actually, I don't. You know, when the police carry out interviews ten minutes after a crime even the people who were standing right there can't agree on the basic facts. And – you know – I studied history at university and that's the same. You think it's about facts but it isn't. It's about the nature of evidence. Who's telling the story, and why?'

I don't know if I believe what I'm saying, but I'm measuring the dimensions of his head. Around us sounds become distinct like separate notes on the piano – the rustle of a newspaper, the scrape of a chair, the clatter of a plate. He keeps me enclosed in his unblinking eyes. His face is strangely transparent – thoughts gather and disperse across it like clouds on a windy day. And OK, so he is good-looking – but I don't want to fall for the old trick, I want to be more original than that.

'Listen, Maggie. If I write about what's happened to your father, then it's not because I'm interested in scandal, it's because I think the way he was treated was unfair. He should never have been arrested and I'm not afraid to say that.'

'Yes, it was wrong.' I can say that calmly but my skin has gone curly. I don't want to have this conversation, but at the same time I do, because there's a part of me that enjoys the drama of this, disgusting though that is. It's an excellent story, and I was there at the centre of it, and I can't resist the appeal of that, because it's never seemed real.

Like when I signed the statement, in an underground room at Gloucester police station, with a smell of stale ashtrays, and an echo like a tunnel, and someone having a furious row down the corridor. Three ballpoint pens tried to save me. I had to sign the statement on every page and they kept on breaking. The policeman tried each one out on a pad, making squiggly lines, and they worked for him, but they wouldn't work for me, and I pressed harder and harder, digging deep ridges into the paper. The policeman kept on laughing, so I had to laugh as well. Ha-ha-ha-ha-ha. An electronic sound, rattling round and round, up to the high ceiling, crossed by pipes as thick as tree trunks. After I'd finally done it, I smiled at the policeman, and shrugged. A formality, his look said, but there was pity in his smile.

I hide my thoughts, in case he can see them. Blood pumps in my fingertips. 'It must have been terrible,' Adam Ferrall says.

'Well, yes, except I didn't know that she was inside the cottage at the time. Then straightaway I went away to Thailand for three weeks, so I wasn't around.'

He nods at me, and his eyes soften with a bedside-manner sympathy, and just for a moment I think – I could tell him it all, the best scoop he's ever had, and he'd be famous, and it would be because of me, and he'd be grateful to me forever, and I wouldn't have to think about it any more. I feel the words buzzing on my lips, as I watch his eyes blink, and blink again.

'You know, it really wasn't fair,' Adam says. 'Because it was suddenly all in the press about how he had been at the cottage earlier that day, as though that was a big revelation, but the point is that he told the police that from the beginning.'

'Yes, of course. Fiona and Dad. Geoffrey and Tiffany. They were all close friends. They were round at our house, or we were round at theirs all the time. But the point is that the press were determined to bring Dad down. Overnight their little darling turned into Beastly Priestley. It was the usual tactic – build-him-up, build-him-up, then knock-him-down.'

'But what do you think did happen to her?' Adam asks.

He pours me some water and passes it to me, but it won't go down my throat. What can I say? If you've got a love affair, and a tin of paraffin and a dead body, then the possibilities are numerous. Don't over-explain, just keep it brief. I must use words carefully, he's a journalist, reading between the lines is his job. My heart flutters around me like a bird.

'I don't know,' I say. 'I assume she had another man. I mean, I don't want to be mean about her, but she easily could have done. She'd have got bored with Geoffrey.'

He nods and watches me with unblinking eyes. I've got to stop this.

'But Tiffany's brothers. They're not happy, are they?' he says. 'I mean, they're not happy with the investigation and the Fire Officer's Report?'

'No, they're not, but actually that report is quite clear. Of course, if you really want to go through it with a tooth comb, and put it all together in a different way, then you can make the evidence suggest a different conclusion . . . But the fact is that the people who wrote that report say that the fire was an accident . . . and anyway none of that's got anything to do with Dad. He wasn't there that night. I mean, I'm sorry for Tiffany's brothers. Very sorry. But they need to accept that there are some things we will never know.'

'Oh – do you think so?' Adam says. 'My guess is that it'll all become clear in time. That's the way it always goes. The truth has a life of its own and it tends to make itself known. As I said, it's what people finally want.' His unblinking eyes stare at me, then he finishes his sandwich, deftly using his knife to stop a last crust from spinning across the table.

Suddenly his mobile phone shrieks the William Tell Overture. I leap so that my knees bash against the table. 'Sorry,' he says, and presses a button to silence it.

My fingers have left sweaty rings on the stainless-steel table and I move my hands to cover them. A coffee machine grinds like a dentist's drill. I look at my watch, and say that I've got to go, and thanks for the hot chocolate. Outside, rain slants against the window and heavy drops slide down the glass, running apart, and then together, through the window dirt.

'Don't go,' he says. 'Wait at least until the rain has stopped.'

'No, really. I'm late.'

'You'll get soaked.'

'It doesn't matter.'

The waitress asks if we want a pudding. Adam takes the menu and holds it out to me. 'You have something,' he says. I'm standing up ready to go, but I take the menu because I don't want to look frightened. He says why don't I have yoghurt and fruit if I'm not very hungry, but I have chocolate mousse cake. He orders that and another cappuccino for himself, made with double coffee.

'I'm sorry,' he says. 'I've upset you.'

'No, no. You haven't. Not at all.'

'It was tactless of me.'

'Don't worry, really. It's fine.'

I shrug and pick at the corner of the menu. Adam sits back on his chair and moves his legs out from underneath the narrow table. His feet are beside me, long black shoes, and thick socks. His shadowed eyes watch me staring at the wilting white tulip. I ask if he minds, and then pick up his bottle of mineral water, and carefully tip the rest of the water into the milk bottle.

'It must be hard having someone well known as a father,' he says.

'No, not really. More of a salutary lesson, to be honest.'

'In what way?'

'Well, for my Dad's generation it was all Glittering Prizes and making their mark, but the point is that it didn't make them happy. I mean, you know Oscar Reynolds? Oil billionaire pouring environmentally unfriendly substances into African rivers? Well, he's a friend of Dad's and sometimes he gets drunk and cries because he really wanted to be Laurence Olivier.'

Adam is laughing.

'Yes, I know. Ridiculous, isn't it? But the point is that

even if he had been Laurence Olivier he wouldn't have been happy. Nothing would have been enough.'

'So you're going to do it differently, are you?' Adam asks.

I shrug and eat my pudding, licking chocolate from my spoon.

'Tell me about Brussels,' he says. 'Why are you going there?'

'I got offered a good job.'

'Better than being a barrister?'

'More worthwhile.'

'What job is it?'

'Aid administration for Poland. I lived in Poland – for a couple of years.'

'Ah.' He wipes cappuccino froth from his upper lip with his napkin. 'So it turns out you're not such a cynic after all.'

'No I'm not. In fact, rather the opposite. It's just that there are some people in life who snigger in the back row, and I'm one of them. But that doesn't mean I don't have any ideals.'

'And do you know Brussels at all?'

'No, but that doesn't bother me. I'm just glad to go abroad again. I want to see a few places, before I settle down. I mean at the end of the day there's almost certainly Labradors and the school run in Fulham, isn't there? So why rush into it.'

Too late, I remember he lives in Fulham.

'God, sorry, is that the time?' I look at my watch. 'Now I really must go.'

He pays the bill and finds my coat. It's a wonderful Doctor Zhivago fake fur, but I'm embarrassed by it now, because it smells doggy when it's wet. As we go, he puts his hand on my back, steering me out of the door, then his watch strap catches in my hair, and he unhooks it while I stand still, feeling the strand of hair pulling right up to my scalp. His skin is smooth, his cheekbones polished. The untangling takes a while. I keep my mouth shut, trying not to breathe too much.

On the pavement outside, in the sharp edge of the wind, he says, 'So when are you leaving?'

'Three weeks. Thirteenth of March.'

'Oh, I see. Well, I might give you a call – before you go.'

Why would he do that? Perhaps he wants to tell me his problems – men usually do; I run a kind of unofficial counselling service for men with relationship problems. They ring up all the time, and invite themselves round, and sit mournfully on my bed, and go on and on about how difficult it is to find a woman to suit them, and they stare into my eyes and say – if only all women were like you, Maggie. But they never do anything about it – they seem to think I'm above all that, or perhaps beneath it.

Or probably he just wants to ask more about Dad.

'You should talk to Gus,' I say. 'He's the person that really knows.'

'Maybe. But I'm a little worried about the nature of his evidence.'

I smile, head towards my bike and flick my scarf over my shoulder, but the wind blows it back in my face, and I taste musty wool in my mouth. The rain has stopped and for a moment there's sun, the first in weeks. He puts my two plastic bags in the basket and I lean down beside my bike and search through my Bermuda Triangle bag for the key to my bike lock. Out of the corner of my eye I can see his shoes still next to me on the pavement. Raindrops shine on them.

Finally I have to lift everything out of my bag. There's a half-eaten bar of chocolate, used tube tickets, a snot-encrusted handkerchief, a Tampax, one of Nanda's letters and a pile of other junk. My ticket for Brussels is caught in the wind, and blows down the street. Adam runs after it, catches it as it flutters against the wheel of a car and dries it on his handkerchief. For no reason, I feel tearful. When I've finally got the key I reach down to try to undo the lock but everything is wet from the rain, and the key won't go in. Still he's standing beside me.

'Let me do it,' he says, so I hand over the key without looking at him. 'You know your front tyre is worn out,' he says. 'You ought to get it fixed.'

'Yes, perhaps.'

'And the gear wire isn't connected either.'

'Yes, I know, I'm just about to get that fixed as well.'

In fact, the gear wire has been like that for two years.

I get on my bike, and sit with one foot resting on the pedal.

'So I'll call you,' he says.

'Yeah, if you want.'

I wobble away on my bike and try not to start expecting anything.

At Moulding Mansions I start packing. One of my old school socks dangles over the gaping jaws of a black rubbish bag. I bin it, I bin it not. Beside me there's a pair of shoes I tried to dye, a manicure set with most of the pieces missing, and a ghoulish plastic monster with orange nylon hair, which Sam won for me at a fair. These things cling. 'Packing is agony,' I say. 'What to take with you and what to leave behind?'

'Maggie, do you really think you've got any choice?' Sam says. He's stretched out on the floor beside me, opening a bottle of wine. Rough-faced, with battered shoes, he's too large for London. He should be tilling the fields in a Thomas

Hardy novel. Like me he's from one of those families where everyone has to do something extraordinary all the time. Except he's not very extraordinary, so he spends his day auditing on the M25.

'So,' he says. 'What's going on with you?'

I open my mouth. 'Perhaps just the edited highlights?' he says.

I drop a cushion on him and push a pile of books into a box. Sam is not at his best. Earlier this week his Australian girlfriend, Debbie, explained her priorities to him. Basically, he comes third after her horse, and her job, but above soft furnishings, and fashion in fifth place. He's decided to give it some time, confident that soon he will supplant the job, if not the horse.

The front door slams. Tyger is back from consulting a witch in Dagenham. Clearly the metaphysical forecast wasn't good. She sidles into my room with a packet of fags in her hand. Stepping over Sam, she pours herself wine, sits in the pink armchair and returns to the subject she's been flogging for days.

'I still don't get it, Maggie, I just don't get it. Why are you going away?'

I don't know what to say. She knows nothing about the voices in my head, the treadmill of my thoughts. I keep packing – hat boxes from the top of the wardrobe, scarves from the end of my clothes rail, a Chinese hat from the curtain rail, postcards from the wardrobe door. Gloves are spread out on the bed like withered hands. Striped woolly ones, long pink satin evening gloves, mittens, and old-fashioned sheepskin motoring gauntlets.

Tyger peers at me over the top of a pair of sunglasses, shaped like flowers, which she's picked out of one of my boxes. 'And what I particularly don't get is how Maggie the

Chess Player – who can't take a decision unless she can see ten moves ahead – decided this without a word of consultation.'

It's true that on this occasion there was no 'to take it, to take it not'. When they rang to offer me the job I said yes before they'd finished the sentence. Later I asked Nanda why I did that and she said – but, of course, my dear, that's how it works. One agonises about small decisions but large decisions make themselves.

'So?' Tyger says. 'So?'

Dougie drifts in, with a joint in his hand, and Biggles cradled in the crook of his arm. He stretches out on the floor, propped against black plastic bags, and falls asleep with his mouth open. From outside in Bridewell Street tyres screech. Upstairs there's banging and dust drops from a crack in the ceiling. I've decided that in Brussels I'm going to rent a flat where everything is white – white walls, white curtains, white rugs on the floor, white sheets on the bed. Nothing like Thwaite Cottages, nothing like Moulding Mansions.

'I mean, this isn't just a bloody flat-share agreement, you know,' Tyger says. 'It's a way of life. You, me, Sam. We've always lived together. I thought we'd all end up in the same old people's home, when the moment comes. But now I don't know what's happened to you, Maggie.'

I don't know what's happened to me either. What she says is right. All of us come from families where there've been more divorces and deaths than hot dinners, so we were never going to do marriage and domesticity, or ambition and Glittering Prizes. But then Sam and I got proper jobs, and I got bored of this Peter Pan world of posh kids trying not to fit in. Or that's what I tell myself.

'I mean, what happened to Maggie the Moral Crusader? Maggie, Defender of the Poor, Oppressed and Wrongly

Accused?' Tyger says. 'Why give up the law when you're just about to make money out of it?'

'I don't know, I suppose the corners I wanted to defend turned out not to be right angles. Anyway I'd rather work abroad. It's anonymous. You can do what you want. I've never really liked London. It's really the most provincial place.'

'Ha bloody ha,' Tyger says. 'More like it's to do with Ned the Nerd. Who frankly isn't worth leaving the country for.' I turn my back on Tyger and step over Sam to lift blankets down from the top of the wardrobe. A good girlfriend is one who can judge the moment to start slagging off your ex-boyfriend. Tyger's timing is not great.

'I've got to say that, with the best will in the world, Ned was actually pretty boring,' Sam says.

'In my view there's a lot to be said for being boring.'

Tyger sighs, takes meat skewers out of her hair and starts picking out knots with a comb.

'No, it's true,' I say. 'Boringness is really underestimated. You know, I'm often standing at a bus stop and I see people there – and they've managed to get themselves out of bed, and they're going to work, or doing whatever else. And I feel like saying – Well Done, Very Good Effort. Because it's actually hard, you know. Even that's hard.'

Tyger stands up and gives me a beady stare. 'You know it seems to me that suddenly all you want is a comfortable little life with a two-bedroom mortgage.'

'Tyger,' Sam says. 'For God's sake, give it a break.'

But Tyger has gone. I should go after her and try to explain, but the truth is I can't be bothered. It's like people who are dying – they check out early, lose interest in earthly stuff. That's what I feel like about this house, it's like I've left already. The air around us is pale blue, sweet and powdery.

Dougie wakes with a start, sending Biggles rolling onto the floor. He struggles to his feet and steadies himself against the wall. 'So what's going on?' he says.

'Dougie. We were just saying life's a bit complicated, that's all,' Sam says.

'Yeah,' Dougie says. 'Yeah, you're right about that.' He stares up at the ceiling and waves one hand high through the air. 'I mean it's like one of those . . . what do you call it? Like an electronic machine, you know . . .' He stops to pull up his trousers. 'All buttons and flashing lights, and you've got no idea how to work it, so you press each button, then you press them all together. Then you hit it, and you cry with anger and frustration.' He picks up Biggles, opens the wardrobe door, realises he's not going to get out of the room that way, and then shuts it again. 'Probably there were Operating Instructions, but you lost them years ago.'

In Cannabis Veritas.

MARCH

Max

Often I think of Tiffany. But in a way that is partial, disconnected. Dipping and wobbling, an image flashes in front of my face, and then is gone. The camera lurches. Suddenly I see a close-up of a single detail. Red fingernails, a bracelet of gold hearts, blonde hair in the dark. I don't know if it's because I can't remember more. Or whether memory is kind.

I met her first when Geoffrey brought her to stay for the weekend at Brickley Grange. What a cliché she seemed. An All American Girl, bright and brazen, with an expensive tan and blonde hair. She ran her hands over the quaint old furniture, and exclaimed over our strange Old World ways. Geoffrey was all over her, embarrassed and proud. I took her for a gold-digger. That was before I knew that she had far more money that Geoffrey has, or ever will have. At dinner, she insisted that she should sit next to me, which certainly wasn't part of Fiona's seating plan.

She talked about the inner journey, working things through, trying to find a place of peace. So very sincere. Too much time in California, I thought.

Isn't it much more important to be honest with yourself

than to have a successful career? That's what she asked, over the roast beef.

Doubtful, I said. The importance of becoming rich and powerful can hardly be overestimated.

But doesn't material success just lead to unhappiness, she said.

We don't really do unhappiness on this side of the Atlantic, I replied. It's just divorce and chemical substances. And occasionally nervous breakdowns, but only for the truly self-indulgent. She didn't like that.

There was a Frenchman staying with us that weekend, and he asked about the difference between English and American English. Tiffany started to tell him about that, but he wasn't clear. But can you understand everything that an American says? he asked. Oh yes, I replied. We can understand everything that Americans say, we just can't understand why they bother to say it.

That made her even crosser. I was enjoying winding her up. Maggie was as well. Tiffany spent a long time explaining to us all this bunkum about feng shui. Then Maggie nodded her head, looking serious and puzzled. So what exactly is the difference between feng shui and having a really good clear-out?

Later, further down the table, there was a drunken conversation about what it would be like if you could know the future. Tiffany interrupted saying that she could read tarot cards. I mean, really. But that's how she was. Very attention-seeking. And I don't like attention-seeking people. Because I like everyone to pay attention to me. Of course, everyone found that ridiculous and started to joke about it. Geoffrey didn't want her upset, so he said of course she could read tarot cards. And so it finished up that she was going to tell our fortunes. But it was all just a drunken game.

She sat in my study and we went in, one by one. I was the last and I tried to sit in an armchair by the fire, but she tapped the leather seat of an upright chair with her pink varnished fingernails, so I sat down beside her. She had turned off the lights except for the green shaded lamp on my desk. There was ringing in my ears. The curtains of my study were drawn. Her fingertips touched mine as she leant over and took my glass from me. You shouldn't drink so much, she told me, and tipped my Irish malt into a plant pot. Typical, that. She had a great taste for Hollywood clichés.

Blonde hair tied back in a ponytail. Swimming-pool eyes. The kind of face you want to slap. The light made a circle around her hands as she laid out the cards. We sat in silence and I fidgeted. From the dining room I could hear people laughing and joking. I saw her looking down at my slippered foot. I moved it under the table. The cards gave me the creeps. Black and spiky line drawings with evil faces on them. I watched her kneecaps, pressed together, under the hem of her skirt. Her perfume was cloying. Her black top showed the strap of her bra.

You're not the man you seem, she said. You hide your face.

I said that's probably a good thing, and she frowned and shook her head so that the leaf earrings shook. I felt like laughing. Then she said she could see a woman, a powerful influence in my life. Probably your mother, she said.

It must be Fiona, I said.

But she said no, it was someone more powerful. Someone who was close and yet distant. I thought about Rosa. A log on the fire popped and crackled, and she leant towards me so I could see the movement of her throat as she breathed. Then the drink and the embarrassment of the situation got the better of me. Perhaps it's you, I said.

She looked at me and she put her hand on my knee. Perhaps it is, Max, she said. I felt like laughing. But she didn't take her eyes off me, and there wasn't any sound from the dining room. She looked at the cards again and she said she couldn't see my future clearly. She nodded her head sadly.

I'll tell you a story about fortune-tellers, I said. I had to clear my throat because my voice had gone croaky. A friend of mine went to see a fortune-teller and he said what you've said – I can't see anything much about your future. And the fortune-teller was really upset.

Well, yes, Tiffany said. When you lay out the cards and you can't see the future, it's worrying. You have to be careful what you say. She was looking at me intently. I was looking at the skin of her neck.

Anyway, you'll never guess what happened, I said. The next week the fortune-teller was run over by a bus. Tiffany was really angry and stamped out of the room. I sat by the fire, poured myself another whisky. But the truth is I was stirred up. Because it does happen sometimes. You do know the future. And I think it happened that night. Her hands on the cards, the strap of her bra, the log falling in the grate. The future was there. The road had divided. I took the turning which brought me to this infernal spot. And somehow I knew it at the time. No way forward, no way back.

Today I'm in London, just for the afternoon. I'm meeting up with Geoffrey. His idea, not mine. Before I head back to Gloucestershire. He's busy, he said, so he'll have to be brief. As though I've got all the time in the world, which of course I have. I wouldn't put up with it, but I'm hoping he'll have some news about this job.

He's a curious chap, Geoffrey, always has been. There's

really no excuse for him except he's an old friend. And finally that does excuse everything. He plods through life in his crêpe-soled shoes and dandruff-scattered tweed jackets. At school he was picked last for every team and was famous for having extraordinarily little pubic hair. At university he was known as Two Brain Drummond but no one took him seriously. Then in the blink of an eye thirty years have gone by and suddenly he's recalled. Energy Minister. Tipped for the Cabinet. Mind you, I could have gone the same route if I'd wanted. But I was never a man to toe the line.

I arrive at his house in Chelsea, ring the bell, ease my finger under the collar of my shirt.

'Geoffrey, good to see you.' He draws me into the house, takes hold of my hand. Then my whole arm. I'm like an actor who's forgotten his lines. That morning comes back to me. When I had to go and tell him that Tiffany was dead. All night we'd been trying to reach him, with no success. He's an insomniac and often unplugs the phone. So I had to come around here. Gus said he'd come for me, but I couldn't let him do that. It was ghastly. I've always been absolutely awful at that kind of thing. No idea what to say. Worse than that I had to resist a terrible desire to laugh. Shock, I suppose.

'Max,' Geoffrey says. 'Max.' He's still got hold of my arm.

'Good for you,' I say. 'Yes.' Still I can't think of the words.

Geoffrey looks worse than ever. Poor sod. Partly it's over-work, of course. But it's not just that, it's grief. Funny, you'd think that if you'd been through that yourself, losing your wife, you'd have lots of patience, but oddly you have less. The awful truth is that Geoffrey, sitting there with his white face and fleshless body, makes me annoyed. There's nothing anyone can say that will help. There is no comfort. You've got to get on with it, that's all you can do.

Geoffrey takes me to his study. His hands are shaky. His

long arms swing and his head is bent forward. He's like something left over from some earlier stage of evolution. He has freckles and sandy red hair, and long legs which don't seem to be part of him. He's forever swinging them around, crossing them, uncrossing them, hooking them over the arms of the chairs. Clearly he's got a cold. He's snuffling and red-eyed.

He sits down behind his desk. From the formal way he does that, and the fact that he keeps clearing his throat, I know there's something wrong. Something more than the normal, that is. This isn't about the job, that much is clear. He starts to chat, but chat isn't Geoffrey's thing. He talks about Maggie. Brussels, what an opportunity for her! The weather. Fiona. How is James getting on at school?

Above his desk there's a photograph of Tiffany. A very good photograph. She'd have made sure that there were no bad photographs of her. And of course, she was a pretty girl. One of the prettiest girls I've ever seen. Features which were rather too large and obvious. Like those heroines in boys' comics. Eyes slanting upwards, mouth shaped like a bow. In the photograph the three of us are standing there together at some formal dinner. I can't remember where. Geoffrey and Tiffany. They were so mismatched. Makes me wonder why he ever married her. She was right out of his league. That always leads to trouble. The problem is that Geoffrey's an innocent. He may have his hands on the levers of power, but essentially he's only just out of short trousers.

Geoffrey's phone rings and he takes the call. It's Leo. I listen to half the conversation. The proposed tax changes, the budget wrangles, whether Robson is really in line for the Defence portfolio. It's like hearing about some thrilling outing from which you've been excluded. Once they'd have been interested in my view. But not any more.

The conversation goes on for a while. Geoffrey sits down, stands up, swings his legs over the back of the chair. Geoffrey, Hugh, Buffy, Angus. We were all at university together. Members of the Citadel Club, which we, in fact, set up. It's attracted a lot of attention in the press, over the years. That's what this journalist asks me about. But it's hard to explain. On the one hand it was about big ambitions. About power. But in another sense it was just a boys' drinking club. It all seems pretty childish now. To dream and not to count the cost.

Geoffrey puts the phone down, starts to recap the conversation, forgetting that I heard half of it anyway. This is an avoidance tactic. I don't like the way he's so twitchy. Come on, Geoffrey, get to the point. He keeps stopping to sneeze or cough. Sorry, he says. Sorry. Frightful cold.

Then he says, 'Look here, Max, I actually wanted to see you on rather a difficult matter.'

I nod.

'Well, the fact is that Tiffany's brothers, and the rest of the family have been talking . . .'

He coughs and snivels. 'Sorry, I haven't offered you a drink. Tea, coffee, something stronger?'

'No, really. I'm fine.'

There's silence.

'Yes, well, as I was saying. The fact is that Tiffany's brothers – well, you know, they had their criticisms of the police, well anyway, they have talked about launching a private prosecution.'

I watch Geoffrey across the desk. Feels like my head's being screwed into a vice. 'And who are they going to launch this prosecution against?' I know but I want to hear Geoffrey say it.

'Well, well . . .'

Geoffrey peers out of the window. 'Max, I must stress, I don't think it's going to come to that. It's just a discussion. And of course I've tried to tell them a thousand times what a bad idea it is.'

'It'll cost them a fortune.'

'Yes, of course it will, and I've told them that.'

'I don't see what they think they'll gain. It was an accident. There's nothing more to be said . . .'

'I'm so sorry, Max . . . You know, they're Americans, and nothing against the Americans, of course, but they do like their pound of flesh.'

I feel like a drink, or a cigarette. It's an effort to sound calm and reasonable. 'Well, obviously, they're very upset. Understandably so. We all are. And they want someone to blame. And if that's their way of coping with this . . .'

'Nothing is decided. I'm still trying to dissuade them. I'm her husband and I must have some say in this. I'm so sorry.'

He burbles on a while longer, sneezing and coughing. I'm not listening. Always I think if I wait just a little longer I'm going to be free of this. But the truth is it'll never end. I realise Geoffrey is asking me a question.

'Sorry, what was that?'

'I was just asking where you are off to now?'

'Back to Brickley.'

'Ah, peace and quiet in Gloucestershire. How I envy you that.'

Patronising sod.

'Sorry, to be in such a rush,' he says. 'I'd have liked more time to talk. When are you here again? We must have lunch one day.'

'Yes, we must. Any time.'

He's relieved now that he's got this conversation over with.

'Actually,' he says, 'Maggie is going to be here on Saturday. I don't suppose you'll be around then?'

'Maggie? I thought she'd gone already.'

'No, no. Any day now, but I wanted to catch up with her before she goes. Saturday lunch seemed the best plan.'

Suddenly it's all agreed.

'And bring Gus along,' Geoffrey says. 'I need someone to do some digging for me and he might be just the man.'

Geoffrey starts to pick up papers from his desk.

'Sorry to hurry you, Max, but I've got to get on. I've a meeting at the House at three. You know how it is.'

'Yes, yes, of course. Although I was going to ask you, just quickly, about that job?'

Geoffrey looks blank.

'The Inquiry job.'

'Ah yes,' Geoffrey says. 'Yes.' He sighs and looks over at me. 'Of course, I did suggest you for that. I'd mentioned that, hadn't I? Excellent solution, I thought. But no go.'

'Oh don't worry,' I say. 'I'm not sure I'd be best suited anyway.'

Bugger, bugger. I needed that job.

Geoffrey shrugs again and gives me a hangdog look. 'Sorry, old chap.'

The last thing I need is his sympathy. He's let me down. And I've been a very good friend to him. He thinks he's got the better of me, but he hasn't. Geoffrey is looking at me intently through his bloodshot eyes. 'The decision was to do with qualifications, that's all, there were simply people with a bit more knowledge in that sphere . . .' He coughs and looks away.

So there are people better qualified than me. Funny that, really.

'But there are many other possibilities, I'm sure of that.

What with your qualifications and abilities . . .' But he knows as well as I do that if there's any gossip about a trial, then there'll be no jobs for me. Somehow we say goodbye. Geoffrey is full of apologies. I am ushered to the door. See you Saturday. Yes, Saturday. I find myself in the street.

I drive back to Gloucestershire through horizontal rain and thrashing winds. I'm feeling pretty shaky. Bugger Geoffrey. Bugger Tiffany. How did I allow her to drag me into all this? What should I tell Fiona when I get home? Nothing. I'll just have to hope it doesn't happen.

Finally I see the lights of Brickley Grange. My spirits lift. The house I always dreamed I'd own. A Georgian facade and a big kitchen table, with everyone crowded around it, eating roast beef. As a child I never had that. It was all jam sand-wiches in the back of Nanda's Austin Seven. This is a house other people admire, a place where I'm on the inside. The only problem is that I've never quite believed in it. I'm always waiting for the grown-ups to come home and tell us off for sitting on the best furniture. And now, of course, it isn't my house any more. Fiona owns it. And if I don't behave then she can tell me to pack my bags.

I open the front door, cross the hall. The house is quiet with James away. I miss him. An outgrown coat of his hangs on a hook. His Wellington boots gather dust on a rack beneath. When Fiona and I married it looked like we wouldn't be able to have children. Test tubes and needles. Ghastly sessions behind hospital curtains. I tolerated it for Fiona. Then after we'd given up, James turned up of his own accord. Looks just like me, and I adore him.

Children are different when you have them late. When I had Maggie I hadn't finished being a child myself. I couldn't see the point of her. But now I see myself in James. Time rolled backwards. Dreadful – watching him go away to school, seeing the cage of life close around him.

In the back corridor my path is blocked by a church pew. I remember now that I bought it last weekend at some auction, despite Fiona's attempts to dissuade me. It is rather large. A barometer hangs above the telephone table. It was given to Fiona and me as a wedding present. I tap it and the needle rocks then settles back at the same point. Stormy.

In the kitchen Fiona is standing at the sink, looking at her watch, her eyebrows raised. A chef's striped apron, rubber gloves. 'Ah, there you are.' She swallows as though she's getting something difficult down. She has big, watery eyes. Untidy hair streaked blonde. There's a leathery, hard-working look about her which I've always found rather attractive.

'Had a nice day at the office, dear?' Her perennial joke, but it falls rather flat now there isn't an office. I nearly go to kiss her, then remember we don't do that any more. At the moment she's at a bit of a loose end. No job for me, no job for her. Invitations dried up. No James to look after. She's chopping up liver. The knife pulls down through the slime of it. My stomach turns. I look away, shuffle through post.

Inevitably our relationship has been pretty tricky since the fire. The pained expression on her face annoys me, although she's got every right to it. She's stuck to me through thick and thin. And I admire her for that. Any other woman would have baled out. She knows I've got my faults and failings, of course. Fidelity has never been my strong suit. Not that I've ever let her catch me out. I love her too much for that. But perhaps over the years she's guessed something. And my arrest upset her a lot. Being married to an adulterer, it's possible. But a criminal – no.

'You've come just in time to help me with some mousetraps,' she says.

'Oh. Do we need them?'

'Yes. A mouse walked right across the floor in front of me this morning.'

'Couldn't we wait until tomorrow? I'll go and buy those traps that don't kill them. Then we can just put them out in the garden.'

'Max, we've tried that before. It doesn't work.'

She stretches each finger of her rubber gloves, until she can pull them off. Then she picks up an evil pile of wood and metal braces and hands them to me. Mr Nipper. That's what the traps are called. I look at the liver on the chopping board. The smell is metallic and bloody. I lay the traps down on the dresser. 'Just let me get myself sorted, then I'll get on with it.'

One in three marriages ends in divorce. Terrible, isn't it? Frankly I find it extraordinary that two thirds last. Domestic routine. That's what holds them together. And the tyranny of possessions. People need possessions so they can feel significant in the world. But men have no talent for possessions, unless they're homosexual. A single man lives in a smelly, cheerless flat with suitcases open on the floor. So finally he has to find a wife. Then every weekend the poor sod's buying a new fan belt for the washing machine. Unblocking the drains. Clearing out the cupboard under the stairs.

Of course, marriage for love is different. Like my first marriage. I was young then and we were at each other all the time. We even argued about how to crack an egg. It mattered desperately that she should crack an egg the same way as me. Wonderful, of course. But normal life becomes impossible. No time for friends, jobs, interests. Finally you pray to be released from it. Funny how I've started to think about that again.

For Fiona and me, marriage is something different. It's not that I don't love her, because I do. But our marriage is the sum of our limitations, we both know that. A marriage of grown-ups. Neither of us is complete. She provides the foundation on which I can build the rest of my life and I do the same for her. She doesn't interfere in what I do. I don't interfere in what she does. But we've been happy enough, or at least we were. That's the funny thing about happiness. Usually you don't know you've had it, until you haven't got it any more.

For both of us marriage was a way out. When we met we were both at a pretty low ebb. Wine, women and song had left me jaded and I'd had an operation on my foot which made it worse instead of better. As an aspiring politician I needed a wife. And her father was an influential man in the Party. As for Fiona – what can one say? She was thirty-seven and broody. A classic panic buyer. A series of disastrous men, culminating in some toad who'd dumped her at the altar. Inevitable really. She's both intelligent and pretty. In a woman it's a fatal combination.

Supper. Usually Fiona is a very good cook. Except just before I was arrested she put the reduction from the lamb gravy into the chocolate sauce and burst into tears. So one does have to be a bit careful. Tonight she's opened a bottle of my favourite Côtes du Rhône, put a cloth on the kitchen table, and warmed some bread.

'You shouldn't have gone to so much trouble,' I say.

I'm always longing for her to behave really badly, let me off the hook.

She lights a candle, pours some wine for me. 'It isn't a trouble.'

As she stands at the cooker, her hand is propped above her

hipbone, her brown fingers spread across the tweed of her skirt. I can see the waistband, a patch of brown skin. A white garment which is probably some kind of thermal vest. I put out my hand to her. She slides away from me, gives me a weak smile.

I tell her about the job. She's full of sympathy but she can't really understand.

'Problem is,' I say, 'I feel rather far from the field of action. I need to be in London more. Keep in touch. You know, without the flat, it is a bit difficult.'

'Really?' she says. 'Really?' She busies herself with plates and a serving dish. 'Perhaps. But I really don't think there would be any point in you getting another flat in London now.'

Which means she's not prepared to give me any money. Even though it's my money. We've had this out before. I get nowhere. There's nothing I can say. I don't have a single card to play.

'Why don't you just stay here for a while? You don't need another job. We don't need the money,' she says.

'But I've no talent for domesticity.'

We both laugh. It's too obvious to be worth saying.

'Domesticity just creates clutter,' I tell her. 'I want there to be room for bigger things.'

'Such as?'

I've no answer to that. Except politics, I suppose. The grand plan, the opportunity to change the world, or the country at least. But it didn't work out like that. Any ideals I might have had were quickly shattered. After a while politics, even at a high level, is just the Women's Institute with ties on.

'The problem is that you always want something more,' Fiona says. 'And I understand that but I find it better to try to make whatever I'm doing at the time interesting because even if you're only buying tomatoes you can still enjoy it.'

'Can you?'

'Yes. It's a question of finding the epic in the everyday. Because life is about buying tomatoes and small things like that.'

'I take your point,' I say. 'But some people have to expect something more or nothing would change. If a person achieves something extraordinary then usually it's because they believed in the impossible.'

'Yes, but only a few people achieve something extraordinary. Many more just waste their lives in the pursuit of a dream.'

I don't know how we started this conversation. It's a long time since we talked like this. And it's strange because just recently Rosa said the same thing, in another way. That happens often. I find myself saving up something that Rosa has said to tell Fiona, and the other way around. I finish the wine. And the liver and bacon. It's a shame Fiona's not interested in me any more. The wine has made me rather perky.

'But do you actually like doing things like buying tomatoes?' I ask.

'Well, I don't mind. It's part of the agreement, isn't it? I mean, in a marriage it usually isn't possible for two people to be doing something extraordinary. Someone has to keep the home fires burning.'

'But do you regret now that it was you?'

'No, not really. Children and houses make me happy. But I did make a sacrifice and I did it partly for your happiness, so I'm sorry that it never made you happy. Or at least it's not so much that you're unhappy. You're just not quite here.'

'I'm sorry.'

'Oh, I don't really mind. It just seems a waste. Paying rent for a house you're not living in.'

We clear up the dishes, switch out the light. I follow her to the stairs. Her hand rests on the polished curl at the bottom of the stair rail. I stop her, put my hand over hers. The stair rail divides us. Her head is higher than mine. A shaft of light from the landing window touches her hair. Blonde, grey.

She tilts her head to one side and watches me. Her eyes in the shadows. Then she leans over and kisses my forehead, before her weary tread ascends the stairs. I follow her. When she reaches the landing, I catch hold of her again. She removes my hand, goes to the door of the spare room.

Maggie

Adam Ferrall telephoned me and I didn't return his call. Then he telephoned again and I was impressed because no one calls twice for me. He asked what I was doing this week. I said I was busy and shuffled papers near the telephone to create diary-consulting effects. Finally I agreed that I'd meet him at the Natural History Museum on Friday. He's got to go there for some fundraising thing. That was the only possibility because it's less than a week now until I'm going away.

On the steps of the museum he leans forward as though to kiss me but it goes all wrong because, as I reach towards him, he moves and I find my face pressed against the collar of his jacket and I wonder if he intended to kiss me at all. We both smile and bluster and he steers me back to the entrance hall, which echoes with drum rolls of laughter and the electric chink of glasses. The space above us is cavernous, with a zigzag of red and yellow bricks, and all around there are media types with rectangular glasses and thick-soled shoes, standing around the big dinosaur, under its snaking tail. This place is different now, all flashing lights and buttons, and low signs in clear writing. Nanda used to bring me when we came to London, when I was a child – that was her idea of a treat.

I'm wearing a new dress, or one that's new to me anyway. I didn't buy it for meeting Adam, of course, but just as a going-away present and I need a new dress anyway. It was in a vintage clothes shop and the skirt is floating grey chiffon, like the wings of moths, and the top of it laces up the back like a Victorian corset, squeezing me together. I did plan to wear some elegant, flimsy little shoes, but then at the last minute I put on my clumpy lace-ups and thick socks. I wouldn't want him to think I've made an effort.

'Let me take your coat,' he says. I'm wrapped up in as many layers as an Egyptian mummy and, after I've taken off my coat, he reaches out to take my scarf and cardigan as well. I feel his hand near me and the cold air on my neck and decide to keep them on for now. He finds me a glass of champagne and straight away he talks about his book and about meeting Dad. I look up at the tail of the dinosaur, swinging overhead.

He envies Dad, he says, because Dad is a man who has had a real opportunity to change things, he's not just looking and analysing, he's actually doing things. And he's a man of principle, because he's stood up for things he really believes in, and not just followed the party line. And on and on like that. Rather too late I start to wonder what I'm doing here. Really I should keep out of the way of Adam Ferrall. But it's like when somebody says – careful that's hot, and then you still touch it. Or it's like when you stand on the edge of a cliff and you want to throw yourself off.

A man comes over and Adam introduces me. He's bearded and bald so he looks as though his head is on upside down. Adam knows this man through work, and after I've been introduced, the man hardly looks at me but talks to Adam about some article Adam is writing. I stand beside Adam, listening, as other people come and go. My legs start to ache and I long for tea rather than champagne. I sit down on a spare chair on my own. It's only recently I realised you can come to parties and not talk to anyone.

Perhaps this is what it's like for wives and girlfriends, their lives bent into the shape of someone else's life. I don't really know about that because I've always been single, although I don't think of it like that. An Unemployed Girlfriend – that sounds better. Recently there was Ned the Nerd, but he didn't amount to much. He lived at Moulding Mansions before Druggy Dougie, and that's really all it was – a house-share arrangement enlivened by occasional fumblings under the bedclothes. Location, location, location. Six months ago he moved out and I've stopped expecting him to call, nearly. And who needs a man anyway, and my life is complete as it is, of course. Except, except . . . Recently I decided – it's compromise time. But even the compromise men haven't worked out.

Adam comes to look for me. I'm so sorry, he says, sorry, but I have to do a certain amount of that, for work. Then he suggests that we go and look at the dinosaurs. We walk through an arch into an enclave, where it's quieter, and peer into a glass case full of dinosaurs' teeth, with brown lines down the side of them, like Freddy's dentures, in the sink at Thwaite Cottages. Our reflections are smudged on the glass – my hair in a cloud around my face, and his head bent down towards me. The babble and splutter of the party echoes through to us, where we stand in a corridor of stone arches. The leg bones of dinosaurs float on glass shelves, and above us a model of a dinosaur is suspended on hidden strings.

'I don't think I really believe in Darwin,' I say.

'Darwin? He's a fact, isn't he?' Adam's hand grips a glass of wine. The same hand that squeezed the bones of my fingers together, the same clean nails, smooth and polished. Reflected in the glass, the profile of his face has a geometrical regularity to it, and I follow the plains and curves of it, mapping them in my head. The top button of his shirt is undone, showing a triangle of white T-shirt. If I touched that sparse hair, would it be bristly – or perhaps soft? A sudden top-shelf-of-the-newsagents feeling flushes through me.

'Well, if evolution exists, then why doesn't it work properly?' I ask. 'Why can't human beings fly? Shouldn't the evolutionary process organise that?'

The shiny tips of Adam's shoes rise up and down as he wiggles his toes. 'It's just that evolution is a slow and imperfect process. And perhaps there's a time lag so we are supplied with abilities after the time when we actually needed them.'

'I'm not sure I agree.'

Suddenly he changes the subject.

'You know there's one thing that puzzles me about your father?'

I shrug.

'He never says anything about his mother and everyone tells me something different. I've been told she was a teacher and an academic and a journalist and a peace campaigner. Then I was told she worked in Africa. Then I was told she used to live with two women and they were all communists.'

'Well, most of those things are true.'

'But where is she now?'

'God knows. Lost in the spiritual supermarket somewhere.'

'Dead?'

'Oh no. Alive. Very much so. In fact, I am going to see her at the weekend, before I leave for Brussels.'

'And is your dad fond of her?'

'Oh yes . . . Well, I don't know. I mean, they go at each other like vipers, and always have done. But that counts as fond in our family.'

Silence. A distant bubbling of voices.

'So what's she like?'

'That's a big question. When she was seventeen she ran away from school to fight in the Spanish Civil War and the police had to prise her, raging and screaming, from a gangplank at Dover. And it's been uphill, or downhill, all the way from there, depending on how you look at it.'

'And the women she lives with?'

'Freddy and Theodora. They're friends.'

'In the sexual sense?'

I purse my lip and give him a don't-be-so-stupid look.

'I'd hardly think so now, since they're all in their eighties. And as for the past, I don't know. They were part of a more private age. People didn't ask.'

'And you've never asked?'

He's beginning to annoy me.

'No, I never asked. Because there isn't an answer, or not in the sense that you want one. Friend, lover, wife, colleague, companion. The choice of words is too limited, isn't it? Not all relationships can be fitted into tidy boxes.'

I want to go home now because this evening hasn't worked out as I planned. I was stupid enough to think that perhaps this was about me but instead it's about Dad. Here I am again, playing the part that he wrote for me. If I don't go home now Adam Ferrall will probably start telling me about his problems.

'What you said about evolution, it isn't right. To me we just seem so badly adapted to the world that there can't possibly be a plan.' My voice sounds as though it has come unstitched. My eyes follow the wide staircase up to the galleries above. We decide to go back to the main hall but it isn't immediately clear how to get there. A corridor twists and turns. Navigation is difficult because we mustn't touch, we must not bump against each other, he mustn't lay his hand on my arm to steer me. The dinosaur bones just look like the litter of so many failed experiments, the wrong shape, put together in the wrong order, abandoned in despair.

At the entrance Adam rummages in his pockets and stares at his fingernails. 'So what are you doing now?' he asks.

'Going home, I suppose. Back to Stockwell.'

'Oh,' he says. 'Oh.'

'Well anyway, it's been good to see you.'

'Yes, yes. Very good. So how will you get to Stockwell?'

'Walk, I think. Or at least I'll walk some of the way.'

'What about your shoes?' We both look down at my black lace-ups and I laugh, so he knows it's all right for him to laugh as well.

'Perhaps I could walk with you? Just some of the way?'

Time goes slow and the space around us shrinks. My lips and fingertips are swollen. 'Yes. Of course. If you want.'

We head out into the darkness. 'You know, I'm quite certain there is a plan.'

'Really?' I say.

'Yes, I'm sure. And one day we will be able to fly.'

Our feet keep time along the pavement. I lengthen my stride to fit with his. Navigation remains complicated. There is a moment when he tries to turn one way and, turning the other way, I cut across his path. We come face to face, too close, and flinch back, out of range. Blue neon light from a shop window flashes over us. He tries to take my bag from me but I don't let him. When we reach a crossing he puts out his hand, as though to hold me back, but then stops before he touches me. It's been raining and the gutters are full and gulp twists of grey water. Showers squirt up from underneath uneven paving stones.

As we wait at a junction near Victoria a lorry goes by and splashes us. Adam gets out his handkerchief, shakes out the folds and passes it to me. I don't want it but he wipes the bottom of his trousers and my shoes. I'm laughing at him because the handkerchief is so small and there's water everywhere but I like it that he tries. When he's finished and folded the handkerchief, we wait for a green man.

'So was there something else you wanted to ask about Dad?'

'No.'

'Oh.'

The brakes of a lorry are released with a hiss. The light has gone green and people are pushing past us. 'It wasn't about your father,' he says. 'I just thought I'd like to walk home with you.' I feel suddenly sick and, when I look down at the pavement, my shoes are covered in water again. We look at each other in the half-darkness. I like the sadness of his face. The lights have changed to red again, so we have to wait. He takes my bag from me and when we walk on neither of us can think of anything to say.

Then suddenly it's easy to talk. Books, films, politics. I have the impression I'm fascinating. It's as though an invisible string has pulled tight between us and there's no slack. I remind myself to enjoy this time, to make the most of it. Because I've been in this situation often enough to know that this is the best bit. Before the excuses, the mute telephone, the tears and the pretending not to care.

We turn into a side street, towards the river, and walk past mansion blocks the colour of luncheon meat. Our footsteps echo in the empty streets and the black windows of houses watch as we pass. We stop so that I can get some gloves out of my bag. Adam holds the bag while I rummage in it. As I put on the gloves, he says, 'You know, I didn't know you were so young when your mother died.'

We walk on and our feet are out of time along the wet pavement. 'She was twenty-three and I was two.'

'I read the press cuttings.'

So my mother is just a column of newsprint in his mind. Does it matter? She's not much more in mine. Just a figure falling, suspended in liquid light, wearing a long coat, as she drops through the grey air, her coat flapping in the wind like the wings of a bird. The rain falls straight, but she falls crooked through it, turning, her ankles and legs straight but apart, a graceful cartwheel fall. Her hair is long like mine and spirals around her. Sometimes the branches of trees stretch out to catch her and I pray each one will hold her but each one bends then gives and she carries on down through the breaking branches.

'An accident like that wouldn't happen now,' Adam says. 'They'd check a building like that more carefully.' He wants a reason, as people always do, because if there's a reason then you can stop it happening again, but people had been stand-ing on that ledge for a thousand years – soldiers, and Welsh noblemen, and Japanese tourists with cameras – and in all of those thousand years it was that moment when it broke.

'Do you still have family in Spain?' Adam asks.

'No. I've seen the house where my mother lived but there's no family there now. Once I thought about going there, after I left university. I thought I'd teach English but this job came up in Poland instead. I don't regret it much because what would have been the point?'

When he peels off my glove and folds my hand up in his, it feels like putting down anchor. We reach the bridge, empty, except for occasional cars. Lights stretch for miles down the river and, below, a boat with a light disappears beneath us. It feels like the blood is flowing down his arm, into mine, and back again. There's a pulse in my palm and I can't work out whether it's his or mine.

'People don't usually ask about my mother,' I say. 'Death is the modern taboo, isn't it? In Victorian times it was sex – putting fig leaves on statues and covering up the curvaceous legs of pianos. Now it's different – you can say what you want about buggery and oral sex and hysterectomies, but talking about death is in poor taste.'

We stand in an alcove and look out down the river.

'Death would be all right if people would actually die,' I say. 'But instead they hang around and you feel a responsibility to them. Because you've got it. Life, that is, and they haven't and so you mustn't be caught complaining and you must do worthwhile things and have a good time. Because every day is reclaimed from . . . well, whatever the other thing is. The reverse of life.'

I feel the wool of his coat against my hand as I stand close to him, with the metal rail pressed against me, staring down into darkness.

'She had no wings to fly.'

When we get to Moulding Mansions, it's one o'clock.

'Is it safe to walk down here?' Adam asks, as we pass a burnt-out car.

'It's where I live.'

At the archway I hesitate, hoping Adam might decide to turn back, but he follows me across the courtyard. I'm hoping that no one will be home, but a light shines through the open front door and in the hall Dougie, in pyjamas and an Australian hat with swinging corks, is standing on a stepladder holding an electric drill. 'Mags,' he says. 'Mags, good to see you. You look amazing. Your hair looks amazing.'

'Well thanks, Dougs.'

'Yeah, I mean it's got all purple and orange snakes in it.'

'Thanks, Dougs, that's great.'

I stand with Adam on the doorstep because it's a bit hard to get any further with Dougie swinging around on the ceiling. Adam is looking a bit shocked. Probably he thought — rich bitch daughter of a millionaire politician with a Chelsea flat and no mortgage. Tyger appears wearing a short skirt and a sheepskin waistcoat with a small T-shirt underneath. She runs pink painted nails through her blonde hair and stands with one leg wrapped around the other. For someone who isn't a mindless bimbo, she does a good act. In the cramped space of the hall I introduce her to Adam. She runs a practised eye over him and I feel as though it's her tongue which is touching him.

Sam comes down to the hall and I introduce him as well and there are far too many of us in too little space and Dougie swinging overhead on the ladder, whistling. Sam looks at me and a light inside him goes on, then off, like the turning of a lighthouse. 'Dougs,' he says. 'Get down off that ladder and come upstairs because I want to say something to you.' He looks at Tyger, who starts to pull Dougie down and suddenly they've all gone upstairs.

After that we stand around awkwardly, glancing around us, holding on to our hands, while we listen to the sound of Sam, Tyger and Dougie trying to be quiet. They're all up for a stabbing. Blood is thumping in tight veins in my head and I'm tired and I want a warm bed and a cup of tea. But at the same time I don't want Adam to go. We don't have anything to say any more. I've ceased to fascinate him so I'm no longer fascinating. The invisible string that ran between us is slack. The silence is as thick as treacle.

'I better get going,' he says.

I walk with him back towards the road, under the archway that smells of piss, and he stops and I stand beside him, the light from a streetlamp wrapped in a circle around us. I should leave him here and walk back inside but I stand beside him, looking at the pavement. The night is holding its breath. I'm too far away from him and too close. I shrug and stand on one leg.

'So what are you doing tomorrow?' he asks.

I consider what would be the right answer, then realise that Adam is going to be pleased whatever I say. How liberating it is to be liked. 'Nothing,' I say.

'Nothing?'

'Well, just waiting for someone to take me away from all this.'

He laughs and leans towards me. 'Well, perhaps I could come round here after lunch? Two o'clock? We could go for a walk in the park and have some tea.'

'Sounds good.'

A doctor's-surgery shiver passes through me. Adam starts to chat about alternative parks and alternative teas and he's not looking at me. I know he's going to kiss me, it's just a question of logistics, of managing it without too much embarrassment, and I wish he'd get on with it, because I'm getting cold, and I want to go to bed.

'I enjoyed the party,' I say, so that silence can't get a grip.

It's hard to think about this and do it. I'd like to kill the chess player that's planning the moves in my head. I want to be overwhelmed but part of me is still sniggering in the back row.

'No matter how grown-up we feel we're all still holding hands behind the bike shed really, aren't we?' I say.

He laughs at me and then leans down, without any embarrassment, and kisses my neck just above my scarf. 'Thanks,' he says. 'I enjoyed myself. One more day reclaimed from whatever.'

Inside, Sam is lying in my bed watching TV and Tyger is sitting on a stack of boxes. My room has been stripped naked. My cardboard life has been packed up. There is no mirror, let alone a mark on it. Blue light from the television flickers over bare walls. I pull off my shoes and get under the duvet, next to Sam, who wraps his arm around me.

'I'd say six out of ten, seven at a push,' Tyger says.

'I shouldn't bother with all this courtship rubbish if I were you,' Sam says, leaning across me to stub out a fag. 'Just drive out to IKEA, buy a flatpack wardrobe, bring it home and assemble it together. If you're on speaking terms after that, book the marquee.'

'So didn't you want to show him your collection of etchings?' Tyger asks.

'Oh, shut up.'

'He did look as though he might have a trouser press,' Sam says. 'But I'm sure you could see it off.'

'It's not like that,' I say. 'I found him really interesting.'

Tyger and Sam exchange mock-serious nods. When I try to think about what Adam and I talked about, I can't remember. It's as though words were just filling up space while some more important communication was taking place.

'Is he a journalist?' Tyger asks.

'Yes. How do you know that?'

'I recognised the name.' It turns out that Tyger knows one

of Adam's colleagues. She would do, of course, because she's like Nanda, she knows everyone. So now Adam fits in somewhere and I have to take account of what other people think of him. He's part of the crowd.

'Marcia had a fling with him,' Tyger says. 'Apparently he's a very good journalist. He won some award. But she got a bit bored with him looking down at her from the barricades the whole time and talking about work and politics. And then he wanted to go on a walking holiday in the Lake District so she binned him.' It occurs to me that, for the first time, Tyger is jealous. Normally if a man's interested in me she's oh-so-encouraging but only because he's never the kind of man she might be interested in herself.

'Wait a minute, he's not the journalist who's writing this book about your dad, is he?' Tyger asks.

'Yes, he is actually.'

'Oh, I see.'

All is now explained. Of course, he doesn't actually like me. Clearly not. What he's after is information. That's what he is about – work and politics. I want to slap Tyger. But the point is – she's right, she's right. And it's dangerous for me to know him, more dangerous than Tyger can possibly understand. This has got to stop. But I want one more day. One more day can't harm. Just tomorrow. Then this stops – definitely.

Nanda

A diamond-edged day, the first day of spring, the last spring I will see, and the sun breaks in waves of pale yellow over the hills, its oblique light touching the edges of dry-stone walls and all the grey of the landscape suddenly made golden. The daffodils are out, growing on the bank, their faces turned towards the sun. I want to die outside in the fresh air, on a morning like this, but I don't know if I will have the choice, and in this matter one cannot learn from the experience of others – how to die well, the final test?

In Burrington there are two undertakers and a few days ago I went into the one which is known to be cheaper and less respectable because I wanted to try out the idea, almost as a joke against myself, and to check that I could do it. Of course, I've dealt with undertakers before, and I'm familiar with the patina of charm that they spread over death. The gentleman there – if I can call him that – explained that there are three different packages called the Worcester, the Wellington and the Windsor, the latter being, as one would suppose, the most expensive. This he said wearing a camel coat, as the front office was cold, and his hands were large and he wore a ring with a stone.

I think perhaps he guessed my situation and that unnerved

him, for although familiar with the dead, and the living, he is perhaps not comfortable with those stranded somewhere in between. For myself, I rather liked the idea of those three different packages, as they seem to add some variety and choice. Defeat I am prepared to accept, but I at least wanted there to be some heroism in it and I thought, privately, in terms of Wolfe at Quebec, or Gordon at Khartoum, or Latimer burnt at the stake, and I imagined it on black and white film, played to clapping hands and rows of open mouths.

But now I have come to suspect that death is a grey gabardine business, and that courage will finally be shown in bending, not breaking – in going quietly, yielding as a green stick does, making no fuss. At least it must be possible for me to stay here and die outside, for under no circumstances will I let them take me away. I think I can rely on Theodora for that, but perhaps not for too much else. Seasons may come and go but her egotism will endure.

I sit on a bench outside my cottage, my head turned up to the weak sunlight, and I think of the day when Max went away to Spain, a day very like this, early morning, with the mists still on the fields, and he was standing at the front gate and Freddy had the car out to drive him to the station, and he had a hat, a battered old trilby of Freddy's, and his clothes and books in one bag. A good-looking young man, tall and strong with thick hair, a handkerchief tied round his throat and boots which were already old and dusty, and he had his guitar with him as well, we had wrapped it carefully in an old piece of eiderdown. From the front gate he waved to me, and turned to go, adjusting the bag hanging on his shoulder, and his shirt blowing in the wind . . .

They tell me now that some young man is writing a book about him but by what right does he do that, I wonder?

What can he possibly know? I suspect his book will contain very little of the truth, for truths are uncovered in unexpected places, and cannot be fitted neatly into the structures which we make and I am the only one who was there from the very beginning.

The past has patterns now and can be organised in my mind. The turnips, I suppose, were really the beginning, at the Medlocks' farm, during wartime, and a young man was there, only the one, the rest having gone away to war, and he was tall and thin with silver hair. His fingers were too white and thin for farm work, and as he passed the turnips over, wrapped in newspaper, we both stopped to look at the lists printed – dead, dead, dead – such brief words, black on white, to express the ending of lives. I was new to Burrington then and, having arrived there from Berlin and before that Prague, I was already worn out with death.

This young man was Arthur Briston, and his family lived in one of the farm cottages and he could not fight, he told me, as his lungs were damaged, and he asked me if I'd like to see a newborn calf and we went to the barn, and the bloody afterbirth was still lying in the straw, and the calf struggled on shivering legs, and as we stood and watched it, he took my hand. It was a wet summer, with the continual smell of rot, and the war so far away he and I struggled to believe in it. We walked often across the Edge, and he was a young man of few words and he could understand nothing about me, but we became very good friends. For him I was a woman, not an intellect. One afternoon a bomber came over, as we lay on a blanket, high on the Edge, picking shells off boiled eggs, and the shadow of it, shaped like a jagged cross, passed across the clear, white skin of his back, and seemed to hover there a moment. Nothing more than a few afternoons of pleasure.

Marriage, children, family life – Theodora, Freddy and I considered ourselves to be destined for higher purposes, the pursuit of wisdom was not to be interrupted by the merely physical, so that when I fell pregnant we did not know what to do. Hot baths, gin and the potions Freddy mixed, made of bark and herbs, had no effect, for Max was stubborn even then, and I should have married Arthur perhaps for he pleaded with me again and again, but I would not even consider it, for I could not face the burden of his love.

You might suppose that an unmarried woman, living with two friends and having a baby, would have caused a great scandal, and doubtless people did disapprove, but they said nothing. The conventional wisdom is that rural areas are narrow and prejudiced and cities are open and liberal but I have rather found the opposite to be true because in the country people see the natural pattern, they know the value of privacy. Nowadays I read all these newspaper reports about pickle-jar babies, homosexuals and three in a bed and ignorant journalists tell us that this is evidence of a changed moral climate, but to me it seems that nothing has really changed except people's willingness to lay bare the details of their lives. There's nothing new, only a sordid desire to share what should be kept private, as I have seen in all those terrible newspaper reports about Max, which I now take care not to read.

During all of my pregnancy I was terribly sick and my face was as green as a spring leaf, and I couldn't eat or sleep, and so I walked all day on the Edge, alone with my mind. I knew from an early stage that the child was a boy and, as he grew inside me, he sucked all my strength for he and I could not share such close quarters. I felt myself invaded and driven back within my own body and as he swelled my skin was stretched tight over his thrashing body and at night I lay awake, sweating, staring into the darkness, alive with anger.

When he started to come, it was earlier than expected and I was far out on the Edge, and it happened as I was bending down to tug at my skirt, which was caught in the gorse, and I felt a shudder which loosened every inch of my flesh. There were clouds rushing low across the sky and patches of sunlight mottled the cropped grass and I kept on walking, my eyes fixed on the black horizon of the Edge, as though this was seasickness, which might shortly abate. Then when I did turn back I found myself in the midst of nothing, trapped between heaven and earth and above me the sky grew narrow . . .

It was Old Mr Medlock from the farm – dead many years ago now – who found me and he came with Arthur Briston, their boots flattening the grass, their voices blowing in the wind as soft as the sheep's wool caught in the gorse, and their hands enclosed my struggling limbs and the sky rolled and swayed above the fencing hurdle which they used to carry me home. It was thirty hours before Max was born and Old Mrs Medlock was there, and I remember the smell of blood, and antiseptic, and the candles burning lower and lower, and the sound of water being poured into a bowl. Sometimes I was conscious and sometimes not, and the night lasted for months, and, oh, how my flesh was shaved from my bones, until I no longer knew whether the bed was beneath me or above and when I finally felt Max slipping from me I would have reached down to push him away if I'd had the strength, and there was no cradle for him, so he was wrapped in a blanket and put in a box on the floor.

I was alone and I lay in bed, torn and bleeding, with my hands gripped across my empty stomach and again and again Max's angry screams splintered the stillness of the night. He would not give up. Oh, how those screams went on, brutal and twisted, so I had to go to him, and I looked at him, writhing in anger, and I could not touch him, and I cried to be released from him, yet still he would not stop and although I lay with my ears blocked against him, his screams went on and on, rising and falling in a bitter, hollow moan.

Then it was early morning and a watery light rippled over the room and I struggled up from the bed on paper legs, and went to look in the box on the floor, and Max was white and transparent, with blue veins and blue eyelids, and I looked down and saw the front of my nightdress stained with milk. His eyes were shut but he held up his hands, like newly bloomed flowers, and as I put out my finger to him, his hands clapped together, then he gripped my finger tight with both hands, and there was a shock in his touch, so that I swallowed my breath, and he opened his newborn eyes. He was heavy in my arms and his head lolled forward and I could not stand, so I lay down on the floor and I pulled open the front of my nightdress, and felt his hand touch my flesh.

It was a long, long time that we lay there, and the world was still as death, and my eyelids heavy, as his mouth tugged at me. Then above us the ceiling of the cottage was lit by the sun, and I stared up at all its lumps and stains, and my eyes followed every branch of every crack. Perhaps I slept, I do not know, or perhaps my eyes were closed, but in my mind that ceiling became a map, and the lumps and cracks and stains turned into mountains, and forests and rivers, so that finally it was as though the whole world was spread out above me, and he and I were there at the centre of it.

It turns out that death is a game of what one should tell and what one shouldn't. The days pass and Freddy, Theodora and I get on with our various projects, and I write letters which make no mention of what is to come, and talk about plans for the future as though I will be there. Yet there is a tension, an awareness of a monster which lies below the quiet surface, and must not be disturbed and anyway – perhaps all this does not matter so very much for why would one want to continue in this landscape of yearning, in this place of longing, endlessly unfulfilled? This world is surely playing out its final scene, and has become a place where people's attention span is no longer than thirty seconds, a place where there is no food you have to chew, a place where one may feel only those emotions sanctioned by celluloid, a place where people are embarrassed by excellence . . .

Now Freddy stamps in with coal from the shed, and as she opens the door an Arctic draught blows, and the letter I was writing floats to the floor. She has the coal scuttle by the scruff of its neck and shakes it over the fire, licking spit from her chin, then she pushes coal down into the grate with the sole of her boot. The knees of her corduroy trousers are caked with mud and she is fractious, and more determined than ever to needle me.

Theodora has finished her writing for the day, and sits in a chair by the fire. Usually she does not like to come to my cottage, because of the mess, but recently she has made an exception and always we only have one fire lit between us, as it is easier to keep warm together. Theodora is currently re-reading all of Proust – evidence, if any more were needed, that she has been on this earth too long. From the window-sill, Theodora is watched by four narrow yellow eyes, which belong to Maud and Agatha, her two Burmese cats, who sit in their sleek blue-grey coats, with smiles on their spiteful faces, and their snake tails wrapped around their paws. The telephone rings but we do not answer it for we prefer to decide who we want to talk to, not the other way around.

Now Theodora raises her head from her book. 'Is this the post?' She pokes at a pile of envelopes on the hearth with her walking stick. I have already looked to check that there's no letter from Max, or from Maggie, but I take the post up from the hearth because Theodora cannot, or will not, bend for it herself. We shake our heads at the state of it, as Bullseye, who is surprisingly nimble for an elderly and overweight Labrador, decided to take charge of it this morning, and I had to get down on my knees to lever it out of his foul-smelling mouth, but fortunately it's the electricity bill that has taken the brunt of his attack.

'So haven't you started the supper yet?' Freddy snaps. She finds this weather difficult, as she is best suited to the out-doors and does not like to be confined, and now she blows her nose, as loud as a trumpet, into a handkerchief.

'If you want to see Max,' she says, 'I don't know why you don't just write and tell him to come.'

My hands slip on the butterfly handle of the tin opener. 'If Max wants to see me, he knows where I am.' Freddy puts the tomato soup to heat on the metal plate above the fire and the tick of the grandfather clock echoes into the corners of the room. Always there is wind here but tonight it must be bad because I feel myself braced against it as it thrashes at the windows. I pass a cup of tea to Theodora and, as she leans towards me, her long hand brushes mine and she smells of face powder and eau de Cologne and she raises the long curve of her eyebrows at me, shakes her head, and adjusts her pink wing-shaped spectacles.

I sit down and Bullseye settles against my feet and levers a back leg round to scratch his ear, flapping it back and for-wards, then he rests his grey muzzle on my knee and his tail sweeps back and forwards across the rug. He gets up slowly and his head is on one side now, and he moves stiffly and he can't get up the stairs any more, so recently I've started to sleep downstairs on the sofa to keep him company. I shall have him put down before too long, for it is only fair that he should go first.

'I do think we've got to accept some responsibility for Max,' Freddy says. I turn my face away from her. How she has fallen into the clichés of old age. She rambles on, and she loses everything, and there are whiskers on her chin, and now she takes bread from a plastic bag, pierces it with the toasting fork and holds it out to the fire. I don't want to discuss Max with Freddy for she understands nothing, nothing. I sit down in my chair and pretend to read.

'It was that school,' she says. 'He should never have gone to that school.' This last is addressed not to me but to Theodora, who lowers her book and looks at Freddy, but without making any comment, as this subject has already been exhausted long ago. It's true that I made a mistake about the school. The truth is that I didn't want Max to be ordinary, that was my crime, and I have paid for it. I knew that he was exceptional and I wanted him to have an exceptional education, so twice a week for four years, after he had finished potato-printing and 'Jack and Jill' at the village school, I drove him to Oxford for private lessons in Greek and Latin and it was a long drive, all across the top of the Cotswolds, and every half hour I had to stop to refill the leaking car radiator, and often the car broke down altogether, and once when that happened we could find no one to help, and Max and I spent the night lying on hay bales watching the stars.

Then when Max was thirteen I organised for him to sit the scholarship exam for a public school and Freddy and Theodora would not speak to me for weeks, but I insisted and, of course, Max was offered a scholarship and I decided he should go. Freddy and Theodora could not understand, because schools such as that are against every principle we have ever held, but then they are not mothers so they do not understand the limits of the rational.

'And he shouldn't have gone to Spain,' Freddy says.

Now she draws closer to the mark, but she will not mention Lucía's name.

There's a smell of carbon and a twist of black smoke rises from the toast. Freddy jerks the fork back from the fire and swears under her breath. 'Not that I blame you,' Freddy says. 'You mustn't think I blame you.' She examines the toast and passes it to me.

I turn it over and it's black so I break it into pieces while Freddy watches me, then I reach down to Bullseye, who stares up at me through milky eyes, and feed him the toast, his tail thumping against my leg. 'I should certainly hope you don't blame me,' I say. 'All this modern rubbish – encouraging the weak and stupid to deny responsibility for their own deficiencies, allowing them to lay the blame for every problem at their parents' door. I don't accept it. People should take responsibility for their own actions.' I brush crumbs from my lap and pat Bullseye's dusty black flank and Freddy turns away and stabs another piece of bread with the toasting fork.

Theodora stretches out a hand to me but the distance is too far and her diamond ring winks for a moment in the light of the fire. She speaks as though she's consulting the authoritative work on the subject. 'Max's problems have nothing to do with us, or with his education.' Her eyes are staring into the fire, her hand moves back to the arm of the chair and her fingers tap up and down, then she purses her lips and closes her eyes and I know that she's thinking of the Wheelbarrow Afternoon, so many years ago, for it was then that we lost him, but of that we never speak.

★

After Freddy has gone to bed, Theodora and I sit on alone, watching the fire.

'Nobody really has a deathbed scene any more, do they?' I ask.

'No, not really,' Theodora says. 'I'm afraid that Dickens must take the blame for that. He overdid it so badly with Little Nell.'

I know that Theodora is angry that I must go first and she wishes all this to be organised without too much inconvenience, and I find that I am much the same. I stand and try to go to my desk to finish writing a letter, but the pain starts – that pain which has become so familiar that I know all its patterns, and how for long periods it hibernates, and then it awakes and becomes restless, turning within me, the first gentle twinge like the kick of an unborn child, then twisting and thrashing, bone clashing against bone, worse and worse . . .

And thoughts come to me of Max and, oh, how I long for him to come home. Just after the fire he came to see me, late one night, and he was in the most terrible state, nearly as bad as the Wheelbarrow Afternoon and I tried to talk to him, yes, I tried – to open the doors to the past, but he only wanted to talk about the immediate problem, what he should say, what he should do, and then I'm afraid that I got angry and finally was very little help to him, and he has not been to see me since. Those one loves, one is least able to help.

Theodora can see the pain in my face, and she wants to offer some assistance, but all she can think of is a cup of tea, and as I do not want to be left while she goes to the kitchen, we go together, and the floorboards creak beneath us and we avoid the patches where the carpet is worn to string. As we reach the step Theodora lays a hand on my shoulder to steady me, although she is the one who walks with a stick. In the kitchen I sit on the bench, bent forward with pain, while she stands with the lidless teapot dangling from her hand, and looks at the kettle on the stove.

Then I start to laugh, because the truth is that she doesn't really know how to make tea, having never done any domestic tasks all her life. I manage to get up and try to take the teapot from her, but she will not let me, and pokes at me with her walking stick, and we stand holding the teapot between us, her hand on the handle, mine on the spout, laughing. Then I make her sit down on the bench and I turn on the stove, and find the tea bags, working with one hand, my other elbow locked against my side.

'You know Old Mr Medlock?' Theodora says. 'Guess what he told me once.'

'What?'

'His wife – you know she got very bad at the end?'

'Yes. I remember.'

Theodora leans forward, and pronounces the words carefully. 'Well. You'll never guess what . . .'

'What?'

'He smothered her.'

'He never did.'

I feel a creaking laugh starting up inside me and Theodora bounces her hand up and down on the top of her stick and starts to laugh as well. 'It took ages apparently . . . ages.' Our laughter crashes around the room, breaking into every dusty corner, flushing the silence out, then I laugh so much that the pain starts, and I have to lean against the sink.

'You know, perhaps you should ask Max to come home,' Theodora says. 'If only because if we do need someone . . . he has had some practice in that line . . .' Theodora rocks back and forwards on her chair, and I remember all the long, long years, and how much we have laughed.

'But I can quite understand Mr Medlock,' I say. 'After all, one doesn't want to go into hospital.'

'Certainly not. Think of all those germs.'

We both look at the state of my kitchen and then laugh again, until our cheeks are wet with tears and I'm tired of the old, old lie that we will be redeemed by love, for laughter, surely, is more likely to be the cause.

When finally we are silent, I turn away and look out of the window into the blackness. 'Mind you, I'm sure there are easier ways.'

'Yes, I'm sure.'

'One must consider.'

Theodora moves her head up and down by a fraction of an inch.

'Yes, one must consider.'

Bullseye and I go to bed downstairs on the sofa for we find it warmer near the embers of the fire, but Bullseye has never been the easiest of bedfellows and always the night begins with him as the pencil and me as the starfish, but it is never long before the situation is reversed. And so I lie awake, with him pressed against my legs, and thoughts come to me of that poor silly American girl, burnt up by her own delusions as much as any fire. How can I explain her? The human mind is strange beyond all reckoning. A person can be, to all intents and purposes, stupid and shallow and yet they can have a few of the higher mental faculties developed to an abnormal degree. That was the case with Tiffany. An idiot savant, I suppose you would say, or a wise fool and, oh, such people are dangerous beyond all measure for they have the propensity to lay people bare, to stumble senselessly across forbidden ground. Maggie and Max mocked her, and she was easy to mock, but the truth is that, without even knowing it, they were scared of her.

One day she came here with Max and Geoffrey and I remember it well, how she had that kind of beauty which is so obvious that it obscures whatever might lie behind. I pitied her for that because, in truth, beauty has more in common with disfigurement than is commonly supposed and she, poor dear, was that kind of woman that men watch but do not see . . . and being an American she had no sense of irony, no sense of humour. At first I thought that she simply admired Max, but then she began to talk to me about him, and we were alone together, because Max and Geoffrey were inside, listening to the news on the radio, talking politics, and she asked a great many questions about Max, and I was telling her this and that – I can't remember really – and then I said, just in passing, that Max has never been very punctual . . . And it was then that I saw it, in her reaction to that, for she jumped at me as though I had poured acid on her, and she was full of angry explanations, and justifications, telling me that I did not understand, that I should not be so harsh. I felt a tenderness for her then and I would have liked to talk to her more openly, but for all her apparent directness, that would not have been possible. For she thought I understood nothing of what she felt but, oh, I understood, yes, above others, I understood . . .

Maggie

To tell him, to tell him not. Voices babble in my head, rehearsing the arguments back and forth. Slowly I make my way to Geoffrey's house which is in Chelsea near the river. The street stretches away from me narrowing towards a low, metallic sky. It is lined by leafless trees, stretching out black and stunted arms. I stand outside Geoffrey's dog-eared house. At the downstairs front window the curtains are shut.

I wouldn't have to tell Geoffrey directly. I could just write to Tiffany's lawyers. I found out their address through my old job and I keep it written on the back of an envelope, folded up in my bag. I can feel it there all the time. Sometimes in crowded places I wrap my hands around my bag, as though making sure the hidden dynamite doesn't accidentally ignite. I go up the steps to Geoffrey's front door.

I imagine all of us – Dad, Geoffrey, Fiona, James, Nanda, me – and we're roped together on the edge of a cliff. My foot slips and I lose my balance. The rope pulls tight. They try to hold me but they can't. One by one, slipping, sliding, screaming, they're pulled over the edge. And then we're falling into a void – friendships drowned in bitter silence, love revealed to be illusion, divorce, prison. My finger stabs at the doorbell.

Geoffrey opens the door. A smile loops across his face like a Christmas streamer. 'Maggie, how wonderful to see you.' He's doing well at the Normal Life Game – except red cracks run through the whites of his eyes as though they've shattered but not yet fallen apart.

I open my mouth, my lips start to make the words – so how is Tiffany? Then just in time I remember and pull the words back inside. I can't believe I nearly said that. But it would seem so natural to ask. I still don't really believe she isn't here. Into the perilous silence I babble greetings.

This is the first time I've seen Geoffrey since the funeral. That was two months after the fire, when the police released the body. Really, there can't have been a body to release but at the funeral there was a proper coffin and by then I'd got into the habit of believing the impossible and so I thought of her inside the plastic oak, pale and perfect, probably still wearing a baseball cap.

She would have enjoyed the funeral. Dad and Geoffrey, milk faces and dark suits, no tears, that would have been in bad taste, but flowers from the American relatives, as thick as a jungle and smelling of sugar. There'd been discussion about a poem to be read. The fundamental rule is that you can't have anything that's been on a tea towel – that's what Dad said. It was the first joke he'd made for a long time.

In the hall I pull my hair back from my face and wipe my glasses on my cardigan. The fanlight throws a diamond pattern on the tiled floor. The props of their improbable marriage are all still here. His worn brogues, under the hall table, next to her trainers, his camel overcoat next to her black mack, his trilby next to her baseball cap.

'You know your father is coming as well,' Geoffrey says. 'And Gus, I think.'

'Oh good. That's nice.'

Just what I need. I follow Geoffrey through to the study. Before the fire he was slow and lumbering but now he buzzes like a bluebottle. His steps bounce and his shovel hands gyrate on the end of long arms. His curly hair is like a bobble hat pulled down too far. Dad always says that he was born with two rows of teeth and had to have an operation to take the second row out.

We go into Geoffrey's study, at the front of the house, and he pulls back the dark velvet curtains, to let in dirty grey light. The grate is empty and the room feels damp and hollow. Grief is encrypted in the air. The shabby, bachelor clutter which I've known since childhood is all still here – the shelves of leather-bound books, the bald carpet, the print of an eagle with its foot chained to a metal ball. But Tiffany had started to make improvements – a watercolour of sugary flowers near the desk, a bowl of pot pourri, dusty now, on a table near the door. Near the window splashes of pink paint – colour tests, quickly done, the flick of the wrist dried on the wall.

Geoffrey pours me sherry, which I don't like. Switching on to auto-chat, I tell him about Brussels and my new job and packing up. He flaps around the room, not really listening, leafing through papers on his desk, sighing, shaking his head. His clothes are too big for him now but, although shrunk, he's not diminished. Grief has reduced him to something stronger and more dense – a man of clay, cast in iron.

'Later I want to show you the orchids,' he says. At the back of the house there's a whole conservatory full of Tiffany's orchids. He excuses himself and goes to see to the lunch. I sit down near the empty grate with my coat still on because of the cold. Everywhere there are photographs. Close to me, pinned above the mantelpiece, there's a recent snapshot of Fiona and James. Fiona used to be pretty before she married Dad – and she had her own career. Then she put on the marriage mask and her face grew to fit in. Now she's out of focus, under-exposed. She wears a Brillo pad skirt and ghastly bi-focals – probably quite useful when you consider all that she needs to overlook.

Most of the photographs are of Tiffany. Dad is in nearly all of them. The nose in different guises, seen from different angles. A laughing nose, wrinkled up, above delighted eyes. A wise nose, pointing down, inquiring, sensitive. An aquiline nose, held high, rising above a bad smell – proud and patrician. In one photograph Dad and Tiffany are play-ing croquet in the garden at Brickley Grange. Tiffany's long legs stick out from underneath shorts – she wears strappy sandals and a baseball cap. A big model-girl smile. After that Dad and Geoffrey pinned me to the lawn with the croquet hoops, and Tiffany didn't much like that, because she wanted it to be her, but no one would ever have dared do that to her. Beside her Dad waves a croquet mallet, his silver hair standing up like wings.

In a tortoiseshell frame Tiffany, Dad and Geoffrey are all together at some formal dinner. Then there's the Texas wed-ding photographs with Dad there as best man. In one shot he walks beside a white-robed Tiffany, coming down stone steps. In his morning suit, slim and elegant, he towers above her. Knowing just how good he looks, indigo eyes turned to the camera, he stretches out a hand to escort her down. Why do I have to tell Geoffrey anything? Why can't he see for himself?

I don't want to look at the photographs any more but they have grown large around me. All those past moments are assembled now. Soon people will step out of the frames and grow life-sized. I shut my eyes but there's no safety in darkness. Images still crowd in on me. Memory leafs back to that night. I let the pages turn. Fire crackles in my head.

I'm home from London, a Gloucestershire weekend, driving back from a party, tired, dizzy-headed. Over the brow of the hill and down towards Brickley. A clear night with a sharp wind carries with it an autumn smell of damp earth and over-ripe apples. Across the fields I see a distant sparkle, like a smouldering coal, not far from Hyde Cottage, where Geoffrey and Tiffany live. I nearly drive straight on home but then I turn down the lane, just to check. I pass through a tunnel of banks and hedges, unable to see more than a few feet ahead, until I turn the last corner.

Then flames tear across the sky in ragged strips of orange and smoke fills the windscreen. I get out of the car and run towards where Hyde Cottage should be, towards the flames, as though I'm going to beat them back. Smoke is in my mouth and my eyes and I'm crying out for help but there's no one there, nothing but fields for miles around. My heel twists on the gravel path and I stumble and fall, kneeling in my shrivelled party dress in the lane, with stones digging into my knees.

The flames reach up like pleading arms and the furnace heat is solid. The cottage is a blurred outline and thick black smoke billows from where the roof should be. A yellow halo lights the dark sky and the flames roar and crash. A storm of black ash blows all around me. The smell is like burning rubber, it clutches at my throat and stings in my eyes.

Partly I'm drained by shock, but at the same time I'm not quite there, because this only happens on television or in other people's lives. I'm separate from the sick excitement inside me, already thinking how I'll tell the story later, planning how I'll go to the phone box in the village, and ring the emergency services, and explain to them how to get here, how to find the entrance to the upper lane. I even imagine a local newspaper report, praising my prompt actions.

Through stinging eyes I see the timbers of the roof collapse. They groan and sigh, as the cottage releases its last breath. The orange heat of the flames is on my face and my chest is squeezed up. I run back to the car, reverse, and drive back up the lane. My hands are shaking so that the car shudders and then plunges across the top road. I have to brake hard to miss the hedge on the other side and it's then that I look back. My mind clicks, sealing the image.

After that I don't remember much. A moment of indecision – should I go straight home or call from the phone box in the village? Doesn't matter, just decide. I called from the village and then went home. Straightaway Dad went back to Hyde Cottage. Then two policemen were at the back door, and Dad came back, and I made cocoa for us in the kitchen. The young policeman – with buck teeth – asked me about my rucksack and, when I told him about Thailand, he said he'd been there two years ago and we got talking about that. He kept looking around Fiona's sparkling kitchen, which made me feel awkward. The older policeman was too polite because, of course, they knew about Dad. They yawned as they left. Past two o'clock, they said, time to get some sleep.

But half an hour later they were back. Tiffany's car was in the garage, they said. This time they were in the sitting room, manoeuvring their boots carefully across Fiona's clean carpets. When they mentioned the car, Dad's forehead folded up in pleats. She often called a taxi and then took the train to London, he said. But she had been at the cottage earlier in the day, he knew that. Strangely, as the truth soaked through me, there was horror but not much shock. Although I hadn't thought she was in the cottage, it was as though I had always known. Dad looked at me with the face of a dead person, and laid his hand, flat, across the side of his cheek, as though he'd been hit. And after that we couldn't look at each other, our eyes were too naked.

Then there were voices rumbling behind doors and telephone calls made. I sat on the front doorstep with my head pressed against a stone pillar. It was as though bits of me were bursting out from inside, and somehow I had to hold on to them, and keep them all together, so I sat with my arms wrapped around me, and my head down. I wasn't crying because it was too bad for that. To start with I didn't think about Tiffany but then I imagined her blue eyes, framed by perfect mascara and perfect eye shadow, and I imagined her flesh, rippled and burnt. Then I choked on the smell of it, and I had to go upstairs and lock myself in the bathroom. None of this was how a tragedy is meant to be, there was nothing heroic about it.

The police didn't ask much, just our names. But I couldn't say mine. The words turned into birds and fluttered in my throat so that I coughed and gagged. Dad said – Magdalena. I tried to tell them that I'm not called Magdalena, always Mags or Maggie, but the words were still battering in my throat and wouldn't come out. We none of us slept. Dad walked back and forwards through the house, suddenly old. At four o'clock he put my rucksack in the car and said we should go to the airport, because that was what had been arranged, a few days before, in some other world. My flight was at seven and he had to go to London anyway and he would drop me off.

I said I shouldn't go but Dad said I must. I refused and Dad and I would have finished up shouting at each other, except the police were there, so I had to do what he said. He and I drove in silence through the early morning darkness

and rain shattering on the windscreen. I sat with a dry handkerchief in my hand and my fists clenched. When we had
been driving for an hour, Dad pulled over onto the hard
shoulder and his fumbling hand took cigarettes and a lighter
from the glove pocket.

'I'm sorry,' he said. Then he said it again. I said that I
didn't want to go away, that I should cancel the trip. But he
said I must go. What about Geoffrey, I said. There was nothing to say. Dad's hands fumbled with the cigarettes and the
lighter, but he couldn't make them work, so I leant over and
lit a cigarette for him. Then I watched the shaking end of the
cigarette in his hand, and the taste of smoke was dry and
flaky in my mouth. On the main road, cars roared and
splashed past us and their headlights touched the silver edges
of Dad's hair, and flashed on his signet ring, as he pressed his
hand against his head. Between the cars there was silence and
then I could hear his breathing, shallow and quick.

There's a crash in the hall as the front door opens. I open my
eyes and sit up. Dad and Gus roll into the room in relentlessly
good spirits. Dad wears his rural-life clothes – a little too neat
and tidy, a Londoner playing at country squire. He bends over
to kiss me, smelling of aftershave, letting his cold hand rest on
my cheek. Gus sits in a straight-backed leather armchair,
lumpy and lardy, his short legs swinging above the floor.
They behave as they always do with Geoffrey, or other old
friends. Everything is political chat and little-boy sniggering.
Sometimes I used to find it amusing, but not any more.

They have various Ealing Voter conversations. Dad speaks
in a flat, nasal whine. 'What I don't understand is why my
granny is lying on a hospital trolley for eight hours in a corridor, when the Government is committing money to
sending our boys to some place I've never heard of . . .'

Gus picks up a magnifying glass from a side table and peers at me. He tips the lens and his eye pours down across the glass. As always that mole on his throat catches against the collar of his shirt. I tend to watch the mole rather than his face. 'So what exactly are you going to be doing for the European Commission?' he asks me.

'Legal reform for Poland. It's a contract for a year but it can be extended.'

'You know the European Commission will be endless men in short-sleeved shirts with rows of pens in their top pockets,' Dad says.

Gus is tapping his shoes up and down, the sound of them slaps on the carpet. He lowers the magnifying glass and then passes it from hand to hand. 'I still don't understand. Tell me more.'

'Well, basically it's aid administration.'

'Ah, Department of the Bleeding Hearts?'

'Lady Bountiful and the Peasants, perhaps?' Dad says. They nod their heads, give each other knowing looks, turn down the corners of their mouths. They're trying to make this like it always was. Maggie – always good for a laugh, the butt of all their jokes, but they haven't the heart for it now, and neither have I.

'Maggie, take no notice of them,' Geoffrey says. He pours more whisky for Dad, then paces, stopping occasionally to hook a long leg up onto the fender, or over the back of a chair, revealing a patch of white hairy leg above an Argyle sock.

'So I understand you've met our biographer?' Geoffrey says to me.

'Adam Ferrall? Yes, I have. Twice actually. He took me out to dinner. He's rather interesting. I like him.'

Dad and Gus look at each other, their eyes opening a little wider.

'I think you'll find there's less to him than meets the eye,' Dad says. 'After all, he's a journalist. All they do is watch. Anyone can do that.'

'I don't think so. Journalists do a very important job. I mean, some of them even die for what they believe.'

Gus and Dad roll their eyes. Geoffrey darts around the place, pouring more whisky. 'Now come on,' he says. 'Don't let's argue.'

'I'm not arguing. I'm just saying that I don't think Adam Ferrall is stupid.'

'Oh no, certainly not,' Geoffrey says. 'In fact, he's undoubtedly rather clever. I mean, he obviously knows how to get his story, doesn't he? I think we should be very worried. Maggie is going to tell him all of our secrets.' Geoffrey laughs but nobody joins him.

Gus's jittery eye clicks. 'I wouldn't credit him with too much guile.'

'Oh really,' Dad says. 'I thought you liked him, Gus. Rather your type. No?'

Gus's flayed skin turns a darker shade of red. I wish Dad wouldn't tease him. He can't help the fact he's one of the many people trapped inside the wrong body. Or the fact he's so tiresomely pudgy and enthusiastic, and always in the way, like a dog, endlessly under your feet or lying in doorways. It's terrible the way Dad uses him – except I suppose people aren't really used unless they want to be.

'So what are you doing now?' I ask him.

'Oh, we ventriloquists always carry on,' he says. 'I may have lost one dummy but I've got another. And at least the current one doesn't try to create his own script.'

'Oh, very funny,' Dad says.

Geoffrey ushers us through to the dining room. He can't cook and his housekeeper is not around on Saturday and so the lunch is sparse. Tinned lobster bisque, toast and Gentleman's Relish, cheese and then rhubarb crumble, made by the housekeeper, keeping warm on the hotplate. Geoffrey serves the soup out of the pan. He doesn't seem to have heated it properly – either that or he's left it too long and it's gone cold again. He switches the stereo on and weighty strains of classical music grind in the background. Conversation turns back to my departure.

'It's all very well you jumping ship and going to Brussels,' Dad says. 'I just don't think it's very fair on Hanbury.'

Hanbury was my former head of chambers and is an old friend of Dad's – not that I got the job that way, I didn't. Now I sigh at the mention of his name. 'You should try working for Hanbury. He's an embarrassment. Women come to see him about their awful divorces, and they cry, and he looks at his watch and says – oh come on, love, this is costing you two hundred quid an hour.'

'So did he sack you?' Gus asks.

'No, Gus. In fact, out of the three people who started with me I was the only person who was offered a tenancy.'

'Oooh, now that's telling us,' Dad and Gus say together in their camp way.

'But I still don't understand,' Gus says. 'Why didn't you take it?'

'I just didn't see the point of it.'

'There's no point in most jobs,' Dad says. 'But people have got to work. I mean, there's no telling what the devils would be up to if they didn't have to go to work, is there?'

I give Dad a beady look. 'Quite right.'

An uneasy silence.

'I just didn't think it was a job that needed doing,' I say.

'Look, eventually everyone realises they're not really needed,' Dad says. 'I mean I'm a politician, an unemployed politician admittedly, but I realised years ago that there's never going to be a voice over the Tannoy saying – is there a politician on this train?'

Everyone starts to laugh, even me.

'When I became a barrister, I knew it wouldn't be about justice,' I say. 'But I did think people might pretend a bit.'

'The role of the barrister is surely just to represent a point of view,' Gus says.

I sigh. 'Thank you, Gus, for that brief glimpse of the blindingly obvious.'

Geoffrey hasn't eaten his soup and he's staring into nothing.

'The legal system leads to unnecessary confrontation,' I say. 'Sometimes all people want is an apology, but no one apologises because they're terrified of the insurance liability.'

'Yeah, man, right on,' Gus says and raises two fingers in a hippie salute. 'When there's been a murder then everyone should have a workshop, hug each other and sort through any childhood traumas.'

'You can take the piss as much as you want but there are other ways of solving these problems. If you talk to Nanda . . .'

I am drowned out by Dad and Gus groaning. 'Oh my God, send her to Brussels immediately.' Dad grips his head in theatrical distress. 'Listen, Maggie, there's not much wrong with the legal system really, it's just that it deals with the probable – with what the reasonable man might think – and that's all right most of the time, except that events are often improbable and men are usually unreasonable, so then you get mistakes.'

I get up to help Geoffrey clear the soup plates away. From the stereo violins creak and whine, straining towards some resolution which is never reached. I feel stretched as tight as the violin strings. Gus is tapping one fat finger up and down on the table and the tic in his eyes is working. Dad picks his teeth.

'I think that whatever the legal system does or doesn't do then the truth tends to come out anyway. Because it is what people want . . .'

'Rubbish,' Dad says.

'It isn't rubbish. And why should it be so unreasonable to expect that the legal system should try to find the truth?'

My voice is too loud and I can feel blood rising to my face.

'Maggie,' Dad says. 'There's no such thing as the truth. In fact, that's the only thing that is true.' Knives scrape across plates as we help ourselves to toast and cheese. Dad pours himself more wine. The violins saw through my head. As I chop at the cheese my knife slips from my hand and clatters onto the table.

'Maggie,' Geoffrey says, stretching out a hand towards me. 'You're being teased. Of course there are truths of a kind and, of course, people should search for them.'

After lunch Dad and Gus are going to watch the dog-racing in Catford and they want me to go. I say no to that. I need to go to the laundrette. In fact, I actually want to go to the laundrette. I like sitting there, in the warm breath of the dryers. There I can keep my head still. Saturday laundrette has become the equivalent of Sunday church-going. Except that today I'll have to go later because Geoffrey wants to show me the orchids.

Dad and Gus say goodbye and good luck in Brussels and leave. Geoffrey takes me into the conservatory. It was built specially for Tiffany, as a wedding present. Like a miniature Kew Gardens with a domed roof, it takes up most of the back yard, a bubble of tropical air trapped under the grey London sky. Inside, the air sweats and sticks to my skin. 'Maggie, look. You see these orchids from Thailand are blooming now? Just what Tiffany and I wanted.'

The orchids are arranged in rows, planted in gravel. A pump whirrs and bubbles, controlling the heat. The orchids are brash colours – electric blue, lime green, vermilion, and their faces have long noses, big ears and spotted throats. Why would anybody want these when they could have the flowers Freddy grows – white field daisies, cornflowers, poppies, and sunflowers? 'Geoffrey . . .' He's turned away from me. I touch a green leaf, brittle and shiny like plastic.

'And these ones as well,' Geoffrey says. 'Tiffany planted these. She would be so glad they're doing so well. Smell this, Maggie, smell this.' He cuts an orchid with secateurs and raises it to me. I swallow its sickly scent, like her perfume. It's orange and pink with veins of yellow.

'Geoffrey . . .' Words curdle in my mouth. Geoffrey cuts another orchid and holds it out to me, his speckled hand shaking. I take the orchid from him and feel the sap of it spreading onto my hand. It's a white flower, with red veins, like a bloodshot eye. An orange tongue pokes out from the centre of it. I look up at Geoffrey, his faded eyes smiling at the orchid in my hand.

'Be careful, Maggie, or you'll break the stalk.' His hands stretch out to protect the flower. Then suddenly I'm crying, tears breaking down my face. I wipe at my eyes, tell myself to stop, put my hand over my face, but tears keep flooding down. I hear Geoffrey's muffled tread, he lifts the bruised orchid from my hand and touches my shoulder.

'Don't, please don't. You'll make it worse.' Tears, warm and silent, keep flowing down my cheeks. Geoffrey steers me out of the conservatory and back to the study, sits me in an armchair, and pulls a handkerchief out of his pocket. He sits down beside me and his brown eyes stare at me, full of pity. 'Maggie, Maggie. I'm so sorry. I didn't realise you were so upset. Sorry, you were trying to tell me, and I wasn't listening.'

I can't say anything otherwise the tears will get worse. I hide my face from Geoffrey and clench my teeth, trying to keep the tears shut inside.

'Maggie, I didn't know you were feeling like this. You should have told me. You should have come to see me.' Before Tiffany, Geoffrey wouldn't have known what to do with a crying woman, but now he takes hold of my hand, and strokes it gently. When I open my eyes he's sitting beside me on a low footstool, legs crossed, one foot rocking. 'It matters to me to know you cared so much.'

'Geoffrey. You don't understand . . .'

'Yes, I do.'

'But Geoffrey, you need to understand how she died, don't you?'

He smiles sadly and shakes his head. 'Maggie, it was an accident, that's all. No matter how much we know, it won't do any good.'

Tears start again when I think of Tiffany's brothers at the funeral, as similar as twins, men contained inside straight lines. Tall and thin, with sharp creases in the fronts of their trousers, lines in their dark hair where the comb had been, and strident rows of even white teeth. They wore dark glasses, both of them, and they did not speak to Dad, or to me.

'There are some things that we will just never understand,' Geoffrey says. I know I should tell him but the truth has become slippery. He fetches me some tea and we sit in silence, watched by all those smiling faces in the photographs. Outside the window the black, stunted tree grows dim as evening falls. In houses opposite lights come on, people pass across the windows, up and down the stairs. Normal life rolling shamelessly on. The tea slides down my throat, leaving a path of warmth all the way inside me. I sit back in the chair. For days and days now I've been packing, trying to get everything ready to go. My hands are ragged and sore. A yawn of tiredness swallows me.

'Maggie, you know what I think?' Geoffrey says. 'I think that although we feel ourselves bound by the physical reality of separation, that isn't really the case. We can decide. In my mind she's still here.' His eyes are alight far inside. He starts to talk about her. His hand lies beside mine on the faded velvet arm of the chair. Do you remember those afternoons at Brickley, when she used to play tennis for hours and hours with your dad? Do you remember that?' His eyes are full of longing. I begin to see it as he describes it, I begin to see how it used to be. He tells me stories about her, all the things that were special to him. The funny things she said, and did. And it's not long before I join in, and so we sit together in a comfortable little world of illusion, warming our brittle hands on the heat of lies.

When I get up to go it's dark outside and the streetlights are on. I go through to the hall. Geoffrey is leaving as well. A car is coming to pick him up to take him to a dinner in his constituency.

'Actually, I've got something for you,' he says. He leans over and takes a pink mohair scarf off the coatstand. 'I've been doing some clearing up,' he says. 'And I wanted to give you something of Tiffany's. I'd thought of some jewellery but I haven't got round to sorting things yet, so why don't you take this, just for now.'

The scarf is fuchsia at one end, fading to a candyfloss pink at the other. I imagine her fingernails snagging in the static hair of it. 'She'd have liked you to have that. And it's just the right thing for this weather, keep you warm. You can wear it in Brussels.'

He reaches towards me as though he's going to put the scarf around my neck.

'No, really, Geoffrey. It's very sweet of you, but you should keep it. You shouldn't give it away.'

'Well, most things I'm keeping but I'd like friends to have something to remember her by.' He reaches forward and wraps the scarf round my neck. It smells of her chemical rose perfume. The fibres of it tickle my skin and my stomach squeezes up like a clenched fist. My neck shrinks away from it but Geoffrey pulls the scarf around me and knots it. I hold my head up high trying to keep my neck away from the touch of it. Geoffrey kisses me goodbye and goes out to the car. Static draws my hair to the fibres of the scarf.

I stand on the pavement.

Geoffrey, stop, don't go, this is what I wanted to tell you, what I never told the police. What I've never said before. Say it, say it. Now. Dad was there that night, I saw his car. It was on the lower lane, nudging out from between the trees. It was a cloudy night, I could have been mistaken, if only I was mistaken, but it was a car with cigar-shaped headlights, tor-pedo-shaped, with an oval grin. Not a car you'd fail to recognise. If only knowing was a process you could put in reverse.

But I don't say it, instead I watch you get into the waiting car, your shattered eyes, your pitted face against my cheek, as you kiss me goodbye. Her scarf still wrapped around my neck, enfolding us both in an air bubble of her perfume. Your long arms swinging, a shovel hand raised to wave goodbye. Stop, wait, let me tell you. But the words are sealed in my head, and so we'll all travel on through the never-never land Dad's made for us.

Your long black car slides away, and I stand in the cold, tears sticking on my cheeks, and that court of law starts again inside my head, the banging of the judge's gavel hitting the back of my throat. Jury, witnesses, police – all are assembled, and me alone in the witness box, suspended above them.

Ms Priestley, do you think that on the night of second October at Hyde Cottage in the hamlet of Brickley your father Max Priestley killed Tiffany Drummond?

Say it, say it.

Yes, I think he did.

JUNE

Max

My luck has turned. I knew it would. I knew they needed me. All because Bill Quigley died, poor sod. Some artery in his heart gave out. Took them some time to notice, of course. But then they got onto me straightaway. They needed a safe pair of hands, someone to fight a Euro by-election at short notice in a constituency where the going can be tough.

And it was tough. I'd forgotten how bad an election campaign can be. No sleep for weeks, endless petty squabbles. Petty issues. Partly it's just the hassle of getting up to speed on the details, but it's also the stress of keeping the whole bloody circus rolling on. But anyway, I won with a majority of five thousand, which is better than Bill Quigley ever had. Of course, it's a load of old eyewash, this election business. But it creates the illusion of choice, and one should never underestimate the importance of that.

What a relief. A job. An opportunity to get out of England. And work that I've never done before. Of course, Europe is a bit of a backwater, but I'm not complaining. Brussels is a pleasant enough place to live. Generally, I'm not much good at abroad. I have a horror of foreign places, particularly the south. There's an excess about them which unsettles me. Olive oil, the rattle of alien voices, the smell of rubbish in the streets. It always brings on a strange sexual stirring. Makes me feel a bit perky. But this country isn't like that. It's comfortingly Northern. Flat and grey. And I've found the perfect place to live.

Good money, plenty of dinners, not too much work. Not that I actually do anything, because the European Parliament has no power. But I create the impression of doing something and that's what counts. It's all sleight of hand. Plaid-slippered and sherry-sipping, the voters of Ealing are terribly impressed. Yes, there is a modern equivalent to the Foreign Legion.

I walk back from the Parliament. A beautiful spring day. New, bright green leaves on the trees. Off the leash. And tonight the swallows are flying south. At last, at last. It's been tricky, what with the election campaign, and having no flat in London. Logistics, logistics. But now she's coming to stay. She'll be able to come here as often as she likes. Rosa. Roosaaah. I roll the name on my tongue. All the time I've been married, I've been seeing her. Eighteen years, on and off. Nothing to be proud of, but there we are.

It was in Green Park that we met, where I was escaping from some appalling meeting. She was sitting on a park bench, eating a sandwich, which was threatening to explode down her T-shirt. She was nineteen then, with surprised eyes and hair that looked like it had been cropped with a knife and fork. Grass stains on her jeans, no make-up. And a camera, of course. She asked if she could photograph me. She liked the image of a pompous older man in a pinstripe suit in a park. That was the flattering way she explained it later.

After the photographs, we had a coffee in some greasy

spoon café. Me busily planning how to get her into bed, without much hope of success. Too young, too alternative, I thought. Then she said it. Just like that. Do you fancy a bit of a fiddle? Or words to that effect. So we went to a grubby flat, where she was staying, near the Tottenham Court Road. Bent the frame of the sofa bed. Afterwards she wanted me to take off my sock. I didn't want to but she wouldn't take no for an answer. She propped my foot on her knee and peeled off my sock with pale, cold hands. I looked away but she stared at the dent and the scar intently. It's beautiful, she said. Like a stain, or a cracked piece of glass. Or a starfish. Yes, definitely a starfish. I laughed at that. Then she placed my foot on the bed, with the sheet underneath it, and took photographs of it. When I left she wrote down her number. Her name in bold writing. Rosa. Roo-saaah. And beside it a careful little picture of a starfish. Yellow paper, green ink.

Now I see her coming up the cobbled square, like a nomad, nothing more than a canvas bag and a camera. She looks as though she's walked from England. She stops at the railing. Waves up at me. The whole of her sways, as though the weight of her waving arm is enough to unbalance her. Her head is tipped up towards me. She's laughing. All day I've been feeling pretty perky, now I can't wait.

I pull open the door as she comes up the steps. Hold the champagne bottle under my arm, point the cork at her. She raises her arms above her head in instant surrender. Pulling her into the house, I put the champagne down on the hall table, push her back against the front door. With one hand over her mouth, I slide the other under her jumper. She laughs and I unlock my fingers from her lips so I can kiss her. Her camera is between us. I try to take it but she won't let me.

I love the elfin shape of her face. She's cool and green, like an underwater creature. Her hands are small and cold. I can hide them completely in mine. I run my fingers over the veins and tendons of her wrist, like the strings of that guitar I used to play back in some other life. She's hardly changed at all since that day in the park, eighteen years ago, except for three silver hairs just at the side of her forehead. Perhaps she never notices them. I always do and feel a tenderness for them.

'I'm so glad you're here.'

She runs her tongue along my upper lip. 'I'm sure that soon sex will be available in pill form,' she says. 'That would be so much more convenient for you, don't you think?' She pulls away from me, twists around on one foot, peers up at the four flights of stairs above us, and the cobwebbed chandelier. I always imagine her as a dancer. She has that same lithe quality, that grace and balance in the way she stands and moves. The body of a boy. Appeals to the paedophile who lurks within.

'What a great house,' she says.

I put my finger inside the waistband of her skirt. She twists my hand away, then kisses me. 'How did you get this house?'

I knew she'd be impressed. She wriggles away from my lips and goes into the sitting room. She stands in the bay window, thick with palms, their leaves pressing against the curved glass. Looks down over the square where there's a park and a green statue of a goddess lounges in an empty pond. Below us the wheels of a pushchair rumble over the cobbled pavement. The sun is sliding down over the houses opposite.

'It's beautiful, isn't it?' she says.

'Yes, pollution does improve a sunset.'

She laughs, raises a hand to trace the twisted art nouveau window frames and stained-glass panels. In the bay window there's a life-sized black and white china dog, who looks out over the square. 'I've called him Rex,' I tell her. She walks through the three rooms which run from the front to the back of the house, joined with double doors. She stares at the chandeliers, parquet floors, green wallpaper patterned with leaves and flowers. 'It's like one of those Victorian glass domes full of dusty flowers or stuffed animals,' she says.

Above us a brass birdcage – mercifully untenanted – swings. On every piece of fabric there's a bobble or a frill, and on every wooden edge there's a knob or a twist.

'Whose is it?'

'A chap I used to know at Cambridge. Willy van der Veken – an oarsman with flamboyant taste in trousers and possible homosexual leanings. Haven't seen him for years actually but I always thought he might come in useful.'

'But is he here now?'

'No, fortunately, he's in Indonesia.'

'Oooh là là! Good old Willy.'

She looks at some of James's pictures which are lying on a chair. He did them at school and Fiona packed them up in a tube for me so I could bring them here. I stand behind her and pull down the neck of her jumper, kiss the bone at the top of her spine. Bury my face in her freshly laundered hair.

'I must take some photographs,' she says.

'Later.'

'Yes, later.'

She wriggles a hand behind her and touches my leg.

'Let me shut the curtains.' She's always careful, much more so than me. But the curtains are made of thick brocade and look as though they'll crumble to dust if we touch them. So I steer her into the middle room, pull her camera over her head. The black strap of it catches against the lobe of her ear. I pour her champagne. As we raise our glasses, we see ourselves duplicated, again and again, reflected in mirrored doors, and above the fireplace. Rosa stands against the wall and shakes off her espadrilles. Then she slides a hand under her skirt, pulls her knickers down, loops them over her feet.

I scrabble around trying to find an object of an appropriate height. There's a footstool but it's too high. I open a cupboard and find a pile of telephone directories. Just the thing. Rosa rummages in her bag and pulls out a tape measure. I stack three telephone directories against the wall. Stand her on them. It's a question of geometry. The angle has got to be right. She passes me the tape measure. Eight inches is the height we need. I lay the blade of the tape measure against the telephone directories. Seven inches. Surely that will do. I kiss her stubbly shins and then her knees. I can't wait any longer. I want to fuck her.

But no. Seven inches won't do. It's got to be eight. She sends me to look for a book. Dusty volumes slip to the ground as I fumble through shelves. One has a spine about an inch wide. I put it under her feet. Measure again. Exactly eight. I take off her jumper. She hasn't got a bra on. My breath stops inside me. Her eyes are level with mine, cool and green. Like a pond on a hot day. I kiss the place where her skin changes from white to brown, where the neck of a shirt would normally be. I let the moment hang, holding back, delaying. Now, every time, I think this may be our last chance.

Slowly, slowly. I kiss her everywhere. The bliss is in the waiting. She holds my hands. When I enter her my face is close to hers, so that I can hear that small gasp she makes. The angle is right. I save up the moments. Turn her around. Kiss the top of her spine, where her hair starts. Shut my eyes.

Then just for a moment I'm back in a rooftop room in Spain, holding a girl with the same smell of lemon and sour white wine.

Afterwards, in a grandiose bedroom, we lie side by side and look at the coved ceiling, miles above. She tells me this and that. A trip to the theatre. The opening of a photography exhibition. I nod and laugh. Blah, blah, blah. But I'm not really listening. All I want to know is whether she's got another man. I'm tortured by that, hypocrite that I am. But I'm not allowed to ask. So all I can do is listen for clues. Who did she go to the theatre with? I'm desperate to ask but it's against the rules.

And that's how it's always been. Just an occasional afternoon or evening. A moment outside real life which leaves the rest of the world looking small and drab. But I want more. I always want more. The life that she and I could have is always running parallel in my head. As soon as I see her, I'm close to the end of when I'll see her. Then I'm waiting again. She doesn't return my calls. She's too busy to meet me. Her petty, stubborn displays of independence drive me mad.

'You know, Rosa, you could come and live out here.'

'Don't be daft. I don't want your life. I've got mine.'

Her life. A rented cupboard in Newington Green, odds and sods of photography jobs. Part-time teaching, an ageing mother rotting in Ruislip. Thirty-seven. No husband. No flat. No children. She says she doesn't want any of that. But it's no way for her to live. I want to buy her jewellery, roses, silk underwear. Or even a car or a flat. But she doesn't want that. Every six months I pay for a new camera lens, or a gas bill. That's the limit of it. Never was a Pygmalion so thwarted.

'Anyway,' she says. 'What about Fiona? Doesn't she want to come here?'

'No. She can't. It's not really possible, with James and all that. Anyway I'll be back at the weekends and pretty often during the week as well.'

Rosa always talks about Fiona as though she's a good friend. Someone we've got to look after. Makes my hair bristle. I don't want her being pleasant about Fiona. Makes me wonder, of course, why I didn't marry Rosa instead. I often ask myself that. Sounds strange but I wanted to save her from being married to me. I didn't want her poured into a mould. Anyway it was too late. Fiona and I were already engaged. Marquee booked, wedding dress bought. Such are the instruments of our love.

'What about Maggie?' Rosa asks. 'Have you seen her yet?'

'No. She doesn't seem to have a phone. Inability to have a telephone and answer it seems to run in the family. But I suppose she'll come round some time.'

'Do you think she's OK?'

'No, not really. But what can I do?'

'Do you worry about her, or about what she knows?'

'Both.'

'I could always ring her,' Rosa says.

I'm surprised by that. Very.

'Yes, you could,' I say. 'If you wanted.'

But really I don't want her to. In my experience, divide and rule is an important principle where women are concerned.

'And Gus?' Rosa asks.

'Oh, he's in fine form. The Continent seems to suit him. He's a new man, with a new image. We must meet up with him some time, you'll find it terribly funny. No more brown trousers and stains on his shirts. Now it's waistcoats and bow ties. And his skin is getting better. About time too – you can't be having teenage acne all your life.'

'You are horrid about him,' Rosa says.

We make love again, then Rosa sleeps. But I can't sleep. Finally I get up, try to open one of the three long windows. But it seems they're nailed shut. I sit in an armchair which looks out over the square. I was trying not to wake Rosa but she sits up, puts on my shirt, comes to sit beside me.

'Max, what's the matter?'

'Nothing.'

'Tell me.'

I laugh and she laughs as well. Usually we don't have this kind of conversation. Usually she doesn't bother me. And that's one of the reasons why I love her. The truth is that women complain a lot about sexual harassment by men, real or imagined. But men could equally complain about intimacy harassment. That need women have to open a window into your head. To know what you're thinking about. Everyone maintains a core of mystery, a place they share with no one. If you love someone you don't try to break into that.

'I suppose questions this journalist asks have set me thinking.'

'Which journalist?'

'The one who's writing this book. What's his name? Adam Somebody. Can't remember. Anyway he was asking about the Citadel Club, of course. And I've tried to explain, but I don't think he really gets it. He's rather a literal-minded sort of lad. He doesn't seem to find the complexities of life at all attractive.'

'So what did you say to him?' Rosa asks.

'Oh, not much really.'

I start to tell her. Of course, she's heard it all before but she's kind enough to let me blather on about the same old things again and again. Blah, blah, blah. The problem is she knows that isn't all. So finally I say, 'You know, just before I left England I was talking to Geoffrey and he told me that I might yet finish up in court.'

'But you can't.'

'Yes, I can.'

I explain it to her. She sits very still on the arm of the chair, holding my hand. She knows it all, of course. I told her everything. She's never doubted me.

'Max,' she says. 'Wouldn't you do better just to tell the truth?'

Just tell the truth and everything will be all right. That's what they tell you at school. But in the world of judge and jury, the truth can be fatal. I've spent enough time defending rogues and chancers myself to know that justice and truth are not the same thing. 'No,' I tell her. 'No. In my case the truth is too improbable. I wouldn't be believed. A reasonable man would convict me. There's no doubt about it.'

'But you didn't do anything much,' she says.

'That's not the point. The point is that I lied and that's all that matters now. If I explained what happened, I'd be finished. Not because of what I did or didn't do but because of the lie. If you're a politician then you're tried by the press and by public opinion. I've seen what happens often enough. Look at poor old Robson. Remember him? My former colleague. His career came to an end over two hundred quid. No one cared about the money, of course, but he lied about where it came from. That's what finished him. In my case everyone would assume there's something more to know. Because why lie to hide nothing?'

We sit together in silence, then she shivers and I take her back to bed.

Always I remember the moment of my arrest. It came out of nowhere. I thought I was a witness, not a suspect. In fact, I'd been helpful. I was the one who provided all the information needed. Went to Geoffrey's house that morning. I was the one who helped him with all the form-filling and telephoning that accompanies any death. I fought off the press, got Tiffany's brothers over from America. Went to the police station to give a statement.

So much time had gone by since the fire. Four weeks. So when the police came to Brickley Grange, just before Saturday lunch, I was worried but not that worried. Fiona opened the door to them, showed them to my study. I was looking out of the window. The terrace, two urns, the path to the swimming pool, the garden wall. Then beyond, miles of open fields. There was a bird sitting on top of one of the urns. Its head cocked to one side, listening or watching. Then suddenly it flew away. When I turned around to greet the police, they said they were arresting me. No handcuffs, no hard words.

I had to go to the kitchen to tell Fiona. She was there with James. So I pulled her into the hall. Shut the door on James. Told her what was happening. Her eyes opened wide and she swallowed hard. But she was calm and I was grateful for that. For her, dignity is everything. One must not make a scene. She asked me what I would need to take with me. Just like a film. The Gestapo knocking at a door. Five minutes to pack. Both of us knew it wasn't like that. Except in a way it was. I went back into the kitchen. James looked up from his aeroplane model. I bent over to kiss him. I'm just popping out, I said. All very calm and quiet.

Except that for no reason James suddenly grabbed a hand-ful of my hair and kept it gripped in his fist. Then he grasped my shirt collar in his other hand. He couldn't have heard what Fiona and I said. He knew nothing about anything. We hadn't even told him much about Tiffany's death. Usually he's an easy child. Yet he clung on and I could see his eyes – so very close to mine, and so very like my own. Like look-ing into a mirror. He just gripped my hair in silence, so that I couldn't raise my head. Fiona snapped at him far louder than was necessary. Behaving like a savage, she said. She wrestled his hands away from me. A chunk of hair went from my scalp. I couldn't look at him. So I went out of the kitchen. I wanted to take my car. The Jag. But the police wouldn't let me, so I went with them. The world looks dif-ferent from inside a police car.

At the station they told me about the Fire Officer's Report. My jacket was at the cottage, they said. There were also the remains of some photographs. And in my jacket pocket there had been a condom. I laughed about that. They even smiled a little. I was relieved that was all they had to say.

I pointed out that I had actually told one of their officers that my jacket was in the cottage. I'd had a coffee with Tiffany earlier in the day. Only later did I realise that I'd left my jacket behind. They knew that. The photographs were also my photographs. Just holiday snaps. My wife and I at Abu Simbel in Upper Egypt. I'd lent Tiffany the photo-graphs because she and Geoffrey also wanted to go on holiday there. As for the condom, it had been there years. It had been forced on me at some AIDS awareness event. I'd never bothered to throw it away.

Then they asked about Tiffany. Yes, I knew her well. Yes, I spent a fair amount of time with her. Yes, I sometimes met up with her without Geoffrey. Of course I did. For God's sake, we're grown-ups, aren't we? It was good that I admitted that I saw Tiffany without Geoffrey. Because the police had been speaking to a lot of people. They could cite times and places where we'd been together. Amazing what apparent friends will say. I rang my solicitor, smoked, drank bad coffee, waited. I was careful not to get angry, not to shout. I was frightened, but not that frightened. I kept clinging to the thought that really they had no information of importance.

The questions went on for hours. Don't ever think you've got any civil liberties. You haven't. There was nothing they didn't know about me. But a simple story, resolutely maintained, is hard to crack. They tried every way. I refused to elaborate. Yes, she and I were friends. Yes, I went to the cottage earlier in the day. The fire? I don't know. No idea. Paraffin in the cottage? Almost certainly she'd used it to light the log fire. Yes, I'd seen her do that on other occasions. I'd seen Geoffrey do the same. People often use paraffin to light log fires. Then why was there paraffin in the kitchen? How should I know? I wasn't there.

Maggie

I love you.
That's what his e-mail says. He sent it two months ago but still I open it every day. Sitting in my office in Brussels, I click on that message and read those three words again and again. I love you. No one has ever said that to me before. Then I go through his other messages. Occasionally there are spelling mistakes and I'm glad about that.

I shut my eyes and think of those shadowed eyes, that one chipped tooth, the tender feel of that cropped head. I remember last weekend, in London, staying in his flat. On Saturday morning I tried to cook breakfast for him, except that having been trained in the Thwaite Cottages School of Domestic Economy, I made a total mess of it. Then suddenly it turned out that the fact that I'd splattered oil across his pristine kitchen, that I'd set fire to one of his tea towels and that I'd scraped the non-stick surface off his frying pan with a metal spoon – all this was suddenly terribly charming and sweet.

And so now I understand – that's how love works. It means that someone looks at you and to them you look good and, for them, whatever you do is fine. Then after a while you begin to see yourself as they see you. You begin to like yourself. Your mop of fuzzy hair becomes luxurious, your lumps become curves, your sharp tongue turns into wit, your funny clothes become stylish – or at least endearing. You are quite changed. At least for as long as that person is looking at you.

Last weekend, after the frazzled bacon and eggs, he gave me a present – a small box wrapped in black and white striped paper. He watched me open it, amid charred tea towel and blackened pan. I was nervous, thinking I might not like whatever was inside. Layers of tissue paper unfolded to reveal a bracelet made of fine gold wires and beads of glass. Tame good taste but I love it because he gave it to me. I look at it now, twisting the wires and beads against the skin of my wrist.

Before, life always felt like a spectator sport. My world was untethered. I used to ask myself – am I a person or just a place where other people's expectations meet? But those three words have enabled me to take possession of my life. Two people have got more weight than one and they take up more space. I feel anchored. My life is substantial. A boyfriend, a new career, my own flat. But isn't it odd that this should happen now? It seems that when one thing is terribly wrong, then other things are miraculously right. Rotten fruit often has a particularly shiny skin.

I look at that message one more time. I love you.

Then I switch off the computer and find my coat. Time to go home.

Apparently elsewhere it's the beginning of summer, but here they don't do seasons, just grey perma-drizzle. This city was built on a marsh and everywhere you can feel the damp rising. I walk through streets that are dirty, disorganised and derelict. When I first arrived here I thought I'd

come to a war zone. The whole place looks like Bosnia or
Beirut on the television. Battered buildings with broken
windows are covered with grime and in the cobbled streets
there are water-filled craters and construction work sprawls
along the pavements. It'll be a nice city when it's finished,
that's what people always say. A smell of oiled metal rises
from the streets, brakes screech and cars rumble over cobbles.
It's as though a piece of the Third World has been trans-
ported to the damp plains of Flanders.

I walk under bridges that smell of piss and through a
Moroccan area that smells of spices. Little girls in exotic silk
stand at front doors, watching with shuttered eyes. I reach
the square near my house, which is lined with red-brick
gabled houses. Tram wires and unused Christmas lights loop
overhead. My flat is in a street like all the rest, dark and deep
as a trench, narrow and lined by once-elegant houses, with
doors and windows two metres tall. I open the front door
and pull back the grille of the antiquated lift. My flat is not
exactly the all white space I imagined but it does have a
marble fireplace, radiators like toast racks, a parquet floor,
and French windows leading onto a curling iron balcony.
Above the fireplace is a long mirror and the rooms are joined
by double doors, like the set of a farce, so that you expect a
maid waving a feather duster to appear, pursued by a man
with no trousers.

I drop my bag on the floor and light the gas fire. When I
first arrived there was nothing in this flat at all. No fridge, no
oven, no curtain rails. Nothing in the sitting room except a
pile of telephone directories and a bare light bulb on a twisted
wire poking out from a jagged hole in the ceiling. For ages I
did nothing to the flat at all. Then Adam started to talk about
coming to stay for the weekend, so I had to make an effort.
I painted the hall bright pink, which the landlady won't

appreciate, and with drawing pins I stuck up curtains made of thin white gauze, which cost the equivalent of a pound a metre in the square. In the kitchen I put a red and white gingham cloth over a flea-market table, and stuck Cartier Bresson posters at angles on the wall, which creates a good accordion-playing-black-beret-and-striped-shirt look.

Nanda says there are three essentials of life – a bed, a bath and bookcases. I've now got all three. And I went out and bought new white sheets, the kind of sheets I've always wanted, part of the all white flat in my mind. Something for Adam, and for me.

A message flashes on my answer machine. Adam. My finger pushes the button. But it isn't Adam, it's Dad. How did he get my number? I walk away from the machine and go into the kitchen. I can't hear his words but the sound of them is slurred and rambling. Clearly it was a very good lunch. I can just imagine him out all afternoon with Gus, drinking, joking. A man of principle, Adam says. A man who has stood up for what he believes. Oh yes, but you should see him when he's been on a bender. One night he jumped out of a first-floor window. As luck would have it there were thick bushes beneath. It's a miracle he's never killed himself.

When the voice comes to an end, I go back to the sitting room and delete the message. So many cities in the world, why did Dad have to choose this one? Before, this felt like my city, a place where I could start again. A place where I could see myself as Adam sees me. Happiness seems to me like a small umbrella. If one person is underneath it, then another person has to be out in the rain.

Tonight I was meant to be going out with two English girls from work. They're the chunky-but-fun types, normally called Pippa or Polly, but in this case called Sarah and Jane. They're coping awfully well with the natives. They organise all sorts of jolly japes, which I find rather hard work, as I don't really do organised fun. They take me to parties in sparsely decorated flats with crooked self-assemble furniture. People from all over Europe are there, partying with a Titanic desperation. Everyone is just passing through. Homesick city. There are sad Scotsmen in kilts, and Spaniards drinking sangria, and Sicilians yearning for the South and the sun.

One gets tired of not understanding. I speak some French but I've never made any effort to become good at it because it's a language I hate. I find it circuitous and flabby – a language for men who want to talk about themselves too much. I exist in a state of verbal confusion. The muscles in my face ache with smiling. Yes. Nod. Smile. Yes. I dread to think what I've said yes to since I've been here. Tonight I decide I'll stay at home. I'm cold and tired and I want to soak in a hot bath. I stand in the sitting room and stare out at the city. Below me the wheels of cars ripple over the cobbles and there's music playing in a bar.

On the table there's a letter from Nanda – prickly hand-writing growing over the envelope. The latest news from the Grannies' Commune. I read the letter this morning but now I pick it up and read it again. Her main news is that Bullseye is dead and I'm sad about that, but also I think spitefully – well, he was only a dog. It seems that in my family there's more than the usual amount of misdirected grief.

I take my new roving telephone, which I've only had for a week, to the window. I dial Adam's number, although I know he isn't in London. Four rings, and then a click. This is seven-three-six, four-nine-two-eight. I can't take your call at the moment but please leave a message and I'll get back to you. His voice is low and it rustles over the softer sounds. I put the phone down before the end of the beeps. Then I dial the number again. This is seven-three-six, four-nine-two-eight . . .

From the window I can see the Palais de Justice with its ring of scaffolding like a crown of thorns. And a gap in the jumbled rooftops, marking out the shape of a cobbled square, bigger than a football pitch, which is where the flea market is. It happens every day – a ragged bunch of stalls and piles of furniture. It's as though houses have been cut open down the middle and spilled all their innards across the cobbles. Books and records, and jewellery and shoes, and old photographs, and hats. People's whole lives are there. Freddy would be in paradise. The morning I spent there with Adam opens up in my mind.

Above the high roofs of Brussels the sky is mottled grey. A blustery wind tugs at trees and lace petticoats on coat hangers and old newspapers in piles. Thin rain comes down at us sideways, blown by the wind, splattering our cheeks and blowing under our coat collars.

On a sheet of tarpaulin, spread with pots and pans, between an old radio and a sewing machine, I spot red shoes made of suede – fifties jazz club kind of shoes with sling-backs and square bows on the front. Dorothy-in-the-Wizard-of-Oz shoes. I stoop down to look at them and touch the blood red suede. 'Unfortunately I don't think they would fit me,' I say to Adam.

'Uuum, and they don't exactly look the most practical shoes,' Adam says.

'Would you mind waiting while I try them on?'

It's an effort to get my boot and my sock off and my foot is suddenly exposed to the cold wind. I hold on to Adam's coat as I balance on one leg, and don't look at his face as I suspect that he might be getting annoyed. The shoes have cream leather insides and worn-out gold writing. The upper edge of them has been stretched into the shape of the last owner's feet. The suede on one of the heels is slightly torn. They look small but strangely my foot slips straight into them so I buy them. And then I buy a wonderful dress made of creamy gold satin with a pattern of big red roses and a 1950s full skirt. Adam probably thinks that these purchases are a little strange.

The rain gets angrier so we go to a tabac for a coffee. One of my neighbours is there – Señor J. Sanchez. I know his name because it's written on his doorbell. He lives in the flat below. He's dark and thin, with untidy black hair and he wears a velvet jacket, and a shirt with too-long collars, and a pair of worn leather slippers. Now he's standing at the bar with a group of Spaniards, including a friend of his who I've also seen before. They are wrapped in overcoats, looking gloomy and cold. We get talking and I long to be able to speak Spanish. Adam asks Señor Sanchez if he likes Brussels.

'If you are taking a flower out of its natural climate then it will die,' Señor Sanchez replies. Both Adam and I are rather floored by that comment, so we nod, smile, and say goodbye.

'Gay, don't you think?' Adam says after we've moved to the window. 'Or perhaps just a bit slimey.'

'Well, Spanish,' I say. 'What can you expect?'

Outside, the rain is still coming down sideways, so I wrap my scarf around my head as we pass under the awnings of stalls piled with fruit and fish and cheese. An old-sock smell rises around us and a chilly smell of fish. Adam has my hand gripped in his. A whole stall is devoted to mushrooms and some of the people there have red-veined country faces, and mud on their boots, so that I think about Nanda. Then we come to a stall where a man is cooking paella and tortilla over a gas stove.

'Let's get some,' I say to Adam. The man cuts through the crisp brown top of the tortilla to where the egg is still runny inside. I breathe in the smell of cooked onions and olive oil. 'Mmm, my favourite thing . . .'

We decide to eat the tortilla straightaway so, standing under the dripping awning of a fruit stall, we break it in two. I stand very close to Adam so that the wool of my coat touches against his suede jacket. There are onions inside the tortilla, brown and sticky, and potatoes, and a hint of pepper. It's hard to eat it without it falling to bits. 'Isn't it wonderful?' I say.

'Mmm,' he says. 'Wonderful – but a bit greasy.'

The rain stops but still glistens on the wet cobbles. I take my scarf off my head and shake back my damp hair. We look at each other, with tortilla still gripped in both hands. The sun is warm on us, and I lean up to kiss him and his mouth tastes of tortilla. He puts his hand on the top of my head and pushes my hair back out of my eyes.

We walk on and I stop to look at old sepia photographs spilt in a pile on the cobbles and resting on top of a commode. Some are wet from the rain. I pick up a photograph and the face of a small girl in a white dress looks out at me. Another photograph is of a group, outside a farm, probably a country wedding. In another a young couple pose next to a palm in a pot and a Grecian column. Their eyes see only the air straight in front of them.

'I feel like I should buy them,' I say to Adam.

'Why?'

'I don't know. It just seems so sad – indecent really, for photographs like that to be here.'

Adam peers down at me, puzzled. I shuffle through the photographs, wiping the ones which are wet on the end of my scarf. The little girl in the white dress has fierce eyes and looks as though she intends to squeeze the life out of the bunch of flowers in her hands. The rain is starting again and Adam wants to go. Still I am holding the photographs. I ask the man behind the stall how much they cost. He names a price, far too much, and I pay him. Adam raises his eyebrows, shakes his head, then bends to kiss my forehead. I hold the photographs pressed against me.

Time for a bath. I've been longing for one all day. I turn on my Roberts radio, which Freddy gave me years ago, and leave it standing on the floor, quietly babbling at me in English. From below, there's the sound of a piano, three or four notes, resolved by a chord – a sound like the beginning of spring. The notes are played again.

My bathroom is painted in so many layers of shiny, peppermint green that there are dried blobs and drips of it on every edge. Cobwebs cling to the knobbled joints of pipework. The bath is one of the reasons why I took this flat. The pot-bellied weight of it rests on elegant, clawed feet, and it's so deep that I can hardly see over the sides of it. I twist the stiff bath taps, and there's a high-pitched squeal and tea-coloured water rushes out.

I wait until the bath is nearly full, then I take a deep breath and plunge a foot in – but the water is cold, so cold that the shock of it shudders up my leg. I hop across the bathroom, and collapse on the loo seat. I think of Nanda, and I want to go home. This has happened before, but always I've been able to re-light the pilot light. Now it won't re-light, no matter how often I try, and I run out of matches, striking them again and again to no effect. I wonder if the

British Embassy would have a hot-water department? I wander back into the emptiness of the sitting room, and stand with my head in my hands, groaning.

I find a T-shirt, and pyjama bottoms, and drag my stiff limbs onto the landing. I think of my neighbour Señor Sanchez. I'll have to give him a try, there's no other choice. In the darkness the chord echoes again in the stairwell. Dust sticks to my wet foot as I go down the stairs. Below me there's an open door and a sliver of light, and a smell of oily foreign cooking. Señor Sanchez always has his front door open. I see that when I walk up the stairs, which I have to do quite often as the lift is always broken. Now, through the open door, I can see a flat like mine with the hall painted the colour of processed peas, and a fringed hessian wall hanging depicting a lurid Mediterranean coastline.

In the sitting room a lamp shines on him as he sits at a piano, his arm moving away from him as he picks out notes. I've made no sound but he swivels around on the piano stool, watches me for a moment, and then comes to the door. He wears the same velvet jacket, the same long-collared shirt, the same pair of worn leather slippers. 'Buenas tardes, señora.' There's a soft hiss to his voice, and his lips roll back over the words, revealing white teeth. Perhaps I could have waited until tomorrow.

'Buenas tardes, señor.' I'm conscious of the low neck of my T-shirt. 'Tengo un problema . . .' My throat is tight and dusty, and I'm at the limit of the language which should have been my mother tongue. 'Uuum . . . the water heater.'

'Ah, si, for the bath.' I hurry back towards the stairs, hearing his slippered feet behind me. 'Si, I know, is difficult,' he says. 'Is a very old system. Not a good system. I help you.' His feet are rooted to the spot, heels together, and his toes turn slightly outwards. His arms wave like a windmill as he talks. His trousers are pulled up too high, and secured with braces. Now he stands beside the bath with his weight on one leg and his hand jiggling change in the pocket of his trousers. If this guy was in a sitcom you'd think he was over-acting – but then that's the problem with living abroad, it doesn't break down racial stereotypes, it reinforces them.

'But you are Spanish?' he says with a grin.

'No, I'm English.'

'Ah, si.' He turns to the water heater. 'You have matches?'

'No, I'm afraid not.' His face is too close to mine and my skin winces. He smells of red wine, and smoke. The light from the bare bulb shines on his high forehead. Reaching down into the icy water, I pull out the plug.

'Wait, wait,' he says, and disappears. I stand beside the bath, shivering, and looking at my peppermint-tinged face in the mirror above the sink.

'What is you name?'

'Maggie.'

He raises questioning eyebrows.

'Well, Magdalena really.'

'Ah, Magdalena.' He makes a short and muscular word of it, with a hiccough in the middle. He strikes a match and turns a knob on the heater. 'Very dangerous, this heater. In fact, not legal. The señora says she has not money for a proper heater, but is no true.'

He mumbles Spanish swearwords and strikes a second match. His fingers are long and stretchy, with too many joints in them. 'I am from Sevilla,' he says.

'Oh really.'

He asks about my job and I explain. 'The European Community.' He shakes his head and turns down the sides of his mouth. 'In Spain perhaps we are not having a good economy or making BMW cars, but we have beautiful wine, beautiful women, beautiful – how you say? – arquitectura. For what are we needing an economy?'

I'd be inclined to agree, but right now I just want my water heater fixed. He lights a match and the flame flares. The smile has gone from his face. 'You are too cold.'

'Yes.'

He removes his finger from the knob and reaches down to turn on the bath tap. He puts his hand under the stream of water. 'Si, si. Is becoming hot now.' He looks up at me, and he's smiling again. 'You like it in Brussels?' he asks.

'I don't know. I haven't been here long.'

I wish he'd go now, but he's watching me with intense eyes that are rather too close together and shadowed on either side of his beaky nose. I remember Adam's sugges-tion – gay? I don't think so. There's silence. I need to say something. 'Do you like it here?'

He shrugs and rolls his eyes. Silence except for the rush-ing water. He's got his eyes fixed on the top of my T-shirt. 'No one can fall in love in this city.'

He stretches that word out like an elastic band.

I sidle backwards to the front door and stand there, hold-ing it open for him. 'Well, thank you. Thank you very much for fixing the water.'

'No problem,' he says. 'You come if you want something. Buenas noches.' He goes out of the door and halfway down he stops and waves a long-fingered hand at me. I shut the door and lock it, then I stand in the steaming bath water, lift-ing one foot and then the other, while the blood throbs back into my feet.

I think of the desk in Adam's bedroom. Even as we lie in bed together I can see it, neatly stacked with political biogra-phies, history books, press cuttings, plastic folders full of interview notes and photocopies of Hansard. He takes care not to talk about his book because he knows that I don't want to know. But in a way it's stupid not to talk because the more you don't talk about something, the bigger it gets. Words limit things.

Sometimes I pretend that in that pile of books and papers he's going to find some proof that Dad is innocent. But, of course, I'm a fool, a total fool, and I know it. Because as he burrows further and further into those papers it's not Dad's innocence he's going to uncover, but my lie. How did I allow myself to be drawn into the situation? The hotplate, the cliff's edge.

I should give him up now rather than wait for the moment when he realises what I really am. I should give him up and find someone else. But there won't be someone else. I've waited twenty-eight years for him. So I make the most of every minute, enjoying the luxury of his love, knowing that it can't last. In my mind I used to criticise Dad for living in a world of illusion. Now I pray – let my lie last just one more weekend.

In the place between waking and sleep my sagging eyes watch the twisted leaves and the faces of animals carved on the foot of the bed. Whenever I ask Nanda about my mother her eyes become vague as sunlight.

What do you remember about her? I used to ask that question. Nanda would shake her head and say – she wouldn't leave the tap running even for a moment. She couldn't understand how we could waste so much water. That's all she said. Now I don't ask any more. I suppose it was all a scandal. English public schoolboy, straight out of Cambridge, suddenly marries unknown Spaniard. An inconvenient mistake.

Now that last weekend at Thwaite Cottages comes back

to me. February, before I left for Brussels. Freddy is building a bonfire in the garden. The mist hasn't lifted all day and there's frost on the ground. I go to Theodora's study.

'Is Nanda all right?' I ask. 'She does seem tired.'

Theodora sits at her desk in elegant layers of silk and wool and peers at me over the top of her spectacles. She has never known what to say to me. I'm in a category marked 'child' and she can't deal with children. If she had to look after me, when I was little, she used to hide in the loo and read a book and I used to watch her through the crack in the door.

'Yes,' she says. 'I think Nanda is tired.'

'But is she all right?'

'Yes, of course. Now don't make a fuss. You know she doesn't like fuss.'

'She doesn't seem particularly pleased to see me.'

I hate myself for sounding so self-centred.

Theodora turns away from me. 'I don't think it's that,' she says. 'I just think that perhaps Nanda has reached the limits of people. Not you in particular, just people in general.'

'What is there after people?'

Theodora looks at me in amazement and shakes her head so that her long pearl earrings swing. The conversation comes to a halt. It's always the same. Theodora, Nanda, Freddy – they've got the Operating Instructions but they're not sharing them.

I go outside and help Freddy carry wood for the bonfire. In the mist we're like ghosts, edgeless and indistinct. The cottages are a shadow in the distance and the greenhouse glistens like an ice palace. Freddy carried a huge branch across her back, staggering under the weight of it. I help her with smaller branches, my nose running in the cold, and my hands covered with damp green lichen. It is getting dark, the mist turning from white to grey.

As always, Freddy terrorises me with her competence.

'Don't drop so many bits . . . and put the branches up higher, can't you?'

'Look, I'm doing my best.'

'Yes, I know. That's exactly what's worrying me.'

The frost rustles underfoot. Twigs catch in my jumper and moss gets stuck under my fingernails. The growing bonfire looks like the ribcage of a dead dinosaur rising up through the mist. Freddy sticks her fork in the ground and undoes her jacket, then wipes her face with her handkerchief. When the bonfire is ready to light I go inside to fetch Nanda.

Freddy reaches into the centre of the fire with a match. A crackle, then a bang, before the flames leap up, roaring through the heap of twigs, and rising high, making the air above the bonfire thicken and shiver. I stand beside it, feeling the heat, blinking as the smoke stings in my eyes. Guy Fawkes figures dance in the golden yellow, forming then dissolving, their limbs flailing.

We watch until the middle of the bonfire has burnt out and there's only white ash left. With a fork Freddy moves the branches that still remain into the centre. The mist is clearing now as the wind rises. The fire blazes and crackles again and our eyes water with the smoke and heat. Then there are no more branches to put on. Nanda bends down to pull at a small branch at the side of the fire. The end is alight and white hot. The flames move down slowly towards her hand. At the last minute she throws the stick back onto the fire. In a gust of wind, the flames flare again, suddenly lighting up her face, her grey hair standing on end and a black smudge on her cheek.

'So what is worrying you?' Freddy says to me.

'What do you mean?'

'Something is worrying you. What?'

'Oh Freddy, don't bother her,' Nanda says.

'I'm not bothering her. It's important to ask these questions otherwise she'll think we just don't care.' Freddy fixes me with a watery-eyed stare. I look up at the night sky, suddenly clear above us, now that the mist has gone. The stars are thickly spread across the blackness.

'Something is on your mind,' Freddy says.

I turn to her and try to think what to say. 'I just don't know what to do.'

'About what?'

'About everything.'

'You do know what to do,' Freddy says. 'Deep down you know. And you just have to trust your feelings.'

'Oh Freddy, how can you talk such rubbish,' Nanda says.

'Is it rubbish?' I ask.

'Yes, of course it is. Just because you're sincere doesn't mean you'll be right. The world is full of people who are sincere – and sincerely wrong.'

'But if I can't trust my feelings what can I trust?'

My question is carried away by a rush of wind into the star-bristled night.

Nanda

Her footprint is all that remains ... marked into the concrete of the path outside Theodora's front door, a wide footprint, with each toe marked clearly, the ball of the foot imprinted deep, but the heel only a shadow, so that the bounce of that step is sealed in the concrete. It's been there so very long, since that day when she stepped across the path, holding Maggie on her hip, her hand raised to shield her eyes from the evening sun, laughing as she felt the wet concrete underfoot, her brown legs under a trailing summer dress, her hair knotted up in a scarf and smelling of sun. A moment gone in a flash, the significance of it not understood. How little we know, how we stumble through the dark.

The time we had of her was too short. When Max wrote from Spain to say he was getting married, I was surprised but not displeased, as I felt a Spanish daughter-in-law must be infinitely preferable to some tiresome girl from the Home Counties, with an obsessive interest in hygiene. Then Lucía came here to stay, and the moment I saw her I recognised her – of course, it's you, I thought, arrived at last, and it was as though I had always been keeping a space open for her.

Her eyes were extraordinary. Maggie has inherited them, dark brown and sometimes midnight blue, still and serene, but with a raw edge, a hidden energy – both of them women with no sense of themselves, no knowledge of their power. It is a type of beauty one sees in Degas' bathing women, a lack of self, and the same quality exists in the photographs Rosa takes, which I saw once in a London exhibition . . .

Lucía's English was rather random but she and I had no need of it. Max spoke to her in Spanish, arguing with her about nothing all the time, except for the evenings when he played his guitar for her, sitting outside on the steps, and he seemed quite changed when he was with her, but I did not know that change for what it was. All that I had put aside in my own life, and so I did not know it when I saw it in him . . . So many mothers are jealous of their daughters-in-law and that I cannot understand. For me Lucía was the natural inheritor of my love for Max. More than that, she was the interpreter of that love, for always between Max and me there had been a distance, an intensity of feeling, and yet a distance. Love, and the denial of love, the fear of what it might do . . .

As a boy Max was fascinated by *Le Morte d'Arthur*, and all those other tales of knights and their ladies and of courtly love, played out at a distance, the desire of the eye. I read him those stories and took him to see medieval castles and houses, with secret gardens, enclosed within walls, and, as those were the images of his childhood, so they became the way in which I thought of him – my knight, playing in the garden with a wooden sword, his hair pale and shining so that every ray of the sun seemed to be focused in on him – and it was a feeling so intense and yet never expressed, until he met Lucía and then I felt that she was the one who would consummate my love for him, and I supplied her in my place, but, oh, it was not to be.

Today Freddy is busy with the wind turbine, our latest project. She has ordered a kit and she intends to use the wind to create our own power system which the manufacturers tell us should create enough for the three cottages, although first we must dig a hole to stand it up, and put a battery, I think, in the shed, but no doubt we will manage that. Freddy gets so upset about it all the time, every setback reduces her to tears for she doesn't seem to understand that at our age there are really no tragedies other than death. In the distance, across the fields, Mr Medlock's men are mending a fence and at four o'clock they'll come over for a cup of tea.

Here, sitting on a bench in the warmth of the sun, I am happy. All my life I have always tended to recognise happiness largely by its absence, but now I am happy, consciously happy. I have arrived at the summit of my own life and, dizzy and breathless, I look down at the tortuous route by which I ascended. The proximity of death has removed a filter from my mind so that I am no longer shielded from the dazzling beauty of the ordinary and so the sight of a flower, a butterfly, a blade of grass, is painful in its intensity. I am living inside a poem. I take deep breaths, sucking in every moment. The future and the past are no longer important. I have been forced into the present and am intent on squeezing every last drop of sensation from it. This is Keats' ideal of a life of sensations rather than thoughts. I focus on each tree, each cloud, and I want to watch each leaf, each bud, each drop of dew. I look up and stretch my eyes from one side to the other of the vast blueness above.

When I see the farm van coming along the track, I go

inside to make the tea. The men come up the path, brushing their hands across their overalls and taking their caps or woollen hats from their heads. 'Good morning to you, Miss Priestley.' They nod to each of us in turn, and there are three of them today and one of them is Young Bob Briston, the grandson of Arthur, dead so many years ago now, and he has the look of his grandfather, as his father had before him, all of them tall, with beautiful silver hair and very blue eyes. Also there is Young Mr Medlock, the son of the Medlock who carried me in from the fields when Max was born. They stand with mugs gripped in their hands. The weather's better, we all agree, there's less of a chill in the air.

The men from the farm start to talk among themselves, in muffled voices, and I feel too tired to stand and so I move back to the bench by the wall and Freddy starts to talk about Maggie. 'She is really most unsettled at the moment. Not that I'd want her to be settled, God forbid.'

Three months now since Maggie went to Brussels – or perhaps even four – and she's not home as often as she was when she lived in London, although she's coming quite soon and I must get her letter out to know if it's next weekend or the weekend after . . . and now Max is in Brussels as well, and she won't like that. He sent me a postcard about a month ago, only three or four lines, and anyway I already knew of his move from other sources. The postcard showed Big Ben and the Houses of Parliament, and there were teeth marks stuck through it, where Bullseye had tried to eat it, one of his final acts of sabotage, and Max's illegible handwriting crawled across the back of it. Since then I have heard no more.

Freddy continues to talk but Theodora interrupts. 'Maggie is not in her prime, youth does not suit her. She will come into her own at forty or fifty. Anyway I do not set too much store by youth . . . it is merely a stage of under-development. After all, no one harbours sentimental notions about the wonders of the mentally handicapped, do they?'

I suggest that perhaps on that question Theodora might not be entirely objective and she nods her head towards me in recognition that I might be right on that point, although not necessarily on any other.

'What I'm wondering,' Freddy says, 'is whether we should think about going to Brussels as part of our trip, although I can't quite think what we will see there that we can't see here. Nowadays there are so many reductions on the trains, and Maggie's letter sounds as though she is inviting us – all that patronising information she provides about how airline companies are perfectly willing to wheel the elderly and infirm through foreign airports, at no extra cost.'

Freddy's butterfly mind goes off on that conversation, and Theodora looks across at me and pokes at my leg with the end of her walking stick – for we've been intending to make a trip now for a long time, and before the war we travelled all over continental Europe and we saw there all that we wanted to see, and much that we didn't . . . and we've always talked of going back and now Freddy presses the point and even I start to talk of it as though I may indeed travel again but really it is Maggie I am thinking about. What can I do to help her? Really I have no wisdom to offer, for as soon as one finds an answer the question changes – and she so much wants me to join in judging him, but judgement is really for the young.

The men from the farm finish their tea, and I watch them go down the path, and how strange it is that these men know nothing of how their forefathers helped us when we first arrived here all those years ago . . . and all they know is that it's a tradition, when working the stubborn land up here, to come and have tea at four o'clock with the Miss Priestleys, but they do not understand why that is, and they are simple men and do not recognise our gratitude.

For it was Arthur Briston and Old Mr Medlock and others long since gone who helped us through our first winter here, and it's doubtful if we would have survived if it hadn't been for them. 'Them daft lasses from London.' That's what they called us, as they rodded the drains for us, fixed the roof, changed the flat car tyres, and explained that even carrots will not grow if you plant them in sodden ground.

We'd come here to escape from the war, from the pain and disillusion of all those new worlds we had wanted to create breaking up around us in violence . . . the thirties, an era of grand plans, the struggle between communism and fascism, all brought to nothing in the horror of war. Evil was ever present. How different is the world today, preoccupied as it is with more personal struggles. Theodora was ill, and Freddy and I were worn out, and we had lived too much, and travelled too far, although, I suppose, we were only in our late twenties then . . .

And so we came to Burrington, just for the day, trying to find out about an early communist community which was founded here in the last century, and then, on an impulse, we bought Thwaite Cottages, empty and partly derelict, for fifty pounds, for we had an idea that we would try simplicity, life on a small scale, and we had some vague and ridiculous notion that it was perhaps our duty to bring liberal and egalitarian ideas to the ignorant natives of Burrington.

However, we had failed to take account of the fact that it was summer when we bought the cottages, and very picturesque they were in the mellow sunshine and dry weather, but when winter came we had no running water, and the wind was so bad that it picked up half the roof of Freddy's cottage and deposited it in a nearby field, and there seemed to be nothing but mud all around us, and the fires smoked and went out, and the very air seized up with the cold, and the car would not start, and we had no idea how to grow vegetables, or paint window frames, or even drive a car, having always had people to do everything for us. Freddy survived better than Theodora and I, for she would not give up and she shouted at us, as we lay in bed under piles of blankets, reading William Morris, and wondering why it did not seem to have turned out quite that way . . .

So long ago now, all of that. The sun has gone in and the air is colder.

I go inside to the kitchen, and Bullseye's basket is still on the floor for I did not get rid of it, as I should have done, and now the harsh solidity of it shocks me. I sit down on the bench to look at it, and his bowl is there as well, the red plastic of it dull and cracked – and the wicker sides of the basket are twisted and chewed, and his blanket is moulded into the circular shape he made by burying his muzzle in it, and walking round and round before lying down . . . After a death the loss is finally measured in the bits and pieces left behind – one is left with a chewed wicker basket and a red plastic bowl, when one wants a dog.

Bullseye at least died as a result of a lethal injection – a kindness that is permitted to animals but not to human beings. Of course, I have made some enquiries myself but I have to take care because if a woman in her eighties claims that she is interested in voluntary euthanasia as a matter of general interest, then eyebrows are raised – one should not have to bargain for death.

All my life, when anything bad has happened, I've always tried not to make a drama out of it – worse things happen, I've always said to myself, but now I find myself at a loss to consider what worse things do happen. Pain grips my side and I press my hand against it, and images run through my head – a hand slammed in a car door, a baby's head crashing down on a tiled floor . . . I must be outside, I want to die outside, I will not let them take me from here. So I sit myself down again, in the cold evening air, next to the place where that footprint lies, half-covered by grass, on the concrete path.

When faced with a disaster the mind fixes on what it can manage, on a small and irrelevant detail, and so finally it is always the wheelbarrow that I remember . . . The rest of it I know only as a dividing point, as a before and after, a moment of savagery which I still fight in my mind, still trying to forgive the world for having allowed it, for it was so much more than one should have to bear – and even now I wake in the night, and brace myself against the thought that it might happen, and then realise that it has already passed, and find that, at least, a relief.

It came with a phone call, slicing through a summer afternoon, with washing blowing on the line, and buttercups scattered across the fields, and a bowl of plums – delicious Pershore plums with golden flesh and pink skins – lying on the table with one half-eaten, when I went to the telephone. I was at home because it was towards the end of the school holidays and I was preparing for the new term and listening to the radio, and Theodora had taken the cats to the vet, and at that time Freddy still worked at the Ministry in London and was only back at weekends.

To this day I don't know who it was who telephoned, or

what they said – an accident, a fatal accident, I understood that, and the person mentioned Lucía and he mentioned Max, and I was sure he'd made a mistake, and then he mentioned Wales, and that was where they had gone for a long weekend . . . Then my mind was filled with towers and turrets and flags waving in the wind, because Max had taken Lucía to see castles, for she'd seen pictures of Welsh castles in a book as a child, and she'd always wanted to visit them, so they'd left Maggie with friends and taken a night train.

I looked out of the window and the washing was flapping and snapping on the line. Then this person asked me if I was on my own, and I said no, and then I had to put down the receiver to get hold of the table, which was moving away from me, and I stumbled around the cottages, bent double, taking hold of pieces of furniture, until I knelt in the kitchen with my hand pressed against my mouth and the side of my head against the fridge and the noise of the radio still babbling on.

After that what I remember is the ship – a toy galleon, which Max had had as a child, carved in wood with cotton sails, from some expensive shop, bought by one of Theodora's London men, and it was his favourite toy, although he ruined it by drawing on the wood in ballpoint pen, and letting the rigging get twisted up. It had always been on the shelf in his room, except that I had given it away a few days before to a child whose family lived in a caravan, because it seemed stupid for it not to be used, and this child's father was going to mend the rigging . . . Except that wasn't the only reason why I had given it away, it was also because of some anger against Max, a stupid argument we had had . . .

Then when I received that phone call I knew I must get the ship back and I knew if I could do that then he'd still be alive, but the family in the caravan had no telephone, and I had no car, and when Theodora came back from the vet, she wouldn't go straight to get the ship, and I shouted at her while she was trying to telephone the police but of course they couldn't tell us anything as we had no idea what had happened, and Theodora couldn't believe that I hadn't written down a telephone number and when I screamed at her it was really myself I was screaming at for having been so stupid. We didn't know, we just didn't know, and we were waiting and waiting for so long and Theodora wouldn't go and get the ship. 'What good will the ship do him if he's dead?' When she said that I knew he wasn't dead, because I could feel him alive inside me, as clearly as I'd felt him when I'd been waiting for his birth, walking back and forwards across the Edge.

When Theodora finally went down to Burrington to find the ship the family with the caravan had gone, and no one knew where, as they were wandering people and there was no way of knowing where to find them, and I felt I'd killed him with my meanness and Theodora said not to be so stupid. In Max's bedroom I stood by the shelf and there was a clean white square in the dust, where the base of the ship had been, and I stood by the telephone waiting and waiting, but then Theodora made me clean the cottage – and so we scrubbed the kitchen floor, and then I stood by the telephone. She made me do the washing, and then I stood by the telephone. Then we weeded the garden, although neither of us ever normally do such things, and after I had washed and swept and weeded everything, we sat on the front wall and I felt the sun burning over me, as it fell lower and lower in the sky . . .

And it was then that I saw a yellow dot which was bigger than the buttercups and I thought it was moving in the distance, and I screwed up my eyes, and stared into the sun, and saw Max's yellow Deux Chevaux, lurching along the bumpy track which leads across the fields. I ran down the track towards the car, stumbling in the ruts, and crying with relief. Max was cramped into the car with his head dropped forward, like a bull ready for the charge, and Lucía was not with him. I wanted him in my arms but he did not stop the car so I ran after it, banging on the roof. When he pulled up outside the cottages he did not get out, so I opened the door. He was sitting inside, quite still, staring. I put out my hand to him, tugging at his sleeve, but he did not move.

Theodora came to look at him sitting silently in the car, staring ahead of him. 'Shock,' she said. 'Tea.' We went inside to make tea, but in the end we never offered it to him, but we sat on the wall and drank it ourselves, watching him still sitting in the car. Theodora suggested that perhaps we should slap him, because he might be suffering from some form of hysteria, and then we went down to the car and tapped his face, but with no result. Feeling a sudden sense of anger and frustration, I pulled hard at his arm, and when he still did not move, I pushed him hard in the other direction. The weight of him yielded under my hands, but it was clear that he didn't even know I was there. What I wonder now is why we never called the doctor – I suppose we were ashamed. Madness, mental illness, nervous breakdown, even then, in the early seventies, were words that could hardly be spoken.

When Freddy arrived back from London, she stood next to the car with her hands on her hips. 'What in God's name is the matter with him?' she said, and leaning into the car, she caught hold of Max and pulled at him hard. 'Oh really, Max, how can you?' She wrapped her arms right around him and pulled and he tipped forward and started to slide, and as the side of his face went down onto the tarmac he didn't even put out a hand to protect himself but lay on his back, quite still, his blue shirt open at the neck, and his sleeves rolled up, his eyes looking up at the sky, and in the evening light our long shadows tipped down over him.

'We'll have to get him inside,' Freddy said. 'We won't be able to do it ourselves. We'll have to get Jack.' Theodora took the car and went down to get Young Mr Medlock, who didn't seem particularly surprised to find Max lying in the lane and he tried to help Freddy to lift him but Max, although slim, is heavy. 'A wheelbarrow,' Jack said. Freddy went to fetch the wheelbarrow while I knelt in the lane next to Max.

'Go inside and make up a bed for him,' Freddy said to me and so I went up to the cottage door, and when I looked back I saw that Jack had lifted Max's body into the wheelbarrow and with Freddy supporting his legs they were struggling up the garden path. In the midst of the appalling, there is always the absurd.

The next morning Max remembered nothing of this. He got up and refused to stay and got in the car and went back to London – all he told us was that Lucía was dead, and it was only later that we learned what had happened . . . and he threw away her clothes, and her books, and the scarves she wore in her hair, and his guitar. He threw away everything except for the bed, because we fought for the bed, and Freddy and I went to London to get it, and brought it home in a van, as something for Maggie . . .

For, of course, she had to come to us, there was nowhere else for her to go, and those first days she ran around on the lawn, unaware, holding up dandelion clocks so that the wind blew away the fluff on them . . . and we were in despair, wondering how we would cope, but it was not long before we saw her as a blessing, a second chance which arrived at a time when our lives were wearing thin – but she, poor child, had only the shallow soil of our grief in which to put down her roots, and yet somehow she thrived. Always she has been an adult, and always she has been relatively unaffected by the strange, twisted state in which Max lives . . . Except now I fear it is no longer so.

Maggie has never known her father – she never saw him at the front gate, waving goodbye before he went away to Spain, she never knew him before the money, and the women, and the drink . . . and I do not know him now either, but I have learnt to understand grief and how it warps and corrupts character, for I have seen it work out its bitter course and felt the deep furrows which it drags across the heart, and how it breaks a crack through the foundations of life, so that the pain is passed on through generations.

After a loss such as that life is unkind, and so we do not speak of the Wheelbarrow Afternoon and its various deaths. I have been waiting so very long for him to come home.

Maggie

On Friday evening Adam meets me at Waterloo Station. 'So how's the job?' he asks.

'Well, I don't know. I mean, how am I to judge if it's the right job for me? I'm floundering around the place, really, aren't I? Just like everyone else, although some of them won't admit it. In the past people had faith. But now the only God is the media, watching us, and dictating its Sunday Colour Supplement values. We read articles about people who are rich or beautiful, and even if the rational part of our minds knows their lives are as small and messy as our own, we want to be like them. And that's the most we've got to hope for – that one day we'll finish up in a Sunday Colour Supplement article. Terrible, isn't it, don't you think?'

'Maggie, Maggie. I only asked how your job is going,' Adam says.

'Yes, sorry. Sorry. Hello. That's what I was meant to be saying, isn't it?'

'Yes,' he says. 'And hello to you as well.' He kisses me and takes my bag.

It is always the same when we meet after a gap of one or

two weeks. He's never quite as I remembered him. Always I have to spend a few minutes reconciling the perfect image that grows in my head with the reality of him. Always I think – just for a minute – oh, it's only you.

'I don't think things are really as complicated as you make them,' he says.

We walk out into the rain together under his umbrella.

We go back to his flat and he cooks supper for me.

I long for a bath but there isn't one here, only a shower.

I had put on sensible clothes for Adam and it feels good to take them off. As I stand under streams of hot water, he pulls back the curtain and comes to stand beside me. He's white without his clothes, like something newborn. I watch the water falling down over me, bouncing off my arms, and dividing into rivulets as it flows down my legs. I move back so that he can stand under the water. Then he pulls me towards him, and rests his chin on the top of my head, and we stand together with the water running down in the gaps between us, with white tiles around us, and the sound of the water splashing down over our feet.

In bed he kisses my breasts where the weight of them lies between us. Then he kisses my belly button and the inside of my leg. Two candles burn on the bedside table. The curtains are shut, their linings enclosing us in a white cocoon. Long-term relationship kind of sex – have a bath, clean your teeth, switch the lights out, do it all very tidily underneath the sheets.

I shut my eyes and listen to the sounds – the ripping open of a condom, the quickness of his breath, the rustle of sheets as he moves me beneath him. The soft hair of that cropped head brushes against my thighs. His hands tickle me and I laugh – but quietly because I'm worried that he won't like me laughing. Then the slapping of his flesh against mine, the pressure of him deep inside me. I'm in love with the fact that he wants me so much. Nobody has wanted me like this before.

And this is all fine, I like it, and inside me that tension builds, the floodwater rising against the dam. But my mind is still sniggering in the back row. I want to be able to have sex, not make an idea out of it. But my head won't shut up and I'm thinking – what's the point of this? What are we trying to achieve? A muscle spasm, that's all. But of course it must be something more or what is all the fuss about? This should be the route into some other world, like Dougie's drugs, or those mystics Nanda reads about. Except that for me sex has never had any wider resonance.

Instead what I think is that his penis inside me carries with it the echo of other penises, not that there have been many of them – usually my relationships don't get that far. But his penis – those other penises – are all the same. They're all digging deeper and deeper, burrowing inside me, all in pursuit of something that just isn't there.

Afterwards he lies beside me, stroking my hair. 'I think we're pretty good at this, don't you?' he says.

'Yes, very.'

'But we need more practice, don't you think?'

'Yes.'

So we practise some more.

Then he gets up to go to the bathroom and I hear him washing his hands.

When he comes back I ask, 'Adam, do you think that two people can ever like all the same things?'

'Why?'

'Nothing. I was just thinking.'

'Actually, no,' he says. 'I think relationships are like two overlapping circles. You know, like Venn diagrams in maths at school.'

He gets into bed beside me and, lying on his front, he traces the shape of two interlocking circles with his finger on the sheet. 'There are some things in the overlap, and some things only in the circles, and you just have to make sure there's always enough things in the overlap.'

'Uum, yes perhaps.'

'Don't you think so?'

'I suppose I thought that some relationships might be like an eclipse, with one circle fitting perfectly over the other.'

He moves across me, and matches his arm to mine, and puts his hand on top of mine. I line up our fingers so that my hand is like the shadow of his.

'I wish it could be just the two of us,' I say.

'It can be,' Adam says. 'It is.'

'I don't think so.'

He shakes his head, gathers my hair in his hands.

'Do you think two people are ever more than the sum of their parts?' I ask.

'Yes,' he says. 'Yes.' He stares into my eyes. 'What's the matter with you? Yes, of course they are.'

I lace my hand into his and lie with my head on his chest, hearing the throb of his heart from far inside. He strokes my hair and the back of my neck. The candles burn straight in the stillness of the room. I watch that stack of books and papers on his desk.

The next day I go to Moulding Mansions. Tyger has cleared up the kitchen in honour of my return, and has cooked spaghetti bolognaise – very sophisticated compared to her normal beans on toast. Dougie isn't around and Sam is too hungover to get out of bed. I'm ready to be annoyed by

Tyger and her questions about Adam but then I find I want to talk.

'The problem is,' I say, 'that I have a suspicion that the reason why Adam and I get on so well is precisely because – although I do really like him – yet somehow I don't care so very much. It's weird. Other men I've been really nice to, and it's got me absolutely nowhere.'

Tyger sloshes tomato ketchup over her spaghetti bolognaise.

'Indifference attracts,' she says. 'That's the thing . . .'

'But why?'

'Dunno. Most of us get less lovable when we fall in love. That's the gloomy truth, I suppose.'

I suck up spaghetti and get it all over my chin.

'The thing about Adam is that he's so simplistic and literal,' I say. 'And it's intentional. Which is amazing in a journalist, amazing in anyone really, and admirable. Often I listen to the things he says and I think – oh come on. Yet that straightforward quality in him does draw like a magnet.'

We move on to ice cream, eating straight from the pot.

'The thing is that – it's like – this is exactly what I've been waiting for. A proper relationship . . . grown-up . . . And Adam seems so right . . .'

'Yeah, but oddly those ones often don't work out.'

I pick up Biggles who is scratching around on the kitchen floor.

'So is Sam just hungover?' I ask.

'Nah,' Tyger says. 'He's a bit crap, to be honest. It seems like he's now somewhere below soft furnishings in the list of Debbie's priorities . . .'

We can neither of us help laughing, although we're sorry for Sam.

I go upstairs and take him some tea.

A hand and face appear from under the side of the duvet.

'We miss you,' he says.

'Oh yeah, course you do.'

But when Adam comes to pick me up I don't want to go. He takes me straight from Moulding Mansions to the station because I'm going home to see Nanda. In the car Adam and I talk about families. He comes from a nice, normal home so he doesn't really understand.

'It's like one day I saw this great big car park,' I say. 'And in this car park there was only one car but it was parked in the worst possible place – crooked and cramped, halfway on a muddy verge, miles from the entrance. So I thought – why ever did that person park their car there? Then it occurred to me that, at the time when the person parked their car, the car park must have been totally full. And that's how it is in families. You don't get to park where you want because by the time you arrive most of the spaces are already occupied.'

Adam nods but I'm not sure he understands. We are in a traffic jam and through the open window there's a smell of curry and petrol fumes. Sun presses down on us through the windscreen. Adam's arm, with his sleeve rolled up, rests on the ledge of the open window, his middle finger tapping up and down.

'How much do you love me?' he asks. It is a serious question.

'I don't know. I suppose I feel a little suspicious of the whole thing. It has been come by too cheaply. Do you understand what I mean?'

'It doesn't have to be difficult.'

'No. But it's just – I mean – I can't really imagine now what it would be like without you. So I wouldn't really know how much I love you – unless you got run over by a bus.'

He laughs at that and then suddenly the traffic moves ahead. One more mile and then he parks the car, insistent that he must come with me to see that the train exists. I buy a ticket and he comes with me onto the platform.

'Sorry,' I say. 'Sorry. That was a bit much, wasn't it? About the bus.'

'No, I like the fact that you're so honest. That's what I like about you.' Around us people are pushing to get on to the train. Voices echo under the high glass roof. Adam is holding my bag and steering me towards one of the train doors.

I catch hold of his arm. 'Adam, I'm not honest. I want to be honest but I'm not. Please don't think I'm honest.'

'Yes, OK. But get on the train or you won't get a seat.'

'No, I want you to promise me. I want you to promise you won't think that.'

'All right. I promise. If it will make you happy.'

He kisses me goodbye and I watch him growing small as the train leaves.

Home. Above me is the black line of Frampton Edge, hemmed by the clouds, and below it Thwaite Cottages lie long and low, their moss-crusted roofs dipping to the ground. I feel drunk on the air and the space. The wind drags at my hair. In the garden plants crawl flat along the ground and the apple trees are twisted to one side. Nothing grows straight up here because of the wind. When I was a child there was a raging storm and a walker was blown off the Edge. He whirled like a spinning top across our garden, and Freddy had to go out on her hands and knees to get him inside.

Nanda is at her front door – a Struwwelpeter figure, brisk

and spiky, with pale green eyes, the colour of willow, and a fuzzy shock of grey hair. Then Freddy and Theodora appear and they're all talking at once, aware of themselves as a comedy, enjoying their own performance. Freddy is gripping Theodora by the arm, trying to stop her moving down the slippery path, and they pull at each other, back and forth, as they fight their way towards me. Freddy is wearing her best cardigan but inside out, to keep it clean. Wind, of course, is said to be one of the causes of madness.

'So how are you?' I say to Theodora.

'Unvanquished, more or less,' she says. As she kisses me her long pearl earrings dance against my cheek.

A vast hole has been dug in the garden for the wind turbine. They wrote to me in Brussels to tell me about that. And I thought – look, call me old-fashioned, call me unimaginative, but shouldn't you get the porch fixed first? Because it's had a prop under it for ten years. But they don't even realise that, because they've lost all sense of time. Like they still talk about the twenty-first birthday present they're going to buy me, and I don't like to say – actually I'm twenty-eight now.

'When the turbine is finished,' Freddy says, 'it will be able to provide all the power that we need. So then we will be quite independent. No one will be able to disturb us.' I nod enthusiastically while staring at the miles of emptiness around us.

Their lives here are like a badly organised camping holiday. Freddy's cottage is the worst. The roof has been covered by tarpaulin now for ten years and half the windows are broken and covered with cardboard. No one except Freddy has been in there for as long as I can remember. You anyway can't get in the door because she's never thrown anything away for fifty years. The place is stacked from wall to wall with boxes of total rubbish, all neatly labelled. Theodora says that Freddy's even got a box marked 'pieces of string too short to do anything with'. And that, says Theodora, constitutes a mental illness. Freddy denies there is any such box.

Inside Nanda's cottage there's a layer more dust on everything and a rancid smell of dog, despite the demise of Bullseye. I step over a sewing machine and collapsed shoe boxes full of letters then sit down by the fire on the orange sofa that goes round three sides of a square, and has legs like upside down radio aerials, and is so low that old biddies from Burrington get stuck in it, and you can see their knickers. Much of it was eaten by Bullseye and his predecessors, but Nanda won't get rid of it because it was designed by a friend who was a famous furniture designer in the seventies. Black-rimmed holes are burnt into the carpet where logs have fallen from the grate. In one corner the floorboards have given way and the hole is stuffed with newspapers.

'Now be quiet,' Freddy says. 'Be quiet.'

She's fiddling with the record player, balanced on a pile of books. These cottages are built out of books. Anthropology under the windows, poetry up the walls, socialism stacked on the desk, French and German under the stairs and history toppling off the mantelpiece. Other people have crazes for golf, or flared trousers, or spinach but Nanda, Freddy and Theodora have crazes for philosophers, religions, languages and worthy campaigns. They devour ideas like vultures ripping flesh from the bone.

There's a scratch and a thump from the speakers as Freddy wobbles the needle. A single note hangs in the woodsmoke air. Debussy's 'Girl with the Flaxen Hair', my favourite, they always play it when I come home. The music falls in a stream of glittering notes. For a moment they stand in reverent silence, listening, but Freddy can never be quiet for long. 'Now what about this boyfriend that she's got?' That's how they talk about me – as though I'm not here. Often I have the impression that I've walked in on a conversation that started several weeks ago.

'Oh now really,' Theodora says. 'Maggie is going to have a brilliant career.'

Freddy starts to make one of her disgusting cigarettes, as thick as my finger, with tobacco falling out of both ends. 'Well, tell us then,' she says.

I try to imagine Adam visiting Thwaite Cottages but my mind won't make the image. 'Well, he's nice,' I say. 'I really like him but I'm not completely sure. He may be a bit boring.'

'Oh dear,' Theodora says. 'You can't have somebody boring.'

'Yes she can,' Freddy says. 'You don't need an exciting man. You need a kind man. Kindness is the criterion by which everyone must finally be judged.'

Nanda and Theodora snort.

'What does he do, this boyfriend?' Nanda asks.

'He's a journalist.'

'Oh, a *journalist*.' With one word Nanda demolishes him.

'It's really no good having one boyfriend,' Theodora says. 'That's bound to lead to trouble. Better to have two, at least.' She would say that, having spent all her life playing Nanda and Freddy off against each other so she can get what she wants.

'I'm going on holiday with him,' I say.

'Oh wonderful, where to?' Freddy asks.

'Seville.'

'Ah, Seville.'

Nanda and Theodora nod and that conversation lurches to a halt.

'And what are his political opinions, this young man?' Nanda asks.

'I don't think he has any, in particular.'

'Well, he should be ashamed of himself.'

'I don't hold with journalists,' Freddy says. 'All those endless articles about the right shade of nail varnish and what the Queen has for breakfast. Who will protect the public's right not to know? That's what I ask myself.'

'Actually,' I say, 'journalists are very important. People aren't hurt by what they know, only by what they don't know.'

They shake their heads at me, appalled by the naiveté of this statement. I notice that behind a chair there's a dried-up dog turd. I ask Theodora about her latest book and she talks about it in a disparaging way – and I can't understand why because her books are wonderful. Everyone finds in them the person that they wanted to find. When I read the reviews I always wonder if the critics have all been reading the same book. 'Is there an autobiography or diaries of Lou Andreas-Salomé?' I ask.

'A few bits and pieces, not much. And to be honest it would make little difference. One doesn't take so much notice of these things. It's all fiction – autobiography more than anything. One should never believe what anyone says about themselves.'

Freddy passes me a box of Road Campaign leaflets and a stack of envelopes. 'Could you stuff those for me?' she says.

They're in their eighties now. I mean, why don't they rest? Retirement is really wasted on the old. Freddy is agitating to be off down to Burrington to go and see some old biddy who's in a bad state. They spend their whole lives worrying about old people, most of whom are years younger than they are. They fuss around getting tea and Freddy starts to cook the supper. Normally they just eat horrid things out of tins but it's clear they now intend something more ambitious. A worrying prospect – riz flambé is a Thwaite Cottages speciality.

I go to the kitchen door. They are cooking on Nanda's wretched old stove.

'Wouldn't you like me to get you a microwave?' I say this to annoy them.

'No,' Freddy says. 'We like life to be about the process of living.'

'Isn't it strange,' Nanda says, 'the way that people in those countries with the most labour-saving devices invariably have the least leisure time.'

'I don't think she should be living on her own in Brussels,' Freddy says. 'It won't do. No one should live on their own.'

'You never know, perhaps she just couldn't face communal living.' Theodora raises her eyebrows and pokes at me with the end of her walking stick. 'Now was Brussels a good idea?' she asks. This is what they always do. They take a decision you've already made and start to unpick it. They make something certain into something uncertain. And it's not just with me. They discuss what President Kennedy would have achieved if he hadn't been shot. I mean really – what's the point of that?

'Brussels is a good idea,' I say. 'But I do feel bad about the other job. Even though I decided to leave, I still feel a bit of a failure.'

'Rubbish,' Theodora says. 'Rubbish. Failure? By whose standards would you be a failure? That's just a judgement. You can agree with it or not agree with it. Anyway, failure opens up all sorts of possibilities.'

'Being bad at things is a perfectly legitimate occupation,' Freddy shouts from the kitchen. Then Theodora begins to ask me about Brussels. The power of the European Parliament? The prospects for the next German government? I don't know what to say. I haven't learnt anything like that in Brussels, I've just sorted out piles of paper and filled out forms. Fortunately, an argument soon breaks out between Theodora and Freddy about federalism and they forget about me. To me their conversation is like Salvador Dali doing words instead of images. Nothing leads where it should. I sit and stuff envelopes, drowsy with the heat from the fire. The music has finished but the record still turns, throbbing and crackling.

When I was a child I didn't really see anything odd about life here. When you're ten years old everything is normal. You're inside your own life so you can't see it clearly. Then Dad's torpedo-shaped red Jag slid over the fields, and he took me away because he was marrying Fiona, and it was time for me to have a proper mother. Nanda said I could go back and see her any time, and Freddy gave me a manicure set with tortoiseshell handles, when I never normally had any presents like that, but still Dad had to pull me out from under the sofa by my ankles, and in the car I screamed so much he had to pay me five pounds to shut up.

But everyone is materialistic at ten, and when I arrived at Brickley Grange I was quickly persuaded by the deep-pile luxury Fiona creates – the heart-shaped soap in seashell dishes in the bathroom, the clown wallpaper in my bedroom. But for all that I never thought of Brickley Grange as home. This place is where I belong, although it drives me mad. Odd how love is expressed mainly in annoyance.

I shouldn't complain because they did their best for me.

It's just that they could never do anything in a straight-forward way. Like when I fell and cut my lip Nanda got the vet to take the stitches out, because it was too far to go to the hospital in Gloucester. And when we had to take a packed lunch to school I never had a Tupperware box with sandwiches in clingfilm, I just had a paper bag with some bread in it, and a knife and a pack of butter. And I was staying with Nanda when my periods started and all she did was sigh, as though periods should have been done away with in the march of progress. And, of course, they never really told me anything about my mother. They come from a generation where people try to forget.

As I go up to bed, I pass Theodora's room and look in through the half-open door. Nanda is there, unfastening Theodora's hair from its two buns. Theodora sits on a chair, wearing a trailing white nightgown. Her hair is long and twisted like seaweed, and it has a greasy sheen to it, but Nanda touches it as though it's made of silk. I envy them, wrapped up together in their silent tenderness.

They were at school together – Nanda, Theodora, Freddy – at a very advanced co-educational boarding school where there were no classrooms or dormitories, no detentions or organised sport. They decided very young that people should always live communally and they have never wavered in that commitment, even if they have never managed to build a commune as big as they would have liked.

Nanda tells me that when she and Theodora were about fourteen they took to sharing a bed. Freddy was jealous – even then – and so she went to tell tales to one of the adults. But that did not work out as planned – all she received was a strict lecture about casting off narrow-minded notions of possession. Under the circumstances it's not surprising that they're all a bit odd.

I go to the bedroom at the back, under the eaves. It's the room where Dad slept as a child, and where I was meant to sleep as well, except it was usually occupied by a refugee, or a single mother with one leg, or someone else you had to pity, so I used to sleep in Nanda's bed, or on a mattress in the kitchen. Now the room is still theoretically mine, but it's full of boxes belonging to a friend of Theodora's who's been having a difficult house move for fifteen years.

As I open the door, the musty air stirs. I flick the switch and a blackbird flaps close to the shadeless light bulb. It quivers like a plucked string, its claws scraping against the wall, and its blue-black wings flapping. For a moment it rests on the curtain rail, and its shiny eyes stare at me, its head turned to one side. Then it dashes itself against the skylight.

Nanda comes up the stairs with a hot-water bottle for me. The bird is sitting on the top of the wardrobe. I show it to Nanda and we shut the door. There are two windows in this room – a skylight and a tiny diamond-paned window, low down and cut deep into the wall. The bird is sitting just below the skylight, looking out at the stars, unable to reach them. We can't undo the latch to let it out, because the metal is rusted up. Nanda opens the other window, her lace-up shoes and woollen stockings shuffling between the boxes.

I point at a broom standing behind the door. 'Why don't we use that?'

The bird starts to throw itself against the skylight, its beak and claws scraping, shedding a feather. It flies close to the open window, but doesn't see the way out. 'No,' Nanda says. 'Just wait a moment. He will find his own way out.'

I get into bed. The sheets smell of other people. Nanda passes me the hot-water bottle and sits down beside me. I put the hot-water bottle down the bed, feel the scalding rubber of it against my legs, then push it down further so that it's under my socked feet. Outside the wind is blowing so that the beams of the cottage creak like the timbers of a ship.

'It'll never go,' I say. 'We'll be waiting all night.'

'I'll put the light out,' Nanda says. 'The glass and the reflections confuse him.'

The pale light of the moon is reflected from a mirror above the mantelpiece. The bird sits perched on the curtain rail. On the end of the bed there's a patchwork blanket, which was Dad's, then mine. Some of my old teddies are propped on a shelf under the window. A line of Nanda's voluminous grey underwear is drying on a rack. On the dressing table there's a wooden writing case Dad gave me as a present.

He used to sit on the bed here when he came to stay for the weekend and we would listen to the radio together. Sometimes the reception was bad and we used to turn the radio this way and that, fiddling with the knob. Once there was no reception at all. Dad told me that people on nuclear submarines are told that if they can't tune in to Radio Four then they should assume that Armageddon has arrived, that World War III has started, that the world has come to an end. The next morning, when I got up and went out in the garden, the world, so miraculously saved, seemed to glitter in silent celebration.

The bird flaps again, throwing itself against the glass.

'Why don't we just steer it out?' I say.

'No, no, just wait.'

Nanda irritates me, the way she sits there, so still and patient, watching the bird. The old-woman hunch of her shoulders, her hands folded in her lap, her knees pressed tight together, the fuzzy outline of her hair. All of that irritates me. A patter of rain falls on the roof tiles and the skylight. Nanda reaches for a tin bowl, white with a blue rim, and rust stains running down the side. She places it under the skylight, on top of one of the boxes. Then she sits beside me again.

'It'll kill itself before it gets out,' I say.

Nanda says nothing.

'I don't want to sit here all night.'

I turn on the light and pick up the broom. The bird swirls above me, flapping against the ceiling. I steer the broom towards it but the bird is nowhere near the window and the broom is too long and unwieldy. I turn the broom, but the bird goes back to the skylight, battering its wings and shitting onto the boxes below. The broom catches against the light bulb and sends it swinging, so that the room tips in drunken lights and shadows. Again the bird flutters against the glass and I smash the broom across the wardrobe door. The bird is close. I feel the breath of its wings in my hair. I put my hand up to shield myself and drop the broom.

Nanda reaches out to take the broom from me but I hang on. We face each other, both of us holding the broom. She will not wrestle it from me, although she wants to. The bird is silent. Suddenly I drop the broom and start to cry – loud, damp crying which has been shut up inside me for weeks. Nanda pulls me towards her. I feel her thin, strong hands. She pulls back the sheets and I get into bed, my head wrapped in my hands, and my knees pulled up to my chin. I hear her moving the patchwork blanket further up the bed. Her hand rests on mine.

'Maggie,' she says. 'Maggie. You know, parents are only people. You can't expect too much.'

I wipe my nose on the sleeve of my pyjamas. The black-bird watches us out of a shiny black eye, its throat and wings trembling. 'Can't you talk to him?' I say.

Nanda shakes her head and sighs. 'I don't know, dear. You know, he and I know each other too well. Our worst fear is of seeing clearly . . . or being seen clearly.'

'I think he won't come and see you because he's lied.'

'Maybe,' she says. 'Maybe. I don't know. All I can say is that your father may be foolish but he isn't violent. Sadly, it's usually harmless people who do the most harm in the end.'

'Still I think he lied.'

'Yes, dear, perhaps. But sometimes people lie in favour of the truth.'

The rain ticks down into the tin bowl. Nanda switches out the light. The bird is against the window again – a dull scratching of beak and claws, the sound of delicate feathers breaking open against the walls. 'I don't know what to do,' I say. 'I don't know what to do.'

'You have no choice about what happened but you can choose your response.'

'I just wish I could have at least one thing that is certain.'

Nanda shakes her head. 'You know, the odd thing is that a person who has got a map that is wrong gets far more lost than a person with no map at all.'

I don't understand what she means. For her this is just an intellectual argument. She doesn't seem to understand that someone is dead. What should I say to her? Your son killed someone? I can't say that to her.

'Maggie. You know, your father needs you. You have more power over him than you know.'

I look up at the bird. It is close to the open window. It hovers, uncertain, moving as though expecting to meet resistance. Its wings flap, its head turns, and then suddenly it flies through the open window, hesitates for a moment, then evaporates into the darkness.

Nanda releases my hand, gets up and goes to shut the window. Then she says good night and goes to the door. As she opens it, her spiky outline stands out black against the light from the landing. She turns away and then looks back at me. 'All I can tell you is that salvation always comes from the most unexpected sources.'

Max

So the noose tightens.

The worst is upon me. A trial.

Geoffrey telephoned to let me know. It was like going downstairs in the dark, finding there's one more step than you remembered. It was early this afternoon when he called yet still I don't believe it. Somehow I thought that because of Lucía I would be spared this. They haven't a shred of evidence against me, but they won't give up. My hands sweat and my stomach churns.

And now Geoffrey is coming round. The last thing I need. I blame this on him. He should have put a stop to it. Now he's in Brussels for the evening. I only got back from England myself ten minutes ago. I wanted a bath and a shave. But he's already here. I can see him in the square, lumbering out of a taxi. He said he'd got to have dinner with the camp followers at nine. I look at my watch. Eight thirty. Not long. Just keep the cabaret rolling on.

At the door he shakes my hand. I mumble greetings, explain that I've just got back myself. Try to appear Hale and Hearty. Sweat pricks the back of my neck. Gus will be here soon, I tell him. Distractions and diversions, that's what I need. I just hope Gus isn't late.

'Let's have a drink.' I pour Scotch for myself and for Geoffrey, feel it burn down my throat. Actually, I'm half cut already as I had a couple of whiskies on the plane. I find myself staring at my shoes.

Geoffrey paces back and forwards. Stops. Places his hand on Rex's china head. He looks as bad as I feel. 'Look, Max, I'm sorry. I've said again and again it's not what I want. It's not going to bring Tiffany back, is it?' There's a crack in his voice as he says her name.

'I'm her husband,' he says. 'You'd think my views would count for something.' Still he talks about her in the present tense.

'Geoffrey, there must be something you can do.'

I can't bear to plead with him, but I must.

He shrugs and shakes his head. 'They're set on it.'

'But Geoffrey, you know what this means, don't you? You understand what's going to happen?'

He looks at me blankly.

'Maggie is going to have to testify in court, and I can't have that. For myself I couldn't care. I'm prepared to go to a hundred courts but I don't want Maggie involved. It isn't fair on her.'

'I'm not sure it will be necessary for her to testify.'

'Yes, it will be. And I'm asking you, Geoffrey, to try to stop this. For her sake. You're her godfather. You know she hasn't had it easy. And now I just don't want her to have to go through this.'

'Oh God,' Geoffrey says and wipes his hand across his face. 'Would you like me to talk to her, would that help?'

'No, thanks. No. It's better for me to deal with it.'

'She's away at the moment, isn't she? Spain? With that journalist chap.'

'Yes.' As though I need reminding of that.

'Rather nice for her really,' Geoffrey says.

How can he be so bloody stupid. I turn, nearly shout at him, then swallow back the words. 'Geoffrey,' I say. 'Tell Tiffany's brothers that you won't let them do this.'

'I've already tried to say that.'

'Well, try again.'

'Yes,' Geoffrey says. 'Yes.'

I try to calm myself. I must be calm. He mustn't know that I'm frightened. I remember Gus on the night of the fire. It'll hold. It'll hold. But not if Maggie has to go to court.

'Of course,' I say, 'I know Maggie wouldn't mind. I know she'd do that for you. But I just don't like her involved. I'm sure you can understand.'

'I'll try,' Geoffrey says. 'I'll try and talk to them again.'

But I've little confidence that'll do any good. Because, in truth, Geoffrey is rubber-spined. I feel let down by him. I've always been a good friend to him, but now he won't help me. I pour myself another whisky.

Geoffrey shakes his head, starts to pace, his shoes creaking over the parquet. From outside there's a tak-tak-tak from one of those pogo-stick road diggers. It makes my teeth wince. For Christ's sake, what are they doing digging holes at this time of night? The weather is wretchedly humid, the sky pewter grey, the air sticky. June this year has a tired, end-of-summer feel. Like August. In the square they've mended the fountain so that now the green goddess disports herself amid arching jets of water. I wish Geoffrey would stop striding around the place and sit down.

'Have they actually set a date for the trial?' I ask.

'Oh no, not yet, it'll be a while. Three or four months perhaps.'

We go through to the back room, hoping that it might be cooler there. The kitchen table is littered with my papers.

I've taken to working here instead of the Parliament. The overgrown garden is wilting. Even in here I can hear the angry battering of the digger. Geoffrey sits on a kitchen chair, crosses his legs, uncrosses them. Moves to another chair, balances one foot on a wine crate. We sit in uncomfortable silence.

Where in God's name is Gus? I don't feel up to any of this, and I've got to get my act together for tomorrow. There's a report on waste management tomorrow and I'm leading the group's vote. Gus has done most of the work, thank God. But I need a couple of hours at least to look through the papers. I look at the clock. Eight forty.

'Of course, it's my fault,' Geoffrey says. 'I wasn't a good husband to her. If I had taken better care of her . . .'

'No, Geoffrey. No.'

God spare me. Geoffrey's face is grey, he presses his hands to his eyes. Crosses and uncrosses his legs again. He's sitting forward, looking at me. His face is flushed and sweating, as though he's in pain. His voice is low and his bloodshot eyes are fixed on me. 'Max. Don't worry, please. It will all blow over.'

I think of Tiffany. Her voice. You lied. You lied. An image flashes in front of my face. The camera lurches. Her clenched fists bash against me. A knife on the stainless-steel draining board. The linoleum floor of the kitchen, a pattern of beige and brown. A red plastic canister with a label on, smudged by paraffin. The photographs melting and bubbling as the match touches them. I've got to stop this.

'Max, there's no need for you to worry,' Geoffrey says.

I turn back to him and pour myself more whisky. He's still watching me. There are deep lines in his face. He's pulling at the cuffs of his shirt. It feels as though that digger is inside my head. Geoffrey is crumpled, with one knee pulled up to the side of him. I'm tingling all over. Either the drink or this ghastly situation.

'I mean, there's no need for you to worry, is there?' Geoffrey says.

I know quite well what he's asking. I wipe a handkerchief across my face. Where in God's name is Gus? I look at the clock. Quarter to nine. I resort to that time-honoured politician's trick of answering the question you'd have liked to be asked.

'Geoffrey, you needn't worry that this will have any effect on you and me because it won't. This has never come between us and I won't let that happen now.'

Geoffrey squeezes his eyes shut. 'It helps that you say that. Because I need old friends more than ever now. I miss her terribly . . .'

I look away from him. What can I say? Nothing. Time is a great healer. Blah, blah, blah. That's the kind of thing people say. Bloody stupid. The truth is that you don't want the days to pass. Because every day is one day further from her. You don't want to forget. Not an inch of her flesh, not a hair of her head.

'Max, I know that Tiffany was fond of you. I know that. And you were fond of her as well, of course. I know that.'

I feel as though I'm being dragged towards the edge of a precipice.

'Yes, of course. I miss her too. We all miss her.'

It would be a relief to talk. Perhaps he would understand. I look at Geoffrey's shattered face and words start. Then the doorbell rings. The sound crashes through the house. My whisky glass goes down onto the table with a bang. I jump up. 'Ah, there we are. That'll be Gus.' My head spins. I put a hand on the back of a chair to steady myself.

'Listen, Geoffrey. Gus already knows about this, and that's fine. He can be relied on to keep his mouth shut. But don't say anything to anyone else, will you? I'm going to have to talk to Maggie, and to Fiona, of course. But I don't want to do that yet. First I want you and me to think of anything we can do to stop this trial. So we'll talk, but other than that, keep it quiet.'

I lay a hand on Geoffrey's shoulder. He looks up at me with broken eyes. 'Now buck up, old chap. Gus doesn't want to see you like this.'

Gus is standing on the doorstep with a pile of papers. He bounces into the hall. God knows why he's so cheerful.

'Gus, good to see you,' I say. 'You're just in time to see Geoffrey.'

The smile slides from his face. 'Geoffrey?'

'Yes, he's just dropped in but he's leaving in a minute.'

Gus pulls a face and whispers. 'Sorry. I should have got here earlier.'

'Yes, you should.'

Geoffrey appears. 'Gus, how are you? You're looking extraordinarily well.'

'Yes, I'm fine. What news from Dear Old Blighty?'

I leave Gus with him, go upstairs to wash my face. I have a sudden longing for Nanda, a longing to go home. I was going to go last time I was back at Brickley. Been meaning to go for a while. Oh well, I'll be in Gloucestershire next weekend. Time enough then. Anyway, she would have no sympathy for me. She never wanted any of this. I never discovered what she did want, but it wasn't this.

Gus calls from downstairs. They're talking shop. Gus lounges back on the green velvet sofa. 'Max, Geoffrey was just saying that they're beginning to take a closer look at this waste management question back home . . . we should be linking into that, don't you think?'

'Should I make some enquiries for you?' Geoffrey asks. 'I could speak to a few people. Because you want to look to the future. You don't want to be stuck out here forever.'

'Yes, good idea. Why not?'

The future may not exist. The doorbell rings.

'Oh no,' Geoffrey groans. 'Already? I've hardly had a moment to talk.'

I go with him to the front door. He pats me on the shoulder as he says goodbye.

I walk back through the house. Gus is rubbing his raw hands together.

'Is everything all right?' he says. 'What did he say?'

Of course everything is not all right. But I don't want to talk. If I talk, I'll have to think. Gus trails after me. Just like that morning after the fire. Wants the role of saviour. Drives me bloody mad.

I pick up the papers that Gus has brought, sit down at the kitchen table. 'Right, let's get going.'

Gus stands beside me and lays the papers out in piles. 'You'll see that I've done preparatory notes for the main reports in Committee tomorrow. I think it's pretty clear.' He looks at his watch. 'I can get in early tomorrow if you want.' He's got his jacket in his hand.

'What? What are you doing?'

'Sorry. I did mention earlier. I'm going out to dinner.'

'Dinner? For Christ's sake, Gus. What do you mean you're going out to dinner?'

He shrugs his shoulders. 'Sorry,' he says. 'I did mention it earlier.'

I really can't have Gus going on like this.

'Of course, I can cancel it,' he says. 'I can easily do that if you want.'

I find my glasses and sort through the papers. I pour myself another whisky. Gus comes to stand beside me again. I light a cigarette, look at him, sigh.

'I can cancel it if you want.'

I say nothing. He turns away and goes to the phone in the front room. I don't know what's got into him. He was the one who wanted to come out here, but now he seems to have lost his enthusiasm for what I'm doing here. Which is all very well, except I rely on him. He and I are in this together, or so I thought.

I leaf through the papers on the Waste Management Report but I can't seem to focus. Gus comes back from telephoning. He stands at the door and bites his lips. I look down at my hands. Outside, the noise of the digger is still rattling through the evening air. The windows of this house are dusty and the air heavy. I feel tired and old. How many days of freedom do I have left? Do I want to spend them doing this?

'Are you all right?' Gus asks.

'My luck seems to be running out.'

'Your luck? Or your nerve?'

Funny, his ability to read my mind. I turn back to the Report and papers.

'For the waste management vote I've worked with Wolfgang on the group list so it should be fine,' Gus says. I look through the list and the fog in my mind clears a little. Work, work. Thank God for work.

'One thing,' Gus says. 'Whatever happens in the vote tomorrow you can expect the Greens to table something on financing before the Plenary vote . . .'

'Well, that'll never pass. We'll tell them to sod it.'

'Don't be so sure,' Gus says. 'The Germans may not back you on that . . .'

'Well, good for them. They can do what they bloody well like.'

Gus's round eyes are shining. 'That doesn't sound like a man who's lost his nerve.'

After Gus has gone I open a bottle of wine. Fall asleep in the chair and wake at four. Outside it's getting light. No point in sleeping. I sift through Gus's notes and the reports again. I feel well prepared. And I'll turn up tomorrow and I'll be good. Very good. Because I always manage to come out best in these situations. That's my talent. Maverick, contro-versial. A master of the political cut and thrust. Or I used to be, anyway.

I walk back and forwards through the empty house, wish that Rosa was here. I stand and stare at James's pictures, stuck up on the wall. Seems strange that I can prepare for this committee, work until four in the morning, just not think about the fire. Or Tiffany. Or Geoffrey. Incredible that I can go on as though nothing is happening. In a few months time I could be in prison. I could be divorced. Deprived of every penny I've got. Disgraced. Robbed of James. Those thoughts are too much. Usually I don't let them start.

But now I sit down in the armchair, in the bay window. Next to the palms and Rex. Beneath the brass birdcage. I take a gulp of red wine. Stretch my head back. Long for the end. Just explain. Tell the truth. That's what Rosa said. It's hard now to remember the truth. If you tell lies you start believing them. And once you start you can never stop. Of course, everyone makes the assumption that I was having an affair with Tiffany. And I can't blame them for taking that view. I'm a dog with a bad name. Fidelity is not my strong suit.

All those endless, bloody stupid questions the police asked. That's what they really wanted to know. Was I attracted to Tiffany? Of course, I said I was. They'd have thought me a homosexual if I hadn't admitted to that. But the point is that I wasn't having an affair with her. I'm no saint but I would never have taken Geoffrey's wife from him. Although I did have sex with her. Once, twice. I don't remember exactly. It was just a passing thing. Nothing serious.

It happened just before Christmas, the year before last. Everyone was snowed in. I couldn't get down to Gloucestershire because the roads were closed. Geoffrey was stuck in Washington. He phoned me from there, worried about Tiffany. She was alone in London. He asked me if I'd go around and see her, check she was all right. I was pleased enough to go. Always an odd time, that week before Christmas. Everyone's off the leash. Christmas lunches, a bit too much to drink. A breath of hysteria in the air. And that year more so than ever due to the snow. Besides which, I was feeling pretty low. Rosa wasn't returning my calls.

So anyway, I went around to see Tiffany. Because I'd been asked to go, favour to an old friend, and all that. In truth, I knew before I went where things would lead. It had been in the air a long time. Ever since that stupid fortune-telling business the year before. Not that I started it. I certainly didn't. She was the one who made the running. But I wasn't averse to the idea. A very pretty girl offers herself to you. What do you do? So anyway, that's how it was. Nothing to be proud of, but there we are. I've no excuse. Drink. Lust. A few evenings together at Geoffrey's house in Chelsea. Just a bit of fun, that's what I thought.

I don't do that kind of thing all the time, mind you. But I was going through a bit of a phase. General view is that you have a riotous youth, then you grow up and become sensible. But that's not my experience. In my thirties and forties it was all marriage, mortgages, jobs, responsibilities. Then I hit fifty. Next thing I know I'm throwing up in wastepaper bins and waking up in bed with women whose names I can't remember. Curious, really. Growing up is a process that can switch into reverse.

Anyway – Tiffany. Yes, she did tell me she was unhappy with Geoffrey. And she told me I wasn't happy with Fiona. That I was meant to be with her. Probably I agreed with her. But that's just the kind of thing you say in those situations. I mean, really, you've got to dress it up a bit. No one wants sex just for sex.

By the end of that week I was actually pretty fed up with her. She wouldn't stop asking me questions. She fancied herself as some kind of amateur psychologist. At first I didn't mind. Everyone likes to talk about themselves, after all. But then she started on about one thing and another. Stuff that had nothing to do with her. In truth, she was pretty tactless. And I wasn't putting up with that. Anyway, by then the snow was clearing, Geoffrey was on his way back. So that was the end of that. Just one of those things. Or so I thought.

But she wouldn't let it rest. Telephone calls, letters, teasing threats. Was I a little in love with her? I don't think so. But I was flattered. I accuse her of a taste for melodrama but perhaps I was as bad. Certainly, we were a bad combination. And, of course, I couldn't avoid her. Because of Geoffrey. Everywhere we went she would corner me. A bad case of intimacy harassment. Often she would turn the screws. But only in a joking kind of way. I'll tell Geoffrey. I'll tell Fiona. Usually I'd manage to jolly her out of it.

Why do men lie to women? She asked me that once.
She's not the first who's asked. An interesting question. But
a more interesting question lies behind it. Why do women
believe things that men tell them even when those things are
patently untrue? Point is, I've never told a lie to anyone
who didn't want to be lied to.

Then the night of the fire. She rang and asked me to go over
for a drink. She knew that Fiona and James were in London
and Maggie was out. I thanked her but said no. It was gone
ten o'clock. I was buried in paperwork. And anyway I didn't
want to see her. Although, of course, I didn't say that. I
should have foreseen trouble. I should have known from her
voice. But, in truth, she often sounded hysterical. For all I
knew she'd laddered her tights. I put down the phone and
started to work.

Ten minutes later she rang again. Started to insist that I
should go around there. I was polite but firm. Then she
started to threaten me. Same old thing. She would tell
Geoffrey, she would tell Fiona. Except this time she sounded
more serious. I really thought she might do it. I was bloody
furious with her. But finally I had to go.

When I arrived I knew she'd been drinking, which she
hardly ever did. She had no head for drink. I'd already had a
few glasses as well, since it was Saturday night. Straightaway
she started in on me. I had lied to her. All the time I'd been
telling her that I couldn't leave Fiona. But it wasn't that at all.
The truth was that I had another woman.

I was shocked by that. Because I'd never told her about
Rosa. Of course I hadn't. And to this day I'll never know if
she actually found out something, or whether it was a good
guess. Or whether it was an hysterical delusion. Anyway, the
point is, she said it with such certainty, I was caught off my

guard. I should have just denied it. But I was drunk, tired, didn't want to be there. Anyway, I admitted nothing. But neither did I deny it with the necessary force. I tried to calm her down, poured her some whisky. She was asking me again and again about this other woman. I tried to say nothing, poured her more whisky. She was angry, hysterical, drunk. But really there was nothing more than that.

I've seen similar situations before. It seems I attract strong emotions in women. They're obsessed by what they can't have. God knows what the psychology of that is, but it's powerful. She told me all the time that she could understand me, that nobody else could. You always know you're in trouble when a woman says that. There was a power in me that she wanted to release. A hidden good. Another speech I'd heard before. Why can't women just leave me alone to be bad? Because I am bad. Undoubtedly. But the irony is that if I finish up in a prison cell, it'll be because of an affair I refused to have. In truth, I might as well have gone to bed with her a hundred times. Hung for a sheep instead of a lamb.

I don't know. What makes me as I am? Nanda would say it's all to do with Lucía's death. Sweet of her to give me the benefit of the doubt. But I think I was just born this way. Not everything has a reason. Just explain. Tell the truth. I don't know. All I can say is that sometimes you strike a match – and you don't know you're in a fireworks factory, until it's too late, and the whole bloody lot has gone up.

Maggie

In Seville people speak to me in Spanish because they think I belong.

Under the furnace heat of the sun, I walk through tightly knotted streets of white houses with red-tiled roofs. Even through my sandals I feel the heat of the stones. Bougainvillea spills down over shuttered windows, green ponds flicker with golden fish and arches are lined with Moorish tiles in a thousand colours. Everywhere there's a smell of sand and dry dust. Echoes ricochet against walls as thick as battlements, voices are muffled by the heat, and oranges shine with a waxy light behind glittering leaves.

I go to visit the house where my mother used to live. I've only visited it twice before but I know it well. It is part of the backdrop of every day. From a hectic market street I turn down a narrow alleyway, cut off from the sun. The house is shut away behind wooden gates and iron grilles. In the shadowed courtyard, I can hear water trickling from a stone fountain thick with moss. In green shadows, under the arches, there are Moroccan lamps hanging low from chains. The windows are blocked out by filigree screens. Creepers hang from the first-floor galleries. Flowers and leaves have fallen but no one has swept them up.

I don't think of this house as belonging to anyone now. I imagine that it was shut up on the day my mother left with Dad to go to England. I imagine the rooms inside draped in white sheets, the chandeliers thick with dust. Waiting for her return. A threadbare green wicker chair under one of the arches is in the place where she left it. She might have left a book on the low table nearby. With one finger I touch the pattern of leaves in the iron grille. The story is that young men used to stand at these gates and watch for their lovers who were shut away inside and they used to bite into the grilles to calm their passion.

I imagine Dad, standing where I am now, and he's like the photograph that Nanda's got of him beside her bed, in the morning mist, wearing a broad-brimmed trilby. He smiles, and squints into the sun, with a handkerchief knotted round his neck, his shirt blowing in the wind. In my mind, he watches my mother's long skirt trailing behind her as she passes through the shadows under the jewelled Moroccan lamps.

Silly, of course, to imagine it like that.

I go back to the hotel where Adam and I are staying. I chose it because it looks rather like my mother's house. Battered and elegant, it operates to its own rhythm, the guests receiving no more attention than the blue shadows that lengthen and shorten, from dawn to dusk, across the tiled courtyard. Battalions of old ladies, swathed in black, carry clinking pails of water and scold threadbare children playing on the curving stone staircases. A dog slouches through the shadows. Another dog sleeps nearby in the sun, occasionally flicking an ear to remove a fly.

Adam has not arrived yet. He will come from London later tonight. I came from Brussels this morning. It's three weeks since I last saw him and I can't wait. At the reception I ask for the key. 'Buenas tardes, señora Magdalena.'

I love the way they say my name. Magdalena. It's a much better name than Maggie – as in saggy and baggy, or Mags – as in hags and rags. Here they say it just the way my neighbour Javier says it. Magdalena – a short and muscular word, with a hiccough in the middle. Perhaps I should call myself Magdalena more often. I suggested that to Adam but he says he prefers Maggie.

Javier remains in my mind. This city is his home. Just before I came away I saw him, which doesn't happen often, although I always hear his music. I was coming back from a party and he arrived back at the same moment, with his friend Pedro. I got into the lift and they insisted on cramming themselves in as well although it's a lift that can only fit two at the most. I didn't know where to look, their bodies were too close to me. The lift shuddered, sending vibrations up our legs, and rattled upwards pulled by metal ropes and weights.

But then when it got to their floor, Javier leaned over and pressed the button so that the lift went down again before the door opened. They both howled with laughter and I smiled although I thought them pretty childish. At the bottom they pressed the up button. We rose again, me peering at the walls and their shoulders, feeling them too close to me, smelling wine. But at the top again they pushed the down button and as we descended they began to sing. A melodious duet – Spanish words, a strange plaintive song, full of yearning. Despite feeling pretty annoyed, I couldn't help but love the way they sang, and the language. Somehow Spanish has a meaning before you understand it.

Again the lift went up and then down again. Still they sang, their heads raised, their voices echoing up and down the lift shaft. I felt like a stiff Brit, trying not to be a spoil-sport, trying to join in the joke but not really managing it. Finally, as we reached the top one more time, I reached over and stopped Javier's hand before it pushed the down button again. His fingers felt small and soft as they touched mine. Laughing, and still singing, he stepped aside and pushed the lift door open. Both of them stood on the landing, bowing in mock courtesy, sweeping off imaginary hats, before they got in the lift and pushed the down button again.

'Good night, Magdalena,' Javier called. I went into my flat but even as I got undressed for bed I could hear the lift still clanking up and down. And as I lay in bed I could hear them still singing and laughing. Mad, totally mad.

I wait for Adam in the hotel room.

It is eleven thirty when he arrives.

Straightaway I know something is wrong. He does not hug me as he usually does but kisses me as though I'm made of paper. I look around the hotel room – tiled floor, long French windows, cupboard of ancient twisted wood. The bed – rather like the bed my mother left me. At the window the floodlit cathedral rising up into the night. The full moon has a red blush to it. Yes, of course, it is too perfect. I should have known that.

He sits down on the bed and pulls me down beside him. A fan creaks and whirs above us. A grey mosquito net is knotted to one side of the bed. He runs his hands through my hair and looks at me with his unblinking eyes. 'Maggie, listen. There's some news I should tell you. Tiffany's family are going to start a private prosecution against your father.'

'What?'

'There's no announcement but I heard.'

Blood tingles in my hands. I shake my head. The pattern

of roses on the bedspread breaks up before my eyes. My stomach has dropped down a lift shaft. I'm suddenly cold. I feel my head moving from side to side. A window opens into the future. Cameras click, Dad is pushing through crowds of journalists and police, a hundred flashlights smack him in the face. Don't let this be true.

'No,' I say. 'They can't.'

'It seems they are.'

The judge's gavel thumps and thumps in the back of my throat. Jury, witnesses, police – all are assembled. Dad and I are caught in a net of staring eyes. There will be pictures of me in the paper. Rich-bitch politician's daughter, and she's not even attractive, and she's wearing the wrong clothes. Geoffrey crumples broken orchids in his hands. Tiffany turns away from us, her face hidden. I alight from a bus, outside a prison, with a queue of other people. I'm going to visit Dad.

Adam is talking but I don't hear. Something has broken inside me. I realise what this means. I'm going to have to stand in a witness box and say that when I arrived home that night Dad was there. Ms Priestley, do you think that on the night of second October at Hyde Cottage in the hamlet of Brickley . . . Not just a sin of omission, not just a matter of signing a form. I think of the full glass of whisky, the newly lit cigarette.

I turn to Adam, wait for him to take me in his arms and comfort me.

'I might have to testify,' I say.

'Yes, perhaps.'

'I can't bear that,' I say. 'But I would have to . . .'

'Maybe. Yes.'

Adam is using new words – perhaps, maybe. The circle of lamplight doesn't reach his eyes. I take hold of his hand.

Underneath it the bedspread roses are jagged and blurred. I don't understand why he isn't looking at me. 'It's what you said. He's just being harassed . . . Don't you think so?'

'I don't know.' Adam gets up from the bed, takes his jacket off and hangs it over the back of a chair. Then he turns and looks at me too directly. 'Are you sure that Tiffany's brothers don't know something more?'

'What do you mean?'

'Well, think. Why would they be doing this if they don't have new evidence?'

I stand up and walk around the bed. I'm clenched tight inside and my face feels swollen. 'Adam, what are you talking about? Of course they don't have any new evidence because there isn't any new evidence . . .'

'Isn't there?'

My anchor is slipping. Breath is trapped in my throat. This was meant to be our perfect weekend – time together in my favourite city, walking in the gardens of the Alcázar, siestas in the afternoon. I should have known I wouldn't be allowed so much. Adam and I are standing on the tiled floor, either side of the foot of the bed.

'Adam, I don't believe I'm having this conversation with you. You know what the situation is. My father has an alibi. Gus phoned him at ten o'clock. The police have traced that call. They know Dad answered the phone at Brickley Grange. Then I arrived back home, and he was still there. So what else is there to know?'

Adam shakes his head. 'No, Maggie. No. Let's be honest. Your father doesn't really have an alibi. You know that. The whole point is that there's a gap, isn't there? A gap of two whole hours. That's what the police were interested in, that's why your father was arrested, that's what this trial will be about. The gap.'

'And so you think he should be in prison?'

'No, I'm just saying he doesn't actually have an alibi.'

'Well, absence of proof isn't proof of absence.'

Adam sits down on the bed and raises his arm to wipe at his eyes. He seems less solid now, and uncertain. A light inside him has dimmed – something more than tiredness or the long journey.

'What is it?' I ask. 'Something happened. What?'

He turns to look at me. 'Nothing. Well – I'm not sure. It's just I don't know what to think any more – about your dad.'

'Why?'

'I realise I don't really know anything about him. All these conversations I've had with him. When one mask comes off there's another one behind it . . .'

'What don't you know about him?'

'Well, take one question, as an example. I wanted to know about your father's father. Nothing much. Just filling in background. But he doesn't talk about him. So I asked a few people, and some said your father was the illegitimate son of an aristocrat, and some people told me he was the son of some big army man. Then I asked your father and he said that his father was killed in the war. So in the end I went to check his birth certificate, and there's no name on it. Just his mother's name. That's all.'

'Well, sometimes a father's name isn't put on a birth certificate.'

'I know. But when I asked Geoffrey he said that your father has no idea who his father was.'

'Well, Geoffrey really shouldn't go around saying that kind of thing.'

Nevertheless, I'm relieved to find that Geoffrey has a little spite after all.

'The point is – your father lied to me.'

'Well, Adam, for God's sake, he's a politician. What did you expect?'

Adam turns to me and his face is grey, as though there are bruises hidden far below the skin. I should never have dragged him into the world of perhaps and maybe. I take his hand in mine. He thinks I don't understand but I do. You put your faith in someone and they're not what they seemed – you're wrong about them, you're wrong about yourself. Why do we need to believe in other people? This book he's been writing – for him it wasn't just about money or career. He looks at me, shakes his head again. 'Perhaps you're right. No doubt it was stupid of me . . .'

'No, I don't think so . . .'

Still I'm holding his hand but something has broken. I'm looking at him now as though I won't see him again, recording every detail – the profile of his downturned face, the shadows under his eyes, the hair that looks bristly but feels soft. I lay his hand down on the leg of his jeans, and press it there for a moment, as though to make sure it will stay. Because I must go now, I've got to go.

I turn and begin to gather together my clothes. I find my shoes by the bed and put them on. Then I go into the bathroom and push make-up, shampoo, toothpaste into my sponge bag. I avoid my face in the mirror. But strangely, deep down, I feel relief. I've spent months dreading this moment. Now that it has arrived I feel that strength which comes when all else has gone. Yes, so here it is. At least I don't have to dread it any more. I'm about to know just how bad it will be.

In the bedroom I pick up my nightdress and T-shirt from a chair and push them into my rucksack. Everything is stained by him – the T-shirt he bought for me, the rucksack which has spent weekends on his bedroom floor, the frumpy lace nightdress which he laughed at, and liked.

'What are you doing?' Adam says.

'I'm going.'

'Whatever for?'

'Please don't argue with me about it. It's better for me to go. I don't want to talk about it. It's just – I can't do this any more.' I kneel down on the floor packing books from the bedside table and a dress from the wardrobe. The book I had been going to lend to him. The dress like moth's wings which I wore that first night.

'Maggie – I don't understand . . .'

I take care not to listen. My hands stumble through clothes, tickets, maps. When I get to Brussels everything will be better. When I get to Seville everything will be better . . . but nowhere in the world is far enough.

'Maggie. Stop it. Wait.' He leans down beside me and catches hold of my arm. The leg of his jeans is beside me, those competent hands grip my rucksack. I mustn't look at him. We wrestle with the rucksack. His hand grips my arm. 'Listen. Listen. I don't know what you're doing but you've got to stop. All these things – your father, the court case. None of this matters. Only one thing matters – I love you. You know that.'

I watch our hands wrestling with the rucksack. My ears are tightly shut.

'Maggie, I thought you loved me. But perhaps I was wrong. Perhaps you just wanted a man who believed in your father?'

'No. It isn't that.'

'Then stay.'

He is pulling at the zips of my rucksack, trying to unpack it. The inside of me goes slack. I want so much to put my arms around him. I want our perfect week in Seville. I want him to stroke my hair and laugh at my jokes. Just let the lies last a little longer. I look up at him and open my mouth to say that I love him but that look of trust on his face stops me. I pick up my rucksack and go to the door. My legs are numb. I can't trust myself to turn around. Everything is swollen and blurred at the edges. I turn the door knob and feel the tongue pull out from its metal groove.

'You lied for him, didn't you?'

I hold on to the door handle.

'He was there that night – you lied for him, didn't you?'

The shock is like a stabbing. My hand grips a place under my ribcage. I turn around. Strangely, the room is all just as it was. The carved wood of the bed, the circle of lamplight, the full moon at the window. And he stands there at the centre of it, upright, calm, watching me with those delving eyes.

'So it's true,' he says.

I am cornered. Nowhere left to run. I put my rucksack down. I need two hands to manage it and the floor tips towards me as I bend down. There's a hole under my ribcage. The muscles in the back of my neck tighten. A pulse thumps above my eye. I stare at the unstable floor. In the courtyard below, people laugh, calling good night to each other. The air around us is as brittle as cut glass. Adam looks as though he's been hit in the face.

'How did you know?' I ask.

'Just a guess. It wasn't so very difficult.'

I wonder how long he's known. I wonder what else he knows. All along he's been walking in chambers of my mind that I thought were closed. In bed, his tongue has been searching my mouth, feeling out the trapped truths. He's been pressing himself inside me to dig out everything that is secret.

'Well, there we are,' I say. 'Very well done. Game, set and match to you. So finally you've got your story. All that time invested has paid off. Your grand scoop. Publish it in as many newspapers as you want. Write it in your book. Why not?'

He comes towards me but I push him away.

'Don't try to make it as though it's all right. I'm a liar. I admit it. Like father, like daughter . . . I lied on a police statement. That's what you wanted to know. Now you know it, so now why don't you leave me alone?'

'Maggie. Listen to me. Only one thing is important . . .'

'Adam, don't be stupid. You don't love me. You love your image of me. It's the same with Dad. You only admired an image of him . . .'

Suddenly anger lights his eyes. I have never seen it in him before. 'Maggie, will you stop talking about your father. Will you just stop talking about him? You don't get it, do you? You've never got it. This is about you . . .'

His anger shakes me but still I form words. 'Like father, like daughter.'

'No,' he shouts. 'No. That's where you're wrong, totally wrong.'

Silence falls on the room with a strange finality. Both of us are played out. I feel as tired as if I'd been fighting him with my bare hands. My throat is so thick that I can't speak any more. My eyes scald with tears. He comes towards me and puts his hand on my arm. He pulls me to him and I rest my head against the familiar smell of his linen shirt, feeling his ribs underneath it, the rise and fall of his chest.

'Listen, Maggie. Listen. There's something important you've got to understand. What happened isn't your fault. Anyone else in your position would have done the same. It's not your fault.'

He sits me down on the bed and holds me against him.

His shirt is suddenly wet with my tears. But inside me relief is unfolding like a luxurious morning stretch. It wasn't my fault. Anyone else would have done the same.

He runs his hands through my hair. 'Poor Maggie,' he says. 'Poor Maggie. It must have been so very difficult for you.' He goes to his jacket and gets out a handkerchief. I dribble and splutter into it. He takes the handkerchief and tries to wipe my face.

'You know, actually it was terribly easy.' My voice is broken by gasps of breath. 'It's only later as the net begins to close . . .'

'Poor Maggie.' He touches my face with his finger, smudging my tears.

He rings the hotel reception and asks for some tea although it's really too late. Then he unpacks my bag and finds my nightdress, passes me a clean handkerchief. I undress slowly and get into bed. He passes me my cardigan and I put it around my shoulders. Still I'm crying, wiping tears from my eyes with his handkerchief. The pale room, the white sheets of the bed, make me feel like an invalid. When the tea comes I drink some of it although it's lukewarm and made with powdered milk. He undresses and gets into bed, pulling me close to him. I put the lamp out but the lights of the city and the moon still shine in at the window. The sheets are smooth and cold. We lie cocooned together, like twins returned to the womb.

'It would be good if we could just go back to before, wouldn't it?' I say. 'You coming to see me in Brussels or me coming to London. Or put the clocks back even further. Go back to a time before the fire.'

'It can still be like that,' he says.

He wipes my face again with his handkerchief and kisses my lips. I hide from him, burying my face against the front of his T-shirt. 'You want me to go to the police, don't you? That's what you want me to do.'

'It isn't about what I want, Maggie. It's about what you need.'

'I know, but Dad . . .'

'This isn't about him . . .'

He turns over, lies straight and pulls my head up so that our faces are close. 'You know, before all this I was going to ask you something. And I suppose I might as well ask it now . . . Nothing has changed. I've got more sure about what I feel, not less. I was going to ask you . . . You know what you said . . . about relationships and boxes . . . well, I was going to ask you if we could move ours to a different box. I had been going to ask you not to renew your contract in Brussels, to come back to London, to live with me . . .'

'Really?'

'Yes.'

'Are you sure? Even now?'

'Even more now.'

'Yes, I know – but living together . . .'

'Yes, of course. I know. It's a bit of a compromise, isn't it? I know it's sometimes better, clearer . . . not to have halfway houses. So we could – I mean, if you want. We could – get married, or something.'

My body has gone stiff. I want to look away but he's holding on to my eyes.

'I hadn't really thought of it . . .'

'Yes, I know . . .'

I realise that I must take care of him.

'Thank you,' I say. 'Thank you very much. I'm flattered, of course.'

My words are too small. What he's saying will not sink into my mind. So he does love me. He really does love me.

I hadn't understood. It's hard to think about this and do it. Voices in my head are babbling, already telling this story to someone else. I force my scattered mind together. What if I got married to him? Then I'd really be in a foreign land. I think of my mother's house – the iron grilles, the striped shadows that they cast.

'Adam, listen. I think you're right. I think I should come back to London. But to be honest I just can't think about it properly. Not while all this other stuff is going on. I don't want us to go into this thing when I'm only half-focused on it. Sorry, I know that sounds all wrong. But do you understand?'

'Yes,' he says. 'Yes. I know, of course – it isn't quite the right moment to ask. But I just wanted you to understand . . .'

'Yes, of course. I do. I do.'

'Probably you should just think about it for now. Keep it in mind.'

'Yes, that's what I'll do.'

An awkwardness is upon us. I turn over and watch the fan creaking above us.

'Maggie,' Adam says. 'I'm not going to tell you what you should do – about your father. All I can say is that I don't think you can keep living like this – and you shouldn't have to either.'

'Yes, I know, I know . . .'

'And I'll help you. To actually do it – to tell the truth, that will be difficult. But you know once it's done everything will be better.'

The clean white world – that's what he's offering me. A place where some things will be certain. And I do want to go there. I wrap my arms around him again. 'You will help me?'

'Of course. Yes.'

We lie awake, waiting for sleep. Pale lights from distant cars pass across the ceiling. I pull my pillow further under my head. The linen is crisp against my face. I look at Adam's clothes, neatly folded on the wooden chair. My rucksack lies on the floor, returned now to its innocence. I am too hot so I pull back the sheets. I look at Adam to see if he's still awake. His eyes stare up at the ceiling.

'Adam, could I ask you something?'

'Yes, of course.'

'Do you think my father could do this to me and still love me?'

He turns to me, his face eyeless in the half-dark.

'No, I don't really think he could.'

Max

Why do women always have to create domestic projects? And more importantly why do their domestic projects always have to involve me? Here I am at Brickley Grange. Beautiful summer afternoon, roses in bloom along the front of the house, air heavy with the scent of flowers and grass. Just the day for a walk. And instead what am I doing? I'm helping Fiona to clear out the cupboard under the stairs. And why are we doing that? Because some friend of hers is coming to stay with a baby. And, of course, babies are well known for spending a lot of time in cupboards under the stairs, aren't they?

Fiona is standing with her hands on her hips giving a stuffed deer one of her Lady Bracknell stares. The deer, which is largely bald, returns her stare through its one glass eye. 'Skip,' Fiona says.

'Certainly not.'

'Max, we do not need Bambi.'

'Yes we do.'

'Don't be ridiculous. This house is overflowing with your junk. You're as bad as your mother.'

'If I want to fill the house with junk I think I should be allowed to.'

Fiona gives me a look which reminds me that this is no longer my house.

'Max, I'm in the mood for clearing things out.'

That's it. I've had enough. I take Bambi out of the back door, hide him in the garden shed. Then I lurk on the terrace with a newspaper and a packet of fags. Of course, this bickering has got nothing to do with the cupboard under the stairs. It's about the trial. She knows about that now. I told her last night, when I got back from Brussels. It was a pretty bloody conversation. I wish she'd shout, or threaten me. That would make it easier. But she was very calm. Her main concern seemed to be about Maggie.

'You must think very carefully,' she said.

I said nothing.

'It's not that I doubt you. You know that I don't. And I'm not worried for myself. I'm quite prepared to put up with anything. You and I are married, and that's what it means. And of course Maggie loves you, and she'd do anything for you, without a question.'

I nodded my head. We were sitting in the kitchen, at the table. The supper Fiona had cooked going cold in front of us.

'I know that you'll put her first,' Fiona said. 'She may have this seeming ability to cope with anything, but really she isn't like that. You know that, don't you?'

'Yes.'

'I would try to help her but she's never had much time for me. It's you she wants.'

'Yes.'

There was silence again.

'There's no reason why she should worry,' Fiona said. 'There's no reason why any of us should worry. This trial is much for the best in my view. It will simply show that there's no truth in all those stupid rumours. It will clear your name.'

'Exactly,' I said. My voice sounded thin.

Fiona started to serve the supper although we didn't finally eat much of it.

'I'm sorry that this has happened,' I said.

What else could I say?

When Maggie was a child she used to ask – Daddy, where would we be if we weren't here? I generally used to give some distracting answer. In my view, it's not a good idea to encourage eight-year-olds to go in for metaphysical specula-tion. But it was an odd question for a child to ask. As though she was already aware of parallel lives. The implications of choice.

Often I think of that question. Roads taken, choices made. I can't help looking back and wondering what brought me here. Other lives go on in parallel. So often a choice hangs on a thread. A slight move one way, or another, and the course of a life is changed. All day, every day, there's a risk. Amazing that anyone gets out of bed really.

Fiona and I nearly didn't marry. Because of Rosa. I think back to that moment when our futures dangled on a thread. The weekend before the wedding. I'd been travelling all week and hadn't seen Fiona. It was Friday evening. She'd taken an earlier train down to her parents' house. Stately pile in Hampshire, avenues of trees, a trout lake. I took a later train. Her parents were away that evening and when I arrived Fiona didn't come out to see me.

I found her in the sitting room. All green willow patterns. Looking out over the lake. The evening was cool and the lake was grey. There was no light in the room. Fiona was sit-ting on the sofa, straight as a nail. She didn't turn around when I came in. On the table was a piece of paper. Rosa. A careful little picture of a starfish. Yellow paper, green ink.

I went to stand beside her. She said nothing. Her parents' house was out in the sticks, and I've never heard silence like there was then. I picked up the note, tore it up into tiny pieces, like confetti, scattered it into the bin. Time went on, although it seemed to have stopped. A creak of shoes, a rustle as I sat down at the other end of the sofa. She was shivering so I struck a match and lit the fire that was laid in the grate. Then I poured her a whisky because I needed one myself. The clunk of the glasses on the table. The tap of the bottle against the lip of the glass. My eyes followed the willow pattern on the sofa over the distance between her legs and mine. Outside it was getting dark and rain came down across the lake in grey sheets.

Finally Fiona and I never talked about that note. The next weekend we were married. So that was that. But I always remember one thing she said. 'Marriage seems like backing a horse. But how can you know, when the race is so long?'

Fiona is clearing away the supper. I have the impression she might be banging a few pots around a little more loudly than she needs to. Of course, she's angry with me. With just cause. But at the moment all I can think about is my survival. I can't be concerned with anyone else.

We are alone. James has gone to a party at a friend's house. And he's staying overnight. I wish he was still here. For the purposes of distraction, if nothing else.

'I thought you were going to see your mother some time this weekend,' Fiona says. 'We won't have time tomorrow, you know.'

'I'll have to go when I'm home again.'

'How is she anyway?'

'Oh, all right, I think. Apparently she's been a bit peaky recently but she's on the mend.' Fiona isn't really interested in Nanda. She's just bringing all that up because if anyone can create a tension between Fiona and me, then Nanda certainly can. Fiona has never found Nanda easy. Don't suppose anyone does. Except, oddly, Rosa.

'Have you talked to Maggie about this situation? About this trial?' Fiona asks.

'Not yet. But I will do.'

'Because if you don't tell her then somebody else will. You must at least be straight with her,' Fiona says. 'Is she still going out with that journalist?'

'Yes, as far as I know.'

'Well, I think that's nice for her. It's about time she settled down.'

Fiona, Geoffrey. They're both the bloody same. You can never be quite sure whether they've genuinely completely missed the point. Or whether their comments are carefully judged. I go to her, where she's standing propped against the dresser, drying her hands on a tea towel. 'Listen,' I say. 'Sorry. Sorry for being grumpy earlier.'

Immediately, she softens. And that's what I wanted. But at the same time I'm annoyed that she's so easily won.

'Don't worry,' she says, and puts a hand out to me. 'We must try not to fight.'

'Yes.'

'And perhaps we will hang on to Bambi. After all, one never knows when one may need a stuffed deer with one eye.'

I laugh at her; kiss her cheek. Half of me is touched by her faith, half of me doesn't want the burden of her goodness. She's a little bit like Gus. Part of her enjoys this situation. It gives her the opportunity to be good to me. What would happen if I became the good man who she so much wants me to be?

'Early night, I think,' Fiona says. I help her to clear up the last of the pots. We put out the light and cross the hall. I follow her up the stairs. On the landing she stops. I hover. She takes hold of my hand. Gently does it. Before she's even noticed I have guided her back to the marital bed. She even comes to kiss my cheek as I'm taking off my cuff links.

What frightens me is that the extent to which you are loved has got nothing to do with being good or being nice. In fact, one is inversely proportional to the other. The people who deserve love don't get it. But the less I deserve, the more I receive.

We lie in bed, sexless as children. Waiting for sleep that will never come.

'Have you seen Maggie since she got back from Spain?' Fiona asks.

'Yes, briefly . . .'

'Did you take her out somewhere nice?'

'No, no. In fact it wasn't like that. I just saw her in the street actually. And it was stupid because I couldn't stop. I was between two meetings. The car was there, people were waiting . . . You know how it is.'

What I don't say is that she was holding up her hair. It was a steaming hot day and she was holding her hair up to cool her neck. Just as her mother used to do. It was lunchtime and she was hanging around at a street corner. Always there's something of the Dickensian orphan about her. Grey and black. Even in the heat. The skin around her fingernails bitten raw. Of course, I couldn't see that but I know. I could almost smell Spain on her skin. If she wasn't my daughter I'd be desperate to go to bed with her.

Always she's so determined not to charm. Sporting one of those rather ghastly trailing hippie dresses she's inclined to wear. Her hair hanging down to the curve of her waist. She was a darker shade of brown than usual. And always she looks so calm, so much part of the scene, whatever it is. Yet also she looks angry, as though she might fire off in a violent temper at any moment. If this were the Middle Ages she'd be burnt at the stake. No doubt about it.

I couldn't stop watching her. Camp followers were trying to bundle me into the car. The sun blazing down. Too hot in my suit. Then two other girls came along and Maggie went with them. All very normal. Any three girls, anywhere. Somehow I expected all this to have left more of a mark on her. It's tricky. A father wants to be worshipped by his daughter. But Maggie has always been hard to impress. Even as a small child she was merciless in the clarity of her vision. There was always a rigid certainty in her. Impressive and unnerving. Why are women so much better than men?

I should have pushed those unctuous minions aside. I should have told the car to wait. Or cancelled the meeting. I should have crossed the road and gone to talk to her. I should have tried to explain. Why didn't I do that? Because I'm ashamed. That's the truth of it.

I dream. One of those dreams when you know it's a dream. But that doesn't help. Tiffany's face is close. Magnified but flickering, like cine film projected onto a white wall. Her pouting mouth screwed up, her blonde hair hanging ragged around her face. The rims of her eyes red, mascara smudged down her face. She's shouting at me. Lurching towards me. Staggering.

You lied. You lied. That's what she's shouting at me. We are in the kitchen. Empty wine bottles on the shiny pine of the kitchen table. A blue and red zigzag pattern on the sofa under the window. The glare of spotlights on the ceiling reflected in a mirror above the fireplace. A knife on the stainless-steel draining board, the jagged edge of an open tin of tomatoes. A box of cigarettes, my brand, empty and crumpled. Must remember to take those with me when I go.

I'm laughing at her because I've seen all this before. It's theatre, and flirtation. Tomorrow things will go on just as they are. I can't see her face but the pattern on the collar of her wool jumper flashes in my eyes. She's going to tell Geoffrey. She's going to tell Fiona. It's a fake world you live in, she says. A world of illusion. I take her in my arms, but her clenched fists bash against me. I lose my balance. Pots and pans on a high shelf flicker towards me.

She picks up the telephone. She's going to ring Geoffrey right now and tell him. I wrestle the receiver out of her hand. She picks it up again. She's going to ring Fiona. This makes me burn red. I've got to find some way to shut her up. I can't go on like this. Pink fingernails pull open the packet of photographs lying on the table. A picture of Fiona at Abu Simbel in Egypt. Heat and dust. Blonde hair blown in a desert wind. My vision tips. I'm trying to take a box of matches out of her hand. She won't let go. She strikes a match, burns her hand. Lights another. A photograph, gripped between her fingers, burns and bubbles to nothing. I tell her to take care. She says she doesn't care if the cottage burns as well.

Tiffany. Tiffany. I try to take her in my arms. I'm laughing at her, trying to make her laugh as well. Of course you're special to me. Of course I'm fond of you. But Geoffrey is my friend. I'm married to Fiona. That's the way it is. You've got to stop this.

She's going to tell Geoffrey. She's going to tell everyone.

There's nothing to tell, I say.

Do I love her? Do I love her? When will I leave Fiona for her? If I don't, then she might as well die. I get angry. I've got to put a stop to this. I've got to shut her up.

Blonde hair in the darkness. Below me, on the cellar steps, blurred. Face running with tears, hands fumbling. There are canisters on the cellar steps, she's stumbling as she reaches for one. She takes the lid off a canister. Red plastic with a label tied on, written in Geoffrey's writing, smudged by spilled paraffin. The kitchen sink, unsteady. Hard to balance. Although there's only a drop of paraffin in the canister, I'm trying to pour it away. The stainless-steel tap turns into soap and slips through my hands. She's pulling the can away from me, it's spilling.

The linoleum floor of the kitchen, a pattern of beige and brown. Stumbling towards the rubbish bin. Tiffany slipping onto her knees with the can in her hands. The grid pattern on the sole of her shoes, a brand name in red. Three flames dancing on the floor, one small, one medium, one large. Then a wave of them, rushing away from us. Her face, the last time I saw it. Everything going slow. Miles to the sink. Hours to get there. Movements heavy, lumbering. Stumbling near the sink on an overturned chair. Stop, stop. Please, stop. Tiffany screaming. The fire suddenly close. The heat of it hitting my face, a curtain eaten in a rush of orange.

I get hold of her. Pull her out of the back door. She's fighting. Stars and moon above. The night open and fresh. My feet crackle on the gravel. She's snaking and writhing on the end of my hand. Flames wave from an upstairs window. Let me out. Let me out. I've got hold of her arm and the buckle of her wristwatch is digging into my hand. She's scratching at me, trying to pull free. Then she's gone and it feels as though she's taken my arm with her. I stand on the drive, waving an empty socket. Stumbling, I run, shouting. My bad foot turns. I stumble. The door of the sitting room is alight all round. A flaming hoop for a circus dog. Smoke everywhere. Choking in my nose and mouth. Coughing up my lungs and my eyes running. The floor on fire. The curtains. Then a groan. A crash. The ceiling comes down. On my knees on the path outside I hear her voice. You lied. You lied.

I wake. Gasp for air.

'Max, Max. What is it?'

I struggle up, breaking the surface, struggling into this familiar room.

I am gripping Fiona's wrist. Holding it tight. We both look down at where my fingers are digging into the white of her arm. I release my grip and draw in breath.

'Sorry. Nothing. Just a dream.'

She holds me against her and kisses me. I am drenched in sweat. She gets up and goes to the bathroom. A shaft of light appears as she flicks the switch. I hear running water.

Still I feel Tiffany pulling against me. Still I try to hold her. I feel the stretch in my arm, lean my weight against it. In truth, anyone would have been thrown off course by what happened that night. But it was worse for me. Because I'd been there before. That moment when something slips through your fingers. Because of that, I thought I should be spared this. Both times it was the same. Death is so easy. Nothing more than sleight of hand. They say that lightning doesn't strike twice in the same place. Believe me, it can.

Maybe if a court convicts me, they would be right. In

some sense I did kill her. By making her into a joke, by failing to see what she felt. Problem is that love is hard to take seriously, when it isn't you that's in love.

Fiona comes back with a glass of water. We sit amidst the crumpled sheets. She puts her arms around me. I turn to touch her hair.

'So is your money still on me?' I ask. 'Even now?'

For a moment she doesn't know what I mean, then she does.

'Yes, always.'

AUGUST

Nanda

All of my life I have been distracted by the ephemeral, I have been confused by the multitude of surfaces ... and now I watch the light changing over the valleys, and it seems that I've never spent enough time looking, before. My mind has always been searching through the future, or the past, and it's only now I realise that all that I was seeking is here, now. This should have been enough, always. How strange that one should have to go to the end of experience, and back again, to find the answer here.

Maggie has come, but at first it's a struggle for me to focus on her. The visions inside my head get stronger every day so that I can watch myself from other places, and I can see people who have been dead for fifty years, but my external vision sometimes becomes confused. There are moments when I have to decide to see, I have to instruct my eyes to look, and then things are sometimes not in the places where they should be – my feet, black lace-up shoes, propped onto a footstool, appear as two trees, far away on the top of a distant hill, and the valleys stretch across the width of my eyes, so close that I can nearly feel the grass and the earth against my skin ... and Freddy's rows of carrots might be close to me, a few yards away in the garden, or they might be miles away, out there where the sun is setting.

It's like that now with Maggie. She appears as a knot of thicker air to the left of my vision, but as soon as my eyes touch her, they flick back again to the far distance, for she is too much in the world and her flesh overflows the normal outline of her body, and she occupies her skin as though it's spacious. I suppose that once I was also at home in my flesh. Yet I have been waiting for her to come because I need her to help me, and I must ask her today, for I must know that I have got the means to decide . . . and so I must ask her soon, soon. I should not have to do this.

'Are you all right, Nanda?' The sound of her voice brings her into focus.

'Yes, dear, I'm all right.'

'Should you go to the doctor?'

'No, no, I've already been. It's just a virus, not much they can do.'

As I speak something nudges me deep inside and I almost welcome the pain now for it is evidence of the battle for life or death going on inside me. Further down the garden Freddy is working on the wind turbine, by the stream, and she works and works all day now so that she doesn't have to see what is happening to me. Sometimes that angers me, but sometimes I am touched by it, and I like to join in her game, discussing what we will do when the wind turbine is finished, talking as always of a grand trip around Europe. Theodora has gone to London, just for the day.

Maggie sits near me on the edge of her deck chair, leaning forward, her long skirt trailing around her and her wrist clanking with bangles as she pulls her hair away from her face. She's so like her mother, in those summer weekends when she came to stay and she found a tin bath in the shed and filled it with water and bathed Maggie in the garden, just here, where we are now, and afterwards she put her own brown, broad feet into the water, with her hand holding her long skirt aside, and her eyes shut at the pleasure of it.

Maggie is swinging one leg and her red shoe flaps on the end of her foot, a strange shoe made of red suede, the kind of shoes women would have worn to a dance when I was a young woman . . . and I do wish she would sit still. People who live in cities don't know how to sit still and if she were silent for a moment she would hear the sounds of the evening. I listen for them always – the voices of the birds becoming softer, the sound of water being drawn up from the earth by a million roots, the earth slowly breathing out the heat of the day.

'Nanda,' she says. 'Nanda. You know my boyfriend?'

'Which one?'

'You know, the journalist. Adam. I've written to you about him.'

The flapping of the shoe has stopped.

'Yes, I remember. You went to Spain with him.'

'Yes, well, he asked me if I would . . . live with him, or even get married to him . . . But I'm not really sure. I don't know if I love him that much.'

'Friendship, surely, is more important – for the long journey.'

'But I want someone I love.'

'You know, this idea that all passion should be expended on one person is a modern idea, and very flawed . . . you should really leave some passion spare for other things. You never know what may take up the slack.'

'But other people who are married? They're in love.'

'Are they? I don't know. Marriage is so very private.'

There's silence for a while, and the sun has nearly gone, and the sky is purple, except for the white line left along the edge of the hills. I can hardly see her now, she is reduced to a shadowed outline. My legs are stiff and my feet are no longer part of me and there is a dampness in the air and I must get up soon and offer her something to eat or drink.

'At least don't marry him out of fear.' I move my stiff legs off the deck chair and feel blood tingle through them for although the evening is still warm I'm cold with sitting still too long.

'It isn't fear,' she says and her voice is brittle.

As I get up I feel that nudging inside me again and I have to tense every muscle to pull myself off the chair, but once I'm up I can move easily, made quick by the pain, shaking . . . She doesn't follow but sits looking up at me and she wants something more. I move my legs through into the hall and then the sitting room, and it's like carrying something that isn't part of me, and I try not to stumble so that she won't worry, but I put my hands on the stair rail and the desk as I pass.

When she comes to the kitchen, the corners of her mouth turn down, and I see the kitchen as she sees it, and it's disgusting, of course, because flies buzz around the rubbish bin, and the sink is full of unwashed plates, and used tea bags rest in the bottom of cups – and there's a saucepan on the stove with dried-out baked beans in the bottom of it and a vase of dead flowers. On the floor there's Bullseye's bowl, and his basket is next to the stove. The place probably smells but I've got used to it.

'Now, I've got some vegetables for bubble and squeak.' I push a rail of washing out of the way and Maggie stands at the door. For myself, I almost take pleasure in the mess, because before too long it will not be my mess any more for even death has some advantages. Occasionally I'm seized by panic, about all the things left undone, and I think about notes I should leave – make sure to get the washer on the tap fixed, and please buy some tomatoes, and check the oven is off before you go to bed. But what would be the point of that? I get a plate out of the fridge which has some cold potatoes on it, and green beans, and cabbage and carrots – there's a cup of dripping left over from some meat we roasted last week.

'Nanda, I don't think I need that much to eat, thank you,' Maggie says. 'Have you got bread? I could just have some toast.' On the draining board there's a plastic packet with a few slices of white bread left in the bottom of it and I switch on the grill and move to lean my hip against the sink, because I feel dizzy . . . For this pain has been battering against me for days now, wearing me away, so that one day I will crumble and fall, and on the ceiling there's a flypaper curling down, caked with dead flies – and now the ceiling starts to spiral around the flypaper, and I'm slipping into sleep, and I wonder where the flies are now.

'Will you come to Brussels to see me when you are a bit better?'

'Yes,' I say. 'Yes. Why ever not?' The butter is hard and my wrists are weak so that it's difficult to spread and too late I notice that there are patches of green mould on the crust.

Maggie steps down into the kitchen and stretches out her hand to me. 'Nanda, let me do that.'

'No, there's no need.' My voice is too loud, and I keep the knife firmly in my hand, and our eyes meet and for a moment I'm drawn in, sucked into the black flecks around the iris, and I know she's frightened, and my hand starts to reach out to her, but I know that I must not weaken. So I give her the plate of toast and turn my back, as though looking for something, until I can go back into the evening air, for I need to be outside and I move slowly, with pain grating deep within.

'Maggie, dear. I wonder if you could help me with something. I might need some pills, but I'm not sure that I can get them here, but there's a place in Amsterdam . . . Would that be too far for you to go?'

I do not look at her but prop myself against the desk and feel for the paper where I've written down the address . . . I should not ask her to do this for me, but there is no other way. I notice her moving behind me back to the kitchen and she thinks that I do not see her sliding her toast into the full pedal bin, for the young always think that the old see nothing.

She comes to my side. 'I'm sure they can send them to you,' she says.

The anger is as bad as the pain now – anger that I should have to bargain for death in this way, but I must have the choice, and I cannot wait much longer and so I fumble and fumble in my desk for the piece of paper.

'But of course I'll go and get them for you,' she says. 'I don't mind going. I'd probably be going some time anyway.'

I give her the address, and we go back outside, and I'm glad to be out of the light, where I can't be seen, and although the sun has gone down now, the night is still warm. I turn the porch light on and fold myself into my deck chair in the twilight, and midges begin to buzz and flicker around us in the pale violet air, and in the light from the porch Maggie's fuzzy black hair stands out around her head like a halo.

'Sorry,' Maggie says, 'but I've got to get back now. I don't want to leave it too late. But are you sure you're all right?'

'Yes, dear. Now don't make a fuss.'

'Nanda,' Maggie says, out of the darkness. 'You know what you said, about Adam.'

I can hardly remember – what I did say about that? I am failing her. I want so much to be able to help, but I don't know if I can, for the space between us is too wide, and I am too tired. After a lifetime seeking wisdom, I have none to offer. 'Maggie, dear, what I said about fear – we were talking about fear, weren't we? I suppose that what I wanted to say is that we're all looking at the world through only one eye, and that's the way it is . . . and you have to consider what you don't know, and what you can't see, as a source of wonder. That is the only way. If you don't, then you will live in fear and that's what many people do, they cling to whatever illusion of security they can find.'

It hurts me now to speak, even my lips are twisted with pain.

'They have that phrase now, don't they? In horror films. They say – the living dead . . . and you know that's an interesting description of a lot of people, people who live in fear. Yes, the living dead certainly exist in their hundreds.'

'And the dead who continue to live?'

'Yes, of course.'

'You know when I was in Spain I went to see my mother's house.' Her voice is quiet, and uneven, forced out from a tightened throat.

'Oh, did you, dear?'

Wind rustles through the trees and an owl hoots. Maggie doesn't say anything more, but sits quite still, and I know that I have betrayed her, but what else can I do? I am too tired for anything more and, in truth, I do not want to pull the grass back from that hidden footprint on the path, I do not want the wound uncovered . . . Although, of course, this conversation about Adam is a mere distraction for he is not the man she wants to discuss. Again, from further away, the owl calls, and the evening is cooler, and the midges are gathering around the light on the porch, and my bare legs are cold and my head floats.

'Well, it's very good of you to come.' My hand reaches out but misses hers which is stretched out in the darkness and I feel too tired to get up . . . and pain flashes through my body, and something between a sob and a groan catches in my throat – but in the darkness she has not noticed. Increasingly I feel that all of life has been a struggle to find receptacles into which to pour an excess of emotion . . .

'Don't get up.' She comes to my side and reaches down to me and I want to hold her, I want to . . . but time pursues us relentlessly, and now the moment has come, and I must let her go into the future, for it is here that our paths divide.

'Maggie, dear.' That is all I can trust myself to say, in case she hears the pain, and I hold her arm for a moment, then she walks away, towards the gate, and she grows small, fading into the purple night and all I can see is her hand waving, as though blown by the wind – and the air closes around the place where she stood. Then I put my hand over my face, spreading my fingers out across my cheekbones, holding together the splintered fragments of my face.

Maggie

Every day I wake up and think – oh no, not this again, I'm finished with this. But then I lace myself up tight, go to work, and play the Normal Life Game. In my mind I can make a rational case about how this is just a bad period of my life. But the truth is that I'm stuck within the confines of today. And today is becoming unmanageable.

It's a terrible thing to be frightened of your own mind. Mine has become like an unwanted guest. I say to it – all right, that's enough now, you've got to leave, but still there's this person crashing around in my head, their voice ranting and arguing all day long. I don't want to live in the same skin as myself any more. The days are taut and edgy. Everything is over-lit and green at the edges.

In my flat a process of decay sets in. My cardboard life is folding up. There's dust everywhere, and piles of dirty clothes, and dead flies, and cereal bowls from a week ago by the bed. I'm ill but it's only a cold. I'd like to be properly ill – a Keatsian bout of tuberculosis, so I could turn into a pale shadow, and cough up blood. Inside I feel ill enough for that. But every day I look in the mirror and see the same disappointingly solid and healthy shape. Biology is meant to be biography – in which case you'd think I could at least be thin.

Out there – in the world beyond the circumference of my head – Brussels has pulled down the blinds and left for the south. August heat burns in empty streets, life is on hold, shadows are short, lone cars rattle over the cobbles. Before my boss left for vacation, he called me into his office and told me what an asset I am to the department. He said that my contract will definitely be extended – and asked if I've thought about trying to get a permanent position. I'd be ideally suited, he said. Shiny fruit, rotten core.

Now nearly everyone else in the office is away – except me, because I agreed to take my holiday later. The grey corridors are silent – a few survivors play cards, smoke, or listen to the radio. The phones ring unanswered. I read books or sit with my head on my desk. At four o'clock I walk home, then lie in bed in a whipped-cream mess of white duvet. Light filters in through my pale gauze curtains. My red suede shoes stand pigeon-toed next to a striped deck chair, scarves are looped on unoccupied picture hooks. Piles of half-read books lie on my packing crate bedside table. My blood runs sluggishly. Adam calls but it's impossible for us to meet because he's away in the States.

One evening I cut my hand with a kitchen knife because my eyes are full of onion tears. I feel so faint I have to sit on the floor for a while. The cut runs across the pad of my index finger. If I squeeze it open there's something white deep inside – the bone perhaps? I wonder if I ought to get it stitched, but the thought of going to a hospital and speaking French and dealing with the medical insurance is all too much. So I wrap my finger up in a handkerchief, go to an emergency pharmacy and buy bandages and lint.

I worry that the cut will become infected, so I keep unwrapping it and bathing it in disinfectant. I do that every day when I get home from work, and this business of dressing the wound begins to fascinate me, and I fiddle with it far more than I should. I like taking off the lint, and laying my hand on the dirty kitchen tablecloth, and squeezing the sliced skin open until I can see the white bone.

At the weekends I don't get up. Javier has gone away and the air pulses with the sound of notes which aren't there. I turn over in bed, and sneeze and wipe my eyes on the duvet, which is less white than it used to be. For hours I watch the window, patches of bright blue sky, a white cloud edged with grey. On the bedside table there's the bracelet Adam bought me. When the phone rings I let the machine take a message because I don't want to speak to Dad. I've decided I hate him, which is a good decision to make. With hate there are no halfway houses, no in-betweens.

Finally I go to see a doctor, and tell him about not being able to sleep, and about the voices. He sends me to a second doctor who's French and specialises in 'maladies nerveuses'. I sit in an office in a modern block somewhere in the Brussels suburbs and watch the corner of a net curtain blowing in the breeze from where the window is open a crack. The doctor smokes, and there's a roar of traffic from outside. We discuss 'mes sentiments' and I begin to understand the point of the French language. I see the value of the circuitous, and imprecise. I tell the doctor that I have no idea why I feel so bad. He prescribes drugs, and talks as though it's flu, and I float back on my bicycle through the suburbs in a sudden, ecstatic good mood.

But in the evening I feel angry because I realise that this doctor is trying to cure me of being myself. Down with shrinks, I think. I've got a perfect right to be fucked up. I take the bandage off my finger and open up the wound to look at the white bone inside. Then I throw the prescription in the bin, and don't go to work the next day, and lie in bed.

The hot-water heater breaks down again, just as it used to when I was first here. With no Javier to fix it, I have to stand at the sink with a sponge and wash myself in cold water.

One evening I take Tiffany's scarf out of the back of a drawer. Candyfloss and fuchsia – the scarf I didn't want to keep and couldn't throw away. The static hair of it sticks to my hands. I suppose the truth is that I was jealous of her. Tiffany, Rosa, Fiona – they all stand in my light. Look at me, Dad, look at me. Contempt has been a good substitute for grief. A line of photographs is propped on my desk – the sepia photographs I bought in the market. Lives are ending all the time, dropping like fallen leaves.

Adam calls from the States. 'You sound bad,' he says.

'No, not really. Just a cold.'

We don't have anything to talk about. That's how it is now.

'Maggie, listen. The longer you leave this situation the worse it will get . . .'

'I thought you weren't going to tell me what to do.'

'Yes, but . . .'

'Listen, sorry, I have to go. My bath is running over.'

I take a day off work and go to Amsterdam to get the pills for Nanda. I don't see why she can't order over the phone. Except probably she would need a credit card and, of course, she doesn't have anything new-fangled like that.

The house in Amsterdam is next to one of the central canals. It's red-brick, tall and thin, with a gabled roof. No curtains or blinds cover vast sash windows that glint in the sharp sunlight. I stand on the doorstep, and wait, looking around me, smelling drains. In the distance a jazz band plays. A barge passes, ploughing a furrow in the black canal water.

From the deck a dwarf-like man watches me. The light here is different — larger, paler. It holds objects still and makes them significant. I want to raise my hands above my head to stop the sky from pressing in on me.

The door is opened by a woman who seems to be expecting me. Her sitting room is bright white with cushions made from kelims on a wooden floor. The sound of wind chimes glitters in the morning air. Burmese cats, like Maud and Agatha, sleep on a white sofa. The woman speaks to me in English and makes me a cup of China tea, amber in colour, tasting of ginger and cinnamon. She shows me the sunflowers on her terrace, over eight foot tall. I sit on the sofa next to the cats. The woman, who is dressed in a flowing orange robe, is silent. I want to stay in her house forever.

As I leave I see Nanda. She's in the distance, walking away, carrying a plastic bag in her hand, her lace-up shoes hurrying around a corner. Of course, when I get to the place she isn't there. I go to a post office — a grey, sixties building in a side street. The sun is frying my skin so it's a relief to step into an interior of shadows. Oddly the post office is empty except for a fraught mother, and a child wailing and screaming in a pushchair. I have to buy a cardboard box to put the bottle in and I wrap it up in a handkerchief from my bag. It's difficult to wrap with my bandaged finger. The bottle of pills weighs nothing in my hand.

The lady at the counter speaks to me in English before I've said a word to her. That's a birthday present, is it? I tell her it is, because she's an old lady with worn-out grey eyes, and I want to see her smile. Then I walk off through the sizzling afternoon, and hear the child wailing all down the street.

A letter comes from Nanda. It's full of descriptions of the shapes of clouds, and the cracks opening up in the fields because there's no rain, and the ladybirds on the terrace. She says that the wind blowing through the cornfields makes waves which roll in towards her, just like the sea. She can hear the wings of birds as they hover above her, drifting through the air. Her words are full of wonder – as though what she sees has never been seen before. I feel jealous.

I write back to her. I've got to do something, I say. I've got to decide something. She writes back – you don't ever solve problems, you only ever move on to a place where they no longer look important.

You could think of your life as a garden, she says. There are all sorts of seeds under the earth, the potential for all sorts of flowers. But you can't tell when any of the seeds might decide to push up through the earth and bloom. Some could come suddenly but others might lie dormant for years. You just have to wait and see. There's no point in shouting at flowers.

I don't find that advice helpful.

Tyger rings up, with Sam and Dougie standing beside her.

'You're in a right black hole, aren't you?' she says.

'No, not really. I'm OK . . .'

'Yeah, that's exactly what it sounds like . . .'

There's a pause while she shouts at Dougie for turning the music on loud.

'So what about Adam?' she says. 'Are you going to marry him. Seriously?'

'I don't know. In Seville I thought I would.'

'Oh, Seville,' she says. 'You should be careful. There are plenty of women who've finished up with total plonkers because the sunset was more than normally beautiful that night.'

'I know, but he was so serious about it suddenly. Men are

such funny things, you don't think they have any emotions, then suddenly it's like the cork going off a champagne bottle, and they're spilling all over the place, and you're scrabbling around for a glass to put it all in.'

'Yes, but getting married. I mean, really . . .'

'OK, OK . . .'

'Sorry . . . Sorry. Listen, why don't you come back to London for a while. We'd really like to see you. It's not the same without you. Come and stay . . .'

'Yeah, maybe.'

Tyger passes the phone to Sam.

'It's your dad that's the problem, isn't it?' Sam says.

I'm shocked that he should see so clearly, and be so direct.

'Yeah, I suppose it is, really . . .'

'There's nothing I can do, is there?'

'No . . . No.'

He cheers me up by telling me stupid stories about the horrors of auditing on the M25. Then he passes the phone over to Dougie, who sounds even less connected than usual. 'Yeah, it is a bit complicated. What with losing the Operating Instructions, and all that.'

He wanders on, full of random words of comfort.

'Friends,' he recommends finally. 'And rabbits . . .'

Javier arrives back from his holiday. He's having a party and he invites me. I say yes, and thanks very much, although I've got no intention of going. On the night of the party I go out to the cinema on my own. When I come back I cook myself a late supper. The noise of Javier's party is so loud that my floorboards seem to be vibrating. Salt and pepper pots jump up and down on my kitchen shelf. Voices babble and someone is thumping away on the piano – it can't be Javier, he never plays like that. Through my open bedroom window a smell of cigarettes and red wine rises up from his balcony.

Two o'clock and I'm lying in bed. The noise from Javier's party is getting worse and worse. The neighbours will be around to complain shortly, I tell myself, and then remember I am the neighbours. I watch the face of the alarm clock. The piano music from downstairs is hectic, crashing through the darkness. I'm too hot, so I get out of bed, and go to the window.

From below – a shriek of laughter, the sound of a glass smashing. Above the jumble of roofs the sky is dark blue, and there's a potato-shaped moon, with a few half-lit stars. On Javier's balcony a crush of people are sitting around a table, or propped against the balcony rail, drinking. A creeper grows along the rail of the balcony. Everybody seems to be twined together like one of those Bacchanalian scenes on Greek friezes. A haze of cigarette smoke surrounds them, and lights from inside the flat touch on one side of their faces.

I can see Javier on the balcony, sitting with one foot propped on a chair. He's dressed more smartly than usual, although his shirt hangs out from underneath a jacket that is too small, and he's still wearing his slippers. He's pouring drink from an earthenware jug and his other hand is on a disembodied leg. I remember what Adam said about Javier being gay. His hand on the leg is white, and the length of his fingers stretches far across the leg. Tiffany's voice echoes from the past – you should wear things that emphasise your waist more, honey. Pink would be such a good colour on you.

I go back to bed, and watch the alarm clock. The luminous blobs move slowly. I sleep for a while then wake at four. I get out of bed and go back to the window. The balcony is empty now, except for a single figure, with a shaggy head, standing on the table. In the blue light the figure is like a satyr or a cherub, with a slight body, and a rounded stomach. I realise that it's Javier. He hasn't got any clothes on.

The piano music is still crashing out from inside the flat, and he's dancing like someone possessed, jumping up and down on the table, twisting, his legs spinning and tapping. His hips are moving to the music and his shaggy hair waves as he jumps. For a brief moment the music stops and he stands quite still, one long-fingered hand stretched above him. He's got something in his other hand, which he's holding down low. It's a bottle, perhaps, with the neck sticking upwards.

As the music starts again, he dances, but more slowly now. Both of his hands are in the air. There isn't a bottle. That's not what it is. I feel as though all the blood inside me is trying to push its way out. Why isn't he embarrassed? I am embarrassed for him. Is he too drunk to know? He doesn't dance like someone who's very drunk. I shouldn't look at him, but I lean forward so that I can see better. I can't stop watching him, as he twists and turns under the fading stars.

The next day I don't wake up until three. I decide I'll go to Dad's house – but it's only a game, a dress rehearsal, because I know he won't be there. The sky is grey and yellow like an old bruise, and the air is tightening. Storm weather. Everything is pale and shallow. The world has been wrung out. My head is swirling and my legs have turned to butter.

It turns out that I've walked past the house where Dad lives several times before. How strange to walk past a house and not know your father lives there. I stand at the railing and look at the naked lady in her panel above the door, and the palm leaves that press against the curved glass of the bay window. The square is deserted, a dog lies on the pavement in a spiral of flies beside a bag of rubbish in the gutter.

The front door opens and Rosa is there. She comes down the front steps. She has the same tortoiseshell octagonal glasses that I remember from years ago. Her hair is surprised, with a green scarf tied in it. A freckle below her eye is like the tear painted on a clown's face. She wears a straight linen dress. I remember the half-open door, her naked back, shaped like a cello, Dad's hand resting on the strings of her spine.

Everything around me seems to be melting like wax. Rosa smiles and says hello, like we're old friends – which in some sense we are. She invites me in, and I slide into the hall, and put my hand on the curl at the bottom of the stair rail. Rosa explains that Dad is at Brickley Grange. She's staring at the bandage on my finger. A necklace made out of a leather thong with a green stone rests against the brown skin above the neck of her dress. I remember that day – the twisted sheets, his white knee, enclosed in the light from the half-curtained window.

At that age I wasn't very keen on skin – it was something that was best kept under vests and woolly jumpers. I'd seen Dad's hairy white legs underneath his shirt tails, and the wrinkled flesh between the stocking tops of old ladies, as they sat on Nanda's sofa, but Rosa's skin was different. It wrapped around her bones neatly, as though it was made to fit. It was as normal to look at as a face or a hand.

She offers me tea, and I follow her into the front sitting room. 'I'm glad you came,' she says. This house is decorated like the French Revolution, as interpreted by a set designer with a limited budget. I hold onto the back of a green velvet chair. A china dog grins at me from the shadows. Everything in my body has settled down into my feet. I wipe a hand across my eyes and sneeze. I mustn't chat with Rosa. I mustn't let this become a pleasant meeting.

'Rosa, I came around to see Dad . . . I came to say . . .' I decide to sit down, because my feet have gone fuzzy, but then the room moves up in front of my face. I've gone over the top on the big dipper. The chair looms towards me – a thump, I find my face close to the parquet floor. I try to pull myself up onto the chair, but then sit propped against it.

Rosa's bony face is close to mine. Her eyes swim like green fish behind her octagonal glasses. She holds a glass of water out to me and asks me questions but the sounds don't make words. I sit up and hold the glass of water.

'Maggie,' she says. 'You're wearing your pyjamas.'

I look down at my plaid cotton legs. 'Yes, I am.' I start to laugh and Rosa laughs as well. All around us there are bars of soap, which have fallen out of my bag. I bought them in the market yesterday. Transparent, flat and oval, they have a green oak leaf in the middle – probably it's not a real leaf, but it's inside the soap, frozen, like an insect in amber.

'I was just buying the soap ready for when my bath works again.'

I explain to her about the bath problem.

'Oh, God – what a disaster. You Priestleys can't last long without a bath.'

It's so weird that she understands that.

'You know you can have a bath here any time you want,' she says.

I get up from the floor and we gather up the soap.

'Why don't you have one now,' she says. 'You might feel better.'

I know that I mustn't do that.

★

The bathroom is on a half landing – pink frilly blinds and plastic wallpaper with blue birds. Rosa finds me a towel, lavender oil, shampoo and a comb. From the window I can see an overgrown garden, an arch and a broken-down summerhouse. I sink into the depths of the bath and spirals inside me begin to uncurl. I turn over and over – awkwardly because of my cut hand. The clouds in my head begin to lift.

Rosa comes in holding a cup of tea. She sits down on the loo seat. I pull my knees up to my chin. She says I can come to the house any time for a bath, and she produces a spare key and drops it into my bag. It occurs to me that she doesn't look well. Her face is too thin and her collarbones stand out. She's transparent and green, like a sour apple.

I've never known what I should think about Rosa. In some ways it offends me that she doesn't look more like a mistress. She should have push-up bras and X-rated clothes. Always I wonder what she does all day – presumably she just sits around waiting for Dad to call, and telling herself that two hours of his time is worth a lifetime of any other man. I've no idea what judgement to make. Is she a tough, independent woman having an affair with a rich and powerful man? Or is she sad and on-the-shelf and used?

She points at a slither of thick cream satin and red roses falling from a plastic bag. The dress that I bought when Adam was here. 'What's this material?' I explain that I have the dress with me because I'd thought of buying a cardigan to go with it. She takes it out of the bag and holds it up. The silk is creased, but inside it you can still see an invisible body, a voluptuous body, cut into its folds and darts. Rosa holds the dress against her and runs her hand down the fabric. It's amazing, she says, and she means it. I'm still sitting forward in the bath, hiding my flesh from her, and drinking my tea.

'Will you try it on?' she says. 'So I can see. Then I could take some photographs of you?'

I don't know what to say. I move my hand across my shoulders.

'Could I do that?' she says.

'Yes, if you want. But why?'

'I don't know – something about the way you look.'

Downstairs Rosa is sorting out camera equipment. She stands by the French windows at the back of the house, picks up a slide and holds it up to the light. I can see the shape of her body through the material of her dress. Her stomach and breasts curve outwards. That sour apple look – I know where I've seen it before. Women who are pregnant – that's it. Rosa has moved from the window. The image has gone. Perhaps I was mistaken. My head begins to blur again.

Rosa opens the back doors of the house and we walk out into the garden. The heat is oily. The garden is lined by high walls and a fretful wind is beginning to tear at the leaves of the trees. I watch a spider hurry back along its extended thread. Rosa takes an ornate chair on spindly legs and stands it by the twisting wrought-iron steps. She sits me down on the chair and makes me face away from her. At the end of the garden there's a door in the wall, and I imagine it opening into another garden, and then another, stretching far away, instead of the grey office buildings that are what's really in the distance. The bath has made me sleepy.

I feel Rosa beside me, and she makes me get up, moves the chair a little, and sits me down again. 'You look so pretty in that dress,' she says.

The wind makes the trees break like waves across the sky, their leaves turn as shields against the wind. Rosa pulls my hair back over my shoulders, and her hands are cold on my neck. I feel like I'm being prepared for an execution. Behind me I hear the click of the camera shutter again and again. Then she takes the chair away and photographs me standing in the same place, arranging my hair once again. Always she turns my face away from her. The camera clicks seem to hit inside me, so that I imagine them like gunshots, unmerciful and dangerous.

Just as she finishes the storm starts. White light flashes on the hem of a cloud, helicopter seeds twist down and smash on the lawn. As the air pulls tight, a bird's scream is swallowed in a yawn of thunder. Rosa and I go inside and stand at the long windows. Two blinks of white light catch the garden unawares, before the rain is sucked down. The air moves more freely in our lungs.

On the table there are piles of Dad's papers – official journals, letters, reports. But there are also some of Rosa's photographs. They show people looking up from everyday situations – unpegging a shirt from a washing line, or choosing fruit outside a grocery store. Or they show people passing in the street, blurred, caught just as they step out of the frame.

'Why do you take photographs?' I ask.

'Oh, I don't know,' Rosa says. 'I suppose it's a way of cheating time. And a way of getting beyond the transient.'

'But these are photographs of transient moments?'

'It's a question of what you think is significant. Yes, a camera would usually be used to record a big moment. Like a ceremony, or a meeting. But that isn't how the mind works. The mind doesn't actually record a fantastic theatrical production, it records a pair of angel's wings, hanging from a hook, backstage. Somehow that's where there's a real permanence.'

'And the people? Why are they only half in the photograph?'

She tilts her head as she considers. Her hand rests just above her stomach. Outside, the rain bounces off the terrace, and the wind tears at the fringes of the trees. 'I suppose what you don't see is more interesting. You know, I painted before I became a photographer, and I used to think that photographs were too bald, too open. But then I realised it doesn't have to be like that. What I do is create a landscape, then the person who looks at the photograph can fill in the details, which means that they're a creator as well. Sorry, I'm never very good at explaining. Do you understand at all?'

We wander through the dust-sheeted house. Flies buzz against the long windows. The rooms are inhabited – a secret presence hides behind the curtains as we come in. Thick crusty wallpaper, frills, oriental carpets, stained glass. The silence is itchy. On the first floor I step into the bedroom she shares with Dad. One of his suits hangs on the wardrobe door.

I walk over to the window and look out across the park to where fruit trees are trained into rigid grids. Then I fiddle with a pair of Dad's cufflinks lying on the desk. I don't want to look at the bed. It is unmade, with the sheets turned back and rumpled up. I imagine the shape of them together, entangled in those sheets.

'Rosa, don't you want Dad to leave Fiona? Don't you want to get married?'

She smiles at me, then laughs. 'No, not really.'

I think of the iron grilles in Seville and Adam washing his hands after sex.

'Do you want to get married?' she asks.

I hadn't expected that question.

'No, not really. Well, maybe a bit, sometimes. I hadn't really thought of it.'

Except I do think of it now.

'I'm not awfully good at possession,' Rosa says. 'Or possessing. And I'm never sure that one person could supply all that one might want . . .'

The silence draws words out of me.

'But are you happy? I mean, like this?'

'You know, I'm not sure happiness is the aim – or not for everyone. For me what's more important is that feeling, when you get up in the morning and life pumps through you like an electric current. It's not happiness, it's something else. Do you know what I mean?'

'That feeling of being out on the edge of something?'

'Yes,' Rosa says. 'You know, some people's lives are just B-plus all the time. They're content, which is fine, except I prefer to try for A – but inevitably that often results in F.'

'Couldn't it be A all the time?'

'No, sadly I think F is always part of A. You can't have one without the other.'

'And if you got married then it would all just be B–plus?'

'Probably. Some people are pioneers and some are settlers.'

We are back downstairs now and I'm looking again at her photographs. Outside it has stopped raining and the sky is clear. 'At least they're black and white,' I say. 'So you don't have to worry about Dad seeing the wrong colours.'

She laughs and holds a pile of photographs in her hand. 'He's so funny because when I do take photographs in colour he says he can't see them properly and he asks me to explain the colours to me. So I have to think up words to describe colours . . .'

My skin turns cold and my stomach clenches. She's

talking to me as though I don't know. But I do know, I do. That was our game. Blue tastes fresh like peppermint, or a sharp winter morning. Red screams and burns your finger-tips and smells like pepper . . . She is standing in my light. English public schoolboy suddenly marries unknown Spaniard. An inconvenient mistake. But yet I exist. Look at me, Dad, look at me.

'I must go,' I say. I pick up my bag and my pyjamas.

'There's no need,' she says.

But there is. I need to get away from her.

'Maggie, listen. Your father is going to be back here on Wednesday . . .'

So now we come to the point.

'Rosa, you know he was there that night, don't you?'

Her eyes do not flicker.

'Maggie, you can't seriously believe he killed her?'

I look out of the windows at the white sky.

'For God's sake, Maggie – your father can't set a mouse-trap.'

'So what did happen then?'

'He made a fool of her – and she couldn't live with that. People can bear anything better than the loss of their self-respect.'

I think of Adam and his book.

'Maggie, you know sometimes what looks like an heroic act of truth-telling is just a way of shifting guilt.'

'I'm not going to court.'

'Maggie, do you love your father?'

Increasingly I realise I don't know what that word means.

'Maggie . . .'

But I am at the front door. She is too proud to plead. The front door opens and sunlight floods into the hall. I turn to say goodbye and then stop. I see into her eyes. For all her apparent calm, she's more frightened than me. I turn and go down the curving steps. She looks beyond me to where a child in Wellington boots splashes through the puddles.

At home my angry fingers switch on the computer.

Blue tastes fresh like peppermint. Red screams and burns your fingertips . . .

I go through my bag and find the address of Tiffany's lawyers. I switch on the computer and try to type a letter. The words won't come. How exactly can I explain this to them? Just keep it short and to the point, businesslike. Just explain what I know – but the words won't come. I sit and stare at black-legged insects lined up on the white glare of the screen. My anger has gone. Outside, the evening light is failing. I save the half-written letter, turn off the computer and lie in bed with the duvet over my head.

Nanda

What will eternity be? Theodora and I talk of this in the late August nights, with my sitting-room window open, me lying on the sofa and Theodora beside me . . . a place where the cobweb-veil between past and present will be pushed aside, a chance to unravel it all backwards – Max's hand reaching for hers on that ledge, and pulling her back, the toy ship still on the shelf in the bedroom, with the washing flapping outside, the shadow of a wartime aeroplane tattooed forever on the pale skin of his shoulder blades . . . the past, the present, the future, assembled together.

Theodora says eternity will be a place where we'll have all the love we craved and did not receive, a place where we'll do all the things we never did, go to the places glimpsed on the horizon but never visited, release all the captive words – and that every pleasure here will be replicated there, but freed from the relentless turning of the clock . . . eternity, beyond, the place of light – now, at last, it is close.

Freddy cannot bear my pain. I wish I could explain that it does not trouble me as much as she thinks. I look down from above and I see my sitting room like a doll's house with the roof lifted off, and I am lying on the sofa and I'm twisted with pain . . . so much so that I feel a distant compassion for myself – and Freddy and Theodora are with me, and they're bent over the bed, then they scurry away to find blankets, or hot-water bottles or glasses of milk. Always they are so very busy – they panic and argue, they stumble around, unseeing. The doctor must be called – no, he must not. Freddy's rough hands grip at a blanket with a red-stitched edge and I see the ivory head of Theodora's walking stick, and the mud on the knees of Freddy's trousers, and the dusty piles of books and letters. And there is Theodora's hair, twisted into its usual double buns – but what a mess it looks now that I cannot do it for her.

I wish I could tell them that they should not trouble so much.

I think of the pills, waiting in my drawer, and days turn into nights, and nights turn back to days, and still I delay . . . although my flesh stinks and leaks and retches, and my right hand lies loose beside me on the bed, crumpled, like an empty glove. Yet at my centre a molten heart continues to beat, and I breathe but the air goes through me, like wind through the timbers of a ruined house – for I need air from the fields, not this bottled air.

I am alone, and with one hand, I pull my feet out from underneath the sheets . . . and even the shivering hurts, and my body is crumpled and shrunken, shallow and bloodless. I rock onto the dead foot, and back again, and the window moves closer, and I stretch out my hand and take hold of the metal catch . . . On the end of it there's a flat spiral of metal, like a snail's shell, moving outwards, passing the same point again and again, and I hold the handle in my hand, running a finger around the spiral.

The window comes open, and I lean against the frame

and, oh, how the night air against my face has a flavour of autumn, and the corn is cut in the fields, and lies in rows . . . and there is the wind turbine, standing in the garden – sleek and white, turning silent and stately in the breeze – and a sliver of moon lies on its back, as though ready for sleep, hanging low over the hills, a moon with faded edges and a pockmarked skin . . .

The light flashes on and I squeeze my fingers round the window frame. 'What are you doing?' Freddy says.

'I want to go out.'

'You must stay in bed. You won't get any better if you don't.' She pulls me back to bed and I lie there holding all the bits of my body together. I cradle the struggling knot inside me in my arms, and feel it settling deep within. Freddy shuts the window, pulls the blanket back over my feet, and runs her fingers through my twisted hair. I hear her pick up the jug from the bedside table, and a glass clink.

Very close I can see Maggie, against the background of the shadowed hills, and the landscape powdered by the moon. She is turned away from me, walking into the shadows, and I have no voice to call her. Her hair covers her back, the ragged ends of it twisting down to the curve of her waist, and red shoes, torn at the heel, swing from her hand as she walks. She wears a pale dress with roses and they bloom red across my vision, blocking out the light. The colour of them spreads like gunshot wounds.

Why do I delay? For what do I wait? For Max, of course. Oh, for Max. For that boy with the wooden sword, fighting in the garden, every ray of the sun focused in on his pale hair.

But the best they will bring me is a man I hardly know . . . Sometimes he comes to see me and he talks about himself in the third person. I could perhaps do this, he says, but Max Priestley the politician couldn't do it. I think this, he says, but Max Priestley could never be seen saying that. When Lucía died he lost so much of himself that he had to invent another person to put in his place. But oh, how I want the real person to come back. However maimed and wretched, I want him to come back. All the structures of this world – all those laws, governments, politics and wars – they are nothing more than grandiose facades which we build to mask the void where the heart should be.

Theodora glides across the room in her velvet dressing gown and sheepskin slippers, the shadow of her thick hair falling around her shoulders. She switches the light on in the kitchen and a bright triangle falls onto the floor and when she comes back she's got a bottle and a glass in her hand – and there's the warm, ginger smell of whisky as she places a glass in my hand and pulls the pillows up behind my head.

'I want to go outside,' I say.

She sits herself down on the bed, crushing the foot I can still feel, and she bends towards me, and as she kisses me, her long hair brushes my cheek. She smells of face cream and talcum powder. Outside, the wind blows and an owl hoots and there's a rush of water from upstairs as Freddy turns on a tap. The material of Theodora's dressing gown rustles as she wraps it more tightly around her and it falls open to reveal one satin knee, and she draws on her cigarette . . . the red point of it making patterns like a sparkler on bonfire night.

'Max,' I say. 'Max.'

'We'll ask him to come home,' Theodora says.

Freddy comes back and pulls the blankets up further around me.

'We're going to ask Max to come,' Theodora tells her. 'And Maggie perhaps.'

'What. Now?'

'Yes.'

'It's four o'clock in the morning.'

'The telephone. We could ring.' Theodora says this as though it is an idea of extraordinary ingenuity and innovation and I start to laugh and the pain is like nails being hammered through the centre of me but still I laugh.

'I think it's for the best,' Freddy says. Then suddenly she starts to cry in long, sniffing sobs.

'We'll wait until six and then we'll telephone,' Theodora says.

We sit and watch as slowly the light at the window turns grey and then pink. There's a mist on the fields and the moon fades. Theodora opens the window and I breathe the autumn air. She and Freddy sit side by side, hand in hand, and they stare at the world as though it is quite new to them.

Eternity, beyond, the place of light, so very close now . . . that place from which we came and to which we return, a place already known, half-remembered, as familiar as home. A place that has always been with me but only as a vague memory – a pattern of perfection – a world to be visited in dreams, a world glimpsed in moments of love, in scenes of dazzling beauty – occasionally even in times of extreme despair. All of my life I have yearned for this place and now I am at the threshold, I have laid aside my flesh, my heart and soul unfold.

Why fight to stay on this earth? A stunted place, half-finished, where evolution struggles to create mutant creatures – blind, imperfect, defeated. I see now that all of my life has been a total waste. Eternity, beyond, the place of light – it was always here . . . Spread out around me, laid out like a feast, and yet I lived famished for the want of it, for I was too busy, always too busy. I thought that I must work for redemption, that I could earn it with my mind, build it with words . . . I must be good, I must deny myself pleasure, I must search, I must understand. How wrong, how totally wrong. For now it turns out that redemption is always here, encrypted in the small details of each and every day . . . Why do we not see it? When it is here always, everywhere, every day of our lives.

Maggie

Finally I go to see Dad because there's nowhere else to go. It's past one o'clock, after a party. Strangely, his front door is open and music thumps from above. I step into the dark sitting room and the china dog grins at me from the shadows. From above there's a crash. Falling furniture? I should go home. I've drunk too much.

Gus appears, coming down the stairs.

'Ah Maggie, how are you?' As though all this is perfectly normal.

'I'm fine, and you?'

'Fine.' He looks different away from England – thinner, with spruce clothes. 'Actually, I'm having a bit of difficulty . . .'

He doesn't have to say because I can already guess. I follow him up the stairs, shivering in my rose-scattered dress. Moonlight shines in from a circular window, glittering on the stair rods. My head hammers with jazz and drink. Candles flicker, their light reflected in the window and the mirror. I blink. Above them Dad seems to be dangling close to the ceiling, framed by the bobbly fringe of the curtains.

'Gus, you bloody useless goon, hold the chair, will you?'

Dad's voice slurs. 'I'll get it open in just a moment. No trouble.'

'Dad, get down from there.'

'I've told him twenty times already,' Gus says.

Dad is standing on a chair, which is standing on the desk, which has been pulled up next to the window. He's got a knife in his hand. His long silhouette bows to me, wobbling on the chair, and he swings the knife upwards with a rabbit-out-of-a-hat flourish. 'Ah, there you are, Maggie. I've been trying to call you. Where have you been?'

He indicates the window behind him, and adjusts his footing as the chair beneath him creaks. 'Just getting the window open,' he says. There are books on the desk, a vase, and a candlestick. Dad's tie is looped over the back of a chair. The room smells of candle wax and red wine. Cigarette smoke is thick in the air and clots at the back of my throat. I imagine him falling backwards, shattering the glass, and dropping into the square below. I should be frightened.

'Max, you're not big, and you're not clever, and you're over-tired, and you're showing off,' Gus says. He and I laugh uncertainly. The chair rocks and Gus's circular shadow stands beside the table, gripping the frail legs of the chair. Dad wags a drunken finger at me and his head moves with it, nodding up and down. Gus and I are like a circus audience, watching a man on a tightrope.

'Max, I'm going home now,' Gus says.

'Well, bugger you. Ooops, sorry. Freudian slip. You can't go home. It's only ten o'clock. Now hold the chair while I get this open.' Gus is staring up at Dad. Strangely, he's quite sober. I reach to lift books and a vase off the table. I don't want to stand too close in case Dad falls on me.

He turns round on the chair, his shoes clattering against the wooden seat. He bends his knees and leans down towards Gus so that the chair wobbles. 'Gus, don't go,' he says. Steadying himself on one of the curtains, he pats Gus gently on the head. Then he takes Gus's glasses delicately in his hands and lifts them up, leaving Gus' face naked. He wobbles, loses his balance, drops the glasses on the floor, and catches hold of the back of the chair to steady himself.

'Shit. Sorry,' he says. 'Sorry. Forgive me.' He starts to laugh, a strange wheezing laugh that convulses him, so that he wobbles again on the chair. Gus blinks and flaps his hands, because he can't see even a foot in front of him without his glasses. I get down on my knees and feel for them under a chest of drawers. Dust from the floor sticks to my hands. My fingers feel the glasses and pick them up. I stretch up to Gus and his fat hands grasp the air until he feels where they are and puts them on.

'Thanks,' he says. My head is starting to ache and my mouth tastes sticky as glue. The jazz shrieks and creaks through my bones.

'Max, I've really got to go home now,' Gus says.

Dad steps backwards and in two giant steps he comes down from the chair, knocking over a china lamp, which smashes, pieces of it scuttling away across the floor and under the bed. Dad sways, then steadies himself against the fireplace. His eyes are blurred, and his shirt is pulled open at the neck. His hair stands up on end, and there's a swollen place on his lip, where dry skin has split open.

'Tomorrow,' he says. 'Perhaps I'll open it tomorrow. I've got time.'

Gus takes the knife out of Dad's hand. Dad fills a glass, spilling it slightly so that a black puddle spreads onto the table. He offers me a drink and I say no. He pushes the glass towards me. I take it and he leans across to get his cigarettes and matches from the mantelpiece.

'Max, sorry, but I'm going home now,' Gus says.

Dad raises his glass to me. 'You know Gus has got his own home now, don't you? With his friend, in a nice little suburb. All very cosy. He's got no time to work for me. He's too busy being a homemaker.'

Gus takes his coat from the back of a chair. There's a rigid smile on his red lips and his hand moves up to pull at his shirt collar. He laughs slightly. 'Max, shut up, will you?'

Dad's leaning back against the desk now. His fingers are fumbling in a box of matches and he's got an unlit cigarette in his mouth, so his voice comes out twisted. 'You know Gus's friend is Belgian. Works at the airport, as a mechanic. All very well, but I just hope he keeps his mind on the job. The aircraft maintenance, that is. I fly from that airport every other week.'

'Max, don't mock me.'

'Ooooh, so–rr–y.' Dad says this in a mock-seductive voice and purses his lips. He gets hold of a match and strikes it. It flares for a moment, then goes out. He swears and shakes his burnt hand. 'You know, before too long I'll have to look for another assistant. What with Gus's personal life and his political ambition – you know he wants to be on a list for the next election, you know that? He's hardly got time to work for me any more.'

Gus puts his jacket on – a new jacket made of cream linen. 'Max, I've always got time to work for you,' he says. 'You know that. But I want to go home now.' Dad puts a hand on Gus's shoulder but Gus moves it away as though it's infected. Gus goes towards the door, taking firm steps, then hesitates and turns to look back at Dad.

His eyes are washed–out and his fat hands hang beside him. I turn the tape recorder off and the silence is sudden and heavy. Gus's jacket is crumpled – he looks like a child at the end of a long day. I can hear the thickness of his breathing. The thin slick of his hair is ruffled. 'Max?' he says.

Dad is lighting his cigarette from a candle. Then he walks across the room and peers at himself in the mirror above the mantelpiece.

'Max?'

Dad doesn't look at him. 'I thought you said you were going.'

Gus's face folds up, he turns and goes out of the room. Looking down over the rail I see his feet stamping as he disappears down the funnel of the staircase. When he reaches the front door he stops for a moment and adjusts the shoulders of his jacket. He turns around and looks up – and for a moment his face lights up. Then he realises it's only me watching him, so he turns and goes.

I take off my red suede shoes and, leaving them at the top of the stairs, I run down on soft feet and stand at the front door. Gus is fumbling around near the gate, twisted, bent over, his head down. At first I think he's looking for something, then I realise he's crying. There's a crumpled whimper, his shoulders shudder. I should go to him but I know he wouldn't like that. It hurts to watch him. Slowly he straightens up, puts out an unsteady hand to the gate and then shambles away across the square.

'Dad, you shouldn't have said that to Gus.'

The beat of the music continues in my head.

'Why have you turned the music off? I thought that you and I might dance.' Dad stands with one hand resting on the mantelpiece, smoke rising around him. He takes a drag on his cigarette and tips his head back, puffing out smoke. His cufflinks glitter in the dark.

He goes to the tape recorder but he can't find the right

button. He comes towards me, takes hold of my wrist and turns me round. His hands are cold and I can feel his signet ring gripping into my finger. As I pull away from him he stumbles and my face is pushed against him. I move my mouth, spitting out the taste of his shirt.

'Don't take any notice of Gus, Maggie. He's just throwing his toys out of the pram. He'll come round. After all, he's not going anywhere very far without me.'

I turn the lights on and we both blink in the brightness – the chair piled on the desk, one of his suits hanging on the wardrobe door, the unmade bed with the shape of Rosa and him folded into it, the silent tape recorder, they jump out at us, large and bright, in the sudden glare of light. My stomach aches with hunger. I blink and rub my eyes, then turn to go.

'No, no, Maggie, don't go. You've only just got here. What do they say?' Dad peers at the ceiling, then shakes his head, as though he's trying to remember. 'Rats, sinking ships. Something like that?'

I go to the door but Dad moves in front of me, blocking my way, and puts a hand against the wall to steady himself. He leans towards me and I can see the stain of red wine on his lips. 'Maggie, don't go.' He's got hold of my arm and he moves me to a chair. Outside in the garden there's a cat wailing. He picks up my glass and passes it to me. 'Listen, I just wanted to say that I'm sorry,' he says. 'About this trial. I'm sorry you've got to be involved.'

He bends down towards me. His fingers on my arm are cold and dry. 'Maggie,' he says. 'You've got to understand. I didn't do anything. It really had nothing to do with me.'

I look up into the garish blue of his eyes. He leans over and kisses me. His lips are dry against mine. I push him away.

'But you were there that night.'

I'm talking to his blue and white striped shirt front. My eyes fix on the pale shadow where my lipstick smudged against him. Suddenly, all my anger goes. I want to lean my head against him. The clock on the mantelpiece chimes two even strokes, which sink into the silence of the room.

'Maggie, I didn't do anything.'

'You were there.'

'That's the fact, not the truth.'

Dad turns away and his shoulders rise in a shrug and then drop. He puts his glass down on a bookcase. I'm cold and I look down at my crumpled dress. The overhead light is too bright and my head is aching. I shade my eyes with my hand and don't look at him.

Dad crosses the room and closes the door. He's looking at the glass in his hand, turning it round and round. He starts to tell me the story of what happened that night. Tiffany's obsession. The way she threatened him. I hate the way he's talking. His words try to hook me and wind me in. His eyes never move from mine. His voice has the rhythm of a hypnotist.

'I don't believe you,' I say.

'Listen. I was drunk. Events got out of control.'

'I don't believe you.'

'Maggie . . .'

'So you stood by and watched Tiffany kill herself? That's what you're saying.'

'No, I tried to stop her . . .'

'Really?'

'Maggie, listen . . .'

'OK, so perhaps you did try to stop her. Well, you weren't much good at it, were you? People do seem to have a habit of dying in front of you, don't they?'

The silence is raucous. Thoughts which have always been hidden are suddenly words and they lie newborn between us. Dad raises a hand to his face. His eyes plead with mine and his mouth opens and shuts with silent words. Then he turns away from me. Please, please, let me have those words back. I can't believe what we are doing to each other. I am more hurt by the damage I have just done to him than by anything he has ever done to me. I step forward to touch his twisted back but, before my hand reaches him, he turns on me, his face twisted with concealed anger. 'Maggie, if I were you I'd be very careful. You lied to the police as well, remember? Perverting the course of justice. It's a serious crime – as you well know.'

I get up and go towards the door but again he stands in front of me.

'So tell me about Spain,' he says.

'Let me go.'

'I like to think about Spain. It's a great place for a romance, isn't it? And you went with Adam, didn't you? No doubt he has some interesting views about me?'

'Actually, I'm going to move back to London and live with Adam.'

'Oh really?' Dad's head is back and his nose is wrinkled up. 'Well, you do surprise me. I wouldn't have thought he'd be your type. A man of many hidden shallows, that's the conclusion I reached.'

If I married Adam, then Dad would spend his whole life despising me.

'Is he good in bed?' Dad's eyes are blue needles in their ring of bloodshot white. He flexes the fingers of one hand and raises his eyebrows at me. Then he smiles so much that the white line of his teeth shows like a snarling dog.

My voice is quiet. 'Dad. It doesn't matter whether you

plead, or whether you bully. I'm not going to turn up at that trial. I'm not going to lie for you any more.'

He stands away from the door, his feet creaking over the floorboards. I move my stiff limbs, open the door, step out onto the landing and put on my shoes. I feel as small and light as a leaf. The stairs go on forever, my feet banging on them, down and down. Where is there to go? Nowhere in the world is far enough. I stop in the hall and wait to hear him behind me but he doesn't come. I leave the front door open.

Outside the square is powdered white. I look up at the moon as it reclines over the neon sign of the Holiday Inn. A strange moon, thin and ragged at the edges, its surface scarred. The latch on the front gate sticks in my hand. I pull it open, and walk down the path, under the clear cold light. I lock my head forward as I walk across the square. My shoes are uncomfortable, so I reach down and pull them off. I imagine him watching me, seeing my hand on the straps. I can feel where he kissed me.

When I reach the other side of the square I look back. The house is white in the moonlight, its fragile minaret slicing into the night sky. The front door is still open. Empty. So this is how big decisions are made.

At the flat, I switch on my computer, and open the file that contains the letter to Tiffany's lawyers. I rewrite it and the words come easily now. Drink babbles over the page and wine throbs in my fingertips. The voices are there in my head, making a case for it, explaining. After I've finished, I read the letter through once, and address it to Tiffany's lawyers, smudging the last line of the address. Then I lick along the seal of the envelope. The edge of the paper slices into my tongue. The metallic taste of blood spreads to the roof of my mouth and down my throat.

From below, the sound of a piano rises, with a smell of olive oil and burnt onions. I wander through the flat, the back of my head still tight with wine. In the kitchen I open the windows and one of my posters rustles in the breeze and slides from the wall, falling like a leaf. In the fridge there's nothing except a pack of butter and yoghurts past their sell-by date. I go back to the bedroom and pull a cardigan over my goose-pimpled arms. Tomorrow I've got to work, but alcohol and anger still press around my veins with a tired energy. A thin wind rustles through the papers on my desk.

'Buenas noches. You will eat some tortilla? Is very good.' Javier stands in my hall, gripping a deep pan in both hands, the handle wrapped in a checked tea towel. Even my toes are breathing in the caramel smell of onion.

'No, no thanks. It's very kind, but I'm going to bed . . .'

My mouth and stomach are weeping with hunger.

'You come down in my flat.'

OK, OK. I follow him past the sunset wallhanging and the spider plants.

'Sit down, please.' His slippered feet shuffle into the kitchen.

I sit down in a black leather and chrome armchair, slide too far back into it, then wriggle forward, and perch on its edge. Javier's sitting room looks like he's just arrived, or is just leaving. Oil paintings are propped against cardboard boxes, and black electronic equipment is packed into corners. Furniture like a 1970s junk shop lurks in the shadows. Two tall lamps, with shades like purple witches' hats, cast oval shadows. A kidney-shaped table pushed against a wall is ringed by moulded plastic chairs which should have Christine Keeler sitting back to front on them. Above the mantelpiece rows of curling black and white photographs are stuck on the wall with pins. A green lava lamp bubbles and sucks like a jellyfish.

Javier comes back with a glass of red wine. 'No,' I say. 'No thanks.'

'Si, si.' Javier has shaved for once, so he looks younger.

'I've already drunk too much.'

'Ah, then – it is the hairs of the dog.'

He's so pleased with that expression that I have to give in. The rioja tastes of wood and smoke and Spain. Javier goes to the kitchen and fetches plates and knives. 'Sorry, in disorder,' he says.

Again I find myself sliding into the back of the chair.

'I like your dress,' he says. 'Es muy bonito.'

'I bought it in the market here.'

'I cannot see well.'

I struggle up, my ears singing, and hold out the dress. He rubs the material between his fingers. 'Let me see more.'

I take off my cardigan and run my hands down the front of the dress to straighten it. He peers down at the material again, and then looks at my face, and smiles. I put my cardigan on, clear my throat, sit down. Javier puts cutlery and plates on a low table near the fireplace. He holds the wine bottle out to me and my chair squeaks as I reach out with my glass. My head blurs as I remember that other bottle which turned out not to be a bottle.

He goes back to the kitchen and brings out the tortilla pan, and puts it down on the tea towel. I give up on my uncomfortable chair and sit on the floor. The tortilla is golden on top and, kneeling beside the low table, he eases out a slice and slides it on to a plate. The egg is still runny and the onions are transparent and fried brown at the edges. There's a tang of pepper as I bite and the potato is soft and heavy with olive oil.

'Absolutely my favourite thing.'

He raises his glass to me and laughs.

'Who are all these people?' I ask, pointing at the curling row of photographs above the fireplace.

He jumps up, plate in hand. 'My family. In Spain. Yes.' He waves his arm and nearly loses the tortilla. He begins to explain the photographs to me, pointing with his fork as he talks. Then he pours me more wine, and watches me as I eat, his dark eyebrows raised, and the white of his teeth showing as he moves his lips back from the hot tortilla. He's holding his fork the wrong way up in his right hand – white pianist's hands which bend like wire.

I ask him about his piano-playing. He plays everywhere he says – bars, as an accompanist, sometimes proper concerts. I ask him if he'll stay here and he doesn't seem to know. 'But is this a good place for a pianist? Wouldn't you have to go to Paris or London to get better known?'

He shrugs his shoulders.

'I am happy,' he says. 'I play for pleasure.'

'And that's all you want – pleasure?'

He doesn't understand. The problem is more than mere language. We eat more tortilla and wash it down with rioja. I'm ashamed of how much I eat but Javier keeps putting more and more onto my plate. I peel off my cardigan. What am I doing here? The middle of the night, rudderless in homesick city, the flat of a man I don't know.

'And you? What is wrong with you?' Javier asks.

So it's that obvious. I start to give him a drink-garbled version of the Tiffany story. Now that I've spoken to Dad, now that I've written the letter, I feel as though I could broadcast the whole thing from a balcony like the Pope's Christmas Day address. Javier's face is full of confusion. 'But this Tiffany – so she was in love very much with your father.

And now she has died because of this. So for what cause does she have complaint?'

I hadn't thought of it quite like that before.

'And your father,' he says. 'So you are arguing with him. Fathers and daughters they are arguing since Jesucristo. It is normal. But still he is your father. You are stuck in him.'

'With him.'

So that's it really. Perhaps it was always that simple.

He finishes his tortilla, goes to the kidney-shaped table and starts to sort through a pile of records. I thought Nanda was the last person in the world with vinyl. The arm of the record player slides out over the record Javier has chosen.

'Now I'm going to play you,' Javier says.

'Play for you.'

The rioja has soaked into my blood. 'Couldn't you play something on the piano?'

He stops the record player. 'Yes, for you I do anything.'

Standing by the piano, the lamplight shines on his high forehead. He's wearing a velvet jacket which is too big and a white shirt with long points to the collar. 'But what do you want?' He spreads his hands palms upwards, summoning music out of the air.

'Can you play Debussy? "Girl with the Flaxen Hair"?'

'Si, si.'

Javier goes to the metal shelves and takes down a file. He searches through it and then, taking out a thin book, he goes to the piano. He sits in a circle of light, flexing his fingers. I wipe red wine from my lips and it leaves a purple stain along the back of my hand. That one note echoes in the early morning silence, and the sound of it expands, before more notes tumble down, and then rise, and fall, and rise again. The sound flows over me, and there are far too many notes for ten fingers. I lie flat on the floor and stare up at the blackness, imagining nothing except sky above. The music ebbs and flows and the rug beneath me vibrates.

When Javier stops playing the air seems bereft. Silence closes around us. Javier lights a cigarette and stands by the piano. 'I'll play some more after a minute.' His face is in the shadows but I can feel his eyes on me. I turn my head to one side and stare across the parquet at the legs of the table, the oil paintings propped against the wall. The zigzag of the parquet jiggles up and down. When I look back Javier hasn't moved. The cigarette burns between his long fingers and his other hand is in his pocket. A sudden twitching starts in my leg. I reach out for my cardigan. 'Thanks so much, but I've got to go.'

'No, no.'

I try to stand up and it's like I've fallen off the edge of a cliff. The floor is rushing towards me. I steady myself against the chair, concentrating on the half-full glass in my hand, being careful to keep the surface of the wine flat. The book-cases and the purple witches' hat go up over my head and rise again beneath me. I steer my feet towards the door.

Javier is standing in the hall, which narrows to a front door so slender I'm not sure I'll fit through it. I balance on one leg like a tightrope walker. The red sunset wallhanging glares. Still I'm holding my wine glass and I wonder why. Javier's hand swims towards me and picks up a strand of my hair. The pull of his hand pricks my scalp. 'You have very beautiful hair.' There's a spot of blood on his chin where he cut himself shaving. At the neck of his shirt there is hair, thick and dark. My stomach lurches, I pull my hair out of his hand and try to move to one side of him. Spider plants brush across my legs. I know I've got to go now. It's very important for me to go now.

'I am in love with you,' he says.

Mediterranean hysteria and alcohol, I tell myself, and congratulate myself that I am still able to be rational. His hand moves towards my glass. Slow, deliberate, like the record player arm. Glass and hand collide, and in action replay the glass unbalances, hangs in the air, spills wine onto my dress. Purple stains spread across crimson roses. This is a scene from a bad play and I want to walk out.

'Oh, I am ve-e-ry sorry.' He takes the glass out of my hand.

The purple stain leaks across the cream silk. I shake my head, pull at the material, staring at the stains. My mind moves like treacle, but the dress is ruined, that much I know, and tears thicken behind my eyes. I go to the kitchen, my foot clattering against a plate on the floor. The sink is in a corner by the window, full of unwashed plates. Brown units, brown lino, orange-brown tiles. The tap lets out a high-pitched whistle and then a sickening groan.

Javier is behind me. 'I'm sorry. Magdalena, I'm sorry.'

I splash water onto my dress. Above me a bulb with a basketwork shade shines a speckled light. Through the window, the street below is silent. No cars ripple over the cobbles. The stain is on the bodice of the dress and the skirt. The water runs through my hands before I can get it onto the dress. I can't tell now which are water stains and which are wine. From behind me Javier reaches for a cloth but I push his hands away.

'You'll have to take your dress off you. It is the only way.'

'No.'

'Yes, you must take it off.'

My hips are pressed against the edge of the sink. The zip of the dress runs down my back like a drip of cold water. Outside the window I look down at the yellow pools of streetlight on the pavement. His hands are on my shoulders.

The dress slides off and there's air all around me. I look down at myself, at the top of my bra, at the curve of my stomach, and shut my eyes. I'm telling the story of this to myself, recording every detail. Voices are babbling in my head, explaining, justifying. I'm not the kind of girl that does this.

Javier takes my hair in his hands. He smells of tortilla, rioja, smoke, something more pungent. I step out of the dress and hold it under the tap, trying to avoid the dirty plates. He's pressed hard against my back. The light in the kitchen sways and the floor is uneven. My legs buzz and my eyeballs stick. The touch of that music is still in my ears, fingers making far more notes than ten fingers ever could. I'm not the kind of girl that does this.

'I love you, Magdalena.'

'No you don't.' I'm pleased with the coherence of that. I push away from him, leave the dripping dress on the back of a chair and go into the sitting room. My cardigan is on the floor and I pick it up. Blood floods into my head and I hold the cardigan against myself. The shadows of the room loom towards me. I go towards the front door. Javier is there and his fingers turn the key in the lock. My throat is tight and a taste of red wine floods back into my mouth. A chasm opens in my stomach. My tongue tastes like leather. So this is how it happens. This is how rape happens. 'No, no.'

He stands in front of the door. There's nowhere for me to go. I turn into the sitting room and feel him behind me. 'No, please, no.' I move to the fireplace, my back turned away from him. Pressed against the mantelpiece, my hands are over my eyes and between the bars of my fingers I see the photographs. A woman's fat legs, in black and white, emerge from under a flowered skirt, and descend like pillars into flat sandals. I feel his hand on my back. I'm not the kind of girl that does this.

'Magdalena?'

'No, Javier, no.'

'Why not?' His hands take hold of the straps of my bra and move them together so that the clasp unhooks. Then he pulls the bra over my shoulders. It brushes against my hips as it falls. 'Magdalena. Come with me.'

He takes hold of my shoulders and turns me round. I lay my hands across my stomach and stretch my fingers out, then watch them, shocked by how inadequate they are to cover me. 'No,' I say, 'no.' But he's pressed against me again and I feel his hand move until it rests on the elastic of my knickers. I'm spilling over with fear, shock, drink . . . something else I don't want to name.

'But you do want.' He starts to kiss me, holding on to the back of my head. My whole mouth is enclosed by his, so it's his breath I'm breathing. I pull away. 'Javier, I don't want . . . Let me go. Let me go.'

He steps back from me and his head is up. He watches me under lowered lids. Then he's laughing at me. His shoulders move upwards and his mouth opens, and he's laughing. First silent laughter, then loud whoops of laughter. He shakes his head, holds up the key to the door. 'If you want.'

I step forward, feel his eyes on my body. My hand touches the key. Want floods through me. I'm caught in blind and struggling need. I lay my hands against his chest. I want our arms and legs to be stitched together, our fingers to merge, our thighs to button. I want throats spliced together, our sinews and tendons made into one frame, our veins soldered so that even our blood runs together.

I lean towards him and kiss his mouth. He pulls off his jacket and his shirt in one quick movement, as though he's peeling off a layer of skin. He's thin and brown, and his flesh fits him tightly. There's even a gold chain hanging on his

chest, like the clichés tell you there should be. I try to cling
to that thought, I try to keep sniggering in the back row, but
the battle is over. My mind is losing its hold. Images break in
on me – twisted sheets, a white knee, iron grilles in Seville.

Javier steers me into the bedroom to an unmade bed,
nearly as big as mine, and a vase of red and white roses on a
packing case. He undoes his trousers and pulls the belt out of
them. Above the bed a wooden crucifix hangs on the wall.
The sheets of his bed are white and I enter the space of
them, and feel their crisp coolness against my skin. I put out
my hand and pull him to me and he kisses me again. A
fumbling of clothes, and sheets, and flesh. He touches me
between the legs, slides his finger into me, and the space he's
opened there seems as wide as a canyon, and I feel like he'll
fit the whole of him inside me.

I kneel beside him as he touches me, my eyes fixed by his.
Then he lies back and pulls me astride him. It's like he's got
hold of my bones. I lean down to kiss his face, his neck, his
arms. When he turns me over he cups his hand over the top
of my head, as he pushes inside me, so that my head won't
bang against the wall. I work my muscles to pull him deeper
inside me, my hands grip his shoulders, somewhere in the
distance I see the quivering of my foot. My mind has
stopped. There are no words here.

Darkness. Headache. Where? Javier's voice. My neck heaves
a lump of clay up from my pillow and I peel open sticky
eyes. Javier's body presses against me, moving me further
over to the side of the bed, where the sheets are cold. He's
speaking in Spanish. My bones are bruised and I'm swollen
inside. I turn my creaking neck and find Javier's hair against
my face. Pedro is standing by the bed.

'Don't worry,' Javier says. 'Go to sleep. He's staying here.'

'What?'

'He's staying here.'

'In this bed?' Suddenly awake, my voice is croaky, and I keep the sheets pulled up to my neck.

'Well, he can't lie himself on the floor.'

'Yes he can.'

'He is my friend. I have to take care with him. He is having some problems in his relations.'

He's not the only one.

I decide to go, except I haven't got any clothes on and I don't even know where my underwear is. Perhaps I'll just get out of bed as I am. Why not? After last night, shame is a redundant concept. I slide crab-wise towards the door. From there I look back and see Javier sitting up in bed, with a puzzled expression on his face, and Pedro is beside him, looking doubtful. Bloody foreigners.

As I go up the stairs, cold air stings between my legs and up my back. In my flat I look for my pyjamas but both pairs are dirty. I find thick socks in a drawer and put them on, and then take my overcoat off the hook on the back of the door and get into bed with it wrapped around me. I've lost layers of skin, and the lining of my coat rubs against the places where I'm raw. What time is it? Half past seven. There's daylight at the window and no chance I'll sleep. The bracelet which Adam gave me is lying on my packing crate bedside table. The gold wires of it are twisted together and I stretch out my hand and try to straighten them. My fingers move over its gold wires and bobbles, but it's too complicated to do it, and my head aches, so I sink my face back into the pillow.

Last night? It won't make much of a rape case. Yes, m'Lord, I took my dress off in Señor Sanchez's kitchen at five o'clock in the morning, as the aforesaid dress had become soaked in red wine. I was drunk. Events got out of control. The tears that are starting turn into a smile. I lean towards the radio and press the knob but there's no sound. I push the knob on and off but still there's no sound. I crawl out of bed and sort through the spaghetti wires, plugs and adapters to check that the plug is in. I crawl back into bed and fiddle with the knob again. The radio crackles and French voices come on, and gales of laughter. I lean over and tune into Radio Four but there's nothing, just crackling. Then I try the World Service. Again, nothing. Armageddon? It certainly feels like it.

Then the telephone starts to ring. The sound is as brittle as a scream in the cool morning air. Each ring is louder and louder, spiralling around the stairwell. I run but I can't find the telephone. Where did I put it last night? By the time I reach it the answer machine has come on, and the caller has rung off. A red light flashes in the darkness, a pulse as regular as the beating of a heart. I press the button but there's no message, just the click as a receiver goes down, a long flat beep, then the machine clicking, rewinding, clicking again. I know it wasn't Dad.

Max

Still Nanda wears the ring I bought for her. It hangs loose on her withered finger. The stone is a tourmaline. Sea green. A semi-precious stone, of course. But more beautiful than diamonds, rubies or emeralds. The ring cost five pounds. I had to save up my pocket money for two years, steal from other children at school. I gave it to her, standing under the apple trees in the garden. She'd been cleaning my shoes with oxblood shoe polish, the stain of it was still in the creases of her hands. She was upset by how much I'd spent on it. I put it on the fourth finger of her left hand. Of course, she's never worn it there.

Around me, the room of my childhood, threadbare and dirty. Pitiful squalor. Peeling flowered wallpaper she tried to paint over, years ago, and never finished. Ghastly fringed lampshades. A rug so moth-eaten you can't tell what colour it is. Layers of soot from the stove. A sickening smell of mothballs and old ladies. Next to the orange sofa the remains of a measuring chart is plastered onto the wall. Ladybirds and butterflies climbing up beside the measurements. She used to mark above the top of my head with a pencil, while I stood, the back of my head against the wall, pushing myself up onto my toes.

Why in God's name didn't she call me before? I'd have paid for all the specialists in Harley Street. But she's always been too stubborn to ask me for anything. And now it's too late. Yellow flesh hangs slack over the bones of her face. Under the bedclothes there's hardly a ridge to mark where her body lies. At the base of her throat there's a flutter of breath. God spare me this.

I force my eyes to her face. Her hair is loose, twisted, stiff as a creeper. Her cheekbones are hollow, and her temples. Pale lips pressed together. Her eyes held shut by a yellow crust. There was always another day to come and see her. I've never understood what she wanted from me. I remember the day I told her I'd been asked to be a Junior Minister. She was in the kitchen, feeding Bullseye. Hacking open a tin of dog food with that old-fashioned stabbing tin opener she has. I wanted her to be pleased. Is that what you want, Max? That's all she said.

Now I cannot look at her face. My mind does not accept this. It comes too soon. I am unprepared.

I go to Theodora. She sits like royalty in her room. How can she be so calm? Selfish old bitch. On top of her head those devilish twists of red hair nod. Her green eyes look me up and down. Her hand is propped on top of an ivory-headed walking stick. When I was a child Theodora did not like me much. And I didn't like her. She frightened me. She wanted Mother all for herself.

'Why didn't you call me sooner?'

Theodora raises a finger to her lips, shakes her head. Then she takes off her glasses, rubs a hand across her forehead. When she looks at me her eyes scorch my flesh. 'You could have come at any time.'

I turn to the telephone. 'I'm going to call a doctor. Do

you know the local doctor's number, or should I call an ambulance?'

'Don't do either, Max, she doesn't want that.'

'If she goes to hospital now, they might be able to do something.'

'Of course they can't do anything. It's stomach cancer. She's had it for months. She doesn't want to go to hospital. She wants to die outside.'

'Don't be ridiculous.'

Theodora snaps her teeth together. 'We do not wish to behave well about this. I will not let her be moved from here. We do not want your help. Let her die as she wants to die. That's all she asks of you.'

This is how it's always been. They never see sense, never do anything the easy way. I turn away from Theodora, go back to Mother. Her head is turning from side to side. It's as though she's saying no again and again. Then her eyes peel open, blink at the ceiling.

'Mother?'

She turns her head. As her lips part in a smile I expect to be able to see through to the pillow. 'Max?' Her voice rattles out with her breath. I clench my teeth, squeeze my eyes together. God spare me this.

Her eyeballs swim in pools of opaque yellow. Filled with incomprehension, disbelief. I can't bear this. I want more time. Don't let her die. I slide her hand out from under the bedclothes, gently, and rest it in my own. It's curved now. An animal's paw. Nothing more than a knot of veins covered by speckled flesh.

'Maggie?' she says.

'She's on her way.'

But, in truth, I don't know about Maggie. Theodora rang her at six this morning but there was no answer. I tried to reach her at the office. Phone rang and rang. I've left a message on her answer machine. That's all I can do. Was it only last night? I shouldn't have said it to her, whatever it was I said. Can't exactly remember. Her dress, that ragged forlorn dress with the red roses. How my sins pile up.

From outside there's a bang like a gun firing, far away. Then crackling. A sound like rushing wind. Mother's head turns on the pillow but she doesn't open her eyes. These sounds are no louder than her breathing but she's heard. 'Burning the stubble. Do you remember?'

Of course I remember. The air wavering in the dense heat, and the black smoke choking my throat. Now I cannot think of it. Images of that other fire flicker in my head. 'I could ask them to wait? Just for a day or two.'

Her breath comes in a tortured rush, and a cough. She squeezes her face together. 'No, no. It's time for it. They must do it while the weather's dry.' Her eyelids flicker as they droop down over her eyes. Her hand is quite still in mine, and cold. I rub her fingers, wonder how long it is since I last held her hand.

Clichéd regrets crowd in on me. I rest my forehead against the palm of my hand. I want new words for this but there are none. I have left undone those things I ought to have done . . . All the times I didn't visit. All the times I didn't call. There was always another day. I turn away from her. It hurts to look. For a moment I'm envious of her. Surely there will be silence in the grave. So much has gone from my life, so little is left. All the people I should have loved, I've disappointed. Everything is at zero for me. Systems shut down.

Her breath comes in a snort, her hand flaps up and down in mine. 'Oh really, Max.' I realise she's laughing. Trying to jolly me along.

'Sorry.' My nose is beginning to run, and because I'm holding her hand with both of mine, I can only sniff.

I get up and go to the window. In the far distance there's the sound of a van or a tractor. A shout from across the fields. When I look out it's bright. Black spots dance across my vision. I see the field, shaved of corn. Stripes of gold and yellow dip and fold with the shape of the land. Down the field a van is parked. Men in overalls are silhouetted against the bright field. Pitchforks, rakes and shovels swing in their hands. They move apart and together again, raising their arms, pointing and planning. Illegal, of course. But still they do it here.

Later those men will come across the field expecting to have tea here as they always do. Theodora will have to tell them that there will be no tea today. She will tell them why. I imagine how they will stand on the path, their caps in their hands. Dazed by the loss. As though a part of the landscape is dying and will not return again in the spring.

'Mother,' I say. She doesn't open her eyes. Her lips move like a baby, sucking in its sleep. She turns her head up slightly, as though reaching up towards light or air.

'Mother, there's something I want to say.' I sit down beside her. Still she doesn't move. I don't know whether she can hear me, whether she'll understand. I stop, wipe a hand across my face. God, I need a cigarette, a drink, both.

Mother turns her stiff neck to look at me and smiles. She's always had a beautiful smile. Still she has a beautiful smile. 'Max,' she says. 'If anyone is going to make last-minute speeches, I'll do it.' A laugh creaks through her empty chest. I start to laugh as well.

I nod my head. 'No, I was just going to tell you. Rosa is pregnant.'

Mother smiles and shuts her eyes. 'You should look after her, Max. You know children should have fathers.'

I bend down towards her, breathe in her bitter smell. Put out my hand to the transparent skin of her forehead. My nose is running, I let out a horrid bubbling sniff. She laughs again and with her hand on the back of my neck she pulls me towards her. Her skin is soft as it rests against my face. I stay like that for a long time, hearing my own breath against her cheek. When she speaks her voice is so close that I feel the vibration of it. 'There's something I want you to do for me. I've got pills from the doctor. In the middle drawer of the desk. There's a white bottle.'

I step over piles of books, push past a sunken armchair. Desk drawer full to the brim with junk. A red-ribboned medal I won in an egg and spoon race, scraps of material, a thimble, reels of cotton, a flea collar. A commemorative coin in a plastic holder. To one side there's a white bottle, I take it to her. A jug of water stands on the table beside the bed.

There are two pills in the bottle. I lean down to her, put them one by one into her mouth. Her gums are red, her grey tongue folds the pills into her mouth. I pour a glass of water, slide my hand round the back of her head. Her hair is stiff and greasy.

'Mother, will you please let me call the doctor?'

'Perhaps. Just an hour or two. Leave it that long.'

I lift her head so she can drink. When she's finished I keep my hand behind her lolling head. A dribble of water runs down between my hand and her cheek. I wait like that, quite still, watching.

She opens her eyes. 'I don't think I'll see Maggie.'

I lay my wet hand on her cheek. Outside the door Theodora's footsteps approach, stop, then retreat. From the fields there's a shout, the clatter of a shovel, the distant trample of feet in the lane. Mother is sleeping. I wait for each breath. I want her to live. I want her to live.

When I look up at the window there's black smoke covering the fields. The air above is blurred by the heat of the flames. I watch a man in cap and gloves reach down, then stand back as a tongue of flame wavers, flares, and then licks a red path across the field.

Maggie

It came with all the shock of long-expected news.

When Dad telephoned I went straight to the station. He had been round to the flat to look for me but I was already at work.

The journey home is long. Stiff-necked, my head rattles against the vibrating window of the train. Belgium, France, Kent. I'm wrapped up inside myself. Scalding tea from a polystyrene cup spills, burns my fingers, tastes of paper. Slough, Reading, Swindon. I-want-to-get-home. I-want-to-get-home. The train rattles and judders over uneven track. Outside, the sky is translucent and the land pale. I bounce the toe of one foot. I-want-to-get-home. I-want-to-get-home. I can still feel Javier between my legs and I tingle with shame. Fields, factories, churches slide across the window. If I'd answered the phone this morning, I'd have been home hours ago.

Dad said – Nanda is dying. But still I'm sure when I reach Thwaite Cottages she'll scurry down the path, with a black scarf wrapped around her shock of grey hair, and her razor eyes searching me all over, curious and critical. My head lolls back against the window of the train. My teeth rattle. I doze and wake to the vague recollection that something terrible is happening. I must ring Nanda, I think. She'll know what to do, but then I remember that that is the whole point . . .

As the taxi turns across Frampton Edge I see the wind turbine. It stands up proud, its white wings turning. And they've been burning the stubble. The taxi rocks over ruts of mud, burnt solid by the summer heat. A bitter, charred smell rises from the scorched fields where a few blackened stalks of corn still stand. The crooked roof of the cottages stands out against the white sky. Shreds of ash are blown across acres of nothing. I stand at the gate. No smoke from the chimneys and silence except for the wind and my heart throbbing in my ears. The front doors are shut and in an upstairs window the curtains are drawn. It feels as though I've been away for a century. As I carry my bag down the path to Theodora's front door the wind slaps at my face and birds rise screaming from the trees below the Edge.

As I stand in the hall, the sound of my bag scraping against the wall is as loud as a landslide and from the sitting room there's the feverish ticking of the grandfather clock. I know that Nanda isn't dead, because a pile of her library books is on the hall table. I push open the door, and Dad is there, sitting slumped in a chair, a cigarette trailing from his hand. Freddy is with him, knitting, on an upright chair by the door. I know that the situation is bad because everyone is calm. People only panic in minor crises.

Dad looks at me with hollow eyes. 'Sorry, Maggie. Sorry. I didn't hear you come.' He sits forward in his chair and digs for a handkerchief in his pocket. He's withered like a plant that hasn't been watered for a long time. I'm not the only person who's come too late.

'Sorry. Sorry I took so long.'

Freddy's knitting needles click in the silence.

'So how are you?' Dad asks.

'Fine, fine.' A ridiculous conversation but we're in unknown territory and familiar customs must be preserved. Freddy looks up and nods her head. I have an urge to shout, but I stand silent, still holding my bag. Dad looks down and then back up at my face. He's still wearing the shirt with my lipstick on it. This conspiracy of calm has to be maintained, if one person cracks it will all go.

'She's dead?' I whisper the words.

'Not exactly,' Dad says.

'No, no,' Freddy says. 'She'll be all right.' She lays aside her knitting and, getting up, she takes my bag from me and puts it down beside the sofa. She's bent up and her slack chin is quivering. 'Just sit down, dear.'

'I want to see her.' I say this too loudly.

Dad struggles up from his low chair, and tips on his feet from heel to toe, as though trying them out for the first time. 'Maggie, it would be better to wait.'

'Why?'

His head moves back and forwards slowly and he stretches out a hand to me. He seems to be made of lead and he blinks again and again. He lays a hand over one eye. 'Please wait.'

I go to the door of Nanda's cottage and my hand slides on the brass door handle. In Nanda's sitting room Theodora is standing facing me, filling the room. There's no electric light and the evening shadows gather in corners. Part of the orange sofa has been moved and there's a gap where it used to be. 'Maggie,' Theodora says. She raises her arms and the sleeves of her cardigan spread wide but her arms aren't stretched out for me, they're raised in a gesture of hopelessness.

'I'm sorry I was so long.' I walk past Theodora, which seems to take hours. The room smells of dust from the stove and dead flowers. The patchwork blanket which used to be on my bed is laid across the end of the sofa. Nanda's hair is loose and knotted but her face is turned into the pillow. Her arm is stretched across where her body should be – a stick arm with a knot of elbow in the middle. Her hand is gripped round the back of the chair beside the bed.

'But I was here three weeks ago.'

The bed they've made for her is by the window. I want to see her face. I want to turn her eyes so she can see out over the fields. I reach out to her and touch the hand gripping the chair. 'Nanda.' I try to unlock her fingers but they're brittle and cold. Someone has taken off her wristwatch and it lies on the table beside her. The second hand continues its solid, even tick. I remember the toast I threw in the bin. I wanted to talk to her, just for one last time. I knew she'd die but I never thought she really would.

She's wearing a nightdress she's had for years. It's pink satin, with a trim of lace around the short sleeves, and it has fallen back to reveal the underside of her arm where the skin is pale and translucent. I think of last night and Javier. How I looked down at our flesh together, the thin pencil line running down from his navel, his hand resting on my ribs, my bottom lip trapped in his kisses.

Nanda twists and a slow moan comes from her skin. I wrap my head in my hands. 'I don't understand why she's like this.'

From behind me, I feel Theodora's arms lock around me. 'Shouldn't we call a doctor?'

'No, dear, she didn't want that. This is a private matter.'

'She's in pain.'

'Sometimes death isn't very tidy.'

'But I want to talk to her.'

'I know, dear, but I'm not sure she'll wake again now.'

I can't cry – the horror is beyond that. I lean my back

against Theodora and feel her solid and upright. I open my eyes and see the mess of Nanda's grey hair and that twisted arm. I want time to move on. Cancel this moment, move on to the funeral and flowers and friends making tea. I don't want her lying there mangled. I don't want the strange animal sounds which come from behind her twisted hair. I didn't know that death would be ugly and indecent. I turn round and bury my face against Theodora.

For a long time I'm like that, tight inside, my face pressed against the silk of Theodora's blouse. I feel her chest rise and fall and breathe her smell of woodsmoke and eau de Cologne. Her hand runs through my hair. When I look at her face the end of her nose is red but her green eyes are steady. I realise that if she can bear this, then I must.

'I should have come before.'

'No, Maggie, you were busy living.'

Theodora pulls a chair forward and sits me down. Then she puts her chair beside me. I look at the knitted squares of the blanket because I don't want to look at Nanda. Her pain is pulling every muscle in my body tight. It's my body which is screaming to be released. My hand strokes the torn pink sheet. Through all the unfolding years I'll be without her. If I marry Adam she won't be there. If I have children she'll never see them. The lights have gone out on the future. There's nowhere to go home to any more.

Theodora and Dad are arguing about pills, their voices grinding together. I stroke the pink sheet. Nanda stirs and twists, her hands still gripped around the chair.

'Pills, what pills?' Theodora says.

'She had some pills,' Dad says.

'I didn't know she had pills.'

'Well, she asked me to give them to her.'

I leave Nanda and go next door. Dad's arm is stretched out, holding a tiny white bottle. It was so light in my hand, that bottle, and with no label on it, only instructions on the top about how to open it.

'I got the pills for her.'

'These pills.'

'Yes.'

'Where did you get them?'

'Amsterdam.'

I look at Theodora but she says nothing. Dad looks out of the window. Freddy has stopped knitting. Outside it's getting dark and I can hear the wind rising, whistling through the trees below the Edge. Dad's arm is still stretched out, stiff, holding the bottle. The ticks of the grandfather clock are short and sharp. A gust of wind moves the timbers of the cottage.

The truth of this bursts on my mind. I step backwards. The tick of the clock is loud in my head. There's a rustle of leaves being blown against the window. The palms of my hands are pressed back against the smooth wood of the clock. I can't believe I didn't know. Now Freddy has understood. Her face collapses and tears spill over her sagging lower lids and run down her face. 'Why didn't she tell us? What if someone finds out?'

'No one is going to find out,' Dad says.

'The lady had cats,' I say. 'Cats like Maud and Agatha. And sunflowers.'

Freddy is rubbing at her face with a handkerchief.

'We can't call a doctor now,' Dad says. 'All we can do is wait.'

'At least it can't be long,' Freddy says.

But somehow I already know that she's wrong.

★

When somebody you love is in pain every second becomes
an hour, every minute a day, every hour a week. The clock
moves but time doesn't pass. I walk through the cottages –
across the hall, Theodora's sitting room, the kitchen, the
corner where Nanda lies. Round and round, back and forth,
like a spider spinning a web, leaving a knotted silver trail.

Everywhere I can hear the sound of her pain. The whine
and grind of machinery failing, a voice shouting from deep
within a cave, the wings of a trapped bird battering against
glass. I clench myself against it. I don't want to think about
Javier but my mind has come loose. I can smell him in my
hair, my breasts are sore where he kissed them too many
times. Underneath my clothes I'm naked.

Dad and Theodora and Freddy move through the same
spaces. Like planets we circle, pass, never meet. Nanda croaks
the same words again and again. They come out from
between her blue lips in sudden whispered breaths. 'The
ship. I've got to get the ship.' Her sitting room is cold. No
one wants to light the fire because the thought that it will
burn on after her death is too much to bear. Her breath rasps
and rasps. Sometimes she's got a strength she's never had
before. She tries to get out of bed and Theodora has to hold
her back. She is like someone possessed. I watch from the
sitting-room door, seeing Dad and Theodora, their long
shadows dancing on the wall, as they lean over her in the
cramped corner of the sitting room. I just wanted to talk to
her one more time.

'What ship?' I ask.

'Presumably the Spanish Civil War ship,' Dad says.

Nanda sits up and her arms beat up and down, her sinews
pulled tight. The rhythm is regular, like a clockwork rabbit
beating a drum. She has twisted out of bed, and lies in the
narrow space at the side of the fireplace, every muscle in her

body tight and her arms still beating up and down. Her nightdress is rucked up at the back and I can see the red knotted veins in her legs. I begin to hate her. I want her to die.

'You'd think at least these pills might have worked,' Dad says.

He kneels on the rug and tries to lift her, but the gap is narrow. She's twisting and one foot sticks out behind where Dad is standing. It flaps up and down, translucent, like the webfoot of a duck. Again and again it slaps on the carpet. Dad gets hold of her and pulls her to him, picks her up, and gets her back into bed. I turn away, my hand gripped over my mouth. In Theodora's sitting room, I walk round and round, then go back and watch from the doorway. There's silence now and Nanda is quiet. I watch the shadows of Dad and Theodora as they move on the wall.

I return to the grandfather clock, but not too often. I let a long time go by before I go to look at it then find that only ten minutes have passed. At eleven o'clock I open the kitchen door in Nanda's cottage, just for somewhere different to go. Everything is the same as three weeks ago. A pan on the stove has got the remains of baked beans dried out inside it, a mouldy chunk of lardy cake is on the window sill. I put my toe on the pedal of the bin and inside I see the toast still lying there, green with mould. I sit down on the bench and finger a dried-out tea bag in a saucer. It has become precious because she put it there.

I think about Adam and I want him here. But it wouldn't do any good. You can love as much as you want, but still it will come to this. I hear Nanda again, her voice calling about the ship.

'We must call the doctor,' Freddy says. 'We must stop the pain.'

'Couldn't we call the doctor, Dad?'

'No. We'll have to wait. Or we'll have to explain about the pills.'

What he means is that he doesn't want me to have to admit to getting those pills. And so we wait, and the pain goes on. At two o'clock I open the back door and go out into the night. Everything is black, there are no stars and the wind is up. Sparks of red still burn in the field like the watching eyes of animals. The night is cold and I find one of Nanda's cardigans on the back of a chair and put that on. Sap, talcum powder, sweat – the smell of her. Freddy comes outside, watches me in the garden and then goes in again.

Around three o'clock Nanda is silent. Theodora and I sit beside her and watch her sleeping. Her arm no longer grips the chair. I can see her face, the face of a dead person. It's so long since I last slept, my head lolls against the back of the chair. I dream – wine spilling on my dress, the feel of Javier's hand inside me, Nanda's yellow face. The tick of the grand-father clock keeps time in my head. I wake, jerking my neck straight, finding that the night is still going on and there's no sign of dawn.

Then the pain starts again and I can't understand it because she seems dead, and yet the pain is still there. It has its own life now. There's nothing left of her except pain. She's still and silent, but struggling for breath, fighting and fighting.

'Dad, Dad, do something. Please do something.'

He comes to the bed and moves me out of the way.

'Dad, please . . .'

My hands are dragging at his shirt.

'Dad, you've got to . . .'

He puts his hand across my mouth to stop my words. For the first time I'm looking at him, really looking at him. The airwaves are clear. All the clatter has stopped. The world has become small. His eyes are ticking round and round. I see the moment when the decision is made. His face hardens into certainty. He takes his hand away from my mouth and touches my shoulder gently.

'Maggie,' he says. 'I want you to look after Theodora and Freddy for a while. Take them outside or make them some tea. Whatever. Just make sure they stay out of here. All right?'

I open my mouth to speak but he shakes his head. I go to Theodora who is standing by the door and I take her through to the sitting room in her cottage. Freddy sits silently in a chair by the fire. I shut the door behind us. Then I make Theodora sit down and I go into her kitchen and try to make some tea. My hands are rattling and I can't do it. So I pour a glass of water. Then I go back to the sitting room. Freddy and Theodora are suddenly old. Pale and grey, they are fragile as moths. The life is going out of them. I give them water they don't want and suggest that we should go outside but they say nothing. I kneel down on the rug near the fire and watch the door, the line of light along the hinge. I force my mind through that crack, press it against his mind. Will him to strength. The waiting is long. Let her die, let her die. I turn my head into Theodora's skirt and press my head against her legs. Her hand presses against my hair.

Then I cannot stay in the room any longer. I must get out into the air. A sob, an inhuman wrenching sob. His, not hers. Freddy wails like a wounded animal, her hands striking the air in tight gestures. Theodora is sitting in silence, her hands held out in front of her, staring into the gap between them. I burst outside and kneel on the path with my head in my hands. The concrete is cold beneath my knees and the wind is dashing across the Edge. The strength of it grows, and slackens, then grows again. There are no stars, and the red sparks in the field have faded, although the air still tastes of burning.

I hear Theodora's voice from inside then the creak of the front door behind me. I turn to see a flicker of movement. I shut my eyes, open them again and Dad is there. He's holding Nanda but she's not a person any more, just a bundle of rags collected in his arms. The porch light shines through her. The wind blows and I think it will take her out of his arms. Both are insubstantial as spirits. Dad staggers on his bad leg. Theodora goes in front of him, showing him the place. The rags tip from his arms onto the bank where the daffodils grow in spring.

I get up and go to him but my foot catches in a rut and I fall. My wrist turns as I go down and I sit in the dew, holding on to my head. It feels as though I've been cut somewhere deep inside. Dad is close and I feel the solidity of him. His shoulders are hunched and his head is bent. He leans down towards me and lays his hand on my shoulder. His shadowed face is crumpled. He raises his hand to shield his eyes. This is the beginning of his death, the loss of his past. He's kneeling beside me. For the first time we're alone.

Ahead of us a hem of grey edges the horizon. The air is damp. We're sheltered from the wind, the silence is as deep as the sky above. It's going to be one of those autumn days Nanda loved. The first day without her. Don't let the sun come up. I don't want to set off on the road away from her. Let me stay here in this day with the touch and smell of her still real. She's on her back, stretched out, with her hair twisted around her. Her skin is as grey as the air above us. One arm is up over her head, her cheek rests against that arm. In the midst of a luxurious morning stretch, life has been peeled away from her. The grass where Dad stood, and where she lies, is flattened to the ground, and light green at the roots. Like everything else in this garden, she no longer grows upright. But her eyes are still open.

SEPTEMBER

Maggie

In this world there are six billion people and none of them are her. She doesn't get up in the morning any more. Six billion people, but the pattern is never repeated. The fire, the lies, I used to wonder what worse could happen, now I know. Mainly what I can't understand is where she is. I expect a face to turn around in a crowd – Maggie, Maggie, there you are. But no. Here today, gone tomorrow. It seems like a trick or a comic turn. I could be laughing, but instead I'm left with loss, raw and jagged. Absence.

When someone dies you're not meant to think about their body. Everyone says – that's just the shell she lived in. But that shell was what I knew best. So I think of her between the bed and the mantelpiece, with her head twisted up, and her webfoot slapping up and down on the rug. I think about her bones in the cold earth of Burrington churchyard, and her hair getting dry and dusty. And Freddy and Theodora – alone on Frampton Edge. Their trio become a duet. Waiting for death. Naively I hoped that death would be in brackets. Normal service will be resumed shortly. But death gets bigger the more you know it.

★

After Nanda died, I stayed on at Thwaite Cottages for a few days. Dad had to go back to Brussels – meetings, lunches, committees, all of that. One evening, unable to bear the emptiness, I went up to Theodora's room. She was sitting at her desk, quite still. Sadness had come upon her like the beginning of winter – the leaves turning brown at the edges, the birds flying south, the first glint of frost. When she turned towards me her eyes looked inwards instead of out.

'Don't give up hope,' I said.

She waved her walking stick at me in a sudden fury. 'What good is hope?' she hissed. 'The person I loved for over seventy years is dead and you talk to me about hope . . .'

'Sorry, sorry . . .'

'Hope is for the soft-headed. Look around you in the world. What possible cause can you see for hope? What evidence can you see that anything is going to get better? Of course it isn't. The people you love get old and die. That's how it is. That's the truth. There is absolutely nothing to be hopeful about.' Again she stabbed her walking stick at me. 'Defiance. That's the best we can do. That's how we survive. Defiance. Just give me a day or two and I will have recovered mine.'

Later she came and apologised to me.

'We are old now,' she said.

Only now I realise how we underestimated Nanda. That's how it is in families – you stand so close to people that you can't see them properly. It wasn't until the funeral that I understood how much she was loved. There was an announcement in the newspaper – peacefully, at home, it said. You can always rely on Dad for a good lie. The service was at Burrington church because she'd left no other instructions. I said we should burn her on a bonfire and dance around the flames, whooping and beating our chests. Or dig her into the compost heap. But Freddy and Theodora allowed Dad to invite the vicar round and even made him a cup of tea. That's how bad it was with them.

It rained the whole day of the funeral so that the roads were half underwater but still people arrived from everywhere. Geoffrey came, and Theodora's book friends, Jack from the garage with his son Dodgy Derek, and the Medlocks, and the men from the farm, looking scratchy in their suits, and flocks of Burrington people who Nanda had taught, their umbrellas crushed together in the porch. They came with their children, and their mothers and their grannies, and Colonel Bampton came, although Nanda hated him, and the postman, and mad Young Mrs Fitzgerald, with a hat as big as a flying saucer.

Adam said there were famous people there – a Minister of Health from some long-forgotten government, a newspaper columnist, two well-known painters, and a chauffeur-driven-Rolls-old-geezer, who rants in the Lords about arms sales. Then hordes of bearded peace campaigners sloshed up the aisle in boots and mackintoshes, so we had to organise a relay up and down the road, through sheets of rain, to borrow extra chairs from the school. There were friends who'd stayed in the spare room, or slept on the orange sofa, and Rosa behind a pillar. People were standing around the font and crowds of children were sitting on the pulpit steps cutting and pasting with glue and scissors.

Freddy and Theodora came late, moving up the aisle with the stately grace of a bride and groom. People put out hands to help them, which they never would have dared before. Freddy was wearing a floppy red hat that Nanda used to wear, and Theodora's hair was a bit of a mess because now Freddy has to do it for her. There was a steamy smell of wet wool and all the lights were on because the rain made it dark outside. Water dripped down the inside of the stained-glass windows. Adam stood next to me, and James was on the other side, pressing sticky fruit pastilles into my hand. Theodora read poems – R. S. Thomas, Gerald Manley Hopkins. People didn't understand but the words made the air tingle.

After the funeral there was tea in the school hall. She had a good innings, people said. She lived life to the full. At least she didn't suffer. She wouldn't have wanted it any other way. Now she's at peace, they said. The last place she'd have wanted to be, I thought. Adam and I pushed through the massed ranks of old biddies together. Some old bloke said – yes, I remember, the granddaughter, an awfully good claret we had, the day you came to lunch. In my head there was a voice shouting – she's dead, she's dead, she's dead.

Adam said – I don't think you should be alone now, Maggie. Yes, I said, yes, and held his hand tighter but I thought about Javier burying his face in my hair, Javier undoing the back of my dress, Javier with his hands protecting the top of my head, as he pushed inside me, deeper and deeper. Then I felt guilty about not feeling guilty. Tyger, Sam and Dougie were nodding and winking, and giving me the thumbs up from the other side of the hall. Tyger in mafia-widow gear, and Sam with a purple swollen eye, and Dougie in a jacket like Joseph's Technicolour Dreamcoat. I wished they'd piss off.

Dad was in fine form, with his hair combed into neat furrows, and a faint smell of aftershave. The room ebbed and flowed, back and forwards, from where he stood. The men from the farm were talking to him – subsidies, set-aside forms, and beef prices. He knows what to say because he gets it off the Archers. Then he was shaking hands with

Bob Briston, their silver heads on a level, and their long noses the mirror image one of the other.

Dad raised a hand, emphasising a point. Those hands . . . Nanda is not the only person I underestimated.

Adam had to go back to London because of a deadline. I stood in the rain, saying goodbye, holding his hand and feeling bloodless. 'Don't worry,' he said. 'I'll be over in two days' time.' He unlocked his car door. 'You know, with every day it'll get easier. You just have to wait for time to pass.' I nodded my head. But I didn't want time to pass. I stood in the road and watched him go, and looked back at the church, its spire slicing the grey sky.

Later there was whisky, as well as tea, because Nanda always liked a whisky. James came to find me, unsticking fruit pastilles from his teeth with his finger. I took him to the tea table to find him a sandwich. Most people had brought some food along. We stood for a long time looking at a cake made by one of the peace campaigners. There was icing on top of it, with a crooked picture of Thwaite Cottages cut out of marzipan. The fields around were marked out in green cochineal, which bled into the white icing. A plastic model of a black Labrador stood up near the front gate, which was made out of broken-up chocolate flake.

Tyger dragged me down a corridor lined with children's rainbow paintings to where Sam and Dougie stood under a corrugated iron porch. 'So are you going to marry him?' she asked.

I looked out at the rain bouncing on the school playground, each drop a sudden flash of concentric rings. I shivered and drank more whisky. 'Yes.'

'Blimey,' Sam said. 'I hope you got rid of the trouser press.'

Dougie coughed and spluttered as he smoked a damp

joint. 'Make sure you get a really big rock,' he said. 'Security for the future. When I was a kid my mum sold her engagement ring and we got a new car and a colour TV.'

I sighed and squeezed up my mouth and dipped the toe of my shoe in a puddle. Then Sam put his arm round me and I started to laugh.

'Problem is,' I said, 'there's this other bloke, who lives downstairs . . .'

Tyger opened her eyes wide, 'Ooooh, you never did . . .'

'No, no. Well . . .'

'In other words – yes,' Tyger says.

'So what's he like – this other bloke?' Sam asks.

'Awful. He's slimey and Spanish and he wears his slippers outside . . .'

Tyger and Sam start to laugh and Dougie splutters.

'Sounds right up your street,' Tyger says.

'Well, don't forget, if all else fails,' Sam says, 'you can always come back to Moulding Mansions.'

When it was all over, except for a few committed whisky drinkers who we couldn't get out of the hall, Tyger said they'd take me back to London. I sat in the back with my head on Sam's knee. Biggles was in a cardboard box next to us because Dougie wouldn't come without him. Tyger drove at a hundred down the motorway although the rain was still thrashing down, and the windows were steamed up, and the air was thick with Dougie's dope. I smoked some of Dougie's joint and started crying, and then slept without dreaming, holding Sam's hand.

Back in Brussels. This morning I went to work, but this afternoon they told me I should go home. So I walk back to the flat feeling like it's me that's dead. The worst thing that could possibly happen has already happened and I'm still here. The end of fear. Above me the sky is hollow. The space seems immense. There's a reckless purity to the day. I am weightless and shapeless with nothing inside me. The simple fact of being alive seems miraculous. People in the street are transparent. I can see their black hearts pumping, counting out life. They watch me as I pass, agog with indifference.

I pass a corner shop and stop to buy supper for Adam and me. He'll be here tonight, arriving on a late train. Under a blue neon sign, I read the headlines of English newspapers. Interest Rate Cuts Hit Industry. Blue-Blooded Bank In Bonking Row. Werewolf Seized In Southend.

At the flat everything is a mess. Still my water heater doesn't work. I should tidy up, but I'm so cold I go to bed instead. I leave my front door ajar for when Javier comes. I know he'll come and I'm disgusted that I can think of him when Nanda is dead. I go back to bed, sleep, and wake to find him standing by my bed.

'Magdalena. Where are you gone?'

I blink awake and wipe my eyes on the duvet.

'What time is it?'

'Five o'clock?'

Javier is grinning until I turn my face to him. 'Oh Mag-da-lena.' He stretches my name out into a long moan. 'Who is dead?'

'My grandmother.'

He's standing with his hands stretched out, and a frown on his face. 'But she was dead still.'

'No, my *mother* is dead already. My *grandmother.*'

Except in my case it's actually the same thing.

Javier lets out a long breath and the whole of him sags. 'But this is terrible.' There are tears running down his face. 'Oh no. Terrible.' He raises a hand to stop the monsoon.

'Oh Javier, don't cry for goodness' sake.' I clutch at the sleeve of his jumper, and the smell of him makes me remember his bed, and the feel of him. He sits down beside me, and kisses my forehead, then holds me in his arms. I can feel his tears on my face.

'You are cold,' he says. 'Wait. I will go and get you a drink.'

I assume he means tea, but he comes back a minute later with a bottle of wine and a corkscrew, and puts them down on my packing crate bedside table.

'You went for the . . .' He makes a digging motion, pressing his foot down onto an invisible spade and shovelling over his shoulder. Despite myself, I want to laugh.

'Yes, the funeral.'

Javier opens the bottle of wine and pours me a glass. Then he takes a handkerchief from his pocket and blows his nose. I haven't eaten for days and the wine makes my stomach churn. 'Javier, I'm all right now, don't worry. You go.' But instead he waters my wilted plants, rings the landlady and abuses her in rapid-fire French about my water heater and goes downstairs to make me some toast. I eat some of it while he pours me more wine and offers to lend me his dirty handkerchief.

'You wait a moment,' he says. He's back a minute later with a pile of photographs resting in his hand. They're curled up with pinholes in the top of them. He sits down beside me and points at a tubular-legged signorina with a black scarf round her head. 'My grandmother. She is dead also.'

He gets into bed beside me and we spread the duvet flat so we can lay his photographs along its white edge. He holds the photographs in his hands like delicate china and I rest my head on his shoulder.

'And the brother of my grandmother. Also dead.' He

flattens the photograph out, folding back a crumpled corner. A toothless man, in black and white, grins in the harsh sunlight outside a flat-roofed house. In the background there's an orange tree like the ones in Seville. His life there, his family – how would it have been, after he was gone? My mother, dead before I even knew her, and her parents, buried somewhere in Seville. Javier is talking, but I don't hear him. The weight of all the dead presses down on me. My blood has stopped still. I'll spend my life doing this or that, and then I'll die like Nanda, and it'll be as though I was never here.

'And my cousin,' Javier says. 'You know, he is dead because of his own lorry.'

'Oh really?'

'Yes, he did not use the . . .' Javier jerks his hand up beside him.

'The handbrake?'

'Yes.'

I try not to laugh but the wine gets the better of me.

Javier shrugs and laughs. 'He was always very stupid, so it is normal that he is dead in a stupid manner.' When I feel Javier's hand on my skirt, I push him away, but his hand continues to stroke my leg, and I like the gentle slow movement of his fingers. I push my head against him, so that everything around me is shut out. I can hear our breathing, and I remember Nanda's breath, rasping all night.

When Javier's hand rises higher on my leg, I move it away. 'No. Javier. I don't want to.' But his hand keeps touching the inside of my leg.

'Javier, you've got to understand – I've got a boyfriend. So I can't do this.'

'Si, si. I understand.'

Still he moves his hand on my leg, and it's better than

being alone, and when I look at his face it's still wet with the tears he cried for her. He pulls at my skirt. 'No. I don't want that.' I push him so hard that he nearly falls out of bed.

He sits up and stares at me, his face angry.

'Javier, I don't want that now. Can't you understand that?'

He takes hold of me by the hair and pulls me towards him. 'You think that because she is dead then you should be dead as well? Is that what you think?' He picks up one of the photographs scattered on the duvet and his eyes are thick with anger. 'All of these people are dead. You . . . insult them. What can you do now? You live now . . .' He reaches forward and his shaking hands start to unbutton my shirt. I pull at his hands, but see nothing because of my tears. He pulls off his jacket and his shirt and throws them on the floor. He's so angry that I wonder if he's going to jump on them. He's pointing a finger at me, and spluttering and spitting as though the words taste bad. 'You waste yourself. You have become . . . an English . . . an English . . .'

I put out my hand to him, and he pushes it away, then suddenly his anger goes, and he kisses me, and laughs. It won't matter if I do this just once more. He gets back into bed beside me, and undresses me slowly, and I watch as though I'm somewhere else. Then he stands by the bed and pulls off the rest of his clothes, struggling on one leg, pulling off his socks. As he gets into bed beside me, the photographs fall from the duvet and rustle down to the floor.

In the sitting room the telephone rings. I hear Adam's voice. 'Maggie. Are you all right? I called you at work, but they said you'd gone home. Listen, don't worry, because I'll be with you in only a few hours, and it'll be all right . . .'

Javier sucks at my breasts like a hungry baby and I stroke the back of his neck.

Adam's muffled voice discusses travel arrangements. 'I've thought about it, and decided that it would be better if I got the seven thirty-six train, rather than the five seventeen . . .'

I used to wonder how Dad could lead double, triple, quadruple lives. Now I realise that all of us are doing that, all of the time. Lives are not all of one piece. I feel Javier's hand between my legs. I am lulled by the rhythm – it's like the rocking of the train as I went home, like Nanda's rasping breath, like the hymns in church. Except something is pricking my back. I reach underneath myself, trying to find what it is, then Javier rolls me over and unsticks one of his photographs from my back. We look at it in his hand and laugh. Then Javier drops it over the side of the bed.

Afterwards Javier says that he's going to teach me Spanish. I admit that I already know a bit. He starts to say words and I repeat them. He makes simple sentences. I try to do the same – and I can do it. My tongue is athletic because the words are already inside me. They come out from behind iron grilles and filigree screens. I talk and talk, making no sense – all that was mute is suddenly shouting.

The effort of it exhausts me. I lie back in Javier's arm. 'In Spanish the verb to expect doesn't really exist, does it?' I ask. 'There's a verb to hope but no different verb to expect.'

Javier thinks about this for a while and then agrees. I look up at the ceiling. Language is culture. Spain – a country where nobody expects anything, where all is random. I begin to fall in love with my homeland.

'You know, for an English person the fact that there are two verbs to be is terribly confusing,' I say.

'But Spanish is right in this, and the other languages are wrong. If you say – I am in Brussels. Then you say – I am tall. This is not the same verb.'

'But surely it should be . . .'

'No, no. The English are stupid. It is quite separate. Of course, of course. The place you are in is only the place you are in. It is not the person you are.'

Later I wake and Javier is playing the piano downstairs.

I'm worried about the sheets. Adam is arriving and I've got to do something about the sheets. I strip them off the bed and hold them up. Light from the window shines through them showing stains like stars, cream against white. I stuff them into a plastic bag and tell Javier I'm going to the Coin-Op laundrette.

I sit on a plastic chair. The machines rumble and breathe hot air. Opposite me a couple are necking and a man is asleep with his personal stereo on too loud. In the street outside a dog pees against a rubbish bin. Two small boys roll dice across the floor, trying to throw sixes. I watch the dice roll. One lands by my foot and balances on its edge for what seems like an hour then falls on four.

I watch the faces of the machines, turning round and round, and when I look away the street outside is turning as well. The white of the sheets, the foam in the machines, the clouds at Thwaite Cottages, always so close. Without Nanda I'm disconnected. She had the strings of the kite. The world is turning fast and my head spins. What will I say to Adam? Another decision. Of course, I must go back to London with him and I must tell Javier that. It's time to reclaim my rational mind.

When the sheets are dry I lift them out and feel their static cleanness against my hands. I push them into the plastic bag and set off home. The air is cool, with the first edge of autumn, and it's getting dark as I wander back through the cobbled streets. The lift is broken so I walk up the stairs, tugging the plastic bag after me. Pedro leans over the stair rail and waves a spatula at me. The first notes of 'Girl with the Flaxen Hair' trickle down the stairs. In Javier's flat the purple lamps throw their shadows over the usual mess.

Javier stops playing and turns to me, drinking beer from a can. I breathe deeply, wriggle my toes, clench my teeth. 'Javier. Listen, I want to talk to you . . .'

'Maggie, Maggie,' Pedro says. 'Let me help you.' He pulls the sheets and duvet cover out of the plastic bag and shakes them out across the floor.

'No. Don't. Stop it.' The floor of their flat is filthy. Javier jumps up from the piano and catches hold of the end of the sheet. They try to fold the sheet between them, moving together in a heel-clicking flamenco dance. Then they toss the duvet cover up in the air. The duvet cover lands across Pedro's head and Javier wraps it around him so they're both lost in whiteness and all I can hear is their laughter.

'Don't. Stop it.' I try to pull the sheet off them but instead they push my head inside it. Everything is white, the light is like snow in the morning and despite myself I start to laugh. I wave my arms but Pedro won't take the duvet cover off my head, it's tight around my face and brushes against the inside of my eyes. I'm being pulled towards the bedroom.

'We put them here,' Javier says. I fumble my head out and see Javier and Pedro pulling the sheets off their bed.

'No.' I pull at my sheet but Javier stretches it across the bed and lies down on it, then pulls the duvet cover on top of him. He reaches out his hand to pull me down beside him but I push him away. 'Javier, I've got to explain to you.' I tug at the sheet again but he won't move. He lies on the bed, his dusty slippers making marks across the white material. Pedro passes him his can of beer.

I start gathering up the pillowcases which are scattered on the floor. 'Javier, you know what I'm saying, don't you?' I'm careful not to look at him.

Javier looks at me and nods. 'Si, si. Your boyfriend. The man which I have seen here. He is very nice, I think.' Javier nods his head, then he turns to Pedro, and the two of them shrug and nod. Clearly Javier is completely unhinged. Why have I only just noticed this?

'Javier, I want to explain to you . . .' Javier gets up and starts spreading the sheet flat around him. I wrestle with Pedro for the duvet cover. Then I stop and move around to the other side of the bed so that I'm in front of Javier. 'Listen to me. That means I can't have a relationship with you.' He doesn't look at me but he nods his head. He hasn't understood. Perhaps I need to explain more simply. 'Javier, I'm not going to get married to you.'

Javier collapses onto the bed as though he's been shot, and lies there laughing, looking up at the ceiling. Then he turns onto his front and his head is tipped up towards me. 'This is good, in fact. Because I'm having a wife and three children in Spain.'

I hold the duvet cover in my hands. Above the bed the crucifix is black against the white wall. Pedro was in the process of putting a pillowcase on but now he stops and swears under his breath.

'What?' I tug at the sheet which Javier is lying on, pulling again and again, as my shoes slip on the floor. 'Why didn't you tell me?'

Javier takes hold of my hands and tries to unwrap them from the sheets. 'But you are not wanting to marry me.'

I fetch the plastic bag, push a pillowcase into it and disentangle one sheet, which is dusty and probably beer-smelling. Of course I don't want to marry Javier. He's a creep. I wouldn't touch him with a cattle prod. And he's completely stupid. 'Get off my sheet. Get off it now.'

Javier, still lying on the bed, pulls my sheet out from underneath him, and rolls up the duvet cover so I can take that as well. I pick up the other pillowcase from the floor. My head spins as I bend down. The pillowcases appear doubled, tripled in my blinking eyes. I push everything into the plastic bag.

'Javier, why don't you care?'

He raises a hand from the bed and catches hold of the hem of my skirt. 'Because you will come back again.' I unpick his fingers, one by one, and then I turn and walk out. I slam the door behind me and stand on the landing with my hand pressed flat on the top of my head.

Max

I stand in the churchyard. Only two weeks ago now.
Seems longer.

Fiona has sent me to do some shopping for supper. The infrastructure of life has got to be maintained, come what may. So I came here to Burrington. As good as anywhere for shopping.

I park the Jag, head for the supermarket. Then decide I might go to Mother's grave. I sit down on a bench beside the church wall. The falling sun is on my face. The hills rise all around. The cut in the earth has not yet healed. Bouquets of flowers wilt beside the granite headstone. Modern death is a poor show. In Victorian times you'd have had a hearse pulled by six black horses with nodding plumes of feathers. Or there's those Middle Eastern women on the television, ripping at their clothes, scratching their faces, wailing. Appalling, but better than this.

Life is suddenly very short. Of course, it was worse with Lucía. She was buried in some anonymous London graveyard. A place she'd have absolutely hated. Partly it was spite, I think. I was so angry with her. It all had to be her fault, otherwise it would have been mine. Stupid. Stupid.

I get up from the bench, walk away from the grave, don't

look back. I pass the school, remember how Mother waited for me there, every day. We'd always walk back home together, all the way to Frampton Edge. No matter what the weather. An old sheepskin coat, she had. I liked the greasy feel of it. Her Wellingtons flapped as we walked. I imagined her hair like an electric shock as we walked under the pylons.

The best day was when she had a migraine. She had to sit down on the verge. I went down the field to fetch some water from the stream. I wiped her head with my handkerchief. She held on to my hand. I was sad when finally she could get up and walk on.

But that was when I was tiny, before I understood. Before I went to houses where faces above my head would exchange knowing nods. This is Miranda Priestley's son. I would be given an extra chocolate biscuit, a distant smile. Ah yes, Miranda Priestley's son. You know, of course. Tight-lipped nods. Eyes turned away. Yes, of course. I wiped chocolate biscuit on their curtains, pushed their children in the nettles.

Now, in my hands, I can still feel Mother's flesh. The dry thinness of it. No different from the cotton of the pillowcase. Down, down. The life going from her. Dreadful, dreadful. Yet the power of it. The sense of right. Joy, something close to joy. Appalling, but true. The one that didn't slip through my hands.

I walk up the hill to the supermarket. Small, dingy place, half the food past its sell-by date, cabbage leaves trodden into the floor. Typical Burrington. I never cared for it much as a place. Reeks of poverty and failure. Too many poets and painters, hippies busking on street corners. I work down the list Fiona gave me – tomatoes, rice, milk, biscuits, eggs, cloves, washing-up liquid, bread. After that I head for the High Street, thinking I'll have time for a quick drink before home.

Then I see the newspaper, gripped between nicotine-stained hands, crossing the road ahead of me. A headline on an inside page. I follow it, my eyes fixed on the top left-hand corner. The photograph. The text shifts and sways as my eyes rush over it. The newspaper folds up. I reach to catch hold of it. The blue duffel coat dodges away through the traffic.

That poor devil, they've got him. That's what I think. There's the smell of blood, the thrill of the hunt. Then I realise it's me. The fox and not the hounds. Cornered. The line of the pavement tips. My breath stops. I look around me. A blue autumn sky. A car horn blares. I'm standing in the middle of the road. A silver car bonnet presses towards me. The blonde in the driver's seat is mouthing swearwords. I move towards the car. The horn blares. I stumble off the road. Fish and chip papers in the gutter.

I rush into a newsagent, pull a paper from the stand. An old biddy at the counter fumbles through her purse. She chats to the old chap behind the till. Hurry up, hurry up. Racks of cigarettes. Plastic jars of sweets. Nice weather. Your mother? Remarkable, isn't it? A loud ticking in my head. Hurry up. I hold the newspaper face down so I can only see the sports on the back page. I won't look at the newspaper until I'm outside. Give it a chance to change what it says. The doorbell jangles. A woman shunts a pushchair past racks of crisps. The other newspaper headlines on the stand. Interest Rate Cuts Hit Industry. Blue-Blooded Bank In Bonking Row. Werewolf Seized In Southend.

Finally I pay. Don't suppose you've got the change, have you? My fingers twitch. Can't get the money out of my wallet. I push the note at him. Take the newspaper, trip over the wheels of the pushchair. Outside everyone is walking away, their backs turned. The grid pattern on the pavement opens and closes like the blades of scissors. I try to read, the paper flaps in the breeze. I press the article I want against a shop window. I read three paragraphs. The wind blows the page shut. Open it, try to read again. It's as bad as it can be. They know I was there that night. New evidence reveals that . . . Who? My mind stops.

I walk back and forwards, up and down the pavement. The words I'll say are forming in my mind. I can explain. There's been a mistake. I didn't harm her. I would never have harmed her. This is all just a misunderstanding. I look at my watch. Half past five. Fiona will know. She'll have heard it on the radio. Or someone will have telephoned. Come to think of it, a couple of journalists left messages this morning. I never returned their calls. Digging dirt about Mother, that's what I thought. Gus – that's who I need. But he's on holiday. The lawyers, Geoffrey. What should I say? It's all going to start again. The police, the newspapers. I'll be arrested. Fiona. Prison.

In the Memorial Gardens I sink down onto a bench. A man walks past with the newspaper in his hand. I turn away. But of course he doesn't know who I am. I'll be all right while I sit here. I put the copy of the newspaper in the bin. But no, I may need it. I pull it out again. I could go up to Thwaite Cottages. Only two miles up the hill. Have a cup of tea with Mother. She'd like that. I'd find her in the sitting room, writing letters. She'd turn in her chair, smile, shake her head. Then I remember she's dead. I get up and walk back to the High Street.

I know I've got to go home. Start explaining. But somehow it doesn't seem reasonable I should have to do that. As

I move the joints of my knees are loose and jarring. A pub at the top of the street is just opening. I go inside. Low beams. I order a whisky. A man rolls in with bristly grey hair. He's a working man with deep lines in his brown skin and sharp blue eyes. For a moment I think he's going to recognise me. I raise a hand to my face. He starts to chat to me about how wonderful the weather is. A smile spreads across his face. When the barman gets him a whisky he pulls an envelope out of the back pocket of his jeans. Coins rattle inside it. Only a man with no money keeps change in an envelope.

'Let me pay,' I say.

He asks if I want to play pool. I say I will, put down the bag of shopping on one of the bench seats. I'm good at pool but it's a long time since I've played. The room with the table in is next to the bar. It's got one frosted-glass window, high up, smells of beer. A dartboard on the wall. The man is fat and, as he reaches up to take down a cue, a line of beer belly appears beneath his T-shirt. He has a ring in his ear, dust all over his jeans. I buy us a second whisky, ask the man what he does, just for something to say.

'This and that,' he says. The skin on his hands is thick and cracked. 'Building mainly, but I've no work at the moment. There's no money round here.' He plays his shot, stands upright, smiles, then laughs. He's about my age, I suppose. Perhaps he could even have been at school with me. Or Mother might have taught him. Probably he lives in the council houses in the back lane. He stands waiting for me to play, his weight on one leg, the corners of his mouth still turned up in contentment. He's got a cigarette in his hand, a twist of smoke rises from it.

He beats me the first time, but it's close. We play again.

'So what do you do?' he asks. I remember the newspaper, the shopping, Fiona. New evidence has revealed that . . .

Who was it? I make such a mess of the shot that I nearly dig a hole in the baize.

'I've nothing to do either. At the moment.'

We both laugh, keep on playing. I win the second game, and get us another whisky. I want to play a third, but he says why not tomorrow, if I haven't got anything much to do. I say why not and we go out of the pub together. We're at the top of the town here. Around us the hills are turning russet. Sheep in the fields and above them white clouds. 'Bugger all around here,' the man says. He's standing beside me, and he breathes in deeply. A gust of wind buffets us. I'm still holding the newspaper. It blows in my hand.

'Tomorrow then?' the man says. He's looking at the newspaper.

'Do you want it?'

'If you've finished with it, yes. Perhaps I'll go and sit in the Memorial Gardens and read it there.' I pass the paper to him. It leaves the feel of newsprint on my fingers. The man raises a hand and wanders away down the hill, his training shoes slapping along the pavement. He walks with a rolling step. I think about tomorrow. Going up to London for a meeting. Back to Brussels. Start of a new term.

Then I know I'm not going back. Not to Brickley and Fiona, or to London, or Brussels. It's over. Finished. I'm not running any more. A weight lifts from me. I shut my eyes and feel the wind on my face. I start to walk and my feet carry me down the High Street as though I'm dancing. I'm not going back. It's finished, finally finished. Burrington looks beautiful. I remember Nanda as I gave her the pills. The dribble of water running down my hand and her cheek.

I can't find where I left the car, wander around looking for it. Finally I walk up the steep hill towards the theatre, find it in the car park there. I've left Fiona's shopping somewhere.

She'll be wondering where I am. Everyone will be wondering where I am. I find some change in my pocket, go to a
nearby phone box. I telephone Rosa, leave a message on her
machine. For a moment I think about ringing Maggie.
Some time I'll have to know. She must have spoken to the
police. I lay my head against the door of the phone box.

When I get back to the car, I worry about the lost shopping. Then remember it doesn't matter any more. I shouldn't
drive, given the amount I've drunk, but if I'm about to be
tried for murder, what does drink-driving matter? That
thought amuses me. How long have I got? Probably only a
matter of hours. I could go back to Spain, to the room I
used to have there, high in the tiled roofs of Seville, with my
one bag pushed under my bed. I could unpack all the years,
turn the handle backwards.

I'm a failure now.

Decide, decide. I must decide. Then I realise that all
responsibility has been taken from me. The fuse is lit. Just a
question of time. Whatever happens will happen. The police
may already be looking for me. I'll get in the car and drive.
Just drive and drive. See where I finish up. I take the road
towards Gloucester, the long road across the top. I open the
window and the wind buffets my face and dries my eyes.
Perhaps I'll drive to Brussels. I reach a straight stretch and put
my foot down and watch the speedometer rise. My mind is
swimming with whisky and relief. It's over. It's over.

The car swerves.

Death is so easy. Nothing more than sleight of hand. A
moment when you could have saved a life. And didn't. What
was I doing when Lucía died? I was blowing my nose.
Ridiculous. Ridiculous. There I was. Blowing my nose.
High up on that ledge. And that's how a life is lost. A split

second. Then someone you love falls three hundred feet and their dear, dear head breaks open on a concrete slab, their eyes spill, their black hair clots with blood. Meanwhile you blow your nose.

Love is short and forgetting long.

Maggie

Adam arrives with the newspaper in his hand.

He shows me the article and the words move over my eyes. The reaction is shock, yes. Except I've already felt all there is to feel. I am out of emotion. This is just another thump on an old bruise.

'Don't worry,' Adam says. 'You did the right thing.'

He has bought me a bunch of white lilies wrapped in cellophane. Their sap leaks onto my hands. The letter I wrote to Tiffany's lawyers still lies on my desk. 'I didn't post the letter,' I say. 'I didn't post it.'

'What letter?' Adam says.

'It wasn't me who told the police that Dad was there that night.'

I pick up the letter. My handwriting crawls across the front of it. The last line of the address is smudged.

'But who said that he was there? Who said that?' I ask.

'I don't know,' Adam says. 'But I didn't say anything to anyone. You know, I would never do that.'

I try to make my mind be hurt by this but I can't believe that it has really happened.

'I promise you I haven't said anything to anyone,' Adam says.

'No, of course not. Of course. I know that.'

In the street below an ambulance siren blares. The truth has a life of its own and it tends to make itself known. That's the way it always goes. I feel myself starting to cry. There should be a map for this, things we should do, procedures to follow, people to telephone. Leave the building by the nearest exit. Do not run. Do not use the lift. But instead we are just staring at the page of the newspaper, the unsent letter, the bunch of white lilies.

The telephone rings. I think – it'll be Nanda. Then I think – no, she never calls. Her death slaps me in the face again. My hand jerks, moving to protect me. Probably it will be Dad on the phone. I go to answer it but Adam is there before me. 'Don't answer it. It would be better not to answer it.' The phone keeps ringing. The sound of it pierces my skull. Adam's finger goes down onto the button that turns the answer machine off. The telephone continues to scream on the desk, the sound getting louder and quicker.

When finally there's silence Adam steers me into the kitchen. He's talking to me all the time. 'This is better for you,' he says. I'm not walking upright because the shock has hunched my shoulders and pulled the muscles of my arms tight. In the kitchen he shuts the windows and closes the curtains. Then he starts to tidy up the mess of dirty pots, papers and books. My hands and feet are numb but blood beats in my lips and inside my head. I think of this news spreading, each person answering the phone, sitting down after the call. All of them hating him.

'You know, Maggie, this is really the best thing that could have happened,' Adam says. 'Because now you're not in any danger. You just say what you've always said. But the police know the truth now – so they're going to be able to start a proper investigation.'

I watch my hand on the tablecloth. Adam wraps his hand round the back of my neck and pulls me to him but I'm stiff and it's hard for him to hug me while I'm sitting down and he's standing up. So instead he makes me tea, lifts a solid bag of sugar down from the cupboard, smashes inside it with a spoon, and puts several large pieces into my mug. His knees touches against mine as he sits down at the table. 'He shouldn't have done this to you.'

I nod and move my knees away from his.

'It wasn't fair of him,' Adam says.

I nod again and try to drink but I hate sugar in tea. The teaspoon is gripped tight in my hand and I move it round the bottom of the mug, scraping hard against the china surface. The telephone rings again and I stand up to answer it. Adam puts out his hand and takes hold of my arm. 'No, Maggie. You've done enough for him. It's not your business.' I look at Adam's eyes, close to mine. I sit down and put my head in my hands while the telephone rings and rings. The sound pulls at the muscles in the side of my neck.

When it finishes he gets up from the table. 'I'll do us some supper.'

On the fridge there's an empty bottle of rioja. 'You don't drink that stuff, do you?' he asks.

'No. The guy downstairs came up for a drink.'

'The gay guy who plays the piano?'

'Yes.'

'He's not bothering you, is he?'

'No, no. I wouldn't say that.'

I watch his back as he cracks eggs into a bowl. He's made a mess of it so there's pieces of shell in the bowl. He tries to hook them out with the corner of a sheet of kitchen paper. I wish he'd just stick his fingers in and get them out that way. This is how it will be when I go back to London. Cooking supper, just the two of us, in a flat together. We eat at the kitchen table, sitting very close. Except that I can't eat. I push omelette around my plate and it sticks to the inside of my mouth. My stomach is rolling like seasickness. The last night before an execution, a pause before the axe falls. Everything seems swollen and significant.

We're clearing the table when the telephone rings again. I turn towards the kitchen door. Adam looks at me and I look away from him. I move to go but Adam takes hold of my arm. 'Maggie?' he says.

I'm holding a plate and I put it down on the table with a clatter.

'Maggie, you've got to get yourself clear of this . . .'

His fingers massage my arm. I pull away from him.

'OK. Let me answer it,' Adam says. 'I can always take a message.'

A moment later he hands the receiver to me. 'It's Rosa,' he says.

'Maggie, do you know where your father is?' Her voice has a serrated edge.

'No.'

'He isn't with you?'

'No,' I say. 'Of course not.'

'Listen, I'm in London and he left a message for me but I don't know where he is. I think he may be in Brussels. Can you go around to the house and find out if he's there? Then I'll come.' Her voice is keeping the lid tight down.

'Rosa . . .'

'Go now.'

Adam is still standing watching me.

'Maggie, are you there?' Rosa says.

'Yes.'

'Will you do that?' Her voice rises and the line crackles.

'Yes.'

I say goodbye and put the phone down.

'Who was that?' Adam asks.

'Oh, no one. Just a friend of Nanda's getting worried about Dad.'

We finish clearing up the plates. Adam goes to the bed-room where he left his bag and returns with a small black and white striped box with a ribbon around it. He gives it to me and I already know what it will be. I open it, sitting at the kitchen table, and inside there's a necklace that matches the bracelet he gave me before. It's made of the same strands of gold. I take the bracelet off and hold it next to the neck-lace, so he can see them lying together in my hand.

He takes the necklace from me and reaches up to put it around my neck. I feel the cold touch of his hands. I lift my hair and twist it onto the top of my head. I feel his breath on my face as he fiddles with the clasp. 'So you'll come back to London now,' he says.

'Yes, I will.'

He kisses me and his tongue against mine is cold.

'You know, I can bring the car over to pick up your stuff. That would be the easiest thing to do. And it doesn't matter if you haven't got a job in London. You can just live in the flat and take your time deciding what you want.'

'Yes.'

I switch on the computer and check the e-mail, although there's no chance that Dad would get in touch that way. Instead I find a message from Tyger. It says – Maggie, where in God's name are you? I tried to call but no answer. What's happening with your Dad? Are you OK? Sam says he reck-ons you always knew. Whatever . . . you did the right thing. Call me and you know I'll come straightaway. So will Sam, and Dougie. Any time. Tyger.

I stand by the computer reading the message again and again. Strange how there aren't really any secrets. I start to reply to the message but Tyger's words go so deep I can't think what to say. I turn off the computer but keep those words close to me. Call me and you know I'll come straight away. So will Sam, and Dougie. Any time.

Adam puts the sheets on the bed, his hands making neat hospital corners. When I pull back the duvet there's a dust mark on the bottom sheet and I put my hand down and brush at it but it doesn't go away. We get undressed and lie side by side under the sheets. Adam tells me that he loves me and I tell him the same. He locks his arms around me and sleeps. I lie awake, my head spinning round and round. Surely now there should be peace. After a year trapped in my own lie, I am released. It's just as Adam says. No one will ever know I lied. This is the end of the story. They all lived happily ever after in a white flat in Fulham.

I watch the luminous blobs on the face of the alarm clock. Do the honourable thing. An accident with a gun. The words pull me out of bed. I stand in the sitting room, my heart pushing against my ribs. I go to the phone but I can't ring his number. The trapped bird scratching against the skylight window, the broom banging, the hot-water bottle against my feet. You have more power over him than you know.

I look at my watch. Half past three. I imagine him alone in that tall house, with the china dog and the unmade bed. Lives, all of our lives, seem as fragile as glass. Each of us trying to grasp a few moments of happiness, every day reclaimed from nothing. What does he have to live for now? Who will take care of him? We are all that is left to each other.

I hold on to my throat. A black figure cartwheels down through the grey air, falling and falling. I see hands stretched out but the figure still falls. Then I am on the edge looking down, and he's beside me. I put out my hands and pull him back. There's that look in his eyes – that look which pulls tight between us. It was there the night Nanda died. The moment when the airwaves cleared. And he did what nobody else could possibly have done.

I pull on clothes, find my bag and coat. I'm just about to leave when I remember the keys Rosa gave me. I check they're still in my bag. Hurry, hurry, I go to the door. But then I stop, go back to the bedroom and look at Adam sleeping, breathing heavily. I think of living with him and waking up to find him always with me. I'm making a bargain here. If I give Adam up then Dad will be all right. Is it a deal, God? Are you listening? Let Dad be all right. Make him wait for me. Dad, I'll do anything for you, anything, but please wait for me. Please keep reclaiming the days.

I look around for a pen and something to write on but in the darkness I can't find either. I mustn't wake Adam. Fumbling, I run my hands across the desk and along the front of my bookshelves. There is no pen. Finally I find a pen in my bag. There should be lots of paper but I can't find a piece big enough so he'll be sure to notice. This can't fail because of a lack of paper. I sort through piles of post on my desk until I find a large envelope.

The flowers he bought are still lying on the dressing table with the Cellophane around them. I stand and watch him. The white of the pillow reflects onto his face. That cropped head, those shadowed eyes, the shape of his face. He is a good man – why wasn't that enough? In Seville he said – do you just want someone who believes in your father? Perhaps he was right. And I'd never have been able to bear the burden of his forgiveness. I'd have to behave well for a hundred years to make it up to him.

I put the necklace and bracelet carefully away in the drawer and touch his shirt where it hangs on the back of a chair. I turn to watch him again. Will he really care that he has lost me? Will he? I suspect not. He will only care that he failed to save me. But he will still know that he was right. He has been right all along. He is invulnerable in his small rightness.

I write – Sorry, Adam. I can't live with you. I can't go out with you any more.

When two people hurt each other, often it's a person from outside that situation who finally pays the price. Nanda, Dad and I – trapped in our secret battles and our fugitive guilt – we have been reckless with other people's lives. I leave the envelope on the floor in the hall. This is a kindness, finally. I look at Adam's face once again then turn away. What's frightening about this is not how hard it is but how easy.

I run all the way to Dad's house, my bag gripped against me, my heart loose inside my chest. When I reach the square I can't breathe any more so I have to walk. There are no lights on at the house. I cross the street and stand on the pavement, then turn, aware that I'm not alone. In a car parked at the kerb a man sleeps, his head dropped forward against the steering wheel. So the vultures gather. On muffled feet I hurry to the front step, push the key into the lock, fall into the hall, and shut the door behind me. Then I stand quite still.

Of course, this is stupid, absolutely stupid. It's all a creation of my mind, there's no reason to think there's anything wrong. I take deep breaths, talk myself into calm. But there's someone in the house, I know it. A sound – faint, blunt. A rhythmic tap which echoes inside me, like the beating of my heart, one beat to every four. I search for a light switch, running my hands around the sides of the doors. Above me, on the half landing, a strand of light shines under a door. I hesitate, watching that light. Tap, tap, tap in my chest. I hesitate, turn into the front room, look out of the window across the square. Lights from a few windows are scattered in the blackness.

I go back to the hall. The space is hollow and the sound of my feet echoes in the darkness. The long windows at the back of the house show the sky starting to turn from black to iron grey. A shadow wavers across the window. For a moment I stop quite still and nearly cry out, then I realise that it's the branch of a palm. I go up the stairs and there's a circular shadow in the shape of the landing window. I pass the light shining under the bathroom door and go up to the bedroom. His coat hangs on the front of the wardrobe door. I remember Nanda's library books on the hall table, her watch still ticking after her death. The room is lit by the streetlights outside. I touch the sleeve of the coat, press the emptiness of the wool between my fingers. Something rustles. I jump back against the wall but it's only the noise of papers falling from a chair where my coat has caught against them.

I look again at the light under the bathroom door. I move down the stairs. The tapping is louder. I put out my hand and slide the handle round. A click, as loud as cymbals, in the stillness of the house. I start to ease open the door. Drops of water are falling from the basin tap. I watch a drop form, then fall. I step into the room. My breath jerks tight. He's in the bath, the white length of him stretched out, his head tipped back against the end of the bath, his throat exposed.

No steam rises from the water, a grey scum has gathered on the surface. His flesh sags down around the bones of his shoulders and chest. One arm hangs down over the side of the bath. I step back from him.

Suddenly he sits forward, splashing water over the sides of the bath and onto my shoes. He presses his head into his hands, groans, and then stares up through blurry eyes. 'Lucía,' he says. 'Lucía.'

'Dad. It's me.' I stand on the wet bathroom floor, gasping. I can still taste omelette like glue in my mouth. He sits back in the bath again with his face in his hands. The flesh on his arms is white and water-swollen, and his hair is flat on his head. His willy floats in the water like a crumpled sock.

'What?' He shakes his head and then stands up, sending water over the floor. The flesh of his legs collects in folds above his knees. I pass him a towel from the rail. He steadies himself on the side of the bath as he manoeuvres a stiff leg. The basin tap is still dripping and I lean over and turn it off.

'Maggie,' he says. 'Sorry. Sorry. Let me go and find some clothes.'

Rivulets of water run down his legs, following the lines of the hairs. I look down at his bad foot — a livid scar shaped like a flower with crooked petals of jagged flesh around it. His two middle toes are bent up like claws. It's seldom that I've seen his foot and I look away.

'Dad, it wasn't me. I didn't tell anybody.'

He shakes his head like a dog and water splashes across my arms. Then he nearly drops the bath towel as he leans down to pull out the plug. 'No,' he says. 'No. Of course it wasn't. I never thought it was.'

'Who was it?'

'Gus,' he says. 'It was Gus.'

I move out of the way while Dad leans over to pick up some clothes on the floor. He's awkward, bending over, still gripping the bath towel, and I want to put out my hand to help him.

'But I don't understand. Gus adores you.'

'Yes.' Dad turns away for a minute and looks over to where the blind is looped up at the window. Then he begins to move past me to the bathroom door, walking slowly, as though his balance is uncertain. 'I was always very fond of Gus. I may have teased him rather but I was fond of him.'

He turns to look at me, his blue eyes settle on my face. 'Maggie,' he says. 'You do look a ghastly colour.'

'Yes, I know. It's stupid . . . I thought . . .'

He shakes his head, smiles. 'Maggie, you should know by now that I am not an honourable man.' He steps out to the landing and stands for a moment in the circle of light that shines through the round landing window. 'But thank you,' he says. 'Thank you for coming.'

'But, Dad, what will happen now?'

'I fear Her Majesty will be deciding that.'

'No, Dad, no.'

I move to stand in front of him. 'Listen, I'm sure if you talk to Geoffrey he can sort it out.'

'No, Maggie.'

I take hold of his arm and the flesh is cold and wet. 'Dad, I'll help you.'

He shakes his head. 'Thanks. It's kind, but no.'

'Dad, please. You can't just give up. You could run away. Let me help you. And Fiona will help you, I know she will.'

'Where would I go?'

'I don't know. South America?'

Dad turns to me, laughs, shakes his head. A ridiculous suggestion.

'Thanks, Maggie. But no. No. It's finished with. I'll hire the best lawyer there is and maybe I'll be lucky. If justice is done then I'll be released. There's nothing more I can do.'

He steps out of the circle of light and goes up the stairs, his clothes gripped under his arm. His head is bent down and he moves slowly. At the bedroom door he turns back, hovering with one foot on a step and one trailing behind him. He sees my hand reaching out towards the light switch. 'No, no.' He waves a hand to stop me. 'Don't put any lights on at the front of the house. Go down to the kitchen. I'll come.'

I feel the minutes dripping away. All these months we haven't spoken and now we're left with only the tail end of this one night. In the kitchen the base of a broken wine bottle sticks up from the table and glass crunches under my feet. Outside I can see the shadows of the garden. My arms are wrapped tight around me. From above water glugs as the bath runs out. The floorboards creak as Dad comes down the stairs. He flicks on the light and we blink at each other across the kitchen table. He's smaller now.

'Careful,' I say. Without his glasses he can't see the broken glass on the floor. He's hovering, uncertain where to put his feet, so I steer him out of the way of the glass, then pass him his spectacles which are on the sideboard. He props them on his nose, sits down, looks at me and smiles. He's wearing old corduroys and a shirt with the sleeves unbuttoned which remind me of weekends with Nanda. The low light hanging over the kitchen table lights the top of his silver hair. He's tired and rumpled but somehow younger. His grandeur has gone. Prospero without his magic.

'I thought that journalist chap was coming to stay? What do you call him?' Dad is leaning forward with his elbows on the table.

'Adam. No, no. Not any more.'

It's hard to think about that.

'Actually, I've got another boyfriend. But he's got a wife and three children.' I start to laugh and Dad laughs as well, the only sound in the early morning. We keep looking at each other and looking away. Dad strikes a match to light a cigarette. We both watch the orange flame as it waves and flickers near the ends of his fingers.

'And he's Spanish.'

'Spanish? Oh, good God.'

We laugh again, enjoying the sound of it.

'Did you know that Freddy and Theodora are going away?' His voice is croaky and he coughs.

'Going away?'

'Yes, last seen in Gloucester buying rucksacks and having a furious row at the ticket office about the evils of rail pri-vatisation, while trying to buy some sort of Eurorailing ticket for the over-sixties. No doubt they'll stop off in Brussels.'

My eyes follow the grain of the wood on the kitchen table.

'Yes, I know,' Dad says. 'Seems indecent really, doesn't it? But they're not the sorts to lie down and die . . .' We start to laugh again.

Then upstairs someone knocks at the front door.

'It's Rosa,' I say. 'She said she'd come.'

'No. She's got a key.' The knocking stops. We wait and it starts again, loud and insistent. Dad looks at me, shuts his eyes.

'I'll go and say you aren't here.'

'No,' he says. 'Just wait.'

I put my hands over my ears. 'Dad, I don't want you to go to prison.'

I can feel the banging against the inside of my ribcage. I wince at each thump. I look down at Dad's foot and it's bleeding because of the broken glass. Finally the knocking stops. Dad doesn't seem to care about his foot but I get some water and make him put his foot up on the table, pulling it forward so it's under the low-hanging light. His foot is pink where the scar is and the tissue is in swollen ridges. It seems strangely personal to touch him there, and I'm gentle, laying my fingers softly on the furrowed flesh. I'm conscious of him watching me. There's a shard of glass stuck in the sole of his foot, and I lift it out, and wipe the severed skin with a tea towel.

'Dad, how did your foot get hurt?'

'I shot it.'

'What?'

'I shot it. You knew that, didn't you?'

'No.'

'Really?' A smile spreads on his face and he nods his head and laughs. 'It was your mother . . . she wouldn't have me when I first asked her. I pleaded and pleaded with her but she thought I was just fooling around.'

Before I can finish with Dad's foot, he gets up again. 'Maggie, there's something I need you to do.' He moves to the sideboard, hobbling on the heel of his cut foot, and picks up his wallet.

'I need you to look after Rosa for me.' He passes me a pile of new fifty-pound notes. 'You need to give her that. And I'm going to write down the numbers of these cards, and you need to take out as much money as you possibly can before they close my accounts.' He moves quickly now, pulling the lid off a pen and writing on the back of an envelope. He turns back to me. 'And you must make her take the money. You must insist.'

A trail of blood is smudged across the floor from Dad's foot. He hands me credit cards and an envelope with numbers written on. 'You know Rosa is pregnant. So you must insist about the money.'

'She's pregnant?'

'Yes. Not part of the plan but there we are. She'll have to stop watching life and start living it.'

I stand and stare at the credit cards then I push them into my bag.

'Listen Maggie, I don't know who is upstairs but they'll be back soon. You must go. There's a door at the end of the garden . . .'

'Dad, I'm not going.'

'Maggie, come on. I want you out of this. Come on.'

He opens the back doors. The sun is coming up and the garden is emerging from shadows. The air tastes as cool and smooth as milk.

'Dad, wait. At least let me do something about your foot and let me find you some proper clothes.' I run upstairs to the bedroom and pick up his socks and tie and find a jacket and the overcoat on the hanger. In the bathroom cupboard I find a pillowcase. I make him sit down and put his foot back on the table and I start to rip up the pillowcase. The sound as it rips is loud and I tug where the seams are until it comes apart. My hands are rattling and I'm making a bad job of it. I don't even know what I'll do with the strips of pillowcase. I start to tie them round his foot but they won't work properly and I swear. One of them falls to the floor. Dad puts out a hand to help me and holds a strip of cotton steady while I tie another over the top of it. When I've finished I try to pull his sock over the swollen mass of cotton but my hands are jolting so badly that I can't do it, so he does it instead. He puts his foot into his shoe with difficulty and it won't lace up. He winces with the pain of it. I make him put on his overcoat.

Upstairs the knocking starts again, the sound of it crashes through the house, bouncing back off the walls. I put my hand over my ears. Please, please stop . . . Leave him alone . . . Don't take him away. Dad takes hold of my shoulders and turns me towards the doors. I turn back against him, clinging to the sleeve of his coat.

'Dad, if only you'd explained that night. It was Gus's fault . . .'

'No, Maggie. It wasn't Gus. It was me.'

'But why didn't you explain?'

Upstairs the knocking has stopped and my words swell in the silence. I look up into his eyes. He holds me by the shoulders. His face caves in and his eyes shut. From between cracked lips his voice is a whisper. 'To have the chance to save the life of someone you love . . . to fail . . .'

He shakes his head, his chin sinking down onto his chest. I raise my hand and touch his face. His hand closes over my fingers, holding them against his cheek. He cannot open his eyes. I lean forward against him and his arms knot around me, pressing me against his overcoat. His hands run through my hair. I push myself against him. Tiffany died for the lack of this. My arms hold him tight. Make this time last, make it last . . .

He stands me back from him and looks into my eyes. 'Maggie, you do believe that I didn't harm Tiffany, don't you?'

His eyes are opaque and I cannot see what lies behind them.

'You do believe that, don't you?' he says.

'Yes.'

I believe him even if it isn't true.

We stand together on the terrace. Cool air brushes over us, tasting of falling leaves. The sun is hidden behind mist, its thin yellow light scattered across the white sky.

'I didn't know about your foot,' I say. 'I didn't know.'

'Silly,' he says, and puts out a hand to steer me down the steps.

My fingers are scrabbling against his overcoat. 'Dad, what shall I do? I don't know what to do.'

He looks down at me and puts his arm around me.

'We none of us know that, sweetheart,' he says. 'Don't expect to know that.'

He kisses my cheek, holds my hand, turns me down the steps.

'Don't worry,' he says. 'You know, whatever happens . . .'

He can't make those three words. My feet are dizzy as I move away from him. They leave a trail in the dew. I look back. The sun is brighter and he squints. Then he raises a hand and smiles and just for a moment he's the photograph that Nanda's got of him all those years ago. At Thwaite Cottages – his shirt blowing in the wind, a ragged trilby, a guitar wrapped in an old piece of eiderdown. My eyes seal that image. I turn away, moving unsteadily down the garden. When I look back, he's gone. The sky above me is untethered. I know nothing. Nothing. Except the reason why I lied for him.